CRY OF THE FIREBIRD

T.M. CLARK

WILDE PRESS

CRY OF THE FIREBIRD

Published by Wilde Press

Edited by Creating Ink

Cover designed by Mecha

Cataloguing-in-Publication details are available from the National Library of Australia www.librariesaustralia.nla.gov.au

Paperback © Published 2024 ISBN 979-8-2230107-6-0

Previously published by Mira, an imprint of Harlequin Enterprises (Australia) Pty Ltd

GENERAL FICTION

This book is written in English as used in Britain and Australia. It has not been Americanised.

ABOUT THE AUTHOR

Zimbabwean-born T.M. Clark combines her passion for storytelling, different cultures and wildlife with her love for the wild in her multicultural books. Writing for adults and children, she has been nominated for a Queensland Literary Award and is a Children's Book Council Notable. When not killing her fans and hiding their bodies (all in the name of literature), Tina Marie coordinates the CYA Conference (www.cyaconference.com), providing professional development for new and established writers and illustrators, and is the co-presenter at Writers at Sea (www.WritersAtSea.com.au). She loves mentoring emerging writers, eating chocolate biscuits and collecting books for creating libraries in Papua New Guinea.

Visit T.M. Clark at tmclark.com.au or

facebook.com/tmclarkauthor
x.com/tmclark_author
instagram.com/tmclark_author
amazon.com/stores/author/B018N3D2QY
bookbub.com/authors/t-m-clark
goodreads.com/tmclark
linkedin.com/in/t-m-clark
mastodon.au/@tmclark
pinterest.com/TMClark_Author
tiktok.com/@tmclark_author
threads.net/@tmclark_author

ALSO BY T.M. CLARK

ADULT NOVELS

- Child of Africa
- Cry of the Firebird
- My Brother-But-One
- Nature of the Lion
- Shooting Butterflies
- Tears of the Cheetah
- The Avoidable Orphan
- Song of the Starlings

PICTURE BOOKS

- Slowly! Slowly!
- Quickly! Quickly!

CULTURAL-SENSITIVITY NOTE

I grew up knowing of the Bushman of the Kalahari as a magical people, and I was in awe of them. Now years later, their name has been changed to San, and many people believe that 'Bushman' is a derogatory term. I have had professors at universities and anthropologists living with the San on the ground both tell me conflicting information about the name that the San were given, and while some have accepted it, some still preferred to be called Bushman. Neither San nor Bushman is a term they chose themselves. This story is not about their name.

I write this story with the utmost respect to the San, to highlight their plight, and bring awareness to the unjustness that is still happening across Africa.

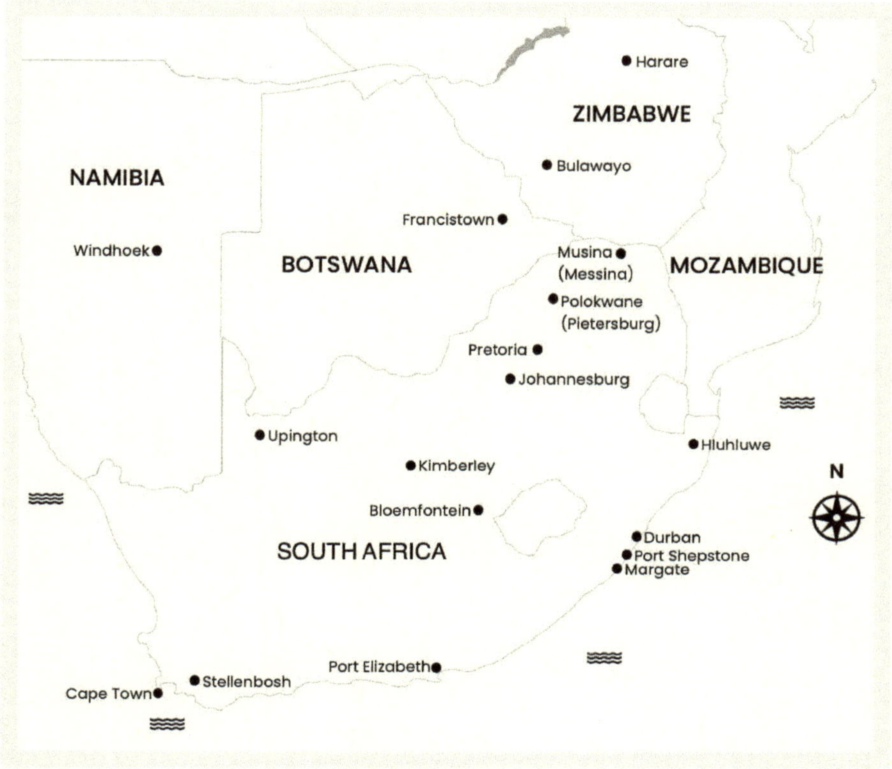
Harare
ZIMBABWE
Bulawayo
NAMIBIA
Francistown
Windhoek
BOTSWANA
Musina
(Messina)
MOZAMBIQUE
Polokwane
(Pietersburg)
Pretoria
Johannesburg
Upington
Hluhluwe
N
Kimberley
Bloemfontein
Durban
Port Shepstone
Margate
SOUTH AFRICA
Port Elizabeth
Stellenbosh
Cape Town

DEDICATION

As always, to Shaun, my love, my life.

Amy Andrews, to pink flamingos!

CHAPTER 1

KIMBERLEY, SOUTH AFRICA, 2017

Quintin Winters pulled his violin, La Angelique, from her bed of purple velvet, along with Fred, his bow, and smiled fleetingly before tucking them under his arm. He walked outside onto the veranda, which looked out over their property, towards their neighbour's game farm. Today there were at least fifty flamingos that had stopped to visit. A few more were silhouetted against the golden sky as they honked and joined those already gathered in the cool water. He and Lily had done extensive work on building a bigger dam soon after Minke, their rescued flamingo, had left them, in the hope that one day, flamingos might visit. If Minke was one of those there now, they would never know.

Beyond the game fence, a herd of majestic eland grazed the small hill, while a group of impala, their tails continually moving to keep the flies at bay, ate against the fence line where a troop of monkeys clambered up and over, using the thick upright pole. Never ones to be imprisoned, they now ran towards the water's edge and an evening drink, chattering madly between themselves, almost as loud as the flamingos.

Buying Hacienda El Paradiso had been one of the best decisions Quintin and Lily had made together. The landscaping had been worth it.

So had the extensive renovations to the house. Their room had been designed to capture just this sight: the flamingos on the dam.

Quintin sat down next to Lily, who was dressed in a pink pyjama top, to watch the sunset. She loved the flamingos as much as he did, and everything they represented to both of them.

He leaned over and kissed her forehead, breathing in her scent. He smelled strawberries. Bessie had obviously washed her hair while he'd been at Kamfers Dam. His own hair was still damp from the rushed shower he'd taken. Her braid was neat, with a pink-striped ribbon at the end keeping it in its place.

He removed the elastic and loosened her silky locks, once so dark, now streaked heavily with grey. Lily only liked to braid her hair at work, otherwise, she preferred to have it free. Like she was.

'There you go, my *wifie*,' he said. 'I'm sorry I'm a little late getting here tonight.'

He rubbed his hands together, creating warmth. Then flexed his fingers against each other, ensuring that the stiffness from being broken all those years ago was massaged out, and they would perform once again as they were meant to. Lifting La Angelique, he tested a few notes with Fred patiently caressing the strings.

She was still in tune.

'There was so much to do at the dam today. The good news is that the breeding season is going well, despite this drought. The dam received a good shower and some decent run-off a few days ago, and now the green algae looks a bit like pea soup all over the place. There are about ten thousand adults still waiting with the nursery chicks. The creche has settled in on the north-western side of the pan. Piet and his trusty Platfontein helpers are making sure that when they roost there, they have no unexpected visitors, either four- or two-legged, to disturb them. There are already three or four chicks who have managed to become airborne, even if for only a moment. The rest are still wandering around, flapping their wings vigorously. They looked like they were attempting to walk on water. Won't be long now and this lot will all be moving on, flying to other feeding pans. It's been a hard slog, but it was so worth all the effort, Lily. The flamingos are safe, they have their warriors constantly watching over them. Only change now is that with money behind them, they can make a difference to the future of the species.'

He began playing his concerto, the slow haunting start, and he watched Lily closely. Quintin let the music wash over them, cocooning them in a time capsule, and as the music rose and fell, he saw her hand twitch.

He smiled and closed his eyes as he reached a particularly intricate run he'd written, allowing his mind to relax and enjoy the music. To enjoy the process of playing to his greatest fan and inspiration in his life. Fred knew the movements and instinctively followed Quintin's heart, and La Angelique's sweet sounds serenaded in the curtain of night. One by one the stars peeked out from the violet sky, and then hearing his music, they brightened.

Quintin felt the soft touch of Lily's hand on his thigh.

He opened his eyes. She was looking at him. Their eyes locked. For a moment, she was free, and they were together.

'I love you, Lily,' he said. 'From that first moment till eternity, you know I was yours alone. I'm not going anywhere. My heart has always been yours, and it always will be.'

She closed her eyes. Slowly, her hand became heavy. He didn't want it to move away, to break the contact.

He continued to play her favourite piece, which he'd composed for her —Concerto for the Flamingo.

CHAPTER 2

BRISBANE, AUSTRALIA, 2010

'You took the job, didn't you?' Quintin said as soon as Lily put down the phone. It was more a statement than a question, and his Austrian accent was strong with disapproval.

Lily turned to look at her husband of twenty-seven years. Quintin had aged beautifully, like a sculpture, and he seemed to get better every year. His hair was flecked with silver and appeared more ash-blond than grey. Although it had thinned, lots of hair remained—hair that he still couldn't control. At the moment, it was stuck up, making him look like he'd just got out of bed. Unable to resist, she reached over and threaded her fingers through the silky strands to smooth it all down. She looked into his blue eyes that were so dark, they were almost purple. They should look older given what they'd seen, but instead, they were vibrant and alive, as if adventure and living had sparked an eternal fire deep inside his soul. And his eyes were surrounded by laughter lines of years spent exploring and enjoying life. Fifty-eight wasn't old at all, they were in their prime years and getting better all the time.

She placed her hand on his arm and nodded slowly.

He pulled away, causing her hand to drop back to her side. 'Even though you know how I feel about South Africa? You still said yes?'

'I did,' she said, crossing her arms. 'And you know why? Ian Hawthorne.'

'That shithead.' Quintin's volume was rising. 'What about him? No, don't tell me. You're working with him again? I swear, Lily, if Ian—'

'He's dead,' she said quickly.

Quintin stopped with his hands midway to imitating a strangling position. 'I can't say I feel anything for that cockroach dying. Hell's a good place for a man like that.'

Lily shook her head. 'There's a little more to it. He was there and things went wrong. Now World Health don't trust his research. They're questioning it. The cherry on top is that they said that he discovered clusters of meningitis but did nothing. Just put it in a report as if it was an everyday occurrence and continued to focus on HIV in the township population. He totally ignored the fact that he was sitting on the data of a killer disease.'

'That's on Ian—'

'That's just it, Quintin. With Ian dead, it's my problem. I know he could be callous and abrasive, and rub people up the wrong way, but now World Health want me to verify the state of things. Imagine that? Sound familiar?' She paused. 'I want to know why he'd do that. Ignore something that was so obviously a looming disaster.'

'Lily, it's South Africa. You shouldn't have taken the job. Not without us discussing it more first.' He shook his head.

She opened her mouth and then closed it. Sometimes silence was a more effective tool than arguing. Instead, she turned and looked out at their view of the ocean and across the bay to Moreton Island. The weather was abysmal, the wind churning the ocean as white peaks leaped across the normally calmer waters.

'How did he die?' Quintin asked.

Turning back to him, Lily said, 'Hijacking. They stole his Land Cruiser.'

'Bloody hell, just one of the reasons we always avoid spending time in the cities in South Africa. It's like the Wild West there. They don't rank Johannesburg as one of the murder capitals of the world for nothing.'

'He wasn't in Johannesburg, he was outside Kimberley.'

'Another city, same crimes. Call them back and tell them you made a mistake, Lily. It's too dangerous,' he said, taking both her hands in his.

She shook her head. 'No, Quintin, I need to do this. It's my chance to disprove him. To make people understand that what happened in Sudan could've been avoided, that they listened to a pig of a man instead of us. Make them acknowledge that they were wrong. That we were right.'

'I don't care about that, it's history,' Quintin said.

'I care,' she said. 'He messed up royally at Zam Zam, and now this. That man should've had his medical licence pulled years ago. He should never have been employed again in any position of authority.'

'You have nothing to prove, Lily. You're an amazing doctor. Do you remember why we stopped going into Africa? Do you remember why we stopped working with NGOs?'

'Of course I remember, but this is World Health—not just some NGO.'

'I don't care if it's Elvis himself back from the dead, it's too dangerous. Last time Africa nearly killed you, and I'm still picking up the pieces.'

'But it didn't. I'm still here. Now Ian's dead, and I can go and—'

'What? Clean up another of his messes? Get another kick in the teeth for it? I don't want to watch that again. Don't ask me to see you go through that repeatedly.' He was shaking his head. 'Lily, you don't have to put us in this situation, just tell them no. You don't have to work. God knows I earn enough for both of us.' He let go of her hands and ran his own through his hair.

'You think I don't know that? It's not the money, my golden rock star. This is about me. About my reputation. After the Sudan fiasco that I warned them about, this is my chance finally to get World Health to acknowledge that they were wrong.'

'They just admitted that when they came crawling back to you and asked for your assistance on this! The admission is there, end of story. No need to go back to Africa and get involved again.'

Lily felt the familiar tears well in her eyes and was damned if she was going to brush them aside. The anger over her treatment a few years back still burned a hole in her stomach when she gave it time to linger. She looked him directly in the eyes. 'I want justice, Quintin. I want them to take what I have to say in my report about Ian and his findings and admit to me, in writing, that I was right. They owe me an apology, a big one.'

He blew out a breath. 'Think about this for a moment before you answer. Is it seriously worth risking your life over? Our lives? Because as much as I hate the thought of you doing this work in a township in South Africa, I hate the idea of you being out there alone without me even more. It's both of us or nothing. That's the way it's always been, and this time wouldn't be any different. But know I'll fight you on safety the whole way.'

Lily waited for her moment, choosing her words carefully. 'Six years ago, I felt like my heart had been ripped out, after Zam Zam. This is my chance to prove to myself that I'm not broken. That I'm tough enough. That I can face Africa again. It didn't destroy me. I'm ready to face the beast again. I love Africa, I was born there, and it's unreasonable that I should be scared to return. I know that you can make your music anywhere, and that deep down you too have a love of Africa. I want this chance to find that stronger me again. To prove to me that while I always knew I was right, I should've stood up and been stronger, more assertive, and perhaps then, Zam Zam might have ended differently for us.'

'Oh, Lily.' He took hold of her shoulders and drew her into his embrace. 'You are strong enough. How can you, after all these years, not know how amazing you really are? But if this is what it takes—then we go back to South Africa. No matter how unhappy I am with the situation there. We go together and find whatever it is that you're searching for. You should know that I would follow you to the ends of the earth if I needed to. I won't let you step into that world alone.'

CHAPTER 3

SOUTH AFRICA, 2010

LILY'S HEART RACED, dreading the changes she knew she would see in the land of her birth. She gazed out the window as the plane prepared to land at O.R. Tambo Airport in the sea of sprawling buildings below, and the tall skyscrapers that marked the financial centre of Johannesburg. The flush of green trees lined straight streets and created a serenity that she knew hid a city that never slept. Where a workforce constantly moved, between the shanties of the townships to the glass monstrosities of the modern buildings, and then later in the day would vacate the working areas and inhibit the smoke and haze of their settlements once again.

No matter where she lived in the world, she still thought of Johannesburg as *her* city. She'd known it when she was growing up, even when she left to go to university in Durban. And she accepted it, even though she now lived primarily in Australia. This ancient land would always be a part of her. From the goldmine dump sites to the exclusive suburbs, Johannesburg always felt like home. Only this time, she was thankful that she was arriving a week after the end of the FIFA World Cup, which had the entire population blowing cheap imitation vuvuzelas that sounded horrendous.

'You okay, *wifie*?' Quintin asked, half smiling as he lifted her hand and kissed it.

She grinned at the old Afrikaans endearment that she'd told him years ago she hated but loved hearing him say in his Austrian accent. 'Just looking at how much it's grown again.'

'You ready? Not too late to charter the next plane and go back to Australia. We have a perfectly good house and recording studio waiting, and you can go work in a private clinic somewhere, see patients, be normal ...'

'Not a chance. We're here now, so close.'

Turning her face back to the window and resting her forehead against the pane, she strained her eyes to see if there was anything recognisable yet.

'Cabin crew, prepare for landing.' The captain's voice came over the speaker system. Lily felt the wheels as they uncoiled from the belly of the plane, and her gut clenched.

Six months in South Africa. When she'd signed the contract papers, it had seemed like a long period of time, but now looking at this city passing below, she knew that it wouldn't be enough.

No matter how many months they spent in Africa, it would never be sufficient to quench her love of the place. Despite her reservations about herself, and her capabilities, she didn't blame Africa for the scars she'd received at Zam Zam. The gross mismanagement of the NGO and the complicity of Ian in the situation—it was his pig-headed view that because they were foreign, they would be safe, that had led him to completely misread the situation.

And she was about to get the chance to prove it now. Although she knew that she couldn't make a decent dent in the community health in Kimberley in just six short months, even if she was double-checking someone else's research.

Dr Ian Hawthorne. An unpleasant man she'd worked with before. According to Marion, her boss at the World Health Organization, the police had just considered his death an ill-fated case of hijacking.

It wasn't going to be easy to step into his shoes. Walking into the World Health private clinic he'd set up, knowing that everyone there was possibly colluding with him. But she needed his last few years of research on HIV in the community of Kimberley, and anything he had about the meningitis patients.

Her specialisation in cluster medicine was an ace up her sleeve and one that Marion was now calling on. As Lily had lived in South Africa through the apartheid era, she knew the dynamics of the country already, which would help speed her investigation into his research along.

Admittedly, both she and Quintin knew they were walking into a viper's nest. Hijackings in South Africa were common enough. She had friends who'd been hijacked at gunpoint, and some had their babies or children in the back seat stolen with the vehicles. Sometimes they'd been found on the side of the road, occasionally alive, a few of them dead. This had become a way of life here. Although the ever-resilient South Africans had come up with a hijack mesh to put on the driver's window to stop the smash'n'grab attacks, it didn't appear to be helping as the hijacks continued.

She squeezed Quintin's hand. He was like the Yin to her Yang and would help them to blend quickly into the community with his music. And while she would be at the clinic all day, at night they'd be in Ian's home, Hacienda El Paradiso, where she'd be able to hopefully understand him more by living in his space.

She heard Quintin's voice in her head: *We've had the displeasure of knowing Ian personally.* They'd worked alongside Ian in Sudan while at the Zam Zam refugee camp when Doctors Without Borders had put out a call for help with the influx of displaced people in the region, and the need for personnel on the ground. The fact that their resilient organisation had packed up and left that camp in 2004 was testament to how bad the conditions were, for both the refugees and the aid workers. But the actual ending, that was all on Ian, every injury, and every death that day, including the two scarred bullet wounds on Lily's shoulder.

According to Marion, Ian had taken a government post in South Africa after the Sudan incident and had been in various NGO positions since then before starting this project about two years ago.

Quintin and Lily hadn't contacted Ian after Sudan, and they'd not even formed a bond with him over the horrific experience. She shook her head, trying to dislodge the memory before it swamped her.

As if sensing she was struggling, Quintin turned to her and smiled. She lifted her hand and ran it down his strong, tanned neck and laid it to rest on his chest, as if touching him could keep her here in the present and away from memories of the past.

'You nervous?' she asked.

'A little. Walking into trouble was once normal for us, but this time, it seems different. It's been a while since we were here. And knowing that Ian was killed doesn't make it easier for me. It's more personal now than your outreach missions and even the refugee camps. Dangerous.' He kissed her hand. 'You know I'll always have your back, but it's South Africa. It's a totally different beast to when you were growing up here, even from when we got married. I'm worried about what we've got ourselves into, that's all.'

'I don't know what I did to deserve you, but hell, I still love you, even all these years later!' She leaned into him. As his lips touched hers, warm and soft, she knew that no matter what Africa threw at them, they would be okay.

They still had each other. And together they would conquer the world.

Lily grinned at Quintin as he indicated to turn the loaded Land Cruiser off the main Midlands Road and onto the unnamed gravel access to Hacienda El Paradiso. Situated twelve-point-two kilometres north of Kimberley's city centre, it was a small, isolated eight-hectare farm within the Roodepan area, surrounded by a six-foot fence topped with razor wire, like all the other properties.

Quintin keyed the code into the control panel, and the metal gates slowly dragged themselves back against the wall, welcoming them into their new semi-rural dwelling.

There were lights on in the house at the end of the long driveway, as expected. They would've been switched on by the live-in maid, Bessie, and her gardener/handyman husband, Lincoln, whom they'd inherited along with the use of Ian's house because the couple had worked for him and had been looking after the house since his death, waiting for someone else to take over.

Despite it only being sundown, Lily looked back behind the Cruiser to ensure the gates had closed and no one had snuck in from outside, a trick they'd been warned had started happening with more frequency in South Africa. They drove towards where lights already twinkled and finally stopped in front of Hacienda El Paradiso, their new home.

Quintin switched off the engine and they both took a moment to take in the wide veranda that surrounded the iron-clad roof and the big windows. The sprawling farmhouse in front of them could've been found anywhere that there was once colonial rule. The Federation style of the English architecture had reached all over the world. However, this house was painted a rustic orange, with thick black burglar bars over each window.

Lily opened her door and stepped out. The cold hit her in the face, and she shivered. She had forgotten how cold Kimberley could get. Right near zero now, the air from her mouth immediately steamed as she blew on her hands and put them under her armpits.

The crunch of the loosely compacted road base under her boots was familiar. Instead of tarmac or bricks, crushed gravel was not uncommon in South African properties with long driveways, and while it sometimes became corrugated in big rains or with the use of large trucks, in a home setting it was generally a good alternative to nothing. She could see the garden was well-tended, its borders neat and trimmed, the bare branches waiting patiently to burst into action again in spring, toughing out the colder months. But then there were those that had been planted especially for winter, their glossy green foliage surrounded by soft petals of white, light purple and pink. 'By the look of this garden, we inherited more than one gardener or at least a service. Look, it's amazing.'

'Probably. There's no way a doctor working full-time would have a smallholding like this without help,' Quintin said.

The front door opened as they walked towards it. A maid was silhouetted against the lights. 'Welcome, Madam and *Baas*. I'm Bessie. I used to look after Dr Ian.' She shook her head and clicked her tongue in a manner that said she was unhappy about his passing and she made the sign of the cross over her chest. 'Mrs Marion told me you were coming to live here, and now I must look after you good-good like I did Dr Ian.'

'Thank you for being here so late to meet us,' Lily said as she stepped into the bright-white light that had flashed on with a sensor as she got closer to the house. She could see Bessie now, standing with a security gate open behind her that would usually have guarded the front door, its thick metal bars making a statement of 'keep out' to anyone who didn't have an invitation. Bessie looked to be in her late sixties, perhaps early seventies, like she should be at home with her grandchildren, not being someone's maid. Her steel-grey hair was plaited neatly, and she didn't wear the customary *doek* that most maids in uniforms in South Africa wore to cover their hair. Even her dress was not some unsightly floral fabric with a matching apron, but rather Bessie wore a long tunic top, like those worn in theatre, and some soft tights. She didn't look like any maid that Lily had ever seen.

'It's good to meet you, Bessie, I'm Quintin, and this is my wife, Lily. Please call us by our names, not madam and boss.'

'Thank you,' Bessie said, holding back the security gate for them.

'I can't wait to see inside; the garden looks beautiful. Does your husband do it all by himself or does he have somebody come in and help?' Lily said.

'Lincoln, he is a hard worker, there is no slowing him down. He also looks after the sheep, goats, chickens, guineafowl and the ducks that Dr Ian had been given by the people who can't pay money, so give him what they can. There is also the little horse, Perdy, and her foul, Dee-Dee, and Pedro the donkey. They are naughty, they eat the flowers in the garden. Sometimes, Lincoln gets help from our friend Klein-Piet, the medicine man, and some of the teenagers from Platfontein that he brings with him, to keep them out of trouble. If there is lots to do, they are hard workers, too.'

'Wow. Didn't expect Ian to help some random teenagers, that's new.'

'No. That was more Klein-Piet's idea. I think Dr Ian just went along with it because teenagers are cheaper labour than men.'

'That's more like the Ian I knew,' Lily said. 'Please don't misunderstand me, it's good that Ian shared his home with all those animals. No one should be alone …' She was fishing for news of an 'other' that might have been off Marion's radar, and Bessie knew it.

'Dr Ian was never alone. We are always here. Come, I have made dinner, and while you have some hot tea, Lincoln can bring in your suitcases and empty your *bakkie*. I have made up your bed with fresh sheets in Dr Ian's bedroom because it is the best room in the house. In the morning, you will agree with me when you see the view out the window. I have cleared out all his cupboards, so that I can unpack your suitcases. Mrs Marion, she told me not to take any of Dr Ian's clothes in case you wanted to keep anything, but she said after you are ready, I can take them and give them to the people.'

'Thank you, Bessie,' Lily said as she walked into the small entrance way. 'But we can unpack our cases, there's no need for you to do that.' The feeling of déjà vu slithered over her, and she stopped, looking around. The house was decorated by a professional stylist. There was no way that Ian could have pulled together the type of collection and style that flowed from one room to another. She had worked with him; he was a slob. His house so far reflected nothing of the man she knew.

As well as the antique furniture, a large original David Shepherd painting dominated the cream wall behind that: a herd of oryx galloping in dry country and dust tufting up from their easy gait across the earth. It was stunning and would've cost a few thousand.

A faint smell of lemon myrtle and wax hung in the air. Lily smiled. She knew that scent well from her own childhood in this country, where maids polished the wooden furniture till it glistened.

'This is the lounge.' Bessie's voice cut into her thoughts, bringing her back to the present, and she took a few steps to catch up to Quintin while looking at the teal curtains and white shutters, and the large cream rug laid over marble-tiled flooring that shone proudly.

'This is the kitchen and the laundry. There is a formal dining room, and formal lounge, and upstairs are all the bedrooms and the office,' Bessie said. 'There is a bathroom downstairs, too.'

'Where do we put the Cruiser at night? When we drove in we could see the large garages next to the house. Perhaps you have the button to open the doors as we weren't given that?' Quintin asked.

'The doors do not open anymore. The *bakkie* stays on the driveway. Dr Ian, he made a hothouse for his flowers inside the garages.'

'Okay, then, expensive car outside where it can be stolen, and flowers in a garage. Interesting choice, Ian,' Lily said.

Bessie carried on walking as if she hadn't heard what Lily had just said.

They reached the dining room, which was an elegant and over-the-top mix of furniture. Large photos of a San, the first people of Africa, in his home somewhere in the Kalahari Desert were framed and hung in sequence along the wall. The pictures were stunning.

Looking around, Lily saw that a tall vase of tightly packed magenta roses in the centre of the table softened the whole room and filled it with their sweet scent. The special touch of a housekeeper, not an interior designer. Bessie had set two places at the large French provincial table.

'I will serve your dinner now. Please leave the dishes, I can do them in the morning. I am in at six-thirty, and then I work until five o'clock, with lunchtime from one to two. I work weekends if you need me to, but that is extra pay. Mrs Marion, she said she told you my wages and that I needed to let you know right away what my working hours were because you might want to change them. Here is Lincoln.'

A big man appeared in the doorway carrying two of the cases. He put them down and stepped into the room, bowing his head in respect.

'Hello, Lincoln,' Lily said as she stepped forward and shook his hand. Quintin followed suit.

'Nice to meet you and thank you for bringing those in. You can leave them there; I'll come help with the rest,' Quintin said as he and Lincoln disappeared, leaving Lily and Bessie in the dining room.

'Bessie, your hours sound fine, but with only Quintin and me in the house, and us mostly away at work, I'm not sure what you'll do all the time.'

'Keeping this place clean is a full-time job. There are six bedrooms. I never understood why Dr Ian moved in here when it was just him. I was always in the house more than he was. The family before he moved in here, they had four children and dogs everywhere.'

'Space, I suspect. It's a luxury that doctors who work in critical situations seldom have. And this house is beautiful, and has so much land outside that he could just walk around and not feel confined. I understand completely.'

Bessie nodded.

'Thank you for cooking dinner. It's lovely to arrive and not have to worry about that.'

'Mrs Marion said this is a new town for you, so I did not want you getting lost on the first night you got here trying to find food. Driving at night is dangerous for people who do not always live in South Africa, to know where to stop and where not to. You could drive into a bad township area. I cannot lose you on the first night that you come into this house. And Dr Ian always liked for me to cook dinner. Make his lunch so he could take it with him, and he ate a cooked breakfast every day with his coffee. But I am happy to learn what you like.'

'Thank you,' Lily said as she reached out and placed her hand on Bessie's arm. 'It's terrible what happened to him.'

'He was a good *baas*,' Bessie said softly, but when she looked at Lily, the warmth of the words did not show in her eyes.

'Let's hope we can make a different standard, then,' Lily said, smiling. 'And we are not too hard to work for.'

Bessie smiled, and this time Lily could see it shine in her crinkled eyes, too.

So, Ian had not been liked by his staff, an interesting first night's observation. Lily was sure that once Bessie got to know her, she would talk about Ian more.

'Right, all inside and the Cruiser is locked,' Quintin said as Lincoln put the last case on the floor in the dining room. 'Thank you both.'

'Great,' Lily said. 'Actually, Bessie, perhaps tonight Quintin and I will serve ourselves. Why don't you take your lovely husband home and we'll see you in the morning.'

'I need to show you the alarm system. Mrs Marion, she said even though she had put it in your letter, I must show you. Make sure you understand, so no *skabengas* get into the house.'

Skabengas—naughty people. Now that was a word she hadn't heard in a while. 'Let's run through that, then you can go. It's late and I hate that we're keeping you from your family,' Lily said.

Bessie looked downwards. 'It's only Lincoln and me here. My daughter—she is now learning to be a nurse at the university in Johannesburg. And my sister, she is in Alexandra. Lincoln's first wife and two sons, they are with God already.'

'I'm sorry to hear that,' Quintin said.

'It is the way now—with the thinnings disease. Dr Ian used to say this disease comes for the old as well as the young. That it is the new plague in Africa. To be feared more than God and his locusts and floods.'

'A harsh way to put it,' Lily said. 'But there's still no cure—at least there are now drugs that can slow it down.'

Bessie showed them the alarm with its two different codes—one for normal usage, and the other as an 'under duress' switch that would alert the security company if there was a problem.

'The cat, Tiger, he is out hunting now, but he will come back inside later. His food is on the counter, but he sleeps on the bed in the spare bedroom mostly. He is a very friendly cat that is also very loud. He talks all the time,' Bessie said. 'Even when I am doing the housework, that cat he comes and checks on me and talks to me from room to room. He is not like any other cat that I have ever met.'

'I had a cat when I was growing up. I'll make sure that he's okay,' Lily said.

'Welcome to your new home,' Bessie said as she left the kitchen. Lincoln was waiting for her just outside. Lily heard the back door close and lock loudly, and then lights appeared along a pathway to the annexed building. Together the couple walked the small distance to their own little detached *ikhaya* near the rear of the house.

'So, this is it, Mrs Winters. Alone at last again in South Africa.' Quintin stepped up to Lily and backed her against the counter-top in the kitchen. He dipped his head and kissed her, and her hands didn't need a second invitation to curl up, wrap around him and pull him closer. Even after so many years together, Lily still couldn't say no to Quintin, and couldn't get enough of him. 'What say we take this upstairs and test-drive that bed, because as much as I want to make love to you here in the kitchen, I suspect that the silhouettes in the window will shock our new helpers.'

Lily giggled against his mouth, then moved her lips along his chin, giving him small kisses all the way to his ear. He shivered and put his head back, granting her easier access to his neck.

Lily whispered against his skin, 'I think perhaps it's a good idea because we both know that dining-room-table sex didn't end well last time.'

'How was I supposed to know that that was a trestle table and we'd both land on the floor!' Quintin said, laughing. 'Come on, *wifie*, let's go.' He ran his hand down her arm, threaded his fingers with hers and gave her a small tug in the direction of the stairs. 'HIV and its cluster meningitis, along with dinner, can wait. I'm starving for my Lily.'

CHAPTER 4

REYANSH PRABHU SMOOTHED his beard and checked that his shirt was tucked in before he took a deep breath and knocked twice on the door of his sister's office. He wiped his palms on his suit pants. Despite the temperature controls within the Ayurprabhu Pharmaceuticals building being just twenty-two degrees Celsius, the sweat continued to bead on his lip.

He cursed for trying yet again to wean himself cold turkey off the drugs. He should have known this wouldn't be the week he could stay away from them.

'Come in,' Mishti barked.

He turned the handle and walked in.

Mishti Prabhu sat behind a huge, lavishly ornate, antique hard-wood desk that was complete with ivory-and-gold leaf inlays. She pushed her chair and it rolled easily on its castors and stood up on heels that defied logic, making her five-foot-seven frame appear like it was six feet tall as she walked towards him.

'Brother, how nice. What a surprise. You should have told me you were dropping in.'

'And have your secretary tell me you weren't here again? No, I need to speak with you urgently in the office, not have you drop by my house talking shop again.'

'Come on, we both know that wife I chose for you is a perfect homemaker. Your house is always neat, tidy and I can't fault her on her management skills as she tells the ever-changing employees what to do. Your staff have excellent cleaning skills, and your wife needs credit for that, even though she gave you those three brats, ruined her figure and continues to milk your bank accounts dry. You really should ask her what she spends the money on. It's clearly not on keeping herself looking nice and trim for her husband.'

He hated that Mishti somehow was aware of the state of everything that went on in his house. He was sure she even knew when he and his wife, Anaya, had last had sex. Somehow, she sniffed out everything.

'It's not Anaya's housekeeping that's under scrutiny though, is it?' he asked.

He saw Mishti frown and knew to get what he had to say over quickly before she started throwing things at him again. 'There has been a development in the lab,' he said in a rush. 'Some of our meningitis fungi died. We've lost the rest of the culture that we were using to put into the new batch of Protease Inhibitors. However, the cultures of the urinary tract infection are doing well, so I can substitute those within twenty-four hours.'

Mishti nodded. She strode to her chair and sat down again, her hands on her desk building pyramids with each finger until she tapped the two pinkies together.

'It's really no one's fault that those cultures died,' he added.

'It sometimes happens with live cultures and fungus, but it is annoying that it happened at this facility. That strain of meningitis has served us well.'

'I still have the source culture, but it will take time to regrow to the amount that we require, that's all,' he assured her.

She nodded again. 'And the urinary tract? Do we have the treatment medication in the same container?'

Reyansh nodded. 'I re-checked that manifest before I came to you. The shipment is on Friday. The pills will be ready on Thursday night.'

She stretched her legs out in front of her and leaned back in the chair.

'There better be no disruption in the supply, Reyansh. It's important that there are no hiccups to the Cape Town shipment. Our shareholders are expecting us to make a profit. We promised them a quality product made with cost efficiency.'

Reyansh sneered. 'You say that every quarter now.'

'I mean it.'

'No, you don't. Why not just say it up front? You want your profit-share cut. It's always been about the money for you.'

'You're wrong. It's about so much more than that. It's about control. Control of our industry, ensuring the family name is the biggest and the most profitable pharmaceutical company in South Africa. About proving to our father that he made the right choice in making me CEO.'

'And you claim credit as if it was all you.'

'The generic cheap drugs were originally your idea, and it was a good one, but now it's about so much more. It's grown, and you need to evolve your ideas along with it.'

'I hate this. You're hurting people and not only those who are already HIV infected. Children, too.'

'Get over it. You have to. For you, it's now a double-edged sword. It's not just about your access to your drug of choice to soothe you, keep you company through the day and long nights. It's about the money, too, isn't it? That lovely wife of yours who likes to spend every penny you earn.'

'I know that.'

'Just imagine how different your life would've been had you not been caught out addicted to our product in the first place and you hadn't had to tell me what you were doing.'

He shook his head. His twin didn't know him. She had never made an effort to understand him since they were in nursery school together. These days were no better; his sister had become the queen of simply taking things from him. Like his best friend, whom she had married and now controlled.

And she'd taken his dreams from underneath him.

She would never acknowledge in public that the manufacturing of cost-effective generic drugs, which had become their bread and butter, had been his idea. His final attempt to prove to their father that he deserved to be given control of the family business. That he could take the company, and make a profit, no matter what. He, the male heir, would ensure that the family name lived on, and that the company thrived, even in the ever-changing South African environment.

Mishti had stolen his idea and perverted it. Distorted his cheap drugs and tainted them. She had proved to their father that by diversifying the idea across different medications, and changing it slightly, they would then cater to the millions of people who were already relying on HIV antiretroviral drugs daily, creating a new market that was just waiting to be tapped into.

An instant market.

Their father had given control of Ayurprabhu Pharmaceuticals to Mishti because of that.

Being the CEO of the family business had been his dream since he could walk, since he used to sit with his father and make pills in their first small laboratory. He learned from a young age how to be the chemist, not Mishti. He was the one who could make the drugs, not his sister with her finance degree. But his father had once again looked right past him and his achievements. Always showing the masses the appropriate affection for his son, but never following through when it counted. He had given his company to his daughter.

'Just imagine if Father knew his precious son was nothing more than a junkie, and his wife a gold-digger who was spending money as if it was water. Poor, poor Reyansh, always the victim. The man who still yearns to be the apple of Father's eye.'

'Why do you taunt me? You got control of the company. I used to idolise you growing up. It was never my fault that I was the male heir.'

'Whatever. I'm not in the mood for a gender-equality argument with you. Just do your job. And do it well so that we don't get caught.'

He shrugged. 'I know my place: I create a market in Africa for African drugs. Our esteemed vice-president of research and your friend Mr Elijah Mbaya's job is to find us new patents that we can make money from, and your part in the big puzzle is to oversee the operations and skim off the profits while keeping the shareholders happy. I know my place, sister-dearest.'

'Then go do it, because if we don't, we can't compete in this industry.'

'I know that, I wasn't born yesterday,' Reyansh said.

'This conversation is over. Get back to work.'

Reyansh bit his lip. He wanted to walk right up to her chair and strike the smug smile off her face. She liked nothing better than to rub in the fact that their father had signed the company to her and left him as just the head chemist. She relished the fact that she had power over him. Her younger brother. One day he would say things to her—like it was her fault that he was addicted in the first place.

Her fault.

Not his. *Hers!*

She was the one who had given him the pills when they were still in school, got him hooked early, and now kept him by the short-and-curlies because if anyone else ever found out that Ayurprabhu's head chemist was addicted to his own drugs, he would be ruined. Anaya would have an excuse to leave him, and the shame he would feel would be devastating. His father, the founding member of Ayurprabhu Pharmaceuticals, would turn away from his weak son.

Reyansh wouldn't survive it.

After all, it had been his father who had insisted that he learn to fight when he was younger. Made sure that if he was ever in a scrap, he would come out the victor. But physical violence was not what was needed in this circumstance. If he did stand up to Mishti in a more forceful way, she would be ruthless. She had proved that she could be, even to those she claimed to love. She had kept her family surname and refused to change to her husband's, even threatening to call off her wedding at one point when it looked like she wouldn't get her own way. And now she had the power to cut off the money that his wife was so good at spending even as it hit their account each month.

Mishti controlled him.

She knew it.

And he knew better than to argue with his older sister, even if it was only by five minutes. She might have the same level of education that he did, but somehow, she was just smarter.

So far, she'd always won.

CHAPTER 5

Ulwazi sat on the friendship bench which the mental health clinic provided as a safe space for lonely or depressed people to meet and find support and friendship. She'd sat here every Tuesday, weekend and public holiday for the past year. She smiled when she thought of how clever she was that she'd manipulated a situation which was supposed to help people into benefitting herself and her family.

Her little mischief of mice—her *igundane*.

It had taken time to unite the *igundane* who spied for her and reported what was happening throughout the whole of Sandton, and she had people sitting on benches in other areas, too, listening to what the women had to say, reporting it all back to her. From Fourways, through Sunninghill, Bryanston and even as far out as Van Riebeeck Park.

She was the intelligence hub. They scampered in and told her the gossip that she needed to know and she never had to pay for it, just give them a favour in return. A job for the daughter in the network. A good word in the boss's ear for a raise by the right person. She traded that information.

Nobody knew better than she did what was happening right under their noses. To any observer, they were just two people sitting on a pretty blue friendship bench. It was the perfect place to collect all the news that she needed from the households in Sandton.

Her office.

For instance, she knew that the madam at number 84 Hunting-don Road was going on an overseas holiday and that she had a big flat-screen TV recently delivered to her house, but she was good to her maid and had also given her a new one when she'd upgraded, and she paid the maid's TV licence. So that information would never be traded. That house, for now, was safe.

The man who lived in number 156 Daisy Street had a big built-in gun safe, and he owned a business licence with a 'dedicated status'. This meant that he could license an unlimited number of firearms and ammunition. He often took a few of these weapons home, especially the semi and automatic rifles, before he went out in his *bakkie* for his job the next day. He never took his key with him, and she knew where it was hidden.

The *igundane* reported that he treated his wife badly. He hit her and locked his children in their rooms as punishment, and the wife was happy to tell Ulwazi exactly where the key was concealed and that it changed places each day of the week. She knew all the hiding places. That house's information had been traded, and some of those weapons were now in Edenvale, safe in her warehouse and waiting for delivery to their new owners.

She had made sure that the wife and children were not there when the attack happened. After all, that wife had sat on this very bench and spilled out her sorrow to Ulwazi. She couldn't hurt the woman, but that good-for-nothing husband, he hadn't died. No, instead of a nice insurance payout for his widow, he was going to recover, and Ulwazi would get to trade information when the time was right again, and make more money from him.

The wife, she could continue to bleat like a sacrificial lamb that she was a victim, but it was her choice to stay there with him. She could always leave if she really wanted to.

The family who owned the townhouse in Ashley Avenue, in Bryanston, was still having staff problems. The Indian madam there changed maids like one would change underwear. Ulwazi knew that mostly the father was just the pay package, but sometimes he liked to take pills. All sorts of different pills. The family were obviously very wealthy, but the *igundane* said that this family itself didn't live like a family awash with money at all.

They had a good security system, but no dog. She would find out what was happening in that house. There had to be something that she could steal or make money from in some other way. She just needed to get a reliable *igundane* into the house.

CHAPTER 6

'Lily, don't move. There's a miniature tiger on the bed between us. Please tell me that's Ian's cat.'

At the sound of Quintin's voice, the cat began kneading the duvet cover and purring so loudly it was as if there was a small engine in the room. It stood and walked up the bed towards Quintin.

'It didn't eat us while we slept, so it must be friendly,' Quintin said.

Lily moved slightly under the covers and laughed.

The cat stopped, as if realising there were two people in the bed, but when Lily put her hand out, he ran to her and headbutted it. Then he yowled.

Lily laughed harder.

He meowed and threw his whole weight against her side as he rubbed from her hip to her shoulder. Turning his bulk over, he showed a striped yellow belly before putting his head under her chin. And then meowed again.

'You are talkative, Stripe,' Lily said as the cat stood and walked over to Quintin, and onto his chest.

'Tiger, she called him Tiger, not Stripe,' Quintin said, frowning.

'You sure?'

'Yeah.'

'Hey, Tiger, aren't you a beauty,' she said.

He half closed his eyes and kneaded Quintin on the chest, purring loudly.

'I guess this means we pass muster with the cat,' Lily said.

'I'm not sure this huge thing is a cat. Look at it, they definitely make them big in Africa,' Quintin said.

Lily looked at the cat that was pinning her husband to the bed. While he did have black-and-orange stripes, he also had a silver streak to his fur. His head was large with tall ears that had tufts at the end, almost like a lynx. His white whiskers were long and thick, sticking out from his expressive face. As she looked at his feet, she could see hair tufting up between the toes. While his coat was shaggy, he was soft to touch, and as she ran her hand over his body, his purrs increased in volume.

'He's beautiful. Just like you. You gained a friend there. I think he must be part-Maine Coon and part-African wild cat. I wonder if Beatrice knows where Ian got him from—he's the biggest domestic cat I've ever seen.'

'Her name is Bessie, believe me, Lily. Thank heavens it's not Beatrice—I would have cracked up laughing every time I said her name. We had a Beatrice at school who was the class clown.'

Lily frowned. 'Okay, Bessie. I'll remember that. Bessie. And her husband?'

'Lincoln. You and names—I swear, you get worse as we grow older. God only knows what you'll be like when we're in our eighties. I'll be introducing myself to you every day.'

'Ha-ha, that's not so far away anymore. It's probably time we stopped joking about that, we're getting older now.'

'We're not ancient, yet. Besides, I sleep with a younger woman, which keeps me from showing my age.'

'Is that so? If that's the case, then I sleep with an old man.'

Quintin reached for her hair, and smoothing it said, 'You're as lovely as ever, and you seriously don't look like you're in your golden years. You don't look a day over fifty. Besides, there are still many years for you to catch me up.'

'You're an idiot, but I love you anyway,' she said, smiling as she put her hand over his.

Quintin laughed.

Tiger meowed and moved back to Lily. Then he walked over their joined hands and headbutted her ear and began grooming her hair.

'Yuck,' Lily said, sitting up. 'I think we need to put a stop to that one right away.'

'Awww, honey, he's just cleaning one of his pride,' Quintin joked, but at the same time, he pulled himself up in the bed and lifted the massive cat away from Lily.

'Since when did you become such a cat fan?'

'This beast is more than just a cat!'

As if knowing that his cuddle time was over, Tiger walked to the bottom of the bed, jumped off with a loud thud, and went to the bedroom door, where he sat down and wailed.

'It's open, you stupid thing, that's how you got in here in the first place,' Quintin said.

But the cat just narrowed its eyes and looked at him again, meowing loudly.

'It wants you to go feed it,' Lily said.

'Why me?'

'Because you're the one who gets up at all hours of the night and will probably have it with you all day while you compose your next album. Look at it. Clearly, it's used to a male feeding it.'

'That's some serious woman logic,' he said, getting out of bed. The cat swished around the side of the door and disappeared, knowing it had got its way.

'Oh, honey, as much as I love the sight of all that maleness, you probably want to put on some clothes. Remember the house came with a maid. Not sure of her reaction being confronted with all that at six-thirty in the morning!'

Quintin stalked back to the bed and kissed Lily loudly on the mouth. 'There are going to be disadvantages to having someone else in the place, and me having to remember to put clothes on in the morning is going to be one of them.'

'I don't know about the view from our window that Bessie said was worth it, but I sure like the view inside!' Lily said.

'Watch your step,' warned Quintin.

Lily avoided a large boulder that projected out into the pathway. 'Thanks,' she said, stepping around it as Quintin loosely adjusted his grip on her hand.

'It's warming up,' he said.

Lily put her face to the sun. 'Once the coldness of the morning's burned off, the day's going to be pleasant. I love the lack of humidity here compared to Brisbane.'

Quintin looked around. Ian's demand for space was obvious. Not a thing on the property was crowded, and nothing was close to the free-standing main homestead, yet even with the illusion of so much land, the property seemed a little claustrophobic to Quintin because of the huge fence that wrapped around the entire perimeter. It reminded him that he was fenced in for security as much as the bad people were fenced out. He'd still be calling in an independent security company. There had been disturbing reports of farmers being attacked on their farms and the re-emergence of 'one-*boer*-one-bullet' within a far-right wing of a political party. He needed to make sure that they, and the staff, were safe.

A pleasant surprise had been finding that one side of the property bordered on a game farm, so that part of the shared fencing was even higher—it was double-fenced with predator wires and had eight strands of wire to keep the large antelope and other game on their side of the fence. The game farm must be well stocked, as they'd seen eland, zebra and wildebeest grazing in the distance.

'I hope that no big cats come for a visit,' Lily said.

'I doubt it, they must have to be vigilant with them. Besides, I'm sure that a zebra tastes much better to a lion than one of the scrawny chickens running around this place.'

Lily grinned. 'Those are our scrawny chickens for at least six months, so if you think they need feeding, then go ahead and play farmer while you're here. Just a reminder that you do have an album to finish. You've promised your record label that it'll be done by June next year.'

They stood near the wooden fence where a small but fat pony ate from a trough, and a grey donkey stood close by, as a little dirty-brown foal ran amok, kicking the air and racing from one end of the paddock to the other as if it was totally unaware that it was chasing its own shadow around. The animals looked happy, but he could see on the donkey where old scabs had healed up on its withers, and on its chest where scarring didn't quite fit with the smooth hair, a sure sign that this donkey had seen its share of troubling times.

Remembering Bessie's comment about them being used as payment for bills, Quintin frowned. Payment for debts. Commodities. Not rescued. He thought about how many animals Lily had saved during their time together. For him, saving animals was a distraction from his music, but he always got roped in when his wife's big heart drove her to protect them.

Ian hadn't been like that. Everything here at his little Hacienda El Paradiso was professionally staged, the picture manipulated. Exactly what had Ian been up to this time?

Something was bothering Quintin. From the discussion with Marion at the World Health Organization, she had said that Médecins Sans Frontières were the primary beneficiaries of Ian's estate, which is what had made it possible for them to move into it, rather than having the property sold off. They'd been given free rein to do what they wanted, as long as it didn't devalue the place.

Ian's job hadn't been connected to the small farm, but they'd suspected that he'd have kept most of his files in his study there. It was something that Lily often did too when she was working on a perplexing problem. It would make it easier for her to continue his research. To their surprise, however, they had found not one notebook or file. Nothing.

'Penny for your thoughts,' Lily said as they walked back towards the house, past the sheep pens, with their neat shelters and stacks of hay that the sheep nibbled at. There wasn't much natural grass left in the paddocks as it was the middle of winter, but the trees that shaded the brown dirt were still green and cast their shadows wide.

'I'm thinking that you knew Ian well enough to recognise those annoying habits of his, and I was wondering if this will work to your advantage when you find his research,' Quintin said.

'Good question. Big point being when I find his research notes and files.'

Quintin smiled. 'I remember how mad his shorthand made you at Zam Zam.'

'I had no idea how to read his charts until you bought me that old Pitmans book. It's strange that he has no paperwork at home.'

'We can ask Bessie when we get back. Perhaps she'll know where it's all been put.'

'Perhaps. She didn't seem overly upset when I mentioned Ian's passing. I think that this wasn't as cosy a set-up as it looks on the surface. Something else was going on here, we just need to figure out what,' Lily said.

'Something here got Ian killed, and until we know what it is, whether simply being in the wrong place at the wrong time or something more sinister, we're going to have to tread carefully with everyone.' Quintin squeezed her hand and drew her closer to him. He'd be there to protect Lily's back, as always.

'I know,' she said. 'I promise to try to step as carefully as I can.'

They got back to the house and were standing near the Land Cruiser, looking towards the garage that didn't house vehicles.

'What do you think of redesigning the garage and making it into a music studio?' Quintin asked. 'Six months is a long time for you to put up with my practising in the spare bedroom, and I know how it drives you nuts when I write something new and play it over and over. If we have a studio here at the house, then you won't have the noise, and I can compose at any hour without disturbing you. Instead of finding a studio in the city and being away from you. I really don't want you here alone.'

Lily smiled. 'Let's go see how hard that's going to be before I agree to any grand design plans.'

Quintin threaded his arm through hers, and they walked together towards the garage. There was a padlock on the door.

'That's weird,' said Lily.

'Lincoln,' called Quintin. 'Lincoln, are you around? We need the garage opened.'

Lily shook her head. 'Since when do you yell for someone like that?'

Quintin said, 'I saw him looking at us coming out—he pretended to be working in the garden. Give him a minute and he'll be here.'

'Can't believe that you shouted for him like that,' Lily said.

'Pot. Kettle. Black. You used to do that all the time. Besides, look, it worked,' said Quintin. 'Less than a minute …'

Lincoln was breathing heavily when he arrived in his blue overalls with some keys jingling in his pocket. '*Baas,* Madam,' he greeted.

'Can you open the garage? We want to see inside.'

'*Yebo,* but Dr Ian, this is—was—his special place.'

Lily reached for Lincoln's arm. 'I'm sorry about Ian, but as you know we've permission to use this property, treat it like our home. Yesterday you told us it was for plants, and that the Cruiser had to stay outside, so we'd like to see the plants that must be very precious to have the whole triple garage and a lock on the door.'

'*Yebo,* Madam,' Lincoln said as he opened the padlock and slowly pushed the door inwards, before stepping inside.

The fluorescent lights flickered on slowly one by one. Row upon row of greenery became visible. The lights gained in brightness as the interior of the garage lit up, and the red glow of the heat lamps dimmed to a lighter pink.

'Wow,' said Lily, 'look at all those.'

Lincoln made his way in front of them as they admired each flower, and as he explained where Ian had got each of them, Lily came to realise how much the collection had become Lincoln's.

'Did you grow orchids before you came to work for Ian?' she asked.

'*Yebo,*' Lincoln said. 'I used to be the gardener at the Orchid Society. But Dr Ian, he talked me into coming and working for him instead.'

'These are impressive,' said Lily. 'What do you think, Quintin?'

'I think the flowers are beautiful, but this room would be ideal as a studio. The only thing it needs is a door into the house so I don't have to come out on a cold morning or during the night to access it.'

'There is a door that the garden hides,' admitted Lincoln.

'Where?' Lily asked.

'Here,' said Lincoln, taking them to the corner of the room.

Here were plants that were definitely not orchids. The plants had distinctive fingers to them and were very green. Lush, as a tropical plant should look.

'Are those dagga plants?' Lily asked.

'For the medicine,' said Lincoln.

'Medicine?' Quintin said. 'These could get us thrown in jail. Maybe you can move them off the property. I know that Ian probably kept his eyes closed to these growing in his hothouse along with the orchids, but Lily and I don't do street drugs.' Quintin's voice was loud and determined.

'These are not mine; these are Dr Ian's. He used to make medicine with the oil. For the cancer patients.'

'Medicine?' Lily asked, frowning. 'What oil?'

'We grow it nice and healthy. Then he used to cook it and mix it in oil, and then he would give it to his patients who are dying.' Lincoln walked to the corner and showed her a five-gallon drum of olive oil sitting on the bench. 'The oil, Madam, this is part of the medicine that we make.'

'Is it still illegal in South Africa?' Lily protested.

'*Yebo,* but Dr Ian always says that it's no good being a doctor if you can't help people, and sometimes his patients are past what modern medicine can help with. Many of these plants are almost ready to harvest again, so the new oil can be made and put into the new bottles with the special droppers. It is important to keep the patients on the oil.'

'What? You planning on continuing to cook drugs? Here?' Quintin asked.

'There are people who need the oil, and the stocks are low. There is hardly any left.'

Quintin ran his hand through his hair and cursed.

'Of course,' Lily said. 'Ian was making CBD oil for his patients. Oh my, Ian. What were you thinking?'

'What happens to us if we keep these plants? What if the police catch us?' Quintin asked.

'I don't know,' Lily said, 'I need to find out what Ian was up to. I need to find his files and read his notes—and the quicker, the better.'

'All the papers, they were taken. After Dr Ian was killed, they broke into the house and they stole everything. All the files in his office and his computer. There are no papers at this house anymore,' Lincoln said.

Quintin moved closer to Lily. 'Who broke in?'

'The police could not tell us. Even Klein-Piet, he came and looked and could not follow them. They got into a *bakkie* and drove onto the tar road, so he couldn't track them, and he is the best tracker the police have.'

'Last night, Bessie mentioned keeping people out,' Lily asked. 'That was why Marion had the alarm system put in. There was a break-in?'

'*Yebo*, after we were told Dr Ian had been hijacked, and then that night, *skabengas* broke in and they made a big mess. They damaged a lot of the furniture, too, and lots had to be fixed and replaced. Like the mattresses in all the bedrooms and the pillows. Klein-Piet said it was like they were looking for something. They even climbed into the ceiling to check in there.'

'Did the police think they found what they were looking for?' Quintin asked.

'They did not tell us, but Klein-Piet said he did not think so. He said there was too much glass smashed downstairs for them to have found everything. Like the people who broke in had a temper.'

Lily shook her head. 'Have they come back again?'

'*Aikona*. From then, we slept in the main house until the alarm was installed. Marion had a separate alarm installed into our *ikhaya*, too. Only then, when we knew that there was armed response monitoring, did Bessie and I sleep easy again.'

Quintin nodded. 'The danger is still here. Nice of Marion to forget to tell you all this.'

'Typical though,' Lily said. 'Remember how little they told us about Zam Zam and what we faced when we got there? At least we know now.'

'We need to make this place more secure, Lily. I'll call in a security contractor this week and fortify. These plants are going. Ian probably got himself involved in a drug war and wouldn't shut up as usual. Now at least we know what the artificial lighting was for.'

'No one sees the lights in the garage. The plants here need the warmth and humidity in the cold of winter. This is why they are inside.'

Quintin blew out a breath.

Lily reached for him and touched his arm. 'There's research showing that there are a lot of benefits from CBD oil. It's been known to help patients with cancer, autoimmune diseases, fibromyalgia and even epilepsy in kids. I'd like to keep them until we know if he was using the oil in his research.'

'There is much that Dr Ian did that was like the medicine man, the sangoma. He learned from Klein-Piet. He is a policeman as well as a medicine man, and he knows that the plants are here. But you also need to know about the other herbs in the garden. Come see by the animals,' Lincoln said, motioning for them to follow.

Lincoln led them down the path, back to the stable area, before turning and spreading his arms wide.

'It's a vegetable patch,' Lily said, looking around.

Lincoln shook his head. 'You are not a gardener, Madam?'

'No.'

'Then I understand. To you, and to others who do not know plants, it looks like a garden with pumpkins and winter beans. But then look closer. There are Dr Ian's poppies, for pure opium, and that scraggly bush, is called *ma-huang*, it is used in Chinese medicine. See the willow that is at the end of the garden? That too is what the doctor planted to help his patients. And over there are his moringa trees. Beech for mental people, and cinchona trees for quinine—to stop malaria. This is also Dr Ian's natural medicine plants. Dr Ian grew lots of plants here to help his patients with being healthy, or comfortable, not in pain anymore.'

Comprehension dawned on Lily. 'You could've hidden these from us. We wouldn't have been any the wiser.'

'*Yebo*, but you are also a doctor, and perhaps you too will learn the plants of Africa now-now. Learn the old traditional medicines. I do not know you yet. You do not know me. But I hope that you will let me and Klein-Piet teach you,' Lincoln said. 'Dr Ian—he told me if something happens, and he dies, and they sold his house, that I must then burn everything. But you are not a sale. Mrs Marion, she said you were another doctor. So, I did not burn anything. My father is one who uses the oil, and I have seen the difference in his life; he has the cancer, and no drugs from the doctor were helping, but now the pain is gone. When Dr Ian died, I could not do as he asked, I could not burn his plants, because I hoped the new doctor would like the plants and continue to help the people of my town like my father and those in the old-age homes.'

'Lily is not a doctor who's ever prescribed non-pharmaceutical drugs, she's—we're both advocates against using recreational drugs,' Quintin said.

Lincoln scratched his neck. 'No, these are not for fun; these are to help people. People in pain. Bad pain.'

'When did he give you those instructions?' Lily asked.

'A few weeks before he was hijacked. Maybe I should not have said anything.'

'Being a hundred per cent honest with us was the right thing to do. Never be afraid to tell us what's going on. We might get mad, but we'd rather know what's happening. With the marijuana plants, it's difficult. We live mostly in Australia, but we travel all over the world, and there are many rules and laws and we need to be careful we don't get into trouble by mistake, as then we won't have that freedom to travel anymore. Quintin's music raises lots of money for people, and if we have our reputation tarnished even by a hint of a drug scandal, then it will hurt many, many people who rely on us to help them get money to help others. Do you understand?'

Lincoln was nodding. 'Mrs Marion, she told me that on the phone. She said that Dr Lily had African roots.'

'What else did she say?' Lily asked.

'That I must look after you both, Dr Lily and the famous musician rock star *Baas* Quintin, that you are important to Dr Ian's work. And if you are happy here and finish his work, then perhaps the house will not need to be sold and maybe I won't need to find another job.'

Quintin snorted.

'You are going to destroy the plants?' asked Lincoln.

Lily looked at Quintin, and she slowly shook her head. 'No. We won't destroy them, not yet, not until I know more of what Ian was up to and I've seen some of these people you speak of. I wonder if this has anything to do with his being hijacked and killed? Having the local doctor as your drug dealer doesn't exactly go down well in some circles.'

'Dr Ian saved many people and helped many, many more with his oil and herbs. People might not like him, but he was a good doctor who let traditional people continue to use their medicines gathered from the land and blessed by the sangoma. He did not force the white medicine on anyone who didn't want it. But he helped with cures for everyone. There are more herbs that he was looking at and that you can harvest from growing seeds and from cuttings that still need to be planted in the spring. You need to talk to Klein-Piet. He will teach you, Dr Lily. He will teach you like he taught Dr Ian.'

'The one who is also a policeman? What if she doesn't want to know?' Quintin asked.

'If Dr Lily speaks with Klein-Piet and still she does not want the plants, I will burn them. The sick people will be very sad, but it is what I will do,' Lincoln said.

'Sounds like I need to speak with Klein-Piet first,' Lily said.

CHAPTER 7

Piet Kleinman, police detective and master tracker, half sat on the edge of his chair and tapped on the desk while he read through the file in front of him.

'Why the tapping, you only do that when you are agitated,' Detective Natalie Hatch said.

'Dr Hawthorne's case. Things amiss.'

'Then you are in luck, look what just arrived.'

Piet rolled his chair over to Natalie's desk. 'What is it?'

Natalie pointed at her computer screen. 'We have a comprehensive reply from *Johies*.'

'The detective in the main Jo'burg office?'

'*Ja*.'

Piet read the typed message.

Re: Hijacking death—extended report request for information.

Case: #203-872-340.

Autopsy Performed: Yes.

Coroner Findings:

Cause of Death: Double gunshot to the right temple.

Manner: Homicide.

Other notes: Multiple contusions consistent with physical assault. Powder burns on skin consistent with close-range discharge of weapon. Broken fingers and wrists, left knee shot.

Weapon: Matched to 9mm used in the following cases:

#203-561-290, #203-870-001, #203-211-892, #208-111-052, #208-528-348.

No further arrests made on any of the above cases.

Files boxed and on their way to you. I have scanned important pages from each, see attached.

Please advise if you need any other information.

Detective Selvin Naidoo

'Can you see the pattern from the case numbers? Three other hijackings and two home invasions,' she said in an almost excited voice.

'Home invasions or farm attacks?' Piet asked.

'Let's take a look.' Natalie's fingers danced across the keyboard as she printed all the case files that were attached.

Piet collected the last pages as they spat out of the printer and spread them on his desk. They both worked in silence for a while, then they laid the papers down in order: autopsy results, crime-scene reports, case notes.

'Home invasions, that means the killer is most likely a city dweller,' Piet said.

'Other hijacks, all in the Johannesburg areas, except Hawthorne outside of Kimberley. The killer and his gun moved far out of his usual target zone for this one.'

'What was so important about Ian Hawthorne? There was nothing special about him,' Piet said.

'*Ag*, come on; he wasn't a likeable man in the slightest. That time you introduced me to him, he was a sexist pig. If that's what he was like to me as a policewoman, I can only imagine how bad he could be. The man gave me the creeps. Reminds me a lot of our new Acting Chief Aarand Chetty.' She dropped her voice for that last part, just in case. 'Slimy and disrespectful to women, argumentative and a moron.'

Piet smiled. '*Ja*, but he loved the African bush; you did not see that side. He would spend hours with me, learning to track, recording all the different names, trying to speak !Xun. I give you that he was not the most pleasant person, but this type of death, it's personal. The beating, the shooting in the knees as if they wanted something from him and he was not giving it over. What did he have that was so important? He was a doctor who was studying the effects of HIV in a displaced population; nothing worth stealing in that.'

'Whatever it was, surely it wasn't worth dying over?' Natalie said.

'Where else were the home invasions?'

Natalie looked over the two cases. 'Sandton and Fourways.'

'Both affluent suburbs.'

'*Ja* … perhaps there is more to this man than you knew. You sure you want to stay on this case, given that you were friends?'

'Totally.'

'Chetty is aware of your personal connection?'

'*Ja,* he was fine with it. But I do not think at the time he was aware of what this case really would become.'

'Meaning?'

'A month ago, when I was investigating the robbery at Hawthorne's house, I asked to remain as the detective on the case. He was adamant that Ian was just in the wrong place at the wrong time. An unfortunate statistic. Not worth investigating, the perfect job for "my type". So, I got to keep it.'

'But to you?' she asked, looking at him.

'It has always pointed to much more. That is why I was digging deeper. The hijacking alone, sure, they just wanted his 4x4. But put the house robbery on the same night, and I smell a polecat.'

'And the fact he's a doctor? You think there's a connection?'

'I have not managed to put a link to that yet, but the killing of foreign doctors on South African soil is not something anyone would want to get into the media. They would have a merry time with it, and it could damage the tourist industry in the area. I do not think Chetty thought about that at all, to be honest. But I think that we should find Ian's killer regardless of who or what he was—there is more to his death.'

'I agree. Chetty is a shithead. Always has been. Should have heard what he had to say about me being on extended leave when he got this temporary appointment. I knew I needed to get back in here or risk being fired in my absence. Let's hope we can solve this before we get our new chief. It's still a few more months before we find out who's incoming.'

'Let's hope so. If Chetty doesn't drive me to drink first.'

'That I would hate to see.'

'Me too. What do the cases say about the other drivers in the other hijackings? Same MO?'

Natalie shook her head. 'Different. The others were all clean. Close-range, execution style. No beatings.'

'They took it up a notch. Either desperate, or this isn't just an ordinary hijacking for a vehicle. They wanted to know something, which comes back to my first reaction: it was personal.'

'Guess the good doctor needs deeper scrutiny now?' Natalie said.

'I suppose so. Good thing Chetty still has not realised it. Remember, I am not exactly in his good graces either. To him, I am just a tracker who happens to have become a detective. My job is to find people at crime scenes, lost kids in the bushveld etcetera. What do I know about hijackings and robberies? It is not something I can track. Do you remember what he said when he had too many spook-n-diesels at Christmas? I am "just one of those Platfontein people, smoking, drinking and gambling my life away."'

'That's bullshit, alcohol talking. A racist remark that belongs in the apartheid era and you know it. He's a fucking loser. Always has been. Who knows, maybe he has blue balls under those pants he wears to work, maybe his wife keeps him on a stingy ration? I would if I was married to that arsehole. The only person he loves is himself. He's a bitter old buzzard, you know like those ground hornbills with the big jowly faces.' She laughed for a moment and then realised that Piet wasn't joining in. '*Ag*, come on, that was funny. I'll download a picture for you.'

Piet just looked at her blankly, shaking his head.

'You do know what a ground hornbill looks like, don't you?'

'Of course I do. But it is an insult to the bird to say that our boss is like him, that is all.'

Natalie laughed loudly and smacked Piet on the shoulder. 'Good one. Okay, look here ... this could get interesting. None of the vehicles in the hijackings were the same, so they are not after parts. A Merc, the only high-end vehicle, then a Mini.'

'Who hijacks a Mini?' Piet said. 'And an older model at that?'

'The same people who next took a VW Jetta station wagon, before Ian's Land Cruiser.'

'Where's your mind going?' Piet asked.

'Down a dark track. This is more than just Ian Hawthorne in this case. There's something else going on here,' Natalie said.

'You have to be one of the most suspicious policewomen on the force, but I agree with you this time.'

'That's what got me into this detective position in Johannesburg. This baby didn't sleep her way to the top, no, she worked her arse off, building cases just like this one.'

'We have work to do, you and I. Right, partner,' he said. Despite Natalie and him being friends since the police academy almost twenty years before, they were the outcasts: the Barbie doll and the tracker. Unlikely friends and undesirable recruits. Together they had survived their training and their postings all over South Africa, and finally, they were in the same town again and actually got to work together.

Right now, Piet wanted to jump in their police 4x4 and rush to Johannesburg and fetch the boxes himself. He was impatient for more information on the cases. He'd already put two and two together and seen it made five. He could feel it deep inside. Almost a slight tremor in his stomach, and he'd learned many years ago never to ignore that instinct. To follow it.

That was what kept him alive in the Kalahari, then in the Caprivi Strip, and across South Africa, once he joined the police force and slowly moved up the ranks. It made him a good cop. It was what had got him promoted to detective. Given him his little bit of freedom inside the force. That, and the fact that he was not only a master tracker but also the best tracker, just as Natalie had pointed out.

Piet sat down next to Natalie again. 'You know, Hawthorne was killed nearer Johannesburg than Kimberley. While we got to process the body, they took lead on the case. Their jurisdiction. Because Chetty had given me the case of the robbery, I requested their investigation notes. A name I know from my past popped up in Hawthorne's file.'

He handed her the papers. 'When I first saw this, I thought it did not look like a normal hijacking, and yet the police officer in charge, Warrant Officer Sithole, has ruled it as one. There is no progress on the case. It has stalled, but when I read through the papers, I saw so much more. It looks a lot like the good doctor was executed in the temple while he was on his knees. It is quite clear from the photos. Add into the mix that his Land Cruiser was taken. And yet, his wallet was still in his pocket, along with a few hundred rand. Who robs a vehicle and leaves the cash? I have seen this execution style before on a case about ten years ago. It involved some gun-running gangs in Pretoria and Johannesburg. I never got to the bottom of the case as I was pulled off it, and it was given to another Warrant Officer —Sithole.'

'Same officer?'

'Same man. He was a new transfer into the department, so to give him cases was not unusual. I have often wondered what happened. So, while I was in the mood for being a nosy parker, I requested the older files, too. And surprise, surprise, it was never solved. The same guy who signed off on Hawthorne's case as being just a hijacking, my old friend—the legendary Warrant Officer Sithole.'

'You think he's a dirty cop?'

Piet nodded. 'I think that not only have we encountered a cop on the take, willing to look the other way, but I have stumbled into the same group of criminals. The gun-runner gangs of Johannesburg. Back then they were small time. I do not know what they are now. Time and the complacency of violence in the new South Africa, they could be much bigger. I cannot help but wonder when I look into the older cases.'

'That Hawthorne might be involved with gangs? With gun runners?' Natalie asked.

'Maybe. His hijacking, his house being trashed. They are related, we just need to figure out how.' He looked at her. 'We should request all the homicide files where Sithole was the main or only case officer. But those will come in as full manual files.'

'Oh great. More paperwork,' Natalie said.

'We need to send a few emails; it would be good to speak with the coroners and the detectives on all those cases. We need to see if there is another gun, see if there are more home invasions with other weapons that were the same MO.'

'*Ja*—okay,' Natalie said. 'If we start with the coroners and move outwards, the paper files of the other related cases from Naidoo should arrive by tomorrow. Then we can sort through them and see what else the detectives have noted. Naidoo did well sending us the important pages, but hopefully there's more useful stuff in the files.'

'Can you do a search for other hijacks and home invasions that Sithole was on?' Piet asked.

'You know that there is a computer on your desk that you have been taught how to use? You remember how to write an email?'

Piet grinned. 'I hate it. You know that. You type so much faster than me. So much easier for you to do it.'

'You, Piet Kleinman are as bad as most of the other males in this office. That's a sexist thing to say!'

'*Nee*, it is not meant like that, you are just better and faster at it,' he quickly said.

'Mmm,' Natalie replied as she opened her email program.

They drafted an email to Dr Ros Juliet, the coroner in Kimberley. Piet had known Dr Juliet since he'd first become a cop and was stationed in the small town of Kokstad before it grew bigger. He'd been sent there because the population was influenced heavily by the coloured Adam Kock, and despite Piet being of San origin, the powers that be had deemed that he would pass as a coloured. The South African Government had still been trying to hide the fact that the San had been brought into South Africa, and that they had played a part in the border wars at all.

Piet slouched back in his chair and massaged his temples, trying to blot out those days. It was a different time then, and one that had been difficult for him and his people.

'You want to have lunch before we send any more?' Natalie asked.

'Is the *rinkhals* poisonous?' Piet said as he grabbed his hat off his desk. 'Lead the way to the Spur, my china.'

The sizzling plate in front of Piet looked and smelled awesome. But the item he loved the most was the deep-fried onion rings.

'Addictive, oily but sublime!' he murmured as he popped one into his mouth.

'That extra saturated fat isn't doing you any favours,' Natalie said. 'Despite what people believe about the Sans' ability to overeat, you can't run if you have a huge pot belly in the front and a big bottom bouncing around at the back.'

Piet laughed. 'Stereotype much? I figure as long as I can still run ten ks and be able to breathe at the end of it, I am doing okay.'

'You need to take better care of yourself, Piet. We're not getting any younger,' Natalie said.

Once many years ago in police college, he'd wanted to be more than friends with Natalie, but that was a different time, when the apartheid regime was strong—and she was white, he was across the colour bar, and only tolerated in the police force because of how he had helped the SADF in Caprivi.

His tribe had been placed in tents in Schmidtsdrift then, while he was shunted from station to station because of his skills. They'd never passed 'go' when Martin had come along and stolen Natalie's heart anyway. Just a few short years later, he'd smashed her heart into a million pieces when he'd died from being caught in a riot in the townships. At least he'd left her the legacy of Breanna, Piet's goddaughter.

'*Ja*, very funny … but talking of age. Breanna's birthday's coming up, what can I get her?' Piet asked.

'I'll give it some thought, perhaps slip it into a conversation with her that you were asking what to get. She'll be unhappy that I came out to lunch with you without her, again,' Natalie said.

'Tell her it was work-related.'

Natalie smiled. 'It's always work-related. She doesn't care, she loves the Spur.'

'Our lunches are more than just work—they are a necessity to survive the police force. Get out of the office once in a while and be real people.'

'I agree,' Natalie said.

'Besides, what type of partner would I be if I did not accompany you to lunch. Martin will come haunt me for not keeping my promise to look after you. Now that you are back from leave, I have a duty to keep you safe.'

Natalie smiled. '*Ja-nee*.' Then she shook her head. 'That promise has been more than kept. Can't believe you finished that whole steak platter.

You sure you're still able to run fast enough to protect my back if I need it this afternoon?'

'I could always run faster and for longer than you could, but maybe not right this minute. Give me at least ten minutes to digest a bit of it first, or I will get a cramp. Perhaps we should visit the gym and see just who has got flabby or not?'

'Nice try. And don't you know it's not polite to say things like that to a lady?'

'*Ja,* you are right. But seriously, I know we can solve this one.'

'You sure you're up to it? He was your friend,' Natalie said.

'All the more reason to find his killer, then,' Piet said. 'Get him the justice he deserves.'

'Right, let's get to it,' Natalie said.

'Idle minds lose brain cells sitting stagnant or some such bullshit about time—is that not how the saying goes?' Piet asked.

'Time is something I fear those men in the hijackings ran out of long ago,' Natalie said.

'Might be so, but at least we have bodies for those dead men. It's a great place to start. Dead bodies tell their secrets to the right coroner.'

CHAPTER 8

KAMFERS DAM, KIMBERLEY

THE CALL of the flamingos filled the African bushveld, their pink bodies silhouetted against the inky-blue sky of the low dawn light, just as the earth welcomed back the sun touching its horizon far in the east. They flew in a large flock to where the Nama Karoo met the grasslands of the Kalahari Savanna. Be it a memory or a natural pull deep inside their bodies, they knew that here there was water they could use to rest. This place was just one small part of the great central South African Highveld Salt Pans system that they used to connect their long journey between their winter feeding areas near the ocean and the summer breeding grounds inland.

Although she'd matured when she was four and had other chicks, Amahle didn't breed every year, but she knew that this would be her time once more. She descended from the higher atmosphere. As the sunlight kissed the earth and shed rose-gold light across the water below, she saw the island.

Home.

It was here that she would dance an ancient ritual when she planned to mate for the season and hatch their chick together. Amahle glided down, swirling on the morning's light breeze as the sun shone on her back. She landed on the water, honking as she joined many of the flock who had flown the same trail, searching the saline lakes of Africa for spirulina algae, forced to move when the waters of one lake receded and the levels of another swelled depending on the season.

She dipped her beak into the cool water, harvesting the nutritious algae within, then smoothly moved towards a few of the other members she knew. But before she got to them, she heard a distinctive honk—one that she was interested in.

It was within a large group of birds, all competing loudly with each other for space as they performed their ritualised group display. They began with a head-flag, honking loudly while they extended their heads upwards and waved them back and forth.

Tightly packed together, the males moved as if synchronised.

She would've recognised Msizi anywhere, with his distinctive dark-red curved beak and impressive pink plumage. His black primary and secondary wing feathers were prominent. Even though from a distance she could only see a black eye, she knew that close up they were a warm golden colour with a purple ring. He moved his body from side to side, his pink legs drumming out a beat of Africa as he danced with a group of males.

Amahle watched as he swung his head from side to side, head-flagging again. She liked that.

The males then began their wing salutations. They stretched out their necks and spread their wings to display their black flight feathers, before they inverted the move. They dipped their heads downwards and moved gracefully, then they lifted their tails upwards, allowing their black flight feathers to point up to the sky.

They marched with their heads in a crook-like posture, as if they'd broken their own necks. Still more head-bobbing and head-wagging with many feathers erect as they danced until finally, the ritual display of bickering began. Loud honking sounded, with some of the males becoming quite aggressive towards others.

A group broke away. Amahle inverted her head and dipped it into the water, feeding. The water flowed through her mouth, through the fine filter in her bill floating on the surface. She sounded out a low murmuring 'murrrh-murrrh-errh' and pretended not to watch Msizi in the smaller flamboyance.

She couldn't help but notice as he performed the preening movements, wing salutes and finally, bows. She stepped out of the water, as did a bunch of females with her, and they joined in the dance. Repeating the males' moves, marching together, head-bobbing, wagging and honking loudly.

All the time flamingos jostled positions within the group, some moved away, and prospective mates stepped closer, hoping to be the one chosen.

Soon they were performing in unison, Msizi next to her, a leg and wing on one side of their bodies extended outwards together, then retracted. Their timing perfect. They repeated it on the other side.

Slowly Amahle walked away, and she lifted her tail feathers. Msizi followed her.

Stopping, she lowered her head and spread her wings, inviting Msizi to briefly mount her from behind. Together they continued a courtship and mating dance, as old as the elephant migration trails that cut deeply into the earth.

Wading together, Msizi and Amahle moved from the shallows of the island. Amahle didn't want to build her nest there in the clay. Instead, they followed a few other birds and nested on the shoreline.

Other sociable neighbours were building their nests around theirs. They manipulated the wet mud together, building a turret, getting it ready for when their single egg would be cradled safely inside the cool nest. Here they were not protected from land predators by the water. They would need to keep an eye out to defend their turrets from hawks and eagles, too, as they lacked the sheer number of neighbouring flamingos sharing their area.

Amahle settled on top of their turret, a foot above the surrounding landscape. Soon she would lay her egg in the mud, and together she and Msizi would begin to incubate their precious offspring. Until then, she had feeding to attend to, and a bond with Msizi to strengthen through dance.

CHAPTER 9

LILY WATCHED as Quintin set up his makeshift studio in one of the spare bedrooms. They had moved out the furniture, brought in a couch, a small table and a kitchen stool for now. They would find a music store and purchase whatever else he needed to get by soon. 'You know, with the morning sun in this room, I'll know when the day breaks and when to come and wake you up, to go do your doctor thing,' Quintin said.

'Very funny, you know that until we find you a proper studio that album you promised the record company won't happen. You can't record in here.'

'I know. But one thing at a time,' Quintin said, taking out La Angelique from her packaging and Fred, his bow that Lily had named for him. 'But, I can play, and I can compose in this room. A recording studio isn't our priority, right now. You are. And getting this Ian thing sorted, and your apology from World Health, that's where the energy will go for now. Getting the album down will happen, as and when it is supposed to. The important part is that we're here together. Like always, we'll work things out.' He leaned over to where she sat on the couch and kissed her.

'Listen to this, my new piece I've been working through in my head. Tell me what you think?' Putting his beautiful old violin under his chin, he played the first few lines of a new composition. He closed his eyes and was lost to the music.

Lily smiled as she looked at his face. His nose still bore the small bump of once being broken, but her eyes were drawn to his hands, which were so beautiful as they stroked the violin and gave the music life. She could see the fine white scars, now so much a part of him. And she thought how once it might have been so different.

It was 1983. Lily was probably the only student who did not scream when Quintin Cornelius Winters stepped on the stage of the sports stadium at Natal University. This was a man who had made violins fashionable again. The protégé who crossed over from the classical into the modern and encouraged a whole new generation to pick up a string instrument and feel its vibrations.

Dressed in black leather pants and jacket with a white T-shirt, his long blond hair tied at the back, his blue eyes sparkled under the spotlight as he waved to the crowd and bowed, first to the conductor and then to the audience, before he removed his jacket.

The roar of the crowd intensified.

Lily studied him. He wasn't half bad; she had expected someone a lot older.

Eventually, after he'd gestured multiple times for people to sit, they quietened down and settled back into their seats. The spotlight widened to show the full orchestra behind him. The conductor tapped his baton on his music stand, and a hush descended over the crowd. Quintin raised his famous La Angelique Stradivari violin, lifted his bow, and the sweet sound of music erupted from the stage.

Lily was lost.

The sound of the classical weavings washed over her, and the stress from her studies and fatigue from her medical residency soon were forgotten as the long, descending tones of the piece he played blanketed her. He played some of his solo works, and the orchestra backed him on several of the pieces.

An hour and a quarter flew past. All too soon the crowd was on its feet again, standing and hooting for an encore. This time Lily cheered.

Quintin spoke to the conductors and turned to address the crowd. 'Ladies and gentlemen,' he said, the accent to his native Austria pronounced—and for the first time, Lily knew what a sexy voice sounded like. 'This is a new piece I've been working on while touring the awesome universities in South Africa. As you all are aware, I'm forbidden from playing on a stage outside of an educational institution, as there are sanctions against South Africa. However, thanks to the cooperation between your great university, I'd like you to welcome to the stage University of Westville music students and their amazing professor, Mark Weeks.'

The hair on the back of Lily's neck stood up. The man had a voice that could tame a rogue lion, it was so deep and smooth, and images of melted chocolate entered her mind.

A group of Indian and black students walked onto the stage and stood near the centre, their instruments ready. The spotlight highlighted two men with drums sitting to one side with a young black singer.

'Please put your hands together for Taahir Pillay, Victor Mvubu, Nomonde Dlamini and the amazing Slidile Magantolo,' Quintin announced.

The crowd gave a polite but muted round of applause. Many people were moving uneasily in their chairs.

A tall man with a beard and round glasses like John Lennon walked onto the stage and bowed to the audience. The conductor once again signalled on his music stand that they were ready to start and entered into a version of Survivor's 'Eye of the Tiger'. While the tune was recognisable, there was an ethnic beat throughout, one that Quintin followed easily on his violin. Slidile Magantolo was a superb singer, her voice powerful and clear, and one that Lily wouldn't mind listening to again. She delivered the performance with conviction, as if she was fighting for survival and recognition up on the stage. Lily cheered along with the crowd.

The concert was finished, the after-party was pumping. The multiracial gathering was not legal, but no one seemed to care as the students from both Westville and Durban campuses partied together. The beat of the music from the speakers could be felt outside the door when Lily walked along the path.

'Come on, it's in the sports centre, in case you couldn't hear. So glad you decided to join us tonight. It's so exciting,' her sister, Rose, said as Andries, her boyfriend, guided them towards the door and into the gym. Almost instantaneously they were pulled right onto the dance floor, and Lily found herself dancing beside Andries, who gyrated next to the man of the evening himself.

Maestro Quintin.

The music flowed through her blood, and she moved with it. Someone passed her a beer in a tall brown bottle, and she passed it on. There was no way she could drink anything when she would be on duty at the emergency room inside of six hours.

One song led into another, and Lily kept on dancing as the group moved together.

Suddenly, people started to scream. The sound louder than the music, and the crowd began pushing Lily towards the back.

Abruptly, the music stopped.

'Raid! Raid! Get out!' someone shouted. 'Raid! Raid! *Gaan uit! Phuma! Phuma!*'

Lily's eyes began to burn. Policemen with guns and rubber truncheons flooded out of the mist and clashed with the crowd. Students were screaming, trying to push towards the exit at the back, but there were more police swarming from there; the crowd were effectively sardined between the two groups of armed police.

Slidile clung to Quintin, begging, 'Help me, they will hurt us.'

Lily couldn't see her sister. 'Rose? Rose?' she shouted. But she only heard others yelling and more tears filled her eyes. Through them, she noticed a policeman look around, and then as if seeing only Quintin and Slidile, he pushed through the other people who were near him and raised his truncheon.

'You black bitch!' he yelled. 'Get your filthy hands off that white man.'

Lily saw the blow coming, and Quintin put his arm up to shield Slidile. She had escaped the bludgeon, but the policeman grabbed her by her braided hair.

'Leave her alone,' Quintin protested, trying to pull her from the big man. 'She hasn't done anything wrong.'

The policeman brought his stick down on Quintin's hands in quick successive blows, hard on the knuckles.

'Stop! Please stop!' Lily ran towards the policeman, begging. She could see that Quintin couldn't hold onto Slidile, although he kept trying to, because the flesh had been split on his hands and white bone showed through, before blood began pumping out.

'Oh my God, my hands. My hands!' Quintin cried, trying to hold them to him.

'No.' Lily tried again to get the policeman to listen to her. 'Enough, please, he's international!' But the policeman hit him again across his face with the weapon. Blood dripped from Quintin's nose as he bent over and vomited.

'I'm Austrian!' Quintin said. 'I'm Austrian!'

'You can be fucking Arnold Schwarzenegger for all I care; you're attending a multiracial party. Consorting with blacks. You're breaking the law here in South Africa.'

Lily watched as the policeman lifted the baton again to hit Slidile. Quintin ran at the policeman, attempting to unbalance him and push him away from her. But the law-enforcement officer was battle-hardy. He turned the baton on Quintin and smacked him across the temple.

Quintin crashed to the floor and didn't move.

All hell broke loose around Lily as two men piled on top of the policeman.

'Rose!' she called desperately again, then dropped to her knees in front of the unconscious musician to assess his medical situation.

Things were a blur until three in the morning, when Lily strode into the back area of the emergency waiting room after driving her car behind the ambulance transporting Rose and Andries. She could feel her heart thumping inside her chest.

'Morning, Dr Church,' the receptionist said as the security guard opened the interior door for her when she flashed her identity pass.

'Hi, Robyn. Do you know if they have put my sister in a cubical yet? She was in that ambulance that pulled in about five minutes before me.'

'Number twelve. She said to make sure that I told you.'

'Thanks.' She passed through the door and walked towards the curtained-off area. The smell so familiar, only this time she knew what it felt like for every single one of her patients' relatives. This was her worst nightmare: having to confront the ER, knowing that once she'd assessed the situation she would need to call her parents and explain how Rose, her little sister, had got hurt while attending a party with her. Rose might be on the cusp of adulthood, but to her parents, she would always be their baby.

She opened the curtain.

Rose was sitting on the chair, wrapped in a blanket. From what Lily could see, she was still relatively unharmed, a few cuts and bruises but mostly in shock. Andries was lying in bed. Monitors beeped next to him, and he had on an oxygen mask and an IV line running into his arm. The paramedics had put bandages across his chest, a clear sign that he'd taken a severe beating. There was a plaster above his swollen, shut eye, obviously covering an awful injury, as dried blood had crusted beneath it. He was lying raised in the bed, normal for a head wound, to help stop the pooling of blood in the eye area. Lily doubted it was going to make a difference; she could see a shiner already.

Bandages were covering his hands, and another looked like strapping to keep a shoulder in place.

'Oh, thank God, you took forever.' Rose jumped up and fell into Lily's arms, sobbing.

'I was right behind you. We couldn't all fit in the ambulance. I told you I was coming.'

'I was so scared. I'm fine. Really. They said I need to keep calm, but Andries's not doing so well. Did you see him when he took on one of the policemen after the bastard knocked out Maestro Quintin?'

'I did. I have to admit, I never knew he had it in him,' Lily said.

'He thought the policeman was going to hit you next, that's why he went in like he did. We both did.'

'I'm okay. He didn't do anything to me. I told you already. You need to sit and calm down, or I'll have you put in a bed. You're in shock,' Lily said, trying to soothe her sister.

'No, don't take me away from Andries.'

'It's okay; it's all going to be okay.' Lily took a deep breath. 'You frightened me. I'm just glad you're alright.'

'Andries is hurt bad,' Rose said. 'The ambulance attempted to fix him up before we got here, but since they wheeled him into this room, nothing.'

Lily squeezed her sister's shoulder. 'It's only been a few minutes, let me look at his chart.'

She read the medical details and then looked up at Rose. 'He's going to be fine. He's marked as non-critical. They'll keep him stable and administer painkillers until the rush of the critical patients is over, then they'll return and ensure that he has nothing else wrong. They will do a CT scan as is common practice with a head wound like his. This is a good outcome; it could have been so much worse.'

'Did you see what happened with Maestro Quintin? I think he's dead. I think they killed him. We could see that cop beating him, and you trying to stop him. Andries pushed me under a table at the back and then rushed in to help, so did Nomonde Dlamini. I never saw an Indian fight like that. He was mad as a snake and just hitting that cop over and over and over. He took a few hits from this other *boer* who initially thought he could bring the two of them down, but Nomonde's a big guy for an Indian, and the *boer* backed away, with both him and Andries standing their ground in front of Maestro and you and Slidile. They kept telling those cops they were just protecting them because Maestro was knocked out, and that Maestro was an international varsity visitor.'

'I know, everything's going to be okay,' Lily said as she wiped the tears from Rose's cheeks.

'Did you tell the ambulance who Maestro was? When they came and took him from you?'

Lily nodded. 'I did. He was seen quickly. They knew he was an important dignitary, but I turned back to find you and Andries.'

'And Slidile?'

'Nomonde was still waiting with her for an ambulance when they took you away and brought you here.'

'I told them you were a doctor at this hospital, and that you were with other people hurt during the raid. They said that we could come here instead of Addington, where they were taking other people.'

Lily nodded. 'Did you see what happened to the policeman that Andries attacked?'

'He went at the same time as Maestro. Andries got him good in his thick *boer* skull and cracked it on the floor a few times with Nomonde's help. He couldn't hurt anyone else after that.'

'Great,' Lily said sarcastically. 'Just stay here. When I get back, we'll need to call Mum and Dad and let them know what happened. Andries's parents, too. You don't want them seeing this on the news. A raid like this one is sure to make one of the radio channels if not the SABC station itself.'

'Where're you going?'

'To find your maestro, and make sure he's okay.'

After that night, Lily spent almost a month checking Quintin's vitals every hour with the nurses, and she grew fond of the ritual. Having undergone a decompressive craniectomy, as well as his hand surgery, the intubation tubes that kept him alive were his friend, feeding vitamins, nutrients and drugs into his blood, taking his waste away, and finally giving him life-saving oxygen as they 'breathed' for him, creating as little stress on his body as possible while he healed. Soon he would be able to breathe and eat on his own again when they were removed. He would need physical therapy after the muscle wastage, but it looked like he was one of the lucky ones and had made it through without noticeable brain damage so far. The odds had been stacked against him, and yet, he was doing well.

Checking the swelling on his hands, Lily watched the pleated grafted skin, which had come from his stomach area, on each of his balloon fingers and across the metal that had been inserted into his knuckles. His hands were immobilised on boards, and she'd observed them, fascinated, as they slowly had begun to shrink again. His head was also clamped in a neck brace in his induced coma.

'He's going to wonder why you're always here,' Staff Nurse Olivia said.

'I'll tell him the truth when he's awake enough to remember it. I've another week of this punishment from Mr Bolleneti for daring to call out a specialist surgeon in the middle of the night. But it gives me enough time to watch him go in for the cranioplasty, and actually witness the neuros tomorrow as they replace the skull piece they previously removed. Then it's back to emergency for me, and normal odd-hour rosters of a final medical residency student again.'

'When you think on it, Mr Bolleneti was actually nice to you, giving you a month of normal working hours. That's not a punishment, it was a reward for daring to break the rules.'

'I think it was his way of making me like the regular hours he keeps, then when I get wrenched back into shift work, I'm going to feel it. Like he said he did after the early-morning and all-day surgery with Quintin's hands.'

'You know, there's a bet going that when he wakes up, he'll be in love with you. I've money on you two getting together before he leaves the hospital.'

'Really? I think you're going to lose. The poor man just had a hole cut in his head. Tomorrow, hopefully they can put that piece of skull back in, and then we still have to wait to see if the neurosurgeon gets it right and doesn't make him a vegetable. And maybe after that, there's still only a forty per cent chance that he'll live past his first year of rehab. Can you imagine if this all goes wrong, and this man can't play his violin anymore, and can't live a normal life?'

'Write the BP in the chart for me one-hundred-and-ten-over-seventy. He's almost awake, don't let him hear anything negative,' the nurse warned.

Lily peeked over her chart at Quintin. His eyes were indeed fluttering, trying to open. 'Come on, you can do it, fight the drugs. Wake up, Quintin,' she said.

Then she was looking into those blue eyes again, and despite them still being a bit dazed, she started telling him their regular lines. 'Don't try to talk, you're in hospital. We need you to communicate with us, using a blink or shrug if you can move your shoulders. Don't try to move your hands; they're immobilised,' she repeated the same thing she'd said to him day in and day out.

His eyes focused, and she could tell that he was now fully awake. She repeated her instruction, and added, 'Do you understand?'

He gave a single blink.

She smiled. 'That's great, we've cognitive controlled movement,' she said, writing it on the chart. 'How many fingers am I holding up?'

He blinked three times. Slow but deliberate movements.

'Good, numerical function.' She looked at the chart and wrote it down. 'Do you have feeling in your foot when I push this pen into the sole here?'

He blinked once.

'And here?' she asked as she ran the pen up the inside.

His toes curled and he blinked.

Lily smiled. 'I believe you have a ticklish spot there, Mr Winters, I'll make a note not to touch there again.'

He attempted to shake his head slightly from left to right.

'Don't do that, just blink rapidly and I'll know that you're saying no. Don't attempt to move your head. You understand?'

One blink.

'Good. Now, going back. Did you feel it when I touched your foot?' Lily asked.

He blinked.

'You did feel it?'

He blinked.

'That means you were trying to say that you don't want Lily to stop touching there, is that it?' Staff Nurse Olivia asked him.

He blinked—just once.

Lily could feel the heat rising in her cheeks. She knew that the blush was unprofessional, but somehow his not wanting her to stop touching his feet was making her want to run her hands instead of her pen up his foot.

Lily cleared her throat. 'Very funny, Nurse. Okay, last one, then we can put you back to sleep.'

He blinked rapidly.

'Sorry, buddy, I know this is gruelling on you, but we're only allowed to have you awake for a short time, then you need to sleep again. It's for your own good. Your brain needs time to heal.'

He just looked at her.

'This last one is going to be a bit harder. You need to tell me if I touch you with something cold or warm. So, one blink for cold, and two for warm. Understand?'

He blinked.

'Can you feel this?' she asked as she touched the centre of his forehead with her stainless-steel pen.

He blinked.

She placed her finger next to her pen but touched with her other hand on his cheek. 'Can you feel this?'

He blinked twice.

'You're doing great. That's fantastic,' she said as she opened his drip and flooded his blood with medication again. 'There'll be a change of shift and a different set of nurses will wake you for your next observation, just letting you know. Good night, I'll see you in the morning,' she said as his eyes fluttered closed.

'I'm taking a second bet in that pool. I reckon you guys will be married before the year is out,' Olivia said with a laugh.

'Lily? You listening still or are you asleep?' Quintin asked, his voice slicing into her mind and drawing her back into the present time. 'I'm listening but lost in a memory, too. That piece is haunting, it transported me to another time.'

'Mexico? Where we slow danced all night in Cancun?'

'No,' she sighed. 'Here in Durban, when we met. I was just thanking the music for bringing you into my life.'

'And I thank medicine for you, although it's also for your stubborn determination, each and every time I'm able to play anything.' Quintin lowered his violin, and leaned over to kiss her.

'No, don't stop, I'm enjoying it, it's soothing.'

'We have so much to unpack.'

'It can wait,' she said against his lips. 'We have all the time to do what we want.'

Lily stretched her back. Looking at the clock on the wall, she couldn't believe it was almost ten in the morning. It was Sunday, after all, so she'd indulged in a leisurely lie-in. The last week at the house had gone quickly, and she was expected to start work at the practice next Monday. But this morning, she had wanted to get into the study and put everything that she had from Marion in order, and read each report and email, to understand what was happening, before she could add to Hawthorne's work.

Tiger's purr changed pitch, and he lifted his head where he sat next to her on the floor. No matter how many times she had moved him, he had come back and lay within touching distance of her hand. Ignoring her papers when they landed on him, he had purred continually, until now. Lily looked towards the door.

Bessie knocked.

'Come in,' Lily said.

'The medicine man, Klein-Piet, is at the gate,' Bessie said. 'He's come to see you.'

Lily stood up and stepped carefully over the stacks of papers, which were sorted into three categories: normal sickness, abnormal symptoms, deceased.

'Klein-Piet, the policeman?'

'Yebo.'

Lily smiled. 'Please let him in, I'll meet him now. Perhaps we can have some tea in the lounge.'

'*Yebo,*' Bessie said. 'Do you want me to take Tiger? Is he bothering you?'

'No, he's delightful company. He's fine where he is, thank you,' Lily said, reaching out her hand and giving Tiger another fuss.

Bessie smiled then left the room.

Lily was eager to meet the man. She'd heard stories as a child of the legendary men of the Kalahari, those who didn't need to drink water for days, who could survive in the desert. She was aware of the socioeconomic problems that had been brought to the newly settled San community. She'd read in Ian's reports that had been submitted to Marion all about the alcohol abuse, violence and staggering jobless rate. It was terrible.

She'd admired the pictures decorating the dining-room wall, but it was only when she'd gone into the office that she'd realised that these were pictures that Ian must have taken himself. Multiple photos, some head-shots, others full body, covered the walls. One of her favourites was who she assumed was Klein-Piet in traditional loincloth with the sun silhouetted behind him, digging some plants out of the harsh Kalahari sand. Others had Klein-Piet and Ian together, standing close but not touching. Obviously, they were friends from what she'd read, but the pictures were a stark reminder to her of how deeply the apartheid laws that had been abolished still affected generations of people. She wondered how long it would take those who had lived through it to begin to accept the change and to learn to live differently.

There were none of Klein-Piet the policeman. Lily frowned.

She wiped her hands on her denim shorts and walked slowly down the stairs, anxious to meet Klein-Piet, but unsure how this get-together would go. Tiger got up and followed her, much like a dog would.

She reached the entrance hall and slipped on her shoes as she heard Bessie talk into the gate's intercom in the kitchen. It was a language like no other; there were clicks, not words, which sounded like something from her favourite movie as a child, *The Gods Must Be Crazy*. She couldn't contain her smile as she walked.

Opening the front door, Lily watched Klein-Piet exit his police *bakkie* and walk towards them. She knew that *klein* meant 'small' from her smattering of Afrikaans that she'd carried with her from her childhood. Being brought up very English in an apartheid society had meant that she wasn't as bilingual as she would have liked to have been.

Now that Piet was closer, it was obvious that he was even shorter than she'd realised. Almost the size of a fourteen-year-old before his growth spurt. He carried himself proudly. His hair was steel grey, cropped close to his head, and his posture that of someone who'd been trained in the military. Someone who was proud—and determined. While he wore a khaki shirt with short sleeves, she could see that his arms were older, the skin taut but devoid of fat deposits. The muscles shaped and the veins strong. She estimated his age to be closer to sixty than fifty. This 'old man' was still as muscular as any other person half his age.

He looked nothing like his photographs. His Nike *takkies* were bright white, despite the dust around, as if they were cleaned regularly and kept in pristine condition. He carried a bag slung across his shoulder, and there was some plants inside that, but with leaves and branches extending upwards and flapping about his head as if it was a feather from a bird of paradise. He lifted his hand and waved. She saw his signature grin from the photographs and couldn't help but return the smile as she walked out onto the front porch to greet him.

'Hello, I'm Dr Lily Winters,' she said, extending her hand to shake his.

Piet looked at her, but instead of a Western greeting, he put his hand on the front of her right shoulder. He nodded and said something that she did not understand as she didn't speak any of the languages of the Khwe or !Xun San community, but she smiled anyway, hoping that the panic of not understanding him didn't show on her face.

Piet began giggling, as if a slow bubble was in his throat, and then it became a full-on belly laugh. 'I think I got you good there,' he said, reaching for her hand and pumping it with both of his wrapped around hers. 'You looked so confused, if not a little terrified.'

'Taken aback, and yes you did,' she said. 'To be honest, I wasn't sure if I would have to try my almost non-existent Afrikaans.'

'I learned Afrikaans and English at the same time up in the Caprivi Strip many years ago. My mother tongue is still !Xun, although I also speak Khwe, Zulu and Xhosa. I hear you are here to take over *Dokotela Meva*'s work. He left a hole in my heart deep inside when he was killed.' Piet's accent was strongly Afrikaans, but it had a different melodic sound in the way he spoke.

Meva. She knew the word and sound of that, and realisation dawned on her—Dr Thorn. He was talking about Ian Hawthorne. Of course—*Dokotela* and *Ameva* manipulated together from Zulu. She was going to be kept on her toes if Klein-Piet always spoke in a mixture of languages.

'Got you again. That was too easy, seriously,' Piet said with a mischievous grin. 'Ian and I were friends, but these things happen a lot here in South Africa, unfortunately.'

Lily shook her head. 'I'm so sorry for your loss. It had been a few years since I last saw him. It's lovely to meet you in person. I feel as if I know you already from the pictures that are in Ian's home. Come on inside. My husband, Quintin, is in the garage and we can join him in a moment.'

'Ian and I had fun when we went camping and looking for plants in the Kalahari. There is much about flora that he taught me and so much that he learned from me. I do miss him,' he said, putting down his bag outside the front door and stamping his feet on the mat before entering the house.

'Talking plants,' Lily said, 'according to Lincoln, there're a few in the garage that you apparently have an explanation for.'

He stayed silent as they made their way to the lounge room.

'Please, have a seat.' She gestured widely to the lounge as she sat on the three-person couch. She watched as Piet sat in one of the overstuffed recliner chairs as if it was his favourite spot. 'There are many plants in the garage, including some medicinal ones.'

Piet smiled again. '*Dokotela* Lily. Do you know that means a flower that blooms in winter? We have been sent another plant doctor to help us.'

'Please just call me Lily.'

'Lily, until your *uBuntu* name finds you.' He grinned and the lines in his face crinkled so deeply she couldn't help but smile back. 'You know, my Afrikaans name found me when I worked for the SADF. They could not say my San name, so I became Piet. Because I could mimic the *Piet-my-vrou*, and the SWAPO soldiers did not know it was not a bird warning of their passing through the veld but me.'

'And Klein?'

'I'm Kleinman, my surname, but when there were two Piets it got confusing. I was the smaller man, so I became Klein-Piet. Now there is only me, so some people just call me Piet.'

'Noted. Just Piet, then.'

Quintin chose that moment to walk in, and Piet stood up.

Lily said, 'Piet, my husband, Quintin.'

They shook hands, and Quintin sat next to Lily. 'So, what did I miss?' Quintin asked.

'You didn't miss anything exciting, got here just at the interesting part. Piet was about to tell us about those plants in our garage.' Lily lifted an eyebrow at Piet.

Piet frowned before he spoke again. 'There is more than one plant on Ian's property that the law says you cannot grow without getting into trouble. I was teaching him the traditional plants of the San. If you are worried about the *dagga* medicine, you need not be. I think that our police force is too busy chasing after the real *skabengas* to come after this tiny medical operation. Maybe also because a majority of them use that oil since they are broken inside.'

'Broken?' Quintin asked.

'Definitely. Some policemen in this town rely on alternative medicine to get through their day, they rely on us. Many people in South Africa have witnessed too much extreme violence, and the stress of living here, it takes its toll, no matter how beautiful the country is. Ian was aware of the PTSD side of the policemen's jobs, but also the need to have medicine that doesn't impair concentration. That didn't contain any THC part of the marijuana plant.'

Tiger came into the room, walked up to Piet and brushed against his legs, before he trotted over to Lily and jumped onto her lap. She stroked his soft fur.

'I see that Tiger has given you the nod of approval. He is a beautiful cat,' Piet said.

'Big, fat and heavy is what he is, but gorgeous. In a few days, he seems to have gone from an outside cat to being Quintin's or my constant shadow.'

'I believe he likes you,' Piet said.

Lily smiled. 'And I him.'

Piet nodded. 'Tiger is a good judge of character. He might have been given to Ian, but he was still wild. With you, he looks like he's ready to be tamed.'

Tiger looked at Piet as if he understood what was being said. 'Spoilt, more like it,' Lily said. 'What about now that Ian is dead? Will the police continue to look the other way?'

'Nothing will happen to you growing the plants and making the oil here. Life goes on.'

'But with no guarantee that we won't be arrested for having those plants?' Quintin asked.

'I cannot guarantee that, but know that the likelihood of anything being found in your garage, be it plant or oil medication, is very slim.'

'Until I find out more about Ian's research, I do want to continue having the plants, be it to prove or disprove him,' Lily said.

'You know my views on those plants,' Quintin said. 'I still believe they should be destroyed, but if you think they're important, and Policeman Piet here says there is little to almost no chance of being raided, then we keep them for as long as you want them here. This is your project.'

She smiled at her husband. It was unlike him to give in so easily.

'Lily, as the new doctor, you need to learn the ways of the medicine man, and all the secrets of the San. Ian was writing them down in a book. It is not good for my ego to admit, but he was better at putting pictures into the document on his computer than I am. The information is important to pass on and to keep safe because the next generation has so much HIV, I worry that soon there will be no one left to carry on the traditions. Not verbally anyway. Already I have lost two apprentices, both to AIDS. Ian suggested that perhaps if I document our medicines in a book, then it will still be here when I am gone, and when the plague of HIV has been beaten by modern drugs, then if there are any San left who are interested, they can learn to read about their cultural medicine in plants and treat with the old ways once again.'

'That's very sad,' said Lily.

'Sad is the fact that they stole his computer when they broke in here, and our book along with it,' Piet said. 'I did not even have a printed copy as we were still busy compiling it.'

'Bessie and Lincoln told us about the break-in,' Quintin said.

'They didn't say anything about your book. Perhaps it could still come to light. Did you look on the practice's computer?' Lily asked.

'*Nee*. Mrs Kilborne, the manager, said that his work computer was only used for work, and she said she checked it. We did not have any reason to push her further and have a look ourselves. There was no break-in at his office, so there was no need at that stage. As far as I know, the book was on his laptop, and here on his home desktop,' said Piet.

'I'm not a computer expert, but I'm happy to dig around a little when I get to work. You never know, she could have missed it,' Lily said.

'On Mondays, he used to come to his outreach clinic at Platfontein,' Piet explained.

'I'll keep that in mind. I'm taking over his office, so I assume his old computer will still be there and his electronic diary, and I'll try to fit in everyone as best I can.'

'That would be great, thank you. It would be sad to have totally lost the whole thing. Ian carried his laptop everywhere. But you know what it is like here—people have so many ways of getting rid of stolen things and not being detected. I would say it has probably been wiped, and is in use again by someone who bought it on the street within a day of it being stolen.'

Bessie walked into the room with a loaded tea tray.

'*Yabonga*, Bessie,' Piet said as he took both the mug and plate that she offered him.

But when Bessie moved out of the way, Lily noted that Piet's tea was served in an enamel cup, much like the servants had been when she was a child, and instead of just biscuits on his plate, Bessie had made a big sandwich with peanut butter and what looked like syrup dripping out of it. The bread was cut like doorstops, and so many memories flooded through her head of times gone by, when she had seen the gardener in her childhood home in Johannesburg get sandwiches just like this with a big mug of tea.

It made her depressed that some things had not changed. She made a mental note to ask Bessie to give him a china cup next time. Medicine man or policeman, he deserved to be treated like an equal. Feeding him as if he was considered below the standard and not allowed to use the same china and mugs in the house as them was not acceptable to her. Although she had grown up simply accepting this as normal, she'd learned better in her travels. But to say something to Bessie in front of Piet would be embarrassing and disrespectful to both of them, so she held her tongue. It would be addressed, and the equality readjusted, but not right then.

'Thank you,' Lily said, taking her tea and a plate with a homemade biscuit on it. Bessie nodded and walked out of the room. Lily knew she was frowning and had to make a conscious effort to smooth it away when she looked back to Piet. 'Did you ask Bessie if she knew where the laptop was? After the break-in?'

'Of course. His laptop, desktop, his camera, all his files were pulled from his shelves and taken. In all my years as a policeman, I have not seen anything like how they methodically packed up his study, then trashed every upholstered surface, as if looking for something else. I am sad that it happened, but personally, I am devastated that our book is gone.'

Lily could see he hadn't finished speaking, so she remained quiet, waiting for him to feel comfortable enough to continue their conversation.

'We had photographs of many plants for the book. I have copies of some, but not all of them. Ian had scanned them into his computer. We had a lot of the text to tell people how to grow them, harvest and use the sap and the fibres for medicines. This bush I have brought for you today, for the garden, is one of those that needs to go in the book. It is not commonly found in this area. It grows further north of here, and on the fringe of the desert.'

'Interesting,' Lily said.

'I guess I am hoping that you will consider working with me on the book, even if we have to start again.'

'I would be honoured, but there are so many loose ends. So much of Ian's life that I'm still finding out about, to put all the pieces of the puzzle together as to what he was doing here, not only with his HIV research, but also the alternative medicines … and your book …'

'I know. Sometimes it takes a while for people to settle in,' Piet said, but his voice petered out as if he had so much more to say but had decided against it.

Lily didn't miss the reluctance. 'You sound like there is more to that statement than just me trying to muddle through Ian's affairs.'

'Do not get me started. But my mind was on all the years it took for the South African Government to give us San a home after we served during the border war to fight for it. Like I said, sometimes it takes a while.'

'How did you come to be living in Kimberley? I thought the San were from further west,' Lily asked.

'Once, I was a Crow—thirty-first Battalion. I fought for the apartheid government against the insurgents from Angola and South West Africa. And yet that same government left my family, my tribe, in limbo, homeless for over twenty years before they granted us land on the outskirts of Kimberley. Before that, we were a people displaced. Kept away from our beloved Kalahari by new laws, and kilometres of farmland between us. We have Platfontein now. After many, many years of living in tents and on handouts, we finally have a place to call home.'

'That's good, at least now you have a home,' Quintin said.

'Yes, and yet, it is different,' Piet admitted. 'As a people, we can be together again, but time has changed a lot. I was one of the lucky ones. I was allowed to continue in the government's employment as a policeman because of my tracking skills, but many were not so fortunate. They had to live off handouts, with no prospects of jobs. We were not trained for anything but living on the land then.'

Lily was shocked but fascinated that Piet was so open about the deplorable situation that the San had found themselves in.

'We were once hunters and gatherers, now we own our land. It is a big responsibility, and my people have many challenges to face and many lessons to learn. We are now becoming farmers. It is very hard, especially those who remember being able to walk the country freely.'

'Understandable,' Quintin said.

Piet sipped his tea and ate his sandwich. When he was done he placed them on the coffee table. 'I always feel like I am cluttering up such a perfect surface when I put the dishes here, but Bessie would skin me alive if I was to take them into the kitchen like I should.'

Lily burst out laughing. 'I take it you don't cross into Bessie's domestic domain often, then?'

'Would you? If I anger her, she might spit in my tea.'

Lily shook her head, not even trying to mask a smile at the image he'd drawn. 'Seriously?'

'*Nee*, she would not, she is too nice for that,' Piet said.

'Come on, I bet you are dying to get that to Lincoln in the garage,' Lily said, moving Tiger so she could stand up. 'I'm more worried about leaving marks on the furniture,' she muttered to herself as she placed her cup on the table. 'What was he thinking decorating like this? It's as if all the furniture belongs in a museum, not in a home.'

'It did not always look like this. Only in the last year or so, he had a decorator come in and make it all fancy. If you were wondering if it was to impress a lady friend, he never had one that I am aware of, and if he did, she did not come to his funeral.'

CHAPTER 10

Quintin opened the outside door of the triple garage and said in a loud voice, 'Lincoln, I brought a visitor.'

'*Dumelang*,' Lincoln called back.

Lily, Quintin and Piet followed his voice.

Piet gifted Lincoln a grin. 'Hello to you, too. It is good to see you again.' They shook hands in an intricate way, as if they both belonged to a secret fraternity.

'Piet brought a new plant,' Quintin said.

Piet pulled it out of his satchel. 'It does not look like much now, but this is a mongongo nut tree. I have waited a very long time for someone to bring me one of these, and it looks like this one might have survived its long trip here.'

'What do you treat with it?' Lily asked.

'Hunger. This is not a medicine plant totally; this is a San community's staple diet in the Kalahari. It is referred to as the *manketti* nut in some places. I have been trying to get my hands on one of these and keep it alive for a few years.'

'A food source?' Quintin asked.

'*Ja*, very high in fat and protein. It can be used traditionally to clean and moisten the skin, like a body rub. And, importantly, this tree is also what we use for our *Nyae Nyae,* the soft-wood sticks used for making a fire. Not the case with this next one, the humble *suurpruim*. While you can eat it, the medicinal value is huge. The roots treat stomach pains, abscesses, colic, coughs, and some have even had success treating malaria and bilharzia. I have not treated either with it, so I cannot say for sure, but the leaves can help eye infections and sore throats. There are two varieties. This one with the hairy leaf is the one that is indigenous to the eastern cape. There is another, but it is different.'

'In Zulu, your plant is called *umThunduluka-obomvu* or *amatu nduluka,'* Lincoln said.

'There you go, already we have three names for it,' Piet said with a smile.

Lincoln potted it in a large bag, and soon both plants were watered and safe on a shelf. 'Now they will be nice and warm and can settle in their soil,' Lincoln said. 'When they are ready I'll take them outside, but not till after winter is finished and there is no more frost.'

Quintin nodded. 'You want to tell me more about the other plants in here? I'm particularly interested in the plants that are also food. When we were in Zam Zam, which is a refugee camp in the Sudan, there was an NGO there that was trying to grow the moringa trees with the refugees. Apparently, they are like a superfood, and according to them they could help world hunger if used right.'

'We have some of those, by the dam,' Lincoln said.

Slowly, they all walked up and down the lines, Piet and Lincoln explaining which of the orchids weren't native to the area. Which of the plants were there for medicinal value, and which for food.

'Many of these saplings that Lincoln has grown here from seeds or cuttings we will take and plant out at Platfontein when they are big enough. The property needs trees, and if you give a household a tree next to their *ikhaya,* they are charged with looking after it. That way, there will always be the food and the medicine plants available to my people,' Piet explained. 'We all brought many seeds with them when they left their home in the north, many grew in Platfontein but many also failed. We even have a few baobab trees being nurtured in backyards.'

'I had no idea,' Lily said.

The overhead lights were on, as was the humidifier, and despite the cold outside, Quintin had stripped off his jumper. Turning around, Lily noticed that he was assessing the room critically.

'What's up?' she asked.

'Ian had insulated the walls and put in shelving, but they are all movable. The lighting is all on cables, attached to the shelving, not all overhead, not part of the structure.'

'So?' Lily asked.

'It looks like he did it himself rather than getting an electrician in to do it—an interesting choice for a DIY job. One that can easily be moved. I still think that this triple garage would make an amazing studio for six months, or perhaps longer if it takes more time for you to find what's causing the meningitis cases. I'd still like to be able to work right here at home. It'd be safer for us if I wasn't leaving you alone in the middle of the night to go to some studio.'

She grinned. She knew that her husband loved her unconditionally, and although he didn't understand most of her work—and had often expressed that he didn't know how she did what she did—he knew that she was really good at it. They'd discussed it many times, and it always came back to the same answer: she needed to make a difference by helping people in need.

He got that.

She didn't mind that Quintin earned more than her by millions. It was never about the money with him, for her, it was always about the consideration he had shown for others, and she loved him for that.

Quintin's babbling drew her back to the present. The pace of his words always sped up when he got excited about a project. 'This space is just perfect, Lily, but while I want to convert it, we can't just have all these plants out in the cold. We'll need to move them. Let's get a purpose-built hothouse for them on the property.'

Lincoln and Piet were both nodding vigorously.

'If we build them a greenhouse outside and move all the plants, we could convert the garages into my studio, and we can all be happy. Doctors, musicians, medicine men and gardeners,' Quintin said.

'*Yebo*,' said Lincoln.

'*Ja*,' Piet said at the same time.

Lily smiled. Sometimes having the money to just do what you wanted to do had its advantages.

'That's settled, then,' Quintin said.

'When are you going to get it?' Piet asked.

'As soon as I can find out where to order one,' Quintin said.

'Is it alright with you if I stay here for a while? Ian used to let me stay in the barn with the horses. I have a few days off, and Lincoln and I need to do some work on the winter garden.'

Lily looked at Lincoln, a frown on her face.

He nodded. 'Truly, Klein-Piet comes and goes. He helps keep the plants in top shape. He is here whenever he has time, like a guest but not. A member of the family.'

'A member of the family who sleeps with the horses? I will not accept!' Lily objected. 'What was Ian thinking?'

'Please do not misread this, Lily. The stables are my choice. I do not get to spend enough time in the open spaces anymore. After we moved from the Kalahari to South Africa, things took a different turn and everything in my life changed. For me, it is a way to be who I am inside. To ground myself with nature, without being in the bush. Ian was a lot of things that many people did not approve of, but being inhospitable to me was not one of his faults. He accepted that I needed my own space, a place to breathe, and he respected that. He enabled me to have it without judgement. He was like family, the type that do not try to change who you are.'

'I'm confused. You rang the bell today. Bessie let you in with the intercom,' Lily said. 'Surely a member of his family would have been given an access code?'

'*Ja.* Except that the alarm system is still very new, added after Ian's death. I could have just crawled through the gap in the fence and used the manual override to open them to let my *bakkie* through.'

'Mmm,' Quintin said. He glanced at Lily, who shrugged her shoulders. 'You can stay, but when the security-fence contractors arrive on Monday, you had best show them that hole. I want it fixed,' Quintin said sternly. 'I need to make this property safer for Lily. I don't want her killed like her predecessor.'

'And not in the stables,' Lily added. 'If you won't stay in the main house as a guest, then there's a perfectly good second cottage I would prefer you use. It even has a veranda, and we can move a bed there so you can sleep outside, if it's that important to you. I'm sure that between us all we can move furniture into it and get that habitable in no time. Ian might have been okay with you sleeping with the horses, but I'm not. I'm so not.'

Piet smiled. 'I already have a key for the cottage, not that it was ever locked before, but just because I chose to sleep in the stables, does not mean that I smelled like a horse all day. There is good hot-water pressure in that cottage.'

Lily shook her head. The man was a puzzle to her.

CHAPTER 11

A WEEK later on the first Monday in August, Lily walked towards the entrance into the Amity Health Clinic, at six forty-five, dressed in her favourite jeans, her lucky shirt and a warm jumper. Her feet were snug in socks and her Ugg boots.

The armed security guard opened the door for her. As she strode into the building that would become her office for the next six months, he said, 'Good morning, Dr Winters.'

'Good morning, and thank you, Michael,' she said, reading his name tag. And was saddened when she realised how fast she'd readjusted to the idea of having a full-time armed security man outside her office.

He nodded at her and went back to standing guard.

She massaged her neck; the cat had moved up the bed and slept on her pillow and kept her awake half the night. She needed coffee. Desperately.

She'd dropped in to meet everyone soon after they arrived, but now she was about to start, she had butterflies in her stomach, which was her usual reaction to any new situation. Settling into the house and getting over the jet lag period was over, and it was time to get to work.

'Dr Winters, you're nice and early for your first day.'

'Thank you, Jacob,' Lily said, shaking the hand of the male receptionist who had rushed to greet her. He was about six feet tall and smartly dressed in clothes that fit his athletic body. 'It's good to be here. Can you show me where the kitchen and the coffee machine are, please? I missed them on my initiation visit.'

Jacob was shaking his head. 'I'll show you to your office and then fetch you a coffee,' he said, leading her down a small passage. He opened a door and she walked in, but he remained outside. 'Mrs Kilborne said to tell you that your passcode for the computer is on your desk in the envelope, with instructions on how to log in. I can help you with that if you need it when I bring your coffee.'

'Thank you, but I can make my own beverages, just show me the kitchen,' Lily said.

Jacob shook his head again. 'Mrs Kilborne will fire me if you make your own. That's part of my job.' He placed his hand on his chest dramatically.

So, office manager June Kilborne was a force to be reckoned with, just as Lily had suspected after her conversation with Piet, particularly considering she had not allowed the policeman into the office to search the computers, but the fact that Jacob was willing to admit it was interesting. 'I'll try to remember that. Please, can you make me a coffee? Full cream milk, no sugar.'

'*Ja*, Doctor, one coffee coming right up,' he said as he headed off to the kitchen.

Lily might live in a First World country now, but she had to remember that she worked in the Third World. Growing up, she'd thought nothing of the maid always waiting on her and her sister, Rose, but once she'd left South Africa, she'd become used to doing things for herself. She and Quintin guarded their privacy fiercely and didn't employ even a cleaner when at home. The estate manager only entered their house in Brisbane when they weren't there to ensure it was ready for their arrival.

Being back in Africa was already changing the way they did that. In the weeks since they'd arrived, they seemed to have integrated into Ian's space just fine. Bessie was a godsend, bringing the tea, making the lunches, and helping Lily with where to shop, and where it was safe to drive and where she must not go at night.

Lincoln looking after the garden and the livestock was a necessity, not a luxury, and as for Piet, he'd drifted in and out, helping where he could with a strength and dogged determination that defied all expectations. The man was pure muscle, and not afraid of hard work.

The new hothouse was up, and while Quintin had multiple bandaids on the various nicks on his skin, he'd managed to avoid more serious injury. She could see that he was enjoying the handyman experience. Building something worthwhile with his hands.

Lily had wondered how Quintin's hands would hold up. Even all these years later, she still worried about them. She'd been by his side when he'd gone through all the therapy to regain use of those precious fingers, and while Quintin now believed the ordeal had made him a stronger person, she still worried that as he got older, the injuries would give him problems and slow him down in his career.

Lily shook her head as if the simple action could clear the cobwebs of yesteryear from her mind. Instead, she focused on her new office space.

It was a typical doctor's room with a large antique wooden desk that dominated one corner, a single patient's chair next to it, and a bed opposite with a washable curtain. She frowned as she realised there was a bulky printer on her desk and a computer with a colossal cathode-ray monitor. Not everyone kept up with technology as much as she and Quintin did. She put down her laptop case and made a mental note to order herself a new flat-screen monitor and compact printer; she'd donate it to the clinic when they left.

Sitting down, she fired up her computer, using the codes in the envelope. She opened Ian's diary while she waited. It was blank for the day, thoughtfully left open for her to settle in. The rest of the week, however, was back-to-back appointments, including blocks booked out for onsite visits to the nursing homes.

She knew that Ian had spent every Monday out at Platfontein, but it wasn't blocked out in her diary—she needed to speak to Jacob to make sure that continued.

Seven o'clock on the dot, her buzzer rang.

'Are you seeing patients yet, Doctor?' Jacob asked.

'Yes, send them in,' she said. She opened her door to wait for her first patient.

Jacob handed her a steaming mug of coffee and a file. 'You'll need these. And lots of luck.' He turned and went to speak to her patient to presumably tell them to go inside her office—it was all clicks. She smiled as Piet was led towards her rooms.

She walked to her desk and turned, motioning for him to take a seat.

He smiled and said, 'Doctor Lily. *Goeie môre.*' He sat.

'*Goeie môre*, Piet,' she said in the worst Afrikaans he'd probably heard in years. 'What can I do for you?'

'As you know, Ian would usually come to Platfontein for his clinic on Mondays, but as you have only just started work today, I did not think that you would have a chance to be visiting. As a medicine man, I need some more antiretroviral drugs issued to the clinic there.'

'You dispense the HIV drugs at the clinic?'

Piet nodded. 'One of the things I do, *Ja*. But the second reason is that I am worried. I have a patient who is beyond the help of my herbs and plants and needs your medicines. Ian used to give me the medications to give to the men who did not want to see a *dokotela* who is not one of the San community. Some of my people, they are too stubborn to come and seek medical help, even when I told them that *Dokotela* Lily was as beautiful as her name.'

Lily smiled.

'Do not laugh. It is true that they are just simple men, but they still need help.'

'I'm smiling because, as you know, I've been away a little while and it's good to see in South Africa some men don't change. Why don't you tell me what is wrong with this one man you're worried about?'

'He has the thinnings disease. You know, AIDS,' he said when she looked at him blankly.

'HIV, or full-blown AIDS?'

'HIV positive, not dying yet. I hope,' Piet said. 'That is why I give them the antiretroviral treatment. They are on tablets all the time, and I give them their drugs sometimes hidden inside one of my medicines for those who do not believe in them and will not take the pills. But now one man is really sick. He told me he had a headache. I gave him tea from the willow tree, but it got worse. I gave him the Panado, and that did not help either. This morning he is vomiting. He says his neck is sore, and he cannot move his head from side to side. But he still would not let me bring him in to see you.'

She frowned. 'If I go see him, will he allow me into his *ikhaya*?'

This time it was Piet who smiled. 'I will tell him that the gods told me that I needed to go find the new angel to come and heal him because *Dokotela Meva* has already become part of the earth.'

'Calling me an angel is dangerous, what happens if he dies? Then I'll be a *tokoloshe* just as fast.'

His smile grew broader, his eyes crinkling up until they were almost invisible. 'Then you will still be called *Dokotela* Lily. To my people, we do not believe in angels anyway; they were brought here by the white man's preaching. To us, if his time on earth is done, then it is the time to be with !Xu, our sky god who looks after the dead souls. We will bury him, and he will become one with the earth once more.'

She shook her head. 'Lily is fine, Piet, but I'm no angel. Give me the names of the men you medicate, and we can see if Jacob can find their files —if Ian had files for them at all.' Taking the last gulp of her coffee, she walked to the door and called, 'Jacob, can you come in here, please?'

She spoke with him softly, then watched as he stood next to Piet and wrote the names on a sheet of paper. 'I'll need a few moments to find these files,' he said, then walked out. Not once had she witnessed any body language from Jacob that suggested she might need to rethink her plans to visit Platfontein with Piet. She felt her bunched-up shoulders relax.

Men in South Africa had always been overprotective of females. It didn't matter who they were; they always took a protective stance. The fact that Jacob hadn't objected while Piet was giving the names meant that she would hopefully be okay going into Platfontein. She knew from Ian's notes that he'd routinely done it, and she was simply stepping into his shoes. The new doctor.

It was a great place to start.

Lily should have known that it wasn't going to be that easy. Platfontein was still considered a township. White women didn't usually go into townships in South Africa.

Mrs Kilborne had insisted that the security guard, Michael, accompany her in her Land Cruiser. While Lily appreciated that she didn't know the situation on the ground, she knew that going into an area with her own militia in the front seat was going to cause more problems than she needed.

Mrs Kilborne eventually gave in—but only because Piet would be in his vehicle and escorting her, too. They'd also compromised on Michael, who had changed out of his uniform into plain clothes. He was not to show he was armed unless Lily was threatened, and his rifle was to be covered at all times unless she was in real danger.

An hour later, they were finally on their way. With Michael sitting in her passenger seat, Lily followed Piet's police *bakkie* into the township.

'We are entering Platfontein,' Michael said as they drove down what still looked to her to be a main road. 'This land was given to the San by the government. It is theirs.'

'So, anyone can live here now?' Lily asked.

'Only the San can live here,' Michael said. 'Before I worked for the clinic, I had never been in this place.'

'You used to come here with Ian?'

'Yes. To help bring the sick people to the hospital.'

'The road to Platfontein has been deserted the whole way. Only one or two people walked along,' Lily said, looking at the odometer. 'And it's roughly fifteen kilometres from Kimberley.'

'Too far to travel daily for work by foot for most from the settlement to the city,' Michael said.

'But what about taxis? They go wherever?'

'Taxis go where there's business and money. The San community have neither. Before they came here, most people knew nothing of them except their old cave paintings. Until a few years ago, many of us living in this area had never seen a San. The situation is hard for everyone—we must learn new languages to communicate with them, and them us. We are one under our rainbow nation, but we are very different, too. The taxis don't go where there is no work, and the people of Platfontein don't go into Kimberley for work, so there is no need for the taxis to have a route. It wouldn't be profitable enough for them, not enough traffic.'

Lily nodded, Michael's explanations slowly sinking into her mind.

'This place is sad,' he continued. 'I have fetched more bodies here with

Dr Ian than in any other township. They come to Platfontein. They drink. The younger ones, they do drugs. They come to this place, and they die here. They do not want to live full lives.'

'But Piet's a policeman, he has a job.'

'Piet is the exception here, Dr Lily.'

Lily frowned as they drove past the tiny Monopoly houses dotted along in straight lines. So different from the traditional way that she knew these people had once lived.

She drove over corrugated roads to a few buildings that stood apart from the others at the end of the row, where Piet had stopped and was already waiting for her. She opened her door and got out to join him.

'This is Moses's home. He is the one who is too sick, and the ambulance will not come here.'

'Why won't they bring an ambulance?' Lily asked.

'They say that we do not pay their fees,' Piet said.

She nodded, understanding that many of the ambulance services were owned by private companies, and they would stop servicing a community who didn't pay. There simply weren't enough of the government ambulances to spread across the whole of the Kimberley area. 'Logistics versus money making the world go around as normal.'

Piet nodded.

She was gathering her bag and noticed that while Michael wasn't taking his weapon out of the Land Cruiser, he was having a good look around, still with his door open and in easy reach of firepower if needed.

'It's a few years since I was last in South Africa, and a lot has changed,' Lily admitted.

'You will not be harmed at this settlement. There are problems here at Platfontein,' Piet said. 'When people see you have come, they know that there is help. You bring hope just driving here. You will most likely have a few other sick people come line up at the main clinic building, too. It will not be an easy day for you.'

'I'm not set up for a remote clinic today, I just came to see Moses. From the symptoms you described, I'm worried he might be another case of meningitis. I'll need to focus on him for now, and we can do an outreach clinic another time.'

'Come, we will think about other problems after we have seen Moses.'

She nodded to Michael, who stood next to the Land Cruiser trying to hide the fact that he was security—a little unsuccessfully to her way of thinking. She walked next to Piet towards the little government-built house.

While each home had power and running water, the buildings were small. As she looked around, she saw that many of the roofs had tarpaulins, with black tyres holding them down, where rain obviously had made its way into the houses. A legacy of the contractors who needed to take more care. There were many neat rows of houses with space in between. Moses's home had a border of aloe plants around it, and the terracotta-hued ground was swept clean of litter and leaves. Half had recently been tilled, and Lily could see some sort of vegetable trying hard to grow through the earth. A group of 44-gallon drums sat at the far end, and a dog hid in the shade of them, too hot, or too scared to get up and bark at them. Its nose was covered by its paw, as if it could see Lily and by default, she then couldn't see it.

She followed Piet inside the home. There was no glass in the windows and blankets had been nailed into the walls to provide some protection from the elements. The floor was concrete and had been polished until it shone in a deep burgundy. A bed on pallets was in the corner—upon it a man lay deathly still. A woman with a cheap Chinese paper fan tried to create a breeze to cool him and chase the flies away when they attempted to settle on his clammy skin or crawl over his gaunt face.

Piet made many clicking sounds before he said, 'We will speak mostly English because *Dokotela* Lily can't speak Afrikaans very good and she can only understand English.'

The woman nodded.

Piet explained, 'I told her hello and that I had brought some help with me today, but now we will talk with you, *Dokotela* Lily, too.' He continued, 'Coti, is Moses awake?'

Coti shrugged and moved out of the way so that Piet and the doctor could stand closer.

'Moses, can you hear me, are you still with us?' Piet asked. There was no response.

Lily snapped on her gloves, then taking her torch, she opened the patient's eye and shone the bright light directly into it. The sensitivity to the light showed immediately.

'How long has he been like this?' Lily asked.

Coti just stared at Lily.

Piet repeated her question to Coti in their native tongue and then continued to translate between Lily and Coti, giving up on speaking a language he thought they would all understand.

'Since the sun came up. He had a good night, but then he was shaking and went quiet. I have tried to give him water, but he cannot swallow it,' Coti said with Piet translating.

Lily attempted to move Moses's head, and he groaned, the stiffness clearly noticeable. 'I suspect this is meningitis, and unless we get him to hospital, he's going to die.'

Piet nodded. 'We have had too many people die of that sickness lately, but not before that ... Ian, he said it was crypto-something or other before, so it probably is again.'

'Cryptococcus, or cryptococcal meningitis,' Lily said, automatically filling in the difficult medical word. 'It's a fungus that creates a swelling of the brain. I need to get Moses to a hospital and give him some antibiotics.'

'Moses does not want to die in a hospital, he wants to die here,' Coti said. 'He said that he spent too many years in the white people's buildings, and before he dies, I must take him out to see the stars as they light up in the sky or the sun as it is dancing across the hot sand of our home. He does not want to be inside.'

'Can we give him the medicine here?' Piet asked.

Lily shook her head. 'I need them to go intravenously. It's safer in the hospital.'

'Ian used one of the other houses that belonged to someone who passed as a clinic. It has two beds in it. I can organise to have someone watch over him while you cannot be here.'

'It will need to be a nurse so they can change his drip bag.'

'There is one here who was a nurse. She trained and worked in the hospitals, but she is sometimes not good.'

'What exactly do you mean?' Lily asked.

'She is my sister. She was supposed to be the medicine woman for our tribe. But she received a severe head injury many years ago. Domestic abuse. Some days she can remember, some days she does not, but if I am with her, she mostly remembers.'

'It's too risky. I need him in hospital to stop him dying.'

'Dying is not the outcome I want for Moses. He is going to the radio station and recording all the stories of where he grew up; he is one who speaks two dialects of our languages. The people here, they need Moses to get better.'

'Then I definitely need him in hospital. Now,' Lily insisted. 'I get that there is no ambulance service, but I want to take him in the Land Cruiser. Coti can come with us. I can give him some pain medication for the trip, to calm him, make it easier, but he needs the hospital to heal fast, to beat this sickness.'

Piet spoke to Coti and the clicks and the gestures from them both never altered in tone. No one seemed to be shouting or dominating the conversation, then Piet turned to Lily. 'She said she has no money for hospital.'

'It is covered under my research project; there is no payment.'

Piet spoke again with Coti.

'She said okay, if it is what will save him, then she will come with him, but you must promise that if he is going to die, you will take his bed out underneath the stars.'

Lily nodded, having no idea how she would keep that promise, but that was a problem for another time. She opened her bag and removed a vial and syringe, before she spoke to the unconscious Moses and gave him some pethidine for the pain he was about to endure during the trip.

Piet went outside, and within a few moments, there were four other men there, including Michael, who appeared with his weapon slung over his shoulder.

'I can't leave it alone, Doctor. If it gets stolen, I'll have to pay for it, and I can help load Moses,' Michael said.

Lily nodded her understanding.

They wrapped Moses in his sheet and carried him to the Land Cruiser. Lily ran ahead to open the back and get the seats laid down before they put him in. From the way they worked as a team, even with Michael's help, she knew they'd had to do this before.

'Come on, let's go,' Lily said as Coti climbed onto the back and seated herself next to her husband, who lay still on the rubber matting.

Lily stopped in the doorway. Moses lay in the hospital bed, tilted up slightly. His light skin dark against the white of the sheets was a reminder to her that this was not where he wanted to be at all. She stepped into the room and stood by the side of the bed, across from where Coti was, and she watched the new set of antibiotics drip slowly into his vein.

'I need some information from you both,' Lily said. 'I know that my Afrikaans isn't good enough to understand you, so we'll need to do this in English. We can go as slow as we need to, but I have to make sure we all understand everything.'

'*Ja, Dokter,*' Moses said, and she smiled.

'I need an honest answer from you both. It's important,' she said. 'I need to find out how you came in contact with this sickness. I know that you and Coti both tested positive for HIV and that you're taking your inhibitors.'

Moses nodded his head. 'I take the medicine that Piet gives me every day, sometimes once, sometimes three times a day. He tells me I have to take it to stay well.'

'Yes, that's good,' she said. 'Now when the other people were sick, those who died, did you go to their house at all?'

'*Nee,*' Moses said, shaking his head.

'Did you, Coti?'

'*Nee.*' She too was shaking her head.

Moses coughed, wiped his nose on a tissue, and then continued. 'When someone is sick it is not like the old days when everyone lived together. Since we moved into the tents, and now into the houses, we have private time. No one wants to know when you are sick except when we do a spirit-and-healing dance. People only want to know when you are better again, so you can help in the community. No one wants to dance anymore for those with the thinnings disease. It never helps, everyone still dies. Maybe not today, or tomorrow, but they die.'

Lily nodded and patted Moses's hand to let him know she understood. She'd heard all about the breakdown of the San traditions. 'Coti, I need to make sure that you're still feeling okay. Perhaps while you are here at the hospital, we can run some bloods, see how your CD4 levels are doing. Can't have you catching anything while you wait with Moses in the hospital.'

Moses nodded. '*Dokotela,* if you can heal this, can you heal my HIV?'

Lily shook her head sadly and patted his hand again. 'Unfortunately, despite so many scientists around the world working on HIV, there's still no cure for it, we can only help you live longer. You're already on the anti-retroviral drugs, so let's concentrate on your meningitis for now. Lucky that the hospital had the right antibiotics for this strain in stock, too, and we didn't have to order anything special in and waste more time waiting on transport getting it here.'

'*Dankie,*' Moses said.

'Don't thank me yet, we are not out of the woods, but we're getting there.'

CHAPTER 12

AT LUNCHTIME, Lily drove back to her office, her mind still on Moses. She needed more information now.

Jacob knocked on her door, a cup of coffee in his hand.

'Thank you, you're a mind-reader, I really need that,' Lily said as he came into her office.

He smiled, deposited it on her desk and turned to walk away.

'Jacob, wait. In Ian's reports to Marion at Head Office, he mentioned these three names of patients.' She wrote them on a piece of paper for him. 'Please, can you bring me their files?'

'No need for me to do that. We have most of the files all scanned and on the computer, and when you see a patient, you record directly into the system. I only gave you Piet's file this morning because his is different; he looks after multiple people. I printed it out for you because you are new, and I thought it would help you to understand the names in his file. Also, because you need the paper copy when you go out there. The wi-fi signal is bad at Platfontein, so you can't work online. I scan any updates you do when you get back and input them for you into the system.'

'That's good news,' Lily said. 'Is it possible to search all the other files of the other patients that had died of meningitis who were seen by this practice?'

'I can look that up on the system and send you the names, or do you want me to show you how to search yourself?' Jacob offered.

'I'd like to know how, thank you. Do you know if there are any files that Dr Hawthorne had, or was expecting from other hospitals or doctors' rooms? For his research?' She took a stab in the dark that Ian would have been in contact with other professionals in his study.

Jacob began to shake his head then stopped. 'Oh, hang on. *Ja*. A box arrived about two weeks after his funeral by courier. I had to sign for it even though he was dead, they insisted. Mrs Kilborne told me to call them to ask them to send it back because he'd crossed over, but they said there was no return address and it was paid for in cash, so I kept it. The lady at the courier company said I should look in the box; if I like what there was then I should take it because he was—well no one would miss it—but I respect the dead. I couldn't open his box. I'm so sorry, I just forgot about it. I'll bring it.'

He disappeared, and she looked around Ian's office that had so quickly become hers. A picture of Quintin and her stood on the desk. Quintin was laughing at something as he played his violin, his head against her chest, and she had her eyes closed. Below it, on the frame, he'd engraved: *Two hearts beat as one.* It had been her twenty-fifth wedding anniversary gift from him.

She sent him a text.

> Thinking of you, hope your day is going well.
> xoxox

Jacob came in with the box and put it on her desk.

'Thank you,' she said. 'Please close the door on the way out.'

'*Ja*, Doctor.'

Lily opened the box. Once she lifted the lid, she could see a note on the top:

HIV+ patients in Galeshewe, 33 per cent of estimated population.

Statistic already higher than national average.

She lifted out a small pile of papers. In the box was all the blood results of people who'd had HIV tests. There were names, addresses and various doctors' or clinics' details, and their results. Lily stared at them for a long time. She flipped through every page, sorting into piles those that were HIV positive and those that were negative.

'What were you doing with this information, Ian?' She muttered.

Her phone buzzed.

Are you going to be late for dinner? Q xoxo

She looked at the clock on her computer. It was already five.

Leaving now. Hugs xoxo

She opened the bottom drawer to put away the files, but she pulled it too hard, and it fell out of the desk.

'Drat,' she cursed. Getting out of her chair, she lifted it by the sides but couldn't get the runners to line up. She put her hand underneath to level it.

'Yikes!' She dropped the drawer and jumped back. Something was under there. It felt too smooth to be the wood. She kicked at the drawer with her foot to turn it over, and saw that it was just a criss-cross of duct tape, with a lump of an object bound securely underneath.

'What have you hidden here, Ian?' she said as she peeled back the tape to expose a flash drive.

'Interesting.' She carefully aligned the drawer to the runners in the desk and glided it back into place, before dumping all the papers inside. She locked the drawers with the key, put that and the drive in her pocket, then switched off her computer.

After dinner, once Bessie had retired for the night, Lily sat at the bench in Quintin's studio. Her laptop was open in front of her and in her hand was the flash drive she'd found.

'Okay, let's see what Ian was hiding,' Quintin said.

'I still feel like we should be telling Piet about this. He's a policeman, and it was hidden.'

'We can tell him if there is something worthwhile on it,' Quintin said. 'Just stick the drive in—my curiosity is getting the better of me.'

'Here goes nothing,' she said, and she slid the flash drive into her computer. 'That's a surprise—no password.' She looked at the directories, clearly named—*Medical Files, Book, Photographs*. She clicked on *Medical Files* first, and a whole array of files and subfolders appeared on the screen. She looked through the codes of each file name but couldn't see anything familiar. She opened one and had a quick read through.

'And?' Quintin asked.

'It's a normal medical file. Patient contracted pneumonia and died.'

'Do you think this might be an electronic copy of the files that were stolen from his home office?'

Lily nodded. 'Most likely. I can make a comparison to those on our system at work.'

'Still doesn't explain why he was hiding it in his office. Do you think he knew he was in danger, or do you think he knew that something in these files was so important that he had to hide a copy?'

'I don't know. He could be conniving, just look at Zam Zam. On the one hand, he organised all those malaria drugs through a back door—right under the politicians' noses. Then he deliberately told Marion that there was no truth in the reports that a rebel force had been spotted just north of us. Despite the fact that we had gone out to look at them gathering in number, waiting while still more reinforcements joined them, and had been discussing how to evacuate. I could never figure out why he stopped the extraction of everyone the day before, so that we were forced to flee in a hail of bullets. Now he hides files on a flash drive and stashes it in his office, hidden but findable. He was always full of secrets. It's going to be hard unravelling them now that he's dead.'

Quintin squeezed her shoulder. 'What's in the *Book* folder?'

Lily clicked there, and multiple files showed up. 'Wow. Look at this. Piet's going to be ecstatic. He didn't lose his book on the San medicinal plants. I don't know what version this is, but we won't be starting again. And it's going to be a great help with getting me up to speed, too.'

'Maybe print him a copy,' Quintin said. 'This is quite an extensive collection. Plant, what it cures, where it's found, and maps, pictures. No wonder Piet was sorry to lose it.'

'I'll print one for him now and text him.' Lily clicked on 'print' and made her way through all the book files, copying them onto her laptop at the same time.

They started browsing through the photos folder. Some just random, others seemed to be headshots. Many had names.

'This is interesting,' Lily said. 'One or two of these doctors I know. But I don't recognise any of these other names. You?'

'No.'

'There is a file here called *Xylophone*. Rather out of place.' She clicked on it. But it asked for a password. 'Damn,' she said. Password-protected files; this might be something.

'You should copy all these files onto your laptop and your home computer and give this flash drive to Piet. See if he can recognise anyone. Can I have a crack at trying to get that password-protected file open?'

'Sure, but first I want to copy across and go through those medical files. See what they are. I want to make sure I understand what's in them before I pass them to anyone.'

Quintin stood up and kissed the top of her head. 'I'll leave you to that fun part; I'm going back to my violin. I was so hoping that there'd be something on there that would just immediately pop and tell us what happened to Ian. I guess I was wishing too much that the danger to you would just be over and done with. Secret files, now there's something I didn't expect from Ian. Can't wait to see what's in them.'

'There might still be something to explain Ian's death, we just need to find it. You said it yourself, why would he hide this flash drive like he did, unless something on here was worth hiding? Those protected files might be it; we just need to get into them.'

'Once you are done, let me know so I can take a run at it,' Quintin said as he walked to the other side of the studio. 'Music on or silent?'

'On. Unless you're planning on using Shirabe—you know I'm not her biggest fan.' The glass violin had been gifted to Quintin by the HARIO Company in Japan a few years ago when they'd first created them. The distinctive sound from this violin was very different to the woody vibrations from La Angelique, his Stradivarius. The sound of the glass one was closer to a Chinese violin.

'Okay,' he said as he lifted La Angelique from her case. 'But I think after you hear the new music I play on her, you might just change your mind. With an orchestra backing, the track will be amazing. Even you'll fall in love with her.'

'I wait to be wowed, then,' she said.

He stuck out his tongue at her, and she watched him for a moment as he got ready and began to do warm-up exercises.

She never tired of watching him play his violins. It was as if he caressed the strings with Fred, and she could see that already he was lost in his musical world. She wasn't even in the room with him when he played with his eyes closed. Just him and his music.

Lily looked down at her computer and began opening the medical files she'd copied across, the music soothing her. Slowly, one at a time, she printed them all out. She silently thanked that she had a laser printer and reams of paper at hand because there were many pages churning out. Going upstairs, she fetched the printouts and, using Quintin's big workbench, started to create new files for each case. Finally, she began collating her notes in Excel.

Age of patient: 66.

Type of influenza: Haemophilus influenzae.

Died: 47th day multi-system failure.

She put in all the main data that she could and repeated the process for each of the files before looking back to where Quintin was practising. Quintin's fringe had fallen across his forehead as he played a more joyful part of his composition, making her smile as she settled down to start working through the data she'd spread out on the bench.

Not long afterwards, one phrase popped out: *P. carinii pneumonia* in adults without known underlying immunosuppressive illness.

Lily sat back and looked at her spreadsheet. Two clusters.

Pneumonia and meningitis.

'Well, well, look at that. Ian, what were you up to and why were you hiding this information?'

She still needed to analyse the drugs used. One or two were flagged as having been used multiple times, and not just one drug dispensed at any time. She had no idea if the original or the cheaper generic drugs had been administered in many of the cases—when she looked at the files, she could not see a pattern.

Although it was past midnight, Quintin was switching violins and getting his headphones ready for his recording session. Lily smiled when she saw that he'd opted for an electric violin instead of Shirabe. As thoughtful as ever while she shared his studio.

'Quintin, I love that you weren't going to use Shirabe, but get her out. It's late, and I need some sleep. I have a visit to a nursing home tomorrow; they always are so emotional for me, so I'll head up to bed. You play your Shirabe; make the right sound first up.'

He frowned. 'Want me to come with you?'

She smiled. 'All the time, but no worries, I'll be good. Don't stop your composing for me. I know you always work well at this time of the night.'

'Composing? Bugger that; I'm dying for you to move so that I get at that flash drive to see if I can find a macro to crack those locked files. Don't you know you have just given me the keys to a treasure map?'

The last dosage of drugs administered should have helped. But Moses had stopped responding to the medication he'd been receiving for the past four days. He was sluggish, his CD4 was just too low, and his immune system too compromised by the disease.

Lily frowned. Moses was calmer, sure, and awake now, no longer slipping in and out of consciousness, but she had expected a better response to the strong antibiotics, as she'd seen with previous patients. It was almost as if he was being given water in his drip bag instead of vital life-preserving drugs.

'Hey, Moses.' She reached for his hand. 'Can you hear me?'

He turned his face to her.

'The nurses are coming to take you to theatre. I need to do another lumbar puncture on you.'

He shook his head.

'I know you are scared, and the last one gave you a huge headache, but this time, we know what to expect, and we'll be able to counteract that with caffeine. I'll be there again, holding your hand, but a specialist will stick a fine needle into your spine and take some of the fluid from there for us to analyse. This will help me to make sure that the drugs are beating your meningitis.'

She had hoped to avoid doing another procedure as they were not comfortable, but now it was necessary.

'Is he going to die, *Dokotela*?' Coti asked, her face lined with stress.

'I'm doing everything I can for him; I'm trying hard not to let that happen.'

'Please remember your promise. If he is dying, you need to take him outside.'

Lily nodded.

The orderlies arrived, and Lily walked with Moses to the theatre. 'I must leave you here. I need to scrub up and accompany the specialist. I'll join you again once we are inside the theatre room, not in the waiting area.'

Moses nodded his head, indicating that he understood, then Lily walked away—her mind full of the meningitis clusters that she knew about.

The flash drive had contained a backup of all Ian's files. Every file had been scanned, and perfect copies were all there, in digital glory now on both her home and work computers. She'd hesitated about calling Piet and letting him know. Her mind was tinged with a little guilt at not sharing all the information with the police, but she pushed it down deep and buried it. After all, she hadn't found anything worth sharing yet.

But at least she'd found his book, and that had made her smile. Looking at it, she had seen the enormous amount of work they'd already done. If even half of what the plants claimed to heal could be true, then the book was bound to not only become a household bestseller, but an accurate account of the San way of medication, ensuring it would never be forgotten.

And she knew that more than a few pharmaceutical companies would be sniffing around the legalities of the book, too. Looking for patents. Looking to secure remedies and ensuring they would get the market share of the drug if they could synthesise it enough and produce it en masse.

She wondered if Ian and Piet had got any legal advice before they embarked on such a book. She knew what a hullabaloo the world had created when the *Hoodia gordonii* and more recently the Devil's Claw plants, both remedies used by the San, were exploited by the pharmaceutical companies of the west. 'Biopiracy' was cited by the lawyers as the parties were in court, trying to come to a settlement.

She'd read most of the reports that Ian had made on the cluster cases, but she was no closer to even suspecting a primary cause. Seven men and three women in Platfontein were dead within the last three months alone. The last thing she wanted was to add another casualty to that number with Moses.

She wondered if it was what had got Ian killed. Did he find what was causing it?

Scrubbing up, her mind still on the cases, she backed into the theatre and stood next to Moses. 'I'm here; I'll be with you the whole time.'

He nodded.

The specialist, Dr Green said, 'Okay, Moses, I see so many people for this procedure that I can't remember, do you speak English or Afrikaans?'

Lily smiled. It was a blatant lie, but one designed to settle her nervous patient.

'Both, but my English is better,' Moses admitted.

'Good because my San is terrible. Can't get my tongue around all those clicks. I'm going to explain what we are doing before I start. I find it helps keep people calmer knowing what's happening.'

Moses nodded. 'Am I going to die this time?'

'You didn't before, did you? It'll spoil my one-hundred-per-cent-no-deaths-on-my-theatre-table record.' Dr Green gave a little laugh at his own joke. 'But we need to find what's happening inside that brain of yours to make sure we can treat you properly.'

Lily held onto Moses's hand. He looked at her and attempted a weak smile. Already she could see that just sitting up had sapped the little bit of strength he had left.

When the procedure was completed, Lily patted Moses's hand. 'Relax, it's all over,' Lily said. 'You did brilliantly.'

'I was very scared, *Dokotela* Lily. Very scared.'

'You covered it well. You did good.' She smiled at him. 'When this is done, the orderlies will wheel you back to your room, and once I have the results, I can decide on your ongoing treatment.'

It was past midnight, and Lily was still at the hospital. She stood at the end of Moses's bed. In all her years of medicine, she had never had a patient with meningitis not respond to their meds. But then, she had never had a patient whose bloods were so bad either. Moses was already crossing into full-blown AIDS; no wonder he had contracted meningitis so easily.

If a person was healthy, you could sneeze on them and they would be fine. If that person had a compromised immune system, however, they would come down with pneumonia. In Moses's case, he'd been exposed to a little fungus somewhere and he'd contracted meningitis.

Both of the spinal taps had the same result. And he should have responded faster to the antibiotics given. She had switched to a higher dose of the IV drugs on hand and increased his oral meds, too.

But Moses was now unresponsive. Four days after bringing him into hospital, and thinking that perhaps she had saved him, she knew that she was losing her duel with Death and his sickle. It was as if Moses's poor body had just had enough, and no matter how many drugs she pumped into it to stop the fungus, it was finished fighting.

The draining of the fluid from his spine should have helped, but she could see her patient was in pain. Despite also giving him pain meds, he had begun moaning even in sleep. He no longer sweated, no longer moved. He was just still. While the groaning was a comfort that he was alive, she could see that Moses was going into organ failure.

Lily didn't understand it. She hated losing patients. She knew that she couldn't save everyone, but she tried—always. To lose someone was to have their death like a tattoo marking on your heart. It was a soul she was forever responsible for.

She didn't want Moses to die. But he *was* dying.

She began questioning herself in her head, questioning every step of the process she had taken since she'd heard about him.

'Coti,' she said quietly to his wife, who had sat vigil beside his bed for the last four days. 'You need to wake up.'

Coti sat up in the chair.

'Remember the promise. Come, it's time,' Lily said. 'There's a battery in the heart monitor, so here, I'll unplug it from the wall. Make sure that and the drip follow.'

Coti nodded again and was ready to wheel her equipment. Lily watched as slow tears seeped from her eyes at the inevitable outcome of the night and wished that it could have been different.

As they passed the nurses' station, Lily said, 'Nurse, the extra blanket, please.'

'Let me call an orderly to help you,' the nurse insisted as she placed the blankets over Moses to ward off the chilly night.

'No, there isn't time to wait,' Lily said.

The nurse went to the top of the bed and began to help.

'Where are we going, *Dokotela*?' Coti asked.

'There is a balcony off the visitors' lounge where Moses can see the stars. I'm so sorry, Coti. I'm so sorry.'

'Thank you for keeping your promise and for staying here. Holding Moses's other hand until he crosses over. Moses would have liked knowing you more. You need to know that to our people, death isn't something we fear. We are born of the sand, and when we die, we return to the sand, and we become part of it.'

CHAPTER 13

The following morning, the sun was barely rising over the purple horizon as Lily looked out the window of the doctors' lounge in the hospital. For once, she thanked the thick glass that separated her from the outdoors because the predawn singing of the Karoo thrush in the big jacaranda trees outside would have been too joyful for her.

She rang Piet's mobile.

'Detective Kleinman.' His voice was not one of a man who'd been sleeping.

'Piet, it's Dr Lily Winters.'

'Official name. What is wrong?'

She took a big breath. Delivering sad news was never easy. 'I wanted to let you know that this morning, just after four, I lost Moses. I'm so sorry I couldn't save him.'

There was a moment of silence on the other side, then Piet cleared his throat. 'He had meningitis. I know you did everything you could to save him, but he will be missed in our community.'

'That was one of the reasons that I called. I don't know what cultural procedures you follow. What do you do for his burial? Who do I release the body to? I was turning to you for help.'

'I'll be right there, Lily, give me half an hour to get to the hospital.'

When Piet arrived, Lily was standing in the doorway watching Coti, who still sat in the same place as she had when they had wheeled Moses back into the room, a sheet over him, the machines silent. She had reached over and put her hand against his body, and there it had remained.

'Thank you for calling me,' he said, and walked to Coti. He had in his arms a soft blanket made of the skin of a springbok that he draped around her. 'Come, Coti, you need to let us take care of Moses. He can become one with the earth. He is with !Xu now.'

A young woman introduced as Elise walked past Lily, her head lowered.

Lily didn't say anything, worried she would do something that might be culturally insensitive. Elise put her arms around Coti and helped her up.

There were other women in the corridor, all waiting to touch Coti and show their support. Lily watched as they quietly walked down the long passageway.

'They are silent now, in respect of those still asleep in the hospital, but wait till they get outside. The women will sing and cry together,' Piet said. 'There is a *bakkie* waiting outside to take them all back to Platfontein, and they will get Coti ready for the funeral.'

'What do I do with Moses?'

'You release him to his people. There are men outside waiting. They are with the private funeral home. They will take his body and we will have a funeral this afternoon.'

'Thank you; they may take his body. Do you need anything else from me?' Lily asked.

'No, I see the release papers on the clipboard at the end of the bed already. They will sign them and give them to your reception when they leave the hospital.'

She nodded.

'You look exhausted; you need to go home and rest.'

'That was the plan. Been a few years since I pulled a full night with a patient,' she said. 'Guess as you get older you don't bounce back so easily.'

'Come on, I'll drive you. Quintin and I can fetch your Cruiser later. You look ready to drop.'

'I would appreciate that, it's been an emotionally draining week,' Lily said.

They drove in silence for a while, across Kimberley and out onto the Midlands Road, Lily lost in her own grief of losing her patient.

'Thank you for all you did for Moses. If you are rested this afternoon, you are welcome to attend his funeral. He will probably have a sort of hybrid Christian-San burial, as many in Platfontein have looked to the church in their time of need, but Moses was not one of them. He was still traditional. I totally understand if you do not want to attend. Funerals are always hard on the living souls,' Piet said.

'Thank you for the invitation, but to see him go into the ground would break me. I have seen too many people lowered into the dark. Way too many than someone ever should have to.' Her mind flashed to Zam Zam and the daily body-washing rituals of the population there, and then placing their corpses into the hard earth because they had died from hunger, or had been ravaged by the conflict between the races. She pushed the scene from her mind. 'I think I was at peace with saying goodbye to him when I took him out to die under the stars.'

'That is a wonderful gift you gave him. In our belief, he is now in the hands of !Xu. That is why it was important for Moses to look at the stars when he died. So that his passage to his god in the sky would be swift and he would not get lost along the way.'

'I'm sorry that despite all the modern medication at my disposal, I was still unable to save him,' Lily said.

'Even the best and fiercest doctor will never win the fight with !Xu. If it was Moses's time to go, then it was time for his footprints in the sand to end.'

Lily gave a weak smile.

'It's good to see you safely home.'

'Safely. Is there even such a thing here at the moment? Ian's killer is still out there, and we still have no idea why he was killed,' Lily said.

'True, but investigations like this take time. We will find the perpetrator in the end. Sometimes it's just something little that helps us catch them.'

'Little, oh that's classic. I wanted to tell you about it on Monday, and I guess we both got busy. I have good news. I've found an electronic copy of your book,' Lily said.

'Where?'

'At work.'

'That news is especially welcome today.'

'Ian had copies of all the different chapters on a flash drive. We can add the new plants that you've brought since we got here. It's a good thing that you and Quintin have taken pictures and written about them,' Lily said. 'The project can continue. I don't know if it's the latest version, but it's a start.'

'I like that we are still working on the book. It is very important,' Piet said.

'The odd part is that the flash drive was taped to the bottom of a drawer. Ian had obviously hidden it.'

Piet drummed his fingers on the steering wheel. 'That is odd. What else was on the flash drive?'

'A number of medical files, photographs, your book. I'm still looking at all the files to see if they are related to my cluster work or not. Quintin was able to crack some files that were password protected, so now I have some of Ian's analysis files showing me the clusters of meningitis he mentioned to World Health. But nothing on his research on HIV, which was the main project he was employed for.'

'Anything else?'

'There is a heap of pictures, too, some of the people I can recognise as we've worked with them before, but many I can't. I don't know if they have relevance to anything. I can tell you that in these medical files, he had more patient information than just from his practice here in Kimberley. He also had files from Johannesburg, Cape Town and Durban, all of the people who had died of either pneumonia or meningitis, and often the files are not of deaths, just of people who have been ill and who then recovered. His files that he had on the analysis seemed incomplete, like he hadn't gone through all the data he'd accumulated.'

'When did you find the flash drive?'

'First day of work.'

'*Jislaaik*, Lily. Who else knows about it?'

'Only Quintin.'

'Keep it that way. Would you mind if Natalie and I came in and did a search of the practice? Perhaps there is another drive hidden there. This is cause for concern. The people who trashed his place, they were looking for something, obviously the flash drive. And if you are saying it is incomplete, and you found it at the office, then we might find something useful there.'

'I'm happy for you to search, just do it neatly—people have to work in that office.'

'You will not even know we have been in when we are done.'

Lily nodded.

'I'll talk to Natalie and see if we can go in tomorrow when there is no one there. It would make it easier for everyone.'

'That's a good idea.'

'In the meantime, if you can give me the flash drive, I would appreciate it.'

'Okay,' Lily said. 'You can have it when we get home. I have copied it onto all my computers; those files are never going to go missing again.'

'Let us hope so.'

'Now that I have the data, I have somewhere to start my analysis and begin looking for the cause of the clusters,' Lily said.

'Everything else aside, I know it is selfish, yet I am seriously delighted that our book has not been lost.'

'I printed out a copy for you—it's at home,' Lily said.

'I look forward to seeing that,' Piet said.

CHAPTER 14

REYANSH READ his email and gave a big sigh of relief. The container had cleared their docking area and was on the move to Kimberley.

He sent a text to his sister.

> Goods left safely from JHB. Await confirmation from distribution in Kimberley.

He opened the drawer and looked at the tablets that he had sitting there, then he slammed it closed again. No use taking the edge off now when he knew that Mishti would come barrelling through the door at any moment. She'd demand to know in what order he thought the sicknesses would happen, as if he already had it mapped out.

He wouldn't know the answer until the replacement stock orders started making their way through the system. Then he'd be able to see which of his drugs were being taken, and then they just had to wait for the corresponding medication necessary to combat the infection. It was still a source of frustration for him that he couldn't tell precisely where the cases were turning up. Thankfully, the new system they were implementing with the suppliers was already starting to show some of that information—it would pay for itself in the end, just the location information alone was worth the cost.

The drugs were perfect.

Now it was spilling out into more drugs. Mishti was getting greedy and had instructed him to expand, again. Not only the HIV-positive people, but into the general population's drugs, too. Her excuse was that there was only so much more pain you could make someone who was HIV positive go through before you killed them, and dead people didn't use pharmaceuticals. She needed them alive, to rely more and more on the drugs.

He disagreed. No one deserved to die because of his skills with chemicals.

He felt a twinge of guilt that now anyone could get caught up in his designer drugs, but the plan was working too well to stop it, and Mishti was demanding more and more variations of contaminants from him.

Anaya was going on again about a new house, and he could never say no to her. She had also wanted another car—a new Mercedes Benz, not just a Toyota Prada. He needed to make sure the money kept coming in, and he needed to keep going with the drugs to achieve that. As long as he gave Mishti her results, she wouldn't expose his addiction to their father, and he still longed mostly for his approval above all others. He always had.

He pushed the guilt aside.

Mishti never questioned him on his drugs knowledge—how he knew which to contaminate. As long as he delivered maximum damage and maximum profit without a chance of being detected. The HIV drugs had been her idea, but what he put into them had been his design.

According to the latest 'confidential' statistics, the HIV national average was only ten-and-a-half per cent. The statistics were a farce; the government had tried to silence the real data that showed the numbers were almost double what they claimed.

HIV in the black population was much higher than any of the other population groups. According to widely published reports, it was higher than twenty-five per cent in the black communities alone.

The population of South Africa was over eighty per cent blacks, and only nine per cent whites. The Indian and the Asians came in at only two-and-a-half per cent combined. But that didn't make him hate the black communities because they outnumbered the likes of him. It made him feel sorry for them. Despite their numbers, they were still misguided by greedy politicians all the time, and people who they believed were on their side and would give them a better life, and ultimately were not.

Their family drug-manufacturing company under Mishti's control was just another in the long line to exploit that.

He frowned, remembering the first drug experiment he'd done for her: HIV retrovirus drugs were taken by the majority of HIV-infected people to help control and inhibit the disease. With a compromised immune system, the designer HIV drugs would deliver the meningitis fungus and the little bit of food supplied for it to survive. And since meningitis was one of the sicknesses those infected would often encounter during their illness, no one would ever suspect anything.

He shuddered at the thought that he was the faceless man behind those who had died. He shook his head.

'They were HIV positive already. It's not like you are giving them the disease, they are already going to die, it's just a matter of when,' Mishti had said.

His own foresight went a little deeper. When he saw the writing on the wall with Mishti pushing his drug ideas further five years ago, he had invested a small nest egg in a friend's business—a funeral home. That was booming, mostly with AIDS-related deaths. There was definitely a synergy between the two companies he cared for.

He looked at the picture of his three children on his desk, his beautiful wife sitting with them, dressed in the best designer clothes. He didn't want to hurt people, but if Mishti told him to, he would do it—for his family.

If he didn't have the money to support his family, they would hate him. Anaya would leave him. She was an unexpected catch that he never wanted to let go. He wondered how she would react if she found out how he earned their daily bread.

At the moment his children were too young to understand, but later when they were adults, would they still look at him with the love and devotion that they did now if they found out?

He couldn't look them in the eye, even in the picture. He reached out his hand and laid it facedown.

He had a job to do: make money. Lots of money. Never mind about his hatred of Mishti and what she made him do. He'd always known that there were consequences for his habit, and all he could hope, now that he was a father, was his kids would never feel the fallout, or have an addiction like he suffered.

The phone rang.

Reyansh looked at the screen on his desk that identified Mishti, and he so wished he didn't have to answer it, but a call was a lesser evil than a visit in person. He lifted the receiver.

'Just checking you're in your office,' she said.

'I'm here,' Reyansh said.

'Then get into my office. Now.' The phone went dead.

Reyansh slowly replaced the receiver—then lifted it again. He bashed it on the cradle until broken pieces started to fly all over his office. He picked up the cradle and attempted to throw it at the wall, but the cord kept it from hitting anything and it fell on the carpet, increasing his frustration.

The action grated on his already frayed nerves. He grabbed the mug on his desk and chucked that at the wall instead. The sound of the cup smashing was satisfying to his ears.

He opened his drawer and popped two pills into his mouth, before checking his reflection in the mirror. Making sure he looked like he had it all together. Not a hair out of place. He took off his lab coat and hung it beside the door so that she would only see his suit. Unsoiled. A veneer over his troubled mind.

Approaching Mishti's office with false confidence, Reyansh started speaking as he opened the door. The quicker he did this, the quicker he could go home. 'The new consignment will be distributed across Kimberley within a few days, and the next shipment for Cape Town leaves tonight.'

'Sit.'

He walked over to the visitor's chair and sat.

'What antibiotics have you put in this container to combat the new contaminants?' Mishti asked.

'Broad spectrum. Amoxicillin/clavulanate potassium packages and paediatric penicillins.'

'Any new oncology drugs?' she asked.

'A few opioids, including fentanyl, gemcitabine and carboplatin, and some of the cholinesterase inhibitors, Donepezil and Memantine, have something extra special in them as well.'

'Meaning? What could you possibly put into an Alzheimer's medication to make their symptoms worse?' Mishti snorted.

'Nothing. They're placebos. Look the same, weigh the same, but made up of cheap fillers, they do nothing. They cost us nothing; they sell for a lot.'

'Placebos? So, what miracle follow-on drugs are used after nothing?'

'None. They're not designed that way. Other than costing us next to nothing to manufacture, so huge profits. Like I said already, it's the perfect drug. But if they do notice that the patient doesn't respond, then the doctors will prescribe other non-generic drugs—which we also manufacture. We get two sets of drugs prescribed instead of just one for the same patient. This lot are the test. If this goes undetected, then I can do a few other drugs without any introduced contaminations, leaving out the expensive active key ingredients.'

'What about the antihypertensive medicines and diuretics? Those worked well last time. Are there more in the Kimberley container?' she asked.

'A variation of both streptococcus and pneumococcus bacteria that causes pneumonia are in those.'

'Old people get sick all the time with pneumonia. Foolproof,' Mishti said. 'Now, we make money quickly off the drugs used to treat it. Who said that South African drug companies couldn't compete with the international cheap drugs coming in? I'm making this company millions, brother. Millions. Now get out of my office and go create more of your magical pills.'

'You'll need to override the quality department again tonight. The testers need to rubberstamp the batch, so we don't fail any ISO auditing.'

'I'll be on the floor at nine o'clock. Is that enough time?'

'Yes. But—' He regretted the but the moment it came out of his mouth.

'But what?' Mishti asked as she raised an eyebrow.

'That quality manager's getting too big for his safety boots. Will you bring him down a peg or two? He's driving me crazy.'

'You're an idiot. Of course he's driving you crazy; he thinks you are a threat to the pompous over-the-top quality system he implemented. Don't lose sleep over things like that. Just do your work and stop thinking about it. Go, get out of my office, do your job and make more of those lovely placebos that bring us more profits.'

CHAPTER 15

ANAYA WALKED through the mall in Sandton city. She loved shopping for clothes and shoes, but hated that she was having to grocery shop after firing another maid. In India, she'd known where everything was, and how to buy the best food so that she could cook for her husband and make him happy. Why couldn't maids in South Africa do things like she wanted them to? It wasn't hard.

She'd had no family support since she married Reyansh. Moving to a new country the day after their traditional marriage, to a man her family had chosen for her, had seemed like an exciting opportunity at first, but reality had quickly set in. Even now, years later, she was still struggling.

She looked at her three children sitting together at the Wimpy having a drink. She was responsible for them, and she was going to make sure they never had to experience what she had growing up. They would never have to marry for money because her family couldn't afford to send her to university. She had been their meal ticket.

Her husband had money—lots of it. His family was rich. They'd paid a nice price for her, once they had seen the doctor's report verifying that she was a virgin. And then Reyansh had stuck his penis into her, and her fate had been sealed.

She would make sure that her children never had to worry about money during their lives. And she would show every last one of those bitches back in India that she could have the best house, and the most perfect life in South Africa. She would make them jealous of her if it was the last thing she did.

Her husband's money would prove to them that she had made the right decision, that she hadn't sold herself short. She had remained pure all those years for a reason, and he might have been a bit older than she would have preferred, but as long as she had access to his money, she would support her mother in the custom her father had never been able to. Her mother would never have to have another 'lover' who wasn't of her choosing again.

Not for her sake. Not anymore.

Her mother used to shop with her in the markets in Mumbai. She would always be there with her. To go bargain hunting with. To accompany her to the temple. But not here. Here she was alone, even after twelve years.

This year, she would turn the big three-zero. When did she get so old? So many years, and still she was not getting everything she wanted. She had been patient, very patient. She did everything a dutiful Indian wife would do. Sure, she knew which shops to buy the best meat cuts to make curry with, and the best shop to buy her spices, but she still missed her mother. She missed her friends. Reyansh worked late at night. He went to work early in the morning. Three children under six were not good company all the time, and she had long given up being friends with the maids. They stole too much from her.

Besides, Mishti didn't like it if she made any friends.

Reyansh had told her to stop seeing them, that all she needed was his family. Mishti ruled over that like a monarch. And so far, Reyansh didn't even seem to realise it. It was worse than having apron strings to a mother; he was attached to his sister by an umbilical cord.

She noticed a kind-looking old black lady sitting on a bench in the shopping centre in front of her, which was painted blue, while all the others she could see were white. It piqued her interest. The woman wore a headscarf that covered her grey hair; her face shone under the lights of the centre. She had a walking stick carved in the form of entwined snakes. Anaya liked snakes—she'd made the journey to the main temple of the Jory Goddess in Belur, Karnataka, during the Hindu festival of Naga Panchami when she was still a schoolgirl. There she'd offered incense and milk to obtain knowledge, wealth and fame.

She wondered what she'd ever done to offend the goddess as none of it had been granted. Even the wealth part hadn't come true. It all belonged to her husband, not her. And she had married him 'out of community of property', so what was his was his, complete with a prenuptial agreement. It was a cruel joke really. Except he didn't know she was squirrelling away a cut of her housekeeping money in an account with her name on it. Just as a backup.

Nobody sat next to the old woman.

Anaya looked at her children, who were shouting at each other again, squabbling about something. 'Just stop,' she whispered. 'I have had enough today. Enough.'

They ignored her as if she wasn't even there.

The old woman on the bench was surrounded by people, but no one sat with her. She was alone. Just like Anaya.

She left the Wimpy and sat down next to the old lady, slumped onto the bench and closed her eyes, hoping that the children would watch each other. She was so tired.

'Welcome to my bench,' said the old lady. 'My name is Ulwazi Dubazane.'

'Anaya Prabhu,' she said as she introduced herself, opening her eyes that she didn't believe had even closed yet. She glanced at the kids as she shook the other woman's hand.

'You look like you're having a bad day,' Ulwazi said.

'A bad day, a bad month, a bad year. Bad life. It all has my name on it,' Anaya said. Then as she realised that she'd spoken aloud, she quickly added, 'It's not too bad, just tiring. How's your day going?'

'Better than yours, apparently,' Ulwazi said, and she chuckled. 'You look harassed and not comfortable at all. Perhaps you need to sit with your children and get a cold drink?'

'If I sit there one more second, I might bang their heads together. They're arguing with each other so much, it's driving me beyond crazy.'

'It can be that way with children,' Ulwazi said.

'Do you have kids?'

'I have one son left, Kagiso, which means "peace". I do not think he's ever given me a day of peace in his whole life. And my two grandsons from my firstborn, Zenzele and Sibusiso, who are still very much part of my life, and I've one great-grandson, Anderson, who lives with me, too, and another baby on the way when its mother finally gives birth. My grandson Sibusiso says that the baby should be called Siyanda, which means "we're increasing", because now he has two baby mouths to feed.'

'You sound like you have it mostly sorted out.'

Ulwazi laughed. 'I don't think anyone really has it all sorted, or I would not be sitting on this bench talking to other women all the time.'

'I'd like to. I'd like to have people say, "There goes Anaya, she has her act together!"'

They both laughed, and Anaya felt a connection with the stranger.

'Welcome to my friendship bench, where you are free to talk with me without any judgement. I cannot solve all your problems, but I can offer a supporting shoulder to lean on and someone to tell your woes. Sometimes it can be a huge load off your shoulders just to talk about your problems.'

'I beg your pardon—I never realised this was *your* bench. I'll leave you alone to do your work,' Anaya said, starting to rise.

'You misunderstand,' said Ulwazi. 'It was made for just what we're doing—sharing as women. Some fancy organisation started these benches as outreaches to women all over South Africa after they apparently worked well in Zimbabwe. To help women talk across the generations and across the colour barriers.'

'What a wonderful idea. I wonder why I never noticed it before?'

'You were busy with your life, and you did not need it then. Seems to me you do now. This is a place of safety. The bench is where you can lighten your load by talking to me and sharing your problems. As women of the world, especially in the new South Africa, we need to stick together. To help each other. We need to listen to one another because most people have forgotten how. If you want to talk to me, I'm here for you. If you just want to sit and close your eyes and be still—well that's good with me, too. I'll sit with you and keep an eye on those children who are now looking at you out of the glass.'

Anaya glanced at her kids. They seemed fine. She turned back to the old woman. 'I'm not ungrateful. And I'm not a bad mother. I just needed a little break. I had to fire my last maid when I caught her stealing, so once more I find myself without any help looking after my children.'

'Being with your children can be very stressful. I'm sorry about your maid.'

'I'm sick of the maids stealing from me.'

'I can understand that. It is our responsibility as mothers and grandmothers—the women of South Africa—to support each other. I have had some training in counselling, and on how to help women in our society. It is important to know that we are never alone when the troubles are piling up.'

'And how much does the service cost?' Anaya asked.

'There is no cost. This is what I do. I volunteer. This is what we ask of many grandmothers—to sit on the bench and listen. It is our way of giving back to our society. We guide and counsel other women, but many of us have lost our families to the thinnings disease, to the wars. It helps the grandmothers to feel useful.'

Anaya watched her children as they began pulling faces at her through the window, before turning back to talk among themselves. Ignoring her once more.

'I can see that you need to talk. You look like the whole world is sitting on your shoulders, and you watch your three children all the time like somebody who is scared they will be stolen from you. As you should, they are your responsibility.'

Anaya shook her head. 'I need help with my children. There is something I would never admit to my husband. Never. He thinks I dress them in good clothes, and we do all the things we want to do, but I'm dying inside. I'm losing me. I want to move to a new house, to a bigger home than my townhouse in the complex in Bryanston. Where we live was fine for a bachelor, but now with the family …'

'I can help you with those problems,' Ulwazi said. 'I wish everybody who sat on the bench had issues that are so easy to help with. The other good suburbs to live in this area if you have some money are Sandton, Morningside, Fourways, even Woodmead. But I personally like Sandton best. I can see that you have lots of diamond rings on your fingers, so I think perhaps Sandton is where you want to look for somewhere to live. You need to go to Pam Golding. They can find you a new home quick-quick. Ask for Joanna; she will help you. Tell her that you spoke with me on the bench.'

'Thank you, I know about Sandton, but I am just feeling overwhelmed and didn't know where to start, but now I do—Joanna. I'll look her up. Can I give you anything? Get you a drink perhaps for pointing me in the right direction?' Anaya asked, once again watching her kids, who were getting ready to leave their table to join her outside.

'Thank you but no. Just know that I am here every Tuesday, weekends and public holidays. Tomorrow it will be another *gogo*, sitting here on the friendship bench. There's always somebody here to listen when you need to talk.'

Anaya smiled, feeling a little better knowing which real estate agent to approach by name. Asking Mishti for that advice was never going to happen.

She was so tired of that evil bitch meddling in her life. Once they moved away from Mishti and her family to a different suburb, things would be different. She might have a chance to change things. To live the life she wanted to live, with her husband and her children. 'Can I ask you something else, Ulwazi?'

'Of course.'

'Can you find me a good maid who doesn't steal?'

'Yes, I know lots and lots of very good, responsible and honest women who are looking for work. It is important to find an honest maid in Johannesburg—lots of maids have light fingers. They can clean out all your diamonds before you notice they are gone. I can find you a good maid by tomorrow morning, and she could be with you while you find a house. She can watch over the children, make sure they have food and are looked after, while you do everything you need to do. You're essential to your family, and you need to make big decisions, so if you have some help from a nice maid it will make your job of being a mother and a wife much easier.'

'Thank you,' Anaya said. 'I'd really appreciate it. Let me go find this Joanna at Pam Golding, and tomorrow morning I'll meet you here for breakfast when the mall opens. And I would like to meet this maid that you can bring along to help me.'

'I will be here in the morning with a good maid for you,' Ulwazi said.

'Thank you again,' Anaya said as she stood up, just in time to collect her children as they ran at her from the Wimpy. She had a real estate agent to contact.

CHAPTER 16

The first of September was officially the start of spring, when everyone got excited that the cold weather would leave, and the long, hot African summers were on their way. But as Piet stood in front of the automatic door to the Kimberley Hospital morgue, he felt no joy. His mind was too occupied with his case load. He stepped aside as it opened for Natalie to walk in first. He followed her through the outer door and into the reception area.

'*Goeie môre,* Detective Kleinman, Detective Hatch,' the receptionist behind the desk greeted them as she pushed a book towards Piet and Natalie. 'Please, can you both sign in? Dr Juliet is expecting you.'

'*Howzit,* Heidi? How's your son doing?' Piet asked as he signed the register. He clipped on his visitor-identification tag and waited for Natalie to do the same.

'He's well, playing rugby this term,' Heidi said.

'Good to hear. He's a strong kid. Tell him I said hello,' Piet said.

'I will. He loved the school visits you guys did last term. He's still raving about how "cool" you two were,' Heidi said as she buzzed the security door.

They walked through the corridor towards the iron gate that separated the morgue from the administration staff, where the town coroner, Dr Juliet, was waiting for them.

Dr Ros Juliet had been old since the day Piet met her back in Kokstad years ago, and she still had the grey-haired style and elegance he remembered. She simply refused to acknowledge that she should retire. He suspected that one day they would find her dead on the job.

'Nice to see you again, young Piet,' Ros said. 'And Natalie, always a pleasure. Wish it was under better circumstances.'

'Likewise,' Natalie said, 'but probably not going to happen in our profession, is it?'

'True. The reason I called you in today was that I've another hijack victim and I thought you should see him for yourselves. This one died three nights ago on the Midlands Road. I'm sure you'll see the report in the police system eventually, but after you spoke to me about your Hawthorne case, I thought you might be interested in this guy.'

'What have we got?' Piet said.

'About a year ago, I had a spate of patients die from pneumonia. What got me is that they weren't all old, or necessarily had a compromised immune system. I couldn't find a link between their deaths. It was like a mini-epidemic. Then just as suddenly, it stopped. This man, who now lies on my table, came here to see me at the time. He was a representative from the fraud department of the medical-aid company ExtraMed. He was asking to see my notes on some pneumonia-death cases as he felt that their company had excessive claims for them, and it was the middle of summer.' She walked to the autopsy table. 'Meet the late Mr Eric Chelmsford. We spoke, and he left just as bewildered as I was at the time. He asked me to keep an eye out for any other "cluster" deaths and to contact him again if I noted anything weird or if I suddenly began to see multiple cases of unseasonal deaths again. We had a few cases of meningitis come through here. I contacted him earlier this week, because although we didn't see him, there was another death quite recently.'

'Moses,' Piet said.

Ros nodded. 'I should have known that you would have ties to him. Your community is tight.'

'His wife, Coti, was devastated, and the new doctor, Lily Winters, too. From what I saw, she took his death quite personally.'

'She's lovely, isn't she? She should be arriving any moment now. I also called her.'

'You called Lily?'

'She's one of the leading specialists in meningitis clusters in the world, and she and I were already going over my files for the other cases and comparing notes. Seems that she's missing a lot of information that she should have had from when she took over from that *slapgat* Ian Hawthorne. She contacted me recently.'

'She did?' Piet asked.

'Yes, frustrating when you take over a research project but only have part of the information. I know Ian was your friend, Piet, but the more I find out about him in death, the more I wonder why? Anyway, back to the late Mr Chelmsford.' She turned to the body on the table. 'He came back to Kimberley three days ago, and we compared notes for the clients of his company, and now he's dead. Not only dead, but he had the same violent death as Hawthorne. I suspect the same calibre gun. Only this time, there was no slug left in his head, only entry and exit. His fingers are broken and his knee is shot out. He had no personal items come through the morgue, so perhaps you need to find out if he had anything else that the police kept when they attended the scene.'

'Any ideas as to what's going on?' Piet asked.

The buzzer went off on the wall. 'That'll be Lily,' Ros said. 'Natalie, do you mind fetching her as I don't want to have to put on new gloves again.'

'Sure,' Natalie said.

'Piet, if you lift that receiver and just hold it up, I'll let them know that Natalie is on her way.'

Piet did what he was asked, and Natalie left the room.

'You know, Ros, if this is an active case you cannot discuss it with Dr Lily Winters—no matter how nice you think she is.'

'Lily's here to discuss the meningitis and pneumonia cases. This poor man just happened to still be on my table,' Ros said.

'And the fact that Lily knew Hawthorne has nothing to do with having her here?'

Ros frowned. 'It has everything to do with it. This man died because I discussed my files with him; Lily needs to understand the danger she might be in. She's analysing the same data. After all, we don't know who killed him or why. But Lily was not even in the country then, so it certainly rules her out as a suspect.'

Piet wanted to groan. Ros was manipulating him into a corner, and he knew it. 'What are you not telling me?'

'I think that you might need to work with Lily on this. These cases are connected—you guys just need to sort out how. You need her to work on the medical side and you're going to need to protect her as you work on the hijackings. I don't want to see her on this table. I think she's now in real trouble, even if she doesn't know or understand it yet.'

'Work with Lily?' Piet said.

If they collaborated, his biggest problem was that Quintin was already jumpy and nervous in South Africa. He had spent thousands upgrading the security around their home, and that was knowing it was only going to be for six months. This case could go on longer than that. This was going to cause complications for Lily when Quintin found out. But Ros was right. The cases were related, which meant that Lily was involved now, and that put her life in danger.

'Think of her as a consultant if you want, but know that when she walks through that door, I expect her to be fully briefed. She needs to understand the implications here. Lily shows a First World naivety, even if she was born in South Africa.'

They could hear Lily's heels walking down the passage as she got closer.

Lily came through the door first, followed closely by Natalie.

'Sorry, am I interrupting?' Lily asked.

'No, you're bang on time. Welcome. You just met Detective Natalie Hatch, and you know Detective Piet Kleinman already.'

'Hey, Piet,' Lily said.

He nodded.

'Right, let's get started,' Ros said. She quickly filled Lily in on the hijacked victim and was soon showing them all the head wounds and the shot-out knee.

'Lily, you need to understand how much danger you're putting yourself in. Both people I have spoken to about these files before you are now dead. Are you sure you want to carry on with this investigation for World Health?'

'I don't have much choice, do I? The clusters are real. I have to find the source—that's what I do. And if it means that we need to do even more on the security front for Quintin and me, then we do it. It's not the first time our lives have been on the line for the good of the population, and I'm sure it won't be the last.'

Ros nodded. 'Okay, then, onto a successful and hopefully safe collaboration.' She wiped her hands on a paper towel and tossed it in the big bin in the corner that said 'Hazardous waste' in bright yellow. 'So that's the hijack victims. Now about the meningitis. I've seen many weird things in my day as a coroner, but I've never known cases to be so unrelated yet connected as this outbreak of meningitis.' She removed her gloves and washed her hands before she moved over to her desk, where she had a heap of files piled up in a Jenga tower.

'You'd expect this type of meningitis in a children's nursery school or even a primary school. Perhaps in a boarding establishment where children are eating together—sharing the same utensils, where they share spit and bodily fluids, and breathe all over each other. The fact that this strain of meningitis is taking so many people that don't know each other, and have no contact, means that there has to be something unusual in common that they have been exposed to—but I can't figure it out. There's no reason for a bacterial infection like this to be spreading.'

'If you are the coroner and can't work it out, who can?' Natalie asked.

'I'm hoping you three,' Ros said. 'I can give you each patient's file, and all the background information I have on the nature of this illness. As you know, I do the coroner work for the city of Kimberley, both private and government. Everything comes through my team and me. The police often call us to private homes when they're questioning deaths by natural circumstances and we have attended to a handful of both prisoner and civilian corpses around this town who also died from meningitis over the last few months. I believe the situation is getting worse, not better.' She handed both Piet and Lily a pile of manila files.

'How many of these did you give to Chelmsford?' Piet asked.

'About a third. I have written in each file if they're his insurance patients or not. Those that weren't, I couldn't share the information with him, just gave him statistics from my analysis. That information is also in there.'

'At least we know where to start looking,' Piet said. 'Having Lily involved will be a definite advantage. If she has a sick patient, we can also observe and learn.'

'I hope I don't lose another one. I'm still trying to understand how I lost Moses in the first place. Having all these autopsy files for comparison will be helpful. Thank you, Dr Juliet, I do appreciate being brought in on this.'

'I hope you can get to the bottom of it. There've been too many unexpected deaths in this town,' Ros said.

'I am sure we will find what is causing these passings,' Piet said.

'It might be a plan for us to start with the old-age-home deaths—it'll be easier to isolate the variables. We'll need to check and compare everything, from the different environments, who was washing the sheets, what washing powders they were using, who was supplying the kitchens their food, everything we can think of. There has to be a contamination point where these bacteria are thriving. Neither the pneumonia virus nor the meningitis bacteria normally lay dormant for long in one's body. I think we might find some of the information needed to build a database and analyse,' Lily said.

'Only if their deaths were deemed to be "suspect" would we have a file on them. Otherwise, we'll need to speak with each of the deceased next of kin for that information,' Piet said.

Natalie said, 'If there is something, we just need time to find it, and who killed Chelmsford and Hawthorne. Thanks for letting us know the MO was the same. It helps with leads when a pattern can be found.'

Ros nodded. 'So many deaths happening. That's the problem. If it's not pneumonia or meningitis that's killing the people of Kimberley, the HIV epidemic is doing its best to try to keep population numbers down.'

'I know how long you have worked here, Ros, and I know how much you care for the people of Kimberley. I believe that we can all work together to figure out what's happening,' Piet said.

Armed with all her new information from both the flash drive and Dr Juliet's file, Lily's analysis was beginning to show some fascinating patterns. But she still needed more information. And there were names of people in her file now who were not dead, whom she could turn to for help.

Lily walked into the paediatric ward and went to the nurses' station.

'I'm Dr Lily Winters. I'm looking for Nurse Kaplan and also Sister Lungu. Do you know if they are rostered on today?'

'Hi, Dr Winters, I'm Sister Thengi Manyuchi. I can look at the roster and see when Nurse Kaplan will be on again. Sister Lungu doesn't work here anymore. She and I were friends. She moved to Port Elizabeth to be nearer her daughter, who was pregnant. I can get you her phone number.'

'Thank you, I'd appreciate that,' Lily said, noticing for the first time the cartoon animal-print apron the sister wore over her uniform. Her hair was neat, plaited and pinned under her little cap, which was fashioned more like a crown in the front, and she had a big, happy smile. Lily had to suppress a grin of her own seeing it. She was always in awe of the care nurses took to make something unique for the kids to feel more at home in hospitals.

'Says here that Nurse Kaplan is on permanent nights, and her next shift is next week, starting on Monday. Is there something I can help you with?'

'Maybe. I'm here as a specialist from World Health—I specialise in cluster diseases. I took over from Dr Ian Hawthorne and I'm trying to get up to speed with his research.'

'Ah, you are that Dr Lily Winters. Dr Hawthorne spoke about you. He said that you did amazing work when you were in the refugee camp in the Sudan. He used to talk about you and your famous husband all the time, like you were personal friends.'

'You knew Dr Hawthorne?'

'I don't think there is a nurse here who didn't know Dr Hawthorne. He certainly had a different way of looking at things. While he kept a protocol for drugs and medical issues, he was very different to the other doctors. He was a big advocate of holistic healing. He said he was sick of the approach to medicine only being chemical drugs. He had many fiery conversations with the people on the board and with other doctors about what their responsibility was to the patient. His views on what was ethically right collided with theirs. He wasn't a popular doctor with the administration, but I couldn't fault his commitment to his patients. This place is a lot quieter now that he's gone. So sorry for your loss of your friend.'

'Thank you. We had a complicated relationship, but I had known him for a long time.'

'So, what can I help you with?'

'I'm looking for information on anything strange that the nurses might have found in the children's ward. I'm looking for unexplained sicknesses. Something which has happened to more than one child. Not a normal sickness like chickenpox, but sicknesses which were either fatal or near fatal. I'm looking for anything any of the nurses can tell me. No matter how insignificant it seems.'

'Actually, a few months ago we had a kid come in with pneumonia—which was not unusual, except about a week later we had a second child come in, and we lost both of them. For a long time, I've wondered if what we'd done to treat them was incorrect and I studied it in my textbooks, and everything the doctors did was right, but we still lost both of the children.'

'Pneumonia? I've seen the same thing in the notes from the adult ward, but they seem to have stopped a few months ago. Any recent cases?'

Sister Thengi Manyuchi shook her head. 'Not pneumonia, but we also have had many children come in with infected sores that shouldn't be infected, almost like something you would see in the tropics. We're not tropical, yet these kids, who have never been outside of Kimberley, are showing tropical abscesses on their legs and arms.'

'What race were they?'

'Black, white, yellow—it makes no difference. It's not discriminating against any one colour within the community.'

'Were they HIV infected?'

'Only a couple were. At first, I thought it was just black kids, but then we had Indians and coloureds. And a few weeks ago, I had four white kids come in with tropical sores that had turned nasty and the parents could no longer treat them through their doctors. It's all children.'

'Can you provide me the names so that we can look them up and see what medication they were on?' Lily asked. 'It might save me a lot of time searching on the hospital system myself, if you can recall them and help me out here.'

'I can call the files up on the computer system. I'm guessing it isn't a coincidence that Ian and I had discussed just this before his death, and now you are asking almost the identical questions?'

'Do you care to elaborate?' Lily asked.

'It made no sense to me why the children died from the infections they had. The medications they took should have cleared them up in no time at all,' she said. 'I have looked at their files multiple times but can't find where we went wrong.'

A call button buzzed as the last of the files on the children she remembered printed out, and Sister Manyuchi gave them to Lily. 'I need to go. Bad timing. If you have any questions, you are welcome to call me or come talk on the floor again. I too would like to know why we are having angels grow their wings too soon.'

Lily nodded and watched as the nurse walked away. The information she'd just gained didn't shock her as much as it should have. What worried her was that this sister had already spoken to Ian about the same things, and Ian had turned up dead not long afterwards.

She had so much to catch up Piet and Natalie on, and yet from the look of Ian's files, she was still behind where he had been in his investigation.

Shaking her head, she began to walk back towards the lifts, her new files tucked securely under her arm. She wouldn't stop digging and investigating until she caught up with him.

CHAPTER 17

THE FOLLOWING MONDAY, Lily stood next to her examination table with a thermometer in her hand and a stethoscope around her neck. Michael sat at the door of her clinic in the little house in Platfontein. That was the only way Lily was allowed to visit her outreach clinic, according to the insurance documents she had read at the office. With Michael and his weapon as part of the deal, or she didn't visit them at all.

Quintin was also with her. She shouldn't have been surprised that both Quintin and June Kilborne had ganged up on her on that one. She hated it. The reminder of having an armed guard present all the time dug a needle into her side. The fact that Hawthorne's killer had still not been found didn't help. Nor did the fact that they didn't know why he had been killed.

Today, Quintin sat at the table, acting as her administration secretary, like he often did at outreach clinics. He was blowing raspberries at her patient and getting no response, which was unusual for him, because kids loved Quintin. He would've been an awesome father if they had wanted children.

David, a boy of about twelve, with big, round brown eyes, stood in front of her with his older sister of eighteen, Elise, and the youngest of the siblings, a toddler, Diamond, sat on the examination table. She was plump as a baby should be, and her hair had been decorated with little strips of coloured fabric. Diamond smiled a lot and was as alert as any two-year-old, even if she didn't respond to Quintin's raspberry blowing.

'Elise, do you know if your mother was sick when she was pregnant with your sister?' Lily asked.

'She didn't have the thinnings disease. My sister is not HIV,' Elise said. 'The *dokotela* took her blood and checked after my mother died at the end of last year.'

'Do you know what sickness she died from?'

'She got cancer in her tummy. I was finishing school—and working at people's houses—making enough money to feed everybody,' Elise said. '*Dokotela* Ian and Medicine Man Piet helped her deliver Diamond early because she couldn't take the drugs when she was pregnant. She was scheduled to have her cut out, but Diamond came early, and my mother could start treatment for the cancer. She was very sick but she lived to see Diamond turn one year old before she passed over. Piet, he made sure my mother had a nice burial, and *Dokotela* Ian, he gave me Diamond and told me to look after her as if she was my baby. I found out then that I was HIV positive, and I know that she is not. She and David both got tested by the clinic here. Both of them are clear.'

'I'm sorry. And I apologise for all these questions, but I need to know if I'm to treat Diamond properly because I have no previous file on her.'

'It is okay, but I do not know all the answers. You are the new *dokotela,* and you need to know all these things. Can you fix Diamond's ears? She's in pain.'

'She has an inner-ear infection. You need to put these drops in three times a day. If you take her swimming or give her a bath, don't let her put her head under the water for at least a week,' Lily said, administering the first lot of drops into Diamond's ears. 'She needs to take this antibiotic.' She put some in a syringe. 'Come on, Diamond, this is nice, taste.' She put a drop on the little girl's lip and Diamond licked it, then reached for the syringe. Lily said, 'Open your mouth,' and she squirted the banana-flavoured medicine in.

Diamond swallowed the medicine as if it was a sweet.

Lily passed both bottles to Elise.

'How do I pay you for today?'

'There is no charge. It's a research clinic.' Lily frowned. 'Why would you think you need to pay me?'

'*Dokotela* Ian always said nothing is for free.'

'What did you pay him?' Quintin asked.

Lily was scared to hear the answer. Taking payment for these clinics was against the organisation's rules of research. Sadly, Lily wasn't surprised to hear that Hawthorne had been charging these poor people just to put some extra cash in his pocket. She'd need to speak to Piet and Natalie to see if they knew anything about it through looking into his finances. She thought of his over-the-top decorated home and wondered if that was where he had hidden the money. In antiques.

'Whatever I could at the time, but today I have nothing. I'm only eighteen, and I already have the social workers on my back all the time telling me that I need to keep my house tidy, I need to do this and do that for my brother and sister. Piet sometimes helps in the house when I don't know how to fix something. Sometimes we can't even pay the electricity bill to Eskom. Billy from two houses down, he offered to disconnect our home from the grid and then reconnect us at the pole, like everybody else and not pay. I wanted to say yes because I put so much money into the machine and we don't get much lights or hot water from it at all.'

'That's good that you didn't illegally connect, it's really dangerous.'

'Sometimes I want to run away—go to a big city where I can get a better job in a bigger house, and it will pay me more, but that means I'd have to be away, and I can't do that to Diamond and David. I need to look after them.' Elise nodded to her siblings with her head. 'I promised my mother I would look after my family.'

'And your social worker? You've spoken to them about this?' Lily asked.

'No, *Dokotela*.' Elise shook her head. 'Social workers come here to take children away, they are not sent to help. I can't tell her that it's all too much.'

Lily frowned. 'I think I need to speak with a social worker here. It seems their roles have changed since I qualified in Durban many years ago. In the meantime, I'll find you some books you can read to Diamond. It might help her settle at night.'

'I can give you one of my chickens,' Elise said.

Quintin grunted. 'We have enough chickens already. And a rooster that crows. Who on earth still keeps roosters around to wake anyone up at four in the morning? Give her our rooster, Lily, free to a good home if she has chickens.'

Lily saw Elise put her hand over her mouth to cover her smile even as she shook her head.

'Diamond needs the protein from the eggs laid by your chickens. And you don't need to take our rooster unless you want him to get more chickens. Quintin is just tired because the rooster somehow got left out of its coop last night, and decided to crow outside our window extremely early this morning. There's no charge for coming in to see me—no one in Platfontein will pay for this clinic while I'm here. Understand?'

'Yes, *Dokotela*. Thank you. I do not want your rooster: he will crow and wake me up instead.'

Quintin laughed, but Lily was distracted as she heard raised voices outside, where people waited for the clinic. In Australia, she would have assumed it was anger, but here in Africa, she knew it could just be excitement, too. People right next to each other talked loudly to ensure that their neighbours knew they were not talking about them. It was a courtesy that was practised in a number of the traditions among the *uBuntu* people. She waited to see which one it was this time.

Piet put his head in. '*Howzit*, Quintin, Lily? I know you are busy with the clinic so I will not stop here long. I wanted to let you know, the flamingos arrived at the dam last night in their thousands. This weekend would be a good one to go look for those plants if you guys want to. The sight will be spectacular.'

'Thanks, Piet,' Lily said.

'Sounds good,' Quintin said.

'I will be at your place on Sunday bright and early, then?'

'Meaning what time exactly?' Lily asked.

'Sixish.'

Quintin let out a low groan.

Lily laughed. 'Hey, Piet, I found something that we need to talk about.'

'Can it wait? I am swamped today, and just got a call into the office.'

'It can,' Lily said. She wasn't sure how Piet juggled all the different duties pulling him in all directions in his life.

'Great, if we do not speak on the phone before, see you on Sunday,' Piet said as he waved and had gone before Lily could say anything more.

'You and Piet are good friends?' Elise asked.

'We have become friends, yes. He seems like a good man to many people.'

'He is. Here in Platfontein, we rely on Piet the medicine man but also Piet the policeman,' Elise said as she picked up Diamond and strapped her to her back with a towel.

'I'm beginning to understand that more and more, the longer I'm here,' Lily said as she looked at Elise. 'Make sure you give Diamond her medicines, and I'll see you back here at the clinic next week to make sure her ear is clear. We don't want to damage her hearing permanently. I'll be in touch about the social worker; someone needs to help you.'

'Thank you, *Dokotela* Lily.'

CHAPTER 18

QUINTIN REACHED for Lily's hand to help her down from the Land Cruiser.

'Thanks,' she said, climbing out and onto the brown grass underfoot.

Piet stood to the side. 'We need to walk to the dam from here. You can hear the flamingos already. Not good to get too close. Perhaps we find a log you can use to make your violins while we are looking for the plants.'

'Perhaps,' Quintin said, although he didn't hold out much hope. He looked around. They appeared to be on somebody's property, but there was not a soul around, just a few fever and camel thorn trees that the area was famous for. He grabbed the safari hat that Lily had bought him so many years ago when they first came to Africa, and he put it on. After slamming the door, he turned on the alarm. 'Come on, then, let's go,' he said, picking up his walking stick that he'd rested against the bonnet. Taking Lily's hand in his, they followed Piet.

'I cannot wait for you to see Kamfers Dam,' Piet said. 'We'll walk around the side and work our way back to here. This part of the dam doesn't belong to Sol Plaatje Municipality. Aiden van Niekerk, the farmer, he knows we are coming. His son Elbie is only eight years old, and he already has to use the CBD oil.'

'Why?' asked Lily.

'He has cancer. We think he's doing okay now he's using the oil, and also some plants from the Kalahari. The big city specialist said the family must get ready to bury him because they could do nothing more. When Aiden was told that, he started to treat Elbie with the oil, and I gave him some bush medicines to try. That was three years ago now and Elbie, he's running around. That one plant, we also can look for today, I use for cancer patients to make the feelings of being so sick go away. I will show you.'

'So many things for us to learn,' Lily said.

'These plants and what they can do fascinate me,' Quintin said. 'But I think I'm more taken with the food plants. There seems to be so much "bush tucker" that could help so many people if it was cultivated.'

Lily snorted. 'You were never interested in plants. What gives?'

'Here they have a purpose. Food. Medicine. Remember at Zam Zam, the moringa trees? They were trying to plant a grove of them to provide food, but the people kept stealing all the plants out of the ground, not letting them become established because they were so hungry for some greens in their diet.'

'I remember that,' Lily said.

'They stole the whole plants? But then they will not have food tomorrow. It is better to leave some of the plant behind,' Piet said.

'Yes, but when they began the project, they didn't educate the population as to why it was being done, just that they needed their help. If they had spent time educating everyone, there might have been a marked difference. Hindsight is a wonderful gift created to haunt us, isn't it?'

'*Ja*, like our flamingos here. Before the Flamingo Warrior people came and told us about them, we did not understand that they were a threatened species, and that we could have a way to look after them. Education helps plenty,' Piet said.

They walked in silence together through the tawny and dry grass that was knee-high, except where it had been grazed low by the wildlife. Scattered trees dotted the landscape as Piet followed what appeared to be a game path through the bush. Eventually, they crested a slight hill and saw Kamfers Dam. The grassy-green colour of the water was clearly visible on the vast expanse before them.

They could see a few small islands filled with reeds on the south side—to the north, the water stretched off into the distance.

'Do you know if the dam is deep?' asked Quintin.

Piet shook his head. 'I am a San—I do not go into water. But this place used to dry up after the rains. No one except the birds swim here. The other animals do not drink here either. The Sol Plaatje Municipality use it as their sewage and stormwater overflow, and now there is water all the time. Except in the drought, then who knows what will happen then. But the flamingos learned to breed here. Especially after Ekapa Mining made the island for them in the middle. And they multiplied.'

'I read about that: didn't they win some huge environmental award?' Quintin said.

'*Ja* man. Everything was a success, until last year, when that island went underneath the water. They did not account for the Sol Plaatje Municipality's incompetence in not diverting water away if big rains came. They knew the levels in Kamfers were to be kept below a certain level, but you know municipalities in South Africa, they just do their own thing.'

'I read in the newspapers that they are expecting big rain again this summer. Do you think we're going to have the same problem?' Lily asked.

'*Ja*. Most likely, Kimberley will always suffer. As long as this municipality and the men involved there are still in charge of the water, they will always expect money in their back pockets in exchange for who to assign it to or not. That is simply how they operate. It does not affect my harvest today though. So, we can be thankful for that.'

'And the flamingos? What happens to them when it floods?' Quintin asked.

'No one did anything when the water rose up and the eggs and the little ones who had just hatched and could not swim yet were drowned.'

'That's so sad,' Lily said.

'It is, and in the papers, they kept saying that they do not interfere with nature. To me it was madness.'

'I take it you don't have any traditional stories about flamingos from others who had seen them before?' asked Quintin.

Piet shook his head. 'I used to live far away in Angola, then we moved south to the Caprivi Strip. There wasn't a lot of water where we came from.'

'Sounds like a different life. Must have been a difficult decision to move?'

Piet smiled. 'No, it was a choice for life. I was on the South African side of that war. I believed that the South Africans were a lesser evil than the communists, even if it meant I had to become a second-class citizen and be called a coloured because my skin is not black. My skin is not white either because I am a San. But at least my family and I would be alive.'

'I can't imagine having to give up my identity simply to stay alive,' Quintin said.

Piet grimaced. 'It was not a choice of identity; it was a choice of dying in the bush or living as a South African citizen, which is what they promised us. It just took them many years after everything that happened for us as a tribe to even get given a home.

'We did not care about what country passports we carried back then, we could always walk through the bush. This is how it has always been done. Out there in the Kalahari, where our ancestors came from, all the San tribes once knew each other. In essence, we are all one people. Even with all the different languages, inside our hearts we are the same. Now governments have put up big fences and country borders, and we are told we as a people are not allowed in the Kalahari anymore. In Botswana, they found diamonds, and they sealed the wells and moved the San away to displaced villages.'

'What about your rights as being previous custodians of the land? They have such a thing in Australia,' Lily said.

'It is diamonds, Lily. No one stands between that industry and profit. Especially not the San.'

Lily shook her head. 'It's Africa; I should have known better.'

'Quintin, to answer your last question, we do not have any stories of the pink flamingo yet.'

'Do you have any other animal you tell stories of?' Lily asked.

'In our culture it is the eland that is special, sacred. We kill them when our boys want to become men. The animal is skinned and the fat from the eland's throat and collarbone is cooked and made into a soup. Then the boy drinks this for … what is the word that will not offend Lily?' He made a gesture with his arm around his crutch area going up and down from his elbow.

Quintin laughed aloud. 'Classic.'

'You're kidding,' Lily said. 'What about the females?'

'There is a ceremony for girls, too, when one of our girls passes into puberty, and she has her first blood. She is put into a special hut. The women all celebrate by participating in the Eland Bull Dance that imitates the mating eland with the men.'

'Why?' asked Lily. 'That doesn't sound like a celebration for her at all. Knowing that everyone will now know that she's menstruating.'

'The dance is so that the girl will stay beautiful, and she will not be hungry or thirsty but have a peaceful life,' Piet said.

'Ah, wow, the boys get potency, and the girls get beauty, health and peace. Can't be too peaceful with all those vigorous males in the village,' Lily said.

Piet and Quintin were laughing. 'I never thought of it like that before. The women, in the end, get all the spoils of the eland,' Piet said.

Lily shook her head.

Quintin was trying to control his laughter but was failing horribly.

'You men are terrible,' Lily said. 'You're like a pack; you stick up for each other no matter what!'

'True,' said Piet. 'Sometimes we feast on elands when there is a marriage. The husband gifts the fat from the eland's heart to the bride's parents. And then later, the bride gets rubbed with eland fat. My people also use our God Kaggen's favourite animal in the trance dance with the shaman.'

'I thought you were a shaman,' Quintin said.

'I am a medicine man. I do not call spirits to myself; I do not try to heal people with magic. I use plants and modern medicines so that my people have the best chance possible. I have too much of the law in me to be a shonky *sheister*. Besides, most shamans are just show-offs and frauds.'

'Do you believe the shaman can cure anyone?' Lily asked.

'I do not, but that is my personal belief.'

'I can understand that,' Quintin said. 'When we were in Zimbabwe many years ago, we met a sangoma. He was both the medicine man and the shaman.'

'They are not normally separated in our culture. It is usually one person and they are often male. But my grandmother was very good with herbs and healing. So, our tribe adapted.'

'Just as well, because it looks like they need your medical skills here at Platfontein, not some hocus-pocus garbage,' Quintin said.

Piet smiled. 'There is room for both. I am lucky; I get to be the medicine man and the storyteller. One day soon, now that we are resettled in this new home, I hope that we will tell new stories of these flamingos and how we made a difference to them.'

'Hang on, you don't swim but you help protect the flamingos anyway?' Quintin asked.

Piet nodded. 'Aiden invited us to be involved. We keep an eye on the birds. To make sure that not too many people come too close to look. There are people who come past the dam looking for free food, and they take the flamingos that fly into the powerlines.'

'So, you and your community actually look after the flamingos?' Quintin asked.

'It is a win-win situation. My people have no work and miss the freedom of space. Aiden needs eyes on his lands. For every person we catch walking on his ground, he gives us some money for the Platfontein school and the community. It also gives protection to all the other birds on the dam. We make sure that their eggs are not stolen either.'

They walked single file in silence for a while. Each lost in their own thoughts on their way to the dam.

They heard the flamingos before they saw them. The en masse honking and chatter from the birds was incredibly loud. They reached the top of the ridge and stood side by side as they looked out over the sea of flamingos, at pink-and-white birds spread over the blue water in an almost Picasso-style live painting.

A few metres in, where the water and the land met, was an island of pink. The beautiful birds flapped their wings and put their heads back down as they moved altogether. Their heaving flock made it look like the island was getting bigger, and bigger, then suddenly they bunched together again, and a wave of changing colours shimmered as some of the flamingos began running and took to the sky. They flew a little way and then elegantly landed once again, gliding onto the flat surface. They settled back down as if whatever had spooked them a few metres away no longer mattered.

Quintin could see that the birds were content living together, safe in their numbers, even if they had to be vigilant on the edge of the water and from attacks above by predator birds like fish eagles and marabou storks.

He turned to watch the amazement on Lily's face. 'Stunning, isn't it.'

'It's mesmerising. There're so many I don't quite know where to look, and which one to concentrate on,' Lily admitted.

'They take my breath away every time I see them,' Piet said. 'It is the true beauty of Kimberley where some raise their babies. Thousands will call this dam their home and return each year to breed.'

'They're beautiful. Do they always arrive so suddenly?' Quintin asked.

'Some of the birds, they stay here always. As long as there is water and food. The Flamingo Warrior who first came to Platfontein to educate the children at school, he said in the last two years there were about one hundred and thirty thousand chicks that fledged from here. It is good to see the flamingos back this year. To many people, the flamingo is seen as food, and it is big enough to feed the whole family.'

'You eat them?' asked Quintin.

'I have eaten them: they taste like chicken and shrimp together.'

'Everyone always says things taste like chicken,' Quintin said.

'These birds are too beautiful to eat,' Lily said.

'*Ja.* Flamingos are beautiful,' Piet said. 'At least now we have a way to make a difference in our community and ensure that they are alive for our children's children.'

'Like volunteer game guards?' Quintin said.

'*Ja,* but it is our youth mostly, so they do not carry guns.'

Lily nodded in understanding.

'From far away, this water looked green, but now that we've walked closer it looks blue,' Quintin said.

'It is green. It is the algae that makes it look blue when you are closer to the water,' Piet said. 'Come, let us get going. We need to go to where the islands are showing further towards the wall from here. It is easier to walk near the water than in the bush along that stretch.'

They walked for a full hour before Piet changed direction and headed towards what looked like a small hill.

'We begin looking here on this island,' Piet said.

'That's an island?' asked Lily.

'When there is water, *ja*. Now before the rains, it is the place where we find the plant I am looking for. When I harvested it, I was careful to leave behind many little tubers, so perhaps today it will be here still, and no other traditional medicine person has come and taken it already.'

'Do you have a problem with that?' Quintin asked.

'Sometimes. My grandmother taught my sister and me—what some might call "the old ways". When I moved to Platfontein, I tried to grow my own plants. I was not having much luck when I met Lincoln, and he had green fingers. When Lincoln went to work for Ian, he said we should begin growing the plants in Ian's garden instead. But not all plants thrive in the cultivated environment, some die. Even Lincoln cannot make the exact same conditions as they have in the wild. This one unfortunately did not grow and had to be rediscovered.'

There was a noise of birds chattering in the area, but there were no trees in the reeds or grasses that clung to the hard-crusted dirt.

'What is that awful smell?' Lily asked.

'Grey-headed gulls. They are very noisy and stinky, too,' Piet said. Using his walking stick to help him, he climbed up the embankment and was on the island. Quintin followed, then put his hand out to help Lily.

'Thanks, hon,' she said, and bent to kiss him.

'*Sis tog*, just like teenagers,' Piet said.

'We've got a licence to do that, and believe me, after all these years it's a good thing. I'm not trading Lily in for a newer model, I like this one too much,' Quintin said, causing Lily to blush even more.

'Lily, she is a diamond. Why would you throw her away for something less precious?'

'She's exquisite, isn't she?' Quintin said as he raised his camera to start taking photos.

'Excuse me, you two, I'm standing right here, while you talk about me like a lump of compressed coal,' Lily said.

'Oh sorry—hadn't noticed you there,' Quintin said with a broad grin.

Lily stuck out her tongue at him.

CHAPTER 19

By mid-September, Lily had increased her clinics at Platfontein to three days a week to attempt to get on top of the backlog of people who needed medical help. That along with the continual contact between the police team and her, and she was ready for the weekend and some down time.

Instead, she was looking at Piet, standing next to his police *bakkie* parked on her driveway. Today he wore a white T-shirt with a 'save the rhino' slogan on it and three-quarter-length shorts. David stood next to him with his little sister, Diamond, perched on his shoulders.

'Hello, Dr Lily,' David greeted her.

'Hello, David. Good to see you and Diamond. How're her ears doing?'

'She's much better. That's why Elise told me I should bring her here with Piet, so that we got away from Platfontein for a little while, and I could earn some money, too. But Elise isn't feeling good today. She's sick.'

'Please tell her to come to the clinic on Monday,' Lily said. 'Piet, why are you carrying spades?'

'You needed new ones, so I picked them up for Quintin from the farmers' coop yesterday. Today we are getting the beds ready in the vegetable garden for some new crops, and we are helping Lincoln in his garden, too.'

'Why're you helping Lincoln plant a vegetable patch? You've been talking about having this weekend off all week.'

'Gardening is how I like to spend my weekends off,' Piet said. 'I wanted off from investigations and crooks.'

Lily smiled. She should have known.

'This afternoon, we planned on harvesting some of the *dagga*. It is time to make CBD oil again, and Lincoln and I can show you how to make it if you want to.'

'I'd like that. Not that I can make it back in Australia, the cops there do not turn a blind eye to things, but it would be good to know how if I ever needed to.'

'*Ja*, you can learn like an *imithi abesifazane*, a medicine woman.'

Lily smiled. 'Why don't we do that this morning?'

'Because this morning you and Quintin were going to the farmers' market to buy all the new seedlings for Lincoln's garden. Quintin discussed this with you at the clinic on Wednesday when I dropped in, remember?'

Lily screwed up her nose; she searched her mind, but it was blank. 'No, but that's okay, I just can't remember it. I've had a lot on my mind. I take it that there are plans for lots of plants going in today?'

Piet nodded. 'Lincoln and Quintin have written a list of what was needed from the farmers' market, so while you're there, you might find that man called Mr Magaso. You tell him who you are. You tell him that you need some more plants for me, and he will bring them here, and we can put them in the new hothouse that Quintin got us.'

'No. Seriously? I tell you what—you come to the market with us, since you know this Mr Magaso, and you talk to him.'

'With you and Quintin?' Piet asked.

'Why not? You, David and Diamond. We can make a morning of it, treat the kids to something special at the market. Surely they have face painting or pony rides, or something there?'

'*Ja*, but—are you sure you want us there with you two lovebirds?'

Lily smiled. 'I wouldn't have asked if I didn't want you there, Piet. Besides, it's also for David and Diamond. Quintin can pay David the same as if he had worked all day. Only this way, he gets to have a bit of excitement, too.'

Piet nodded.

At that moment, Diamond seemed to realise that she knew Lily and started moving up and down on David's shoulders, her arms outstretched, wanting to get to her.

'Hello, sweetie,' Lily said, taking the little girl from David. 'You're so precious.'

Diamond looked at her with big brown eyes and grinned.

'Here,' Piet said, taking the spades off his shoulder and loading them onto the boy, 'take these and go find Lincoln. He is probably in the hothouse. Tell him there is a change of plan, then come back here so we can all go to the market.'

David passed the loaded nappy bag to Piet with a grin and walked towards the garden beds.

'I got an email this morning. The IT department got onto that flash drive you gave me, and they found hidden files within those Quintin could not get into,' Piet said.

'Hidden files?'

'There is more—they had military-grade encryption, too. Ian was definitely trying to hide something. To be honest, I am actually more comfortable with going with you to the market, because I was going to have to warn you to be extra careful, to stay with Quintin and not wander off alone, not stop for anyone on the roads. But now I will be with you, so that is one less thing to worry about.'

'You worry about me?'

'All the time, Lily, all the time.'

'Aww, that's sweet, Piet.'

'*Ja,* not so sweet when you think about why. Someone might be after you now, Lily, and we need to protect you.'

'Thank you, it means a lot to me that you think like that. Now this little lady and I are going to get ready for a morning in the market. Whoever they are, they will not make me hide inside.'

Piet shook his head. 'I will be here when you guys are ready to go.'

'Come on, sugar, let's go find Quintin and get moving,' Lily said as she walked back to the house and opened the door.

Lily walked into the studio and was immediately immersed in her husband playing one of his new tunes. His eyes were closed as he played on La Angelique, Fred dancing back and forth over the strings. Silently she moved closer, but Quintin had a sixth sense for when she was around, and he opened his eyes and winked at her.

'Don't stop on my behalf,' she said.

'I won't,' he said. 'Give me another three minutes and this one will be done.'

'I'll be waiting,' she said, and took a stool from the counter and sat on it, Diamond still attached to her, but now listening intently to the music. She closed her eyes and listened to the rhythm and was lost in the moment as the sweet sound of the notes vibrated through the ancient wood and washed over her.

The music faded, and finally, silence filled the room. Diamond blew a raspberry and spit bubble, and Lily was woken from her trance.

'Time to go already?' asked Quintin.

'I would rather stay here and listen to you all day,' Lily said.

'You've always been my biggest fan. Who's this?'

'And proud of it. You remember this little lady? This is Diamond—one of Piet's extended family. She's coming shopping, and I asked David, her older brother, too. Piet is also outside waiting—going to be a full car.' She filled him in on the file encryptions.

Quintin walked over to her, hugged her tightly and kissed her head. Diamond reached out her arms for him. 'Really?'

'She wants to come to you,' Lily said as Diamond continued to reach for Quintin.

Quintin put his hands around the little girl's waist and held her securely, placing her on his hip. 'Hello, Diamond, nice to see you again.'

Diamond blew him a raspberry and giggled, running her fingers into his beard then holding onto it tightly.

'That's the most I have heard her vocalise since I met her at the clinic,' Lily said.

'Hang on, little one, a bit less tugging on that, it hurts,' Quintin said as he eased her fingers loose. 'You sure it's a group outing to the market?'

'Yes, I'm sure. Actually, I've been hankering for some biltong and some dry *wors*. I'm hoping we'll find some there.'

'Why not just make your own? I like that you make yours at home,' he said.

'Yes, that's because in Australia they eat that horrible jerky, which tastes nothing like biltong, and they don't make *wors*, so I have no choice but to make it. What time does the farmers' market open?'

'Now-ish. Lincoln insisted it was better to get there early,' Quintin said. 'Let me put La Angelique away and we can get going.'

The Beans Se Bos Country Market was a flea market, with homemade goods, antique furniture and plants for every household, so no one went home empty-handed. The smell of *braai* and *boerewors* rolls permeated the air and mixed with the smell of hundreds of people milling around in the African sunshine. Despite the cooler weather, the sun was already beating down on everybody when they got to the market. Umbrellas with tables underneath as well as a few gazebos were scattered around in an orderly manner, and people milled around in between.

Quintin stopped at the first bake store they came across. '*Koeksisters*, been a while since you made those.' He handed over the money and popped the sugary delicacies into his mouth. He smiled. 'That alone was worth the visit. You want some?' He offered around and watched as David carefully fed his sister and gave her exactly half of his sweet delight.

Quintin gave him another one. David went to feed more to Diamond.

'No, Diamond has probably had enough, but you are welcome to eat the whole thing, David,' Lily said.

They walked slowly up and down the aisles, and Quintin watched as an African lady walked past with three children trailing her and one on her hip. They were well dressed, and she was on a mobile phone, and yet she didn't carry a bag to put her purchases in. He turned and checked that Lily had her bag securely over her shoulder and across her body as she usually did when they were in a crowded place. He moved his own wallet from his back pocket to the front of his jeans, remembering the time he'd had his wallet stolen by pickpockets when they bumped into him in a crowded market.

He watched the woman and the children as they walked slowly along, touching things, not really looking at them. They seemed to be concentrating on a couple walking in front. The tourists were obviously foreign, and while Quintin could see the man was tall, the woman next to him appeared petite and almost fragile. Her handbag was hanging loosely on her shoulder.

'Back in a second,' he said to Lily as he detoured past the suspected pickpocket family. He could hear the couple talking in German, which was distinctly different to the Afrikaans all around.

'*Entschuldigung*,' he said in German to the strangers, 'you might want to secure that bag better. This is Africa, and you're foreign. You'll be targeted with it hanging loosely like that. You should carry it like my wife over there,' he pointed to Lily, 'and make sure that your money, if not on a waistband or in a bumbag underneath your clothes, is secure in the front pocket, where it is less likely to be stolen,' he said.

Lily didn't know what was being said, but the lady looked at her and then she secured her bag across her chest. Lily gave her a little wave and smiled.

Quintin stopped and waited by the store as the suspected pickpockets walked past and picked up the pace, knowing that they'd been spotted, and moving on to find another victim. Quintin smiled because today he'd foiled at least one bag snatch. But not before the woman with the mobile phone still glued to her ear had glared at him for warning her intended target. He grinned back and greeted her politely, but she ignored him and pushed on. She had people to see and rob.

'Talented, polite and nice enough to want to warn a stranger that she's about to be robbed. Be still my beating heart,' Lily said as she linked her hand into his.

'Just because I'm not in Africa all the time doesn't mean I want other people to suffer what I had to learn the hard way,' he said.

They walked around the market, stopping to buy a jar of marmalade made with brandy. Lily bought her biltong and a packet of dry *wors*, and then they headed towards the plant area. Luckily, it was right next to the face painting.

'Piet and I'll be with the kids over there, while you sort out all the plants and do your gardening thing here,' Lily said.

'Sure,' Quintin said as he dug the list from his pocket and watched as David took Diamond to get her face painted.

He spoke with one of the vendors, who quickly had a couple of boxes packed full of seedlings—he even offered to take the boxes to the *bakkie*. When they were done, the vendor pointed to where Quintin and Lily would find the last vendor that they were looking for.

'Look at Spiderman and the fairy,' Lily said when Quintin joined them in the kids' area.

'Oh, so beautiful,' Quintin said.

'You're saying that I'm beautiful? As Spiderman?' David asked.

'Definitely not beautiful,' Piet said, rolling his eyes at Quintin. 'You are rocking that Spiderman look.'

Quintin shook his head. 'As a person, totally beautiful inside and out, but as Spiderman, you're actually a tad scary looking.'

'Awesome,' David said with a smile. 'But Diamond is beautiful?'

'Your sister looks like a little fairy with all that glitter and pink all over her face,' Quintin said.

'Almost like a flamingo,' David said.

Quintin and Piet laughed.

They took pictures on their phones, and then Diamond put her arms out to Quintin to be carried. She put her head on his shoulder and rubbed her eyes.

'Someone has had a full-on morning and probably needs a nap. Your Mr Magaso is just over there. I can sit here with the kids while you go and talk to him,' Quintin said.

'Thanks,' Lily said, kissing him. 'David, will you look after Quintin and Diamond for Piet and me until we get back? Make sure no one comes and paints his face while I'm not looking?'

David's shoulders appeared to puff outwards, and between giggles at the thought of Quintin with a painted face, he managed to say, 'Yes, Dr Lily, I can do that for you.'

Mr Magaso had an umbrella with 'Standard Bank' written all over it. Underneath that, he had a small round table and two chairs. The table was covered with skins, and he sat in traditional clothing of a Zulu sangoma. His headdress was made out of ostrich feathers and the head of some poor lion which must have died many years ago—the hair had been reduced to patches of shiny leather in places. His large stomach was well-rounded thanks to an ample beer belly. Covering his shoulders, he had a kaross made from *dassie* skins which was old and worn with holes right through. On the table in front of him, he had an assortment of bones and stones that he tossed for people and told their fortunes, or warned them of impending danger. He seemed to be alternating between the two options as they watched.

'Come, sit out of the sun while we wait,' Piet said.

'He is another medicine man?' Lily asked.

'Yes, when he is free. We need to go sit in his chair, pay the fee, and have your fortune told—only after that can you tell him who you are, and then he will acknowledge me sitting beside you.'

Lily looked at Piet and raised her eyebrows. 'Are you serious? I'm to sit there and listen to his rubbish for ten minutes?'

'That is the way it is done,' Piet said. 'It is always a show.'

When the next customer left, Lily stood beside the chair and Mr Magaso motioned with his hand for her to sit.

'Fifty rands for your fortune,' he said.

Lily rolled her eyes. 'Fifty rand? That's a rip-off, you and I both know that. You're just going to tell me now that I'm going to win money and my life is going to change, which is exactly what you've been telling every second person while we've been here waiting in the queue. And if you don't tell me that, you're going to tell me that I must be careful of one person who is in my life causing trouble and hiding like a snake. Now I've told you a fortune that you were going to tell me; I don't have to pay you fifty bucks.'

He looked at her and let out a belly laugh. 'I think that you are the new *dokotela* that Piet here has been telling me about. You are too clever to be just any customer.'

Lily smiled and extended her hand. 'I'm Dr Lily Winters, and it's good to make your acquaintance, Mr Magaso.'

They shook hands.

'Piet, good to see you here. It is not often that you come to the market. Sit, sit,' Mr Magaso said.

'Today is a special day. I came with Lily and her husband, and we brought some of the Platfontein children for an outing. They have not got to experience this market before now. I think they like it,' Piet said.

'This is good to hear. You are always helping your people,' Mr Magaso said.

'Talking about helping people, we need more plants delivered to Lincoln. Can you do that today?'

'*Yebo*,' Mr Magaso said. 'How many?'

'About thirty. Lincoln said to make sure they were the same medical strain as the last ones. He does not want any of the other plants, just the medical ones,' Piet said.

Mr Magaso nodded.

'Are you a medicine man like Piet?' Lily asked. 'Or are you a shaman?'

She felt Piet stiffen next to her and she wondered if she had just broken some traditional barrier, but she would take this opportunity to ask questions anyway.

'*Yebo*,' Mr Magaso said. 'I am both. I am a Zulu, so we are called a sangoma. I can call the spirits, and I can heal people, too.'

'So, you have patients that you treat with your medicines and you make them better?'

'Yes, all the time. I can see that Piet did not know you would be asking these questions of me because this is the first time I have ever seen him on the edge of his chair. Why do you ask this?' Mr Magaso said.

'No, we had not discussed it. Only that I would meet you, as I am interested in the CBD oil that we make from your plants. But I haven't had a chance to see how it is made yet, because at the moment all my time is being consumed with patients that keep dying from meningitis and pneumonia in my clinics,' Lily said. 'So I am reaching out to other doctors and asking if they are having the same problems. Hoping to discuss my problems and perhaps find a solution.'

Mr Magaso clicked his tongue. '*Eish*. That is very sad news that you are a doctor and you cannot stop them dying. Especially as you have all the modern medicines at your fingertips.'

'For some reason, the medicines I'm trying aren't working, and I've no idea why. I was wondering if you've been experiencing the same thing with the people you've been treating,' she asked. 'And it's not just the elderly. Young people have also been dying.'

Mr Magaso looked into the distance and squinted his eyes before he looked back at her. 'I have had a few people who have died no matter what medicine I gave them—neither from the old traditional route nor the modern medicine that I got from a doctor in Upington. There was nothing that this *ubuthi wezokwelapha* could do. It was just their time to cross over to their ancestors.'

Lily bit the inside of her lip. 'I know that we've only just met, Mr Magaso, but could you tell me the names of the people who died so I can include them in my investigation?' she asked.

'I'll make you a list,' he said as he lifted the skin off the table to get a briefcase from underneath. He took out a pad of foolscap yellow legal paper and a pen, and he began to write in a neat and concise script the names of seven people. When he was finished, he tore the paper off the pad and gave it to Lily.

'Thank you, Mr Magaso, I appreciate this.'

She could still feel the tension radiating from Piet.

'Dr Lily Winters, you're good at bargaining, but you still owe me fifty rands for spending time with me today. I will add it onto the bill for the plants when I deliver them to Piet and Lincoln at your house. Please make sure that you have the cash waiting with them.'

Lily shook her head in wry amusement. 'Sure, and thanks again for your list of names.' She put the list in her bag.

'Those are only the people I can remember straightaway, but I will go home and I will think hard on this, and if I remember someone else, I will write it on a paper and give it to Piet.'

'Thank you, Mr Magaso. One more thing before I go. When people die in a rural settlement, do you have to register their death with the authorities?'

'*Yebo*. We have to make another paper for the new government even when someone dies. We now have more papers for the dying than we got when we were born. You must have the same in your white medicine world? Dr Hawthorne, he said there was too much paper for doctors everywhere.'

'I fear this time, he was right, that there are even more papers in my world. Thank you, Mr Magaso, I never realised you knew him,' said Lily.

'Briefly, but it is good to meet you.'

She massaged her temples, realising that the longer she stayed in South Africa and attempted to find out what was happening with the clusters, the more she found that there was a more personal connection between the communities and Ian.

She stood up to leave. It was only then she noticed that Mr Magaso was sitting in a wheelchair. She wondered how she'd not seen that before until she remembered that his legs had been covered by his cloak of skins; they were only visible because he'd moved it to get his briefcase out.

'Thank you for your help. See you next time,' Piet said, shaking Mr Magaso's hand. 'Come on,' said Piet. 'Quintin is coming towards us; he might need our help.'

Lily smiled at the efficient way that Piet had got her out from under Mr Magaso's umbrella and onto the pathway.

'You done?' Quintin was by her side almost instantly. Diamond was fast asleep on his shoulder.

David manoeuvred himself in between Piet and her. She saw Piet put an arm over his shoulder as they started walking and she grinned.

'That was quite a talk you had going on,' Quintin said. 'Looked intense.'

'Yeah, it was interest—'

The force that hit Lily in her chest knocked her off her feet. She fell backwards, the back of her head smashing into the hard, compacted ground of the market pathway.

She saw stars.

Her jaw ached. Her head throbbed.

Gulping air, she tried to breathe, but it felt like someone had hit her with a sledgehammer in the chest and was still standing on it.

'Lily!' Quintin shouted.

His voice was muffled, and he was blurred when she looked at him. She could hear Diamond screaming.

She lifted her hands, trying to rub her eyes to clear her vision. They were wet. Tears were natural given the intense pain she'd just experienced. She ran her hands across her face. There was a ridge running from her jawbone to near her eye—she could feel it.

Slowly, air seeped back into her lungs. She turned her head towards where Piet had been just a second before but he was gone. She could make out the legs of a man who was running away from them; she knew they belonged to Piet, in pursuit.

'Lily?' Quintin said as he bent down and held her face in his hands. 'Lily, stay with me.'

She could hear Diamond crying and realised that Quintin had given the baby to David to enable him to check on her, but Diamond was shaken and scared, and David was doing what he could to comfort her.

The noise of the market returned; it burrowed into her throbbing head, loud as a freight train. Air rushed into her chest, and she could finally breathe normally.

She put her hand over Quintin's. 'I think I'm okay, just winded,' she said as she sat up. Quintin was crouched beside her, holding her steady, ensuring she didn't flop back down, as she lifted her knees and put her head in between them to steady the dizziness that washed over her. She felt a pain in the top of her arm on the inside.

'Maybe a small concussion,' she said, 'going to have a bruise on my inside left arm. That hurts more than my face.'

'I'm going to call an ambulance,' Quintin said.

'Might be an idea, but I would rather go home. I'll take some paracetamol and rest with you on the couch.' She looked down. Her T-shirt was torn at the sleeve, and her handbag that had been over her shoulder was gone. 'How bad does it look?'

'You took quite a shoulder-slam. It might have been a latch or something on his pack that got your face because he was taller than you. I've seen worse: it's just a scratch from what I can see. We'll need to get it clean to look properly. And I'm calling that ambulance.'

She beckoned to David and took Diamond. She put her arm out to include him in the hug. 'It's okay; I'm okay. We're all going to be just fine.'

Tears spilled from David's eyes. 'I thought he killed you, Dr Lily.' He bent down and put his arms around her.

With Diamond's head on one side of her and David's on the other, Lily looked up at Quintin.

He hugged them all together.

'I'm not dead. And Diamond was nice and safe with Quintin. He held onto her tightly, so she didn't get hurt. We're just shaken.'

Diamond hiccupped and wriggled, no longer screaming, now just restless. Quintin stepped back, giving them room. David let her go, but remained close, his hand still touching her.

'What was in your bag, Lily?' Quintin asked.

'Other than my purse and the money I had in it for the market, there was nothing special in there, only the list that Mr Magaso just gave me of patients. You have the Cruiser keys on you, so he's not getting the car, and he didn't get the house key or anything. Oh no, my mobile phone was in there. Our pictures of the face painting.'

She could see Quintin quickly checking his front pockets.

'All present here. We still have some on my phone, so all is not lost. And yours might have already loaded up to the cloud. We can cancel that phone and organise another one for you. Not like anyone can get into it, you have your screen lock on, don't you?'

'Always.'

'Right, I'm calling the ambulance.'

'No ambulance. I'll be okay. But you can call Piet. Find out if he got the guy and where he is,' Lily said.

'On it,' Quintin said.

Quintin had his phone out and was calling, but he kept a hand on her shoulder as if he was worried she would disappear. David and Diamond clung to her still. Where she should have felt anger at what happened to her, she didn't. But she was as mad as a snake that the incident had upset the kids' beautiful day out. Their painted faces were now both streaked with tear marks, and clearly wiped all over both Quintin's and her shirts, and the market magic had been stolen from them.

'Sorry, Dr Lily, that man stole your bag and hurt you,' Mr Magaso said after wheeling himself out towards them. 'I find it so hard to believe that in the new South Africa so many people turn to crime and stealing rather than putting in an honest day's work. This is not a reflection of who we are as a people; we are better than this.'

'I guess I looked like an easy target,' Lily said.

'You? No! Look around,' Mr Magaso said, shaking his head. 'There are many other women here with bags on their shoulders only, easier targets than yours. That was a bag snatch like I have not ever seen before. That man wanted your bag and something in it, and he attacked you.'

CHAPTER 20

Lily had been home a few hours and had at last stretched out on the couch to watch TV after completing all the paperwork that Piet and Natalie had made her fill in about what had happened.

The youngster had outrun Piet, and there had been a car waiting. Piet had run the plates, but they were stolen, so they were no closer to knowing who had attacked her, or what they were really after.

A call came in on the house phone. Lily answered it.

'Dr Lily?'

'Yes?'

'It's Elise. It's an emergency. Coti won't wake up. I tried and I tried, but she is sweating and sleeping.'

'Do you know if she took something to make her sleep?' Lily asked, rubbing her temple.

'No. She has been sick for a day, maybe two. Piet asked me to keep checking on her for him, but something is wrong, and I can't get Piet on the phone.'

'We're coming. Try to keep her cool until I get there,' Lily said. 'Are the kids okay? Did they settle in back at home?'

'*Yebo*. Sorry about the bad ending to the day, they seemed to have loved the market. David seems taken with Spiderman now.'

'We will have to try it again another day, see if we can erase the bad memory of me being attacked there, make it all glitter and sugar again,' Lily said.

'I think they would like that.'

'Right, you see to Coti, I'm on my way.' Lily hung up and immediately rang Piet, who picked up on the first ring.

'Lily?'

'Elise has been trying to reach you.'

'I just plugged my phone into my *bakkie* charger. I am about to leave the station.'

'I need to get Coti into hospital. Sounds like she has gone into a coma. Can you meet us at the turn-off into Platfontein? Quintin can drive.'

'I will be there. Lily, you sure you are feeling up to this? Perhaps if I bring her in—'

'She will be in such pain if it is meningitis. She'll need something to help her at least with that before you move her, and you don't have anything you can give intravenously.'

'Nee.'

'It will be okay; Quintin will be with me. We need to save Coti. I'll be fine,' Lily said.

She put down the phone and stared at it for a long time. Of all the days, why today? Could Africa throw any more at her?

Lily administered the antibiotics into the drip in Coti's arm. She watched as the steady blip of the heart monitor continued and rubbed her eyes. The massive headache that she'd got from the bump on the back of her head that morning wasn't helping at all. Nor the bouncy ride into Platfontein that Quintin had undertaken with her. Despite arguing with her, he already had the Land Cruiser keys in his pocket and was walking out the door, still telling her why it was a bad idea. She loved that man and the way he cared so fiercely for her. Always wanting to protect her from the cruel world out there.

She wrote up the chart that hung on the end of the bed. As she went to place it back, she dropped it on the floor, where it clattered loudly as it struck the tiles. Slowly, she bent down and picked up the clipboard which had landed facedown. She turned it over to look at her notes.

When she'd written it, it had been as clear as day in her mind, and she knew what she'd commented on, but on the paper was just chicken-scratch. Nobody would be able to read it.

During her training so many years before, one of the doctors had said that nurses needed to be able to read a doctor's writing, and despite the old joke about how poorly they wrote, they were encouraged to always write as neatly as they could.

She couldn't stop the shakes.

'Doctor, are you okay?' Staff Nurse Jones asked as she came into the room.

'Fine. I think. Tell me, do you ever have trouble reading my writing on the charts of my patients?'

The nurse looked down. 'I do, but Sister Newman, she says it's legible, and she tells me what you have written.'

'So, you find it difficult usually?'

'Yes, but it's still not as bad as some other doctors. Most days it's okay. Why do you ask?'

'I just tried to read my own writing.'

'Let me look.' She took the clipboard from Lily and studied it for a moment. 'Doctor, this isn't your writing. This is just straight lines. I don't think that even Sister Newman could read this.'

'Thank you, Nurse,' she said, taking back the chart.

As a doctor, she was no idiot; she knew something was wrong. So much for her small concussion that she managed to talk Quintin out of calling an ambulance for. She rubbed her cheek and could feel where the scab had formed across the cut she'd received.

'You look a little pale. Perhaps your fall affected you more than you realised today.'

'I'll have a rest now that Coti is stabilised. I couldn't leave her alone, even after what happened today. I'm just tired, that's all.'

'If you say so. Get some rest. Now that your patient is here, the other doctors can look after her. Go home; a doctor is no use to her patients if she's sick.' The nurse put her hand gently on Lily's arm and then walked away. The door closed behind her.

Lily held the board close to her chest as she sank to the floor. She hung her head, trying to stop the nausea and the clamminess as it rippled over her skin, the feeling of knowing that something was wrong.

She had taken quite a knock on her head. She really should have it checked.

She flicked over scenarios of what could have caused her writing to become illegible. Loss of a fine motor skill could be caused by a few factors. Simply knocking her head in the fall, a small swelling in the brain, cervical spinal stenosis, but there was a pain associated with that, and she wasn't displaying any other symptoms. Ulnar nerve entrapment. Again, a huge pain accompanied that. She wrote that off and dug deeper. A brain tumour. She'd had no pain; she was tired. Cancer.

'No. Think of lesser illnesses that cause a degenerative loss of motion, Lily,' she said quietly to herself. 'Don't jump to the worst-case scenarios. Stop the self-diagnosis.'

There was a gentle knock on the door, and a second nurse entered the room. 'Dr Winters, are you okay? Nurse Jones asked me to check in on you.'

'I'm not sure, Sister Turner,' Lily said as she read the nurse's badge. 'Perhaps. Would you mind writing up these notes for me as I seem to be having a problem getting things down on paper tonight.'

'We couldn't believe you came in; the talk of the hospital is that someone attacked you at the market just this morning.'

'I thought I was okay. Seems I hit my head harder than I realised. I need to record what meds she's been given, her temperature and vitals.'

'I'll organise that. But let's get you into a chair and make sure that you're okay before we see about your patient and her chart,' Sister Turner said as she took Lily's arm and helped her off the floor and into a visitor's chair.

'You know, we can take you into MRI and do a quick scan, see what's happening in there, make sure it's just a concussion.'

'I'm pretty sure it is only that. There's no reason for it to be anything else. I'm tired, my head hurts, and you're right, I need to get home. I'm probably more shaken up than I wanted to admit to myself. Stunned that someone would do that to me. To anyone.'

'Come on, Dr Winters,' Sister Turner said, 'let's go down and have that MRI to iron out any doubt that it is just a concussion. You can never be too sure. I'm clocking you out for the night.'

'Please get Quintin; he's waiting for me in the doctors' lounge. Tell him where you took me,' Lily said.

A day later, Lily was back at the hospital and by Coti's bedside again. Coti had not improved.

'Come on, you need to fight this,' Lily said quietly. She looked at the drip; Coti would need new antibiotics soon. She rang the call bell.

Nurse Jones walked in. 'Hey, Dr Winters, good to see you on your feet and looking so much better.'

'It's good to feel better, too. Believe me, doctors make the worst patients.'

'Tell me about it,' Nurse Jones said. 'So, it was just a concussion?'

'Yes, all clear now. But I'm glad we did the MRI; I never got a chance to say thank you to you for getting Sister Turner involved.'

'It was the least I could do,' the nurse said.

'Thank you anyway,' Lily said.

Nurse Jones smiled. 'Was there something you needed; you used the call button?'

'I'm increasing Coti's dose of antibiotic. Add another ten millilitres of Cefotaxime.'

'I can do that, but you will need to write me a new script. The generic of that is out in pharmacy, and I got their last one this morning for her dose then. I know they have the non-generic, even though it's more expensive, but they want it by name or they won't dispense it to us.'

'That's fine, she falls under the research project, so here you go,' she said as she dug her pad from her pocket and wrote out the script. Careful that she could see her printed writing correctly and anyone else could read it, too. It seemed to take a long time.

'Is that all?' Nurse Jones said.

'For now. If you can administer that directly into her drip and flush with saline, I'll be back to check on her in four hours.'

Nurse Jones nodded and left the room.

'Come on, Coti,' Lily said, 'you have to pull through. I can't lose both of you.'

CHAPTER 21

Heritage Day on the twenty-fourth of September was marked as the day that the rainbow nation celebrated its cultural diversity, but to Lily, it would always be King Shaka's day. The images of masses of men, dressed in traditional Impi cloths, gathering at his graveside to celebrate the last of the great Zulu conquering kings, had always been a memory that had lived with her from her university days in Durban. Taking advantage of the public holiday, Lily had spent most of the day at the long bench in Quintin's studio, listening to his music as his work soothed her. Tiger sat in an old box on the benchtop, half spilling out of it but purring all the time. He seemed as content as a cat could be.

She could feel her shoulders relaxing.

Coti's rapid response to the new brand of antibiotics had been nothing short of remarkable, and she had pulled through. Sure, she would be on tablets for a while yet, but she was already home and being cared for by the other people in Platfontein.

Now that Lily was there more regularly, the women of Platfontein were starting to trust her, coming to her with their problems, and she was finding out more and more about the interesting San and their customs.

She still needed to get to the bottom of the HIV epidemic and verify the research handed in by Ian, but her contact with the women and her access to their stories was going a long way to seeing the impact on their social structure. Even without HIV, their move to Platfontein was destroying it.

Lily was looking at all the past patient notes on each person who had died of pneumonia or meningitis. Clutching at straws, she'd entered everything. And finally, she was seeing a pattern.

She took in a quick breath. 'Oh, my hat. I think I've found it.'

'What?' Quintin asked.

'I think I've found something,' Lily said. 'Something big and concrete and you need to come and have a look.'

'About time you had a break. What is it?' Quintin asked as he came over and sat next to her on one of the other stools.

'See here. There was a lot of pink in the analysis of the medication that the meningitis patients had taken before they got sick. Those are HIV blockers.' She turned a page. 'This now, see the majority of green medications? Those are meningitis drugs.'

'And?' Quintin said.

'Drilling further down. Same patients. Looking at those with meningitis, only two-thirds had spinal taps, and different hospitals, so different equipment with those, so I can rule equipment out.' She turned back to the second page. 'This is where it gets interesting. This is the page for everybody who had pneumonia. Not so many pink flags, HIV, but enter the two new drugs, yellow and orange tabs are: Donepezil and Memantine. These patients were all on Alzheimer's medication,' Lily said.

'So, what are you saying?' Quintin asked.

She wanted to be wrong. She dreaded that she was right.

'Hang on, I have to show you one more quickly. Paediatric patients. Those who died as well as those who had just been ill. Same smattering of pink tags but, look, a new dark-green tag is dominant. Liquid paracetamol. I think it's the drugs that are causing the clusters.'

'Show me again,' Quintin said.

As she turned back to him, she took a deep breath and said, 'I've been analysing the files with people who were ill and people who died. One of the questions on the medical reports is which medications they were on before they got sick. You know—common medications that everyone takes, along with vitamin supplements. I was coming up blank with everything else trying to find a common link, so I also analysed the medications they were given in the hospital once they'd presented with the sicknesses. I still have gaps, but I'm pretty sure that I have the answer.

'For pneumonia and meningitis patients, most have been on HIV inhibitors, or they've been on Alzheimer's medication. The paediatrics patients were all given liquid paracetamol. These are the only three drug groups that I'm certain of; there are others, too.'

'You're sure of this?'

'I triple-checked. I couldn't believe it myself. We are dealing with either substandard or tainted pharmaceutical drugs.'

'Are you ready to tell Piet and Natalie?'

'There is more. The drugs that we've been giving the patients in hospitals to combat the infections also appear to be tampered with. I can't prove this one conclusively like the others, I will need more time to research and go through pharmaceutical records at the hospital, but I'm pretty certain I'm onto something there. I want you to check me first; make sure that I'm not drawing the wrong conclusion.'

Quintin put his hands on either side of her face. 'If you are right, this could mean that you could be in more danger than before. That little escapade at the market was not just a random attack. They thought you had the flash drive on you. Someone knows you have all the files to figure this out.'

Lily nodded her head. 'I need Piet and Natalie to look into it further with me. But I'm one hundred per cent sure that there are contaminated drugs in South Africa. I have to narrow it down to exactly who's manufacturing them, or distributing them; it might be any company, South African or international. But that is what is causing the meningitis clusters I came here for.'

Quintin held her hands. 'Your safety is my main concern. Having found this, what else can we expect to happen?'

'I don't know. This is unprecedented. I can speak with Marion, find out her opinion.'

'I think perhaps Piet and Natalie should be called in before you tell Marion. Let them know what you're all really up against.'

She nodded.

He hugged her. 'Well done for finding it. I'm so proud of you. You okay?'

'Yeah, I'm super excited to find what was causing the clusters, and at the same time, inside I'm strangely calm. Wanting now to find who did this and make sure they pay for every life they have impacted. Every person they made ill or murdered.' Her voice rose a little at the end.

Tiger peered out from his box, stretched and walked over to her, as if knowing that she needed some attention.

Lily reached out and took the cat in her arms. 'You stay safe here, but no medications for you either, just in case.' She buried her face in his soft fur until he wriggled, wanting to get down.

'I know it's late, but you should call Piet and Natalie and share the news.'

'You realise it's Saturday night and it's already after ten,' Lily said.

'I don't think they'll care,' Piet said. 'If it's important we need to tell them, remember? No matter what time.'

CHAPTER 22

Piet and Natalie sat at Lily's dining-room table, files spread around them. The sun was rising outside, taking the sky from its inky blues into the gentle mauves of dawn.

Quintin cleared the empty coffee mugs in front of each of them.

Piet rocked back in the chair. 'Thanks, Quintin.'

Lily smiled as he walked past and touched her shoulder.

'So, mainly HIV-positive people are dying. That is some sick joke. I mean, yes, they have compromised immune systems, but they are on their meds, they do not just die randomly anymore,' Piet said.

'I'm amazed by the complexity of your analysis and what you've found,' Natalie said. 'I can't believe that someone would use a drug made to prolong life to deliver a death sentence. It seems so unfair. My guess is it's personal. It's someone with something against people with HIV, or against old people, but I can't put a finger on why children? What type of sick person wants to kill children?'

'I agree. It makes no sense. Why kill somebody who is already going to die?' said Piet.

'Perhaps it wasn't to kill them, but it was just to make them more ill,' Lily said. 'In the private sector, sick means hospital and more drugs. The more drugs you sell, the more money you make.'

Natalie shook her head. 'Even in our old-age-homes cases, this scenario works. Sick means high care or the ER if you're bad enough.'

Piet scratched his head. 'Does not work for the prison system though. Too sophisticated to have come from inside there, it has to be an external factor. It is easier to simply bribe a guard if a prisoner wants to get out and go home. Anyway, some of these men were only on short sentences, a couple of months, and for most of the prisoners, it is much better than being on the street, so it makes no sense that they would want out in the first place. They do not have to be sick and go through the infirmary to get out. I can understand the maximum-security prisoners attempting to take that route, but that was only two out of all those deaths.'

'If you're sick, doctors will keep throwing everything at you until you improve—or die. Usually more drugs. If one antibiotic doesn't work, you try another,' Lily said.

'*Shoo*. I'm still stuck on how a drug company could be making viruses and bacteria for the same people they are supposed to heal, just to make money,' Natalie said.

'The pharmaceutical companies have an astonishingly bad track record of tainted drugs. Sometimes in error, sometimes by a single person. Perhaps a whole company. They're driven by profit. Profit for their board members and shareholders,' Lily said.

'I made more coffee,' Quintin said, coming back into the room with a tray.

Natalie put her hand up for one.

'You are mainlining coffee again,' Piet said. 'I'm just pointing it out because you took such pains to cut down.'

Quintin put Natalie's coffee in front of her and a packet of biscuits on the table.

'That was before we pulled my first all-nighter in years. Are you going to open those Romany Creams that are in front of you or just stare at them?' Natalie asked.

'Hint taken,' Piet said, opening the biscuits and offering them to Natalie first.

Natalie took one, dunked it in her coffee and ate it. 'Bliss. Coffee and chocolate. My favourite meal to get my mind back on top of its game when on little sleep.'

'You always were one for sweet things,' Piet said.

She looked up and out of the big sliding doors at the view of the valley below the house. 'You know, you guys have an amazing view here.'

Lily said, 'I don't get to look at it that much, but I guess when you see it at dawn, it is pretty.'

'Natalie, you have a view just as stunning. What is really on your mind?' Piet asked. 'Talk, what is troubling you?'

'It's Breanna's birthday in two weeks. All I can think of is, there are tainted drugs out there and she might not make it if she somehow takes them. Seeing these kids die because of medication that their parents gave them to help them, it breaks my heart. When I get home, I'm going to just hold her close. Is it selfish of me to be grateful for having such a healthy daughter?'

'You have a daughter?' Lily asked.

'Almost thirteen in body but thirty in her head,' Natalie said. 'Quite frankly, knowing all this now, I'm scared for her.'

'I can imagine.'

Natalie took her phone off the table and held it out to Lily. 'This is Breanna.'

'She's lovely,' Lily said.

'I think so, I'm really lucky that she's not one of those teenagers who only communicate with a grunt in the morning and when they get home from school. She texts all the time, checking in on me, and she sends me pictures of clothes she wants me to buy her.'

Lily smiled. 'That's great that she talks to you about clothes. I see many mothers whose daughters at that age are already butting heads with them. Looks good for both of you if you're still communicating.'

'I'm lucky, and at least this way, I can still sort of control what she wears, and she can dress appropriately and not like a skank. I don't remember shops selling clothes for me to dress like a thirty-year-old hooker when I was a teenager.'

'At least you get clothes pictures. Your daughter sends me pictures of cute kittens and dogs needing new homes, and big puppy eyes, saying please convince Mum for me,' Piet said.

'I never realised that you were partner-partners,' Lily said.

Piet shook his head and put his hands up. 'I am Breanna's godfather.'

'And her way to owning a puppy, apparently,' Lily said.

They all laughed at that.

'I just wish I could wrap her in cotton wool and keep her safe forever from the outside world,' Natalie admitted.

Quintin brought Lily her coffee and sat down beside her.

'I would be just like that, too, if I had kids. I would suggest that you go home and toss any medications you have in the bin. Or better yet, bring them here so we can have them analysed. We'll need samples of newer and older medications of all brands,' Lily said.

Natalie nodded. 'I'll do that. For her birthday I wanted to take the day off, spend time with her shopping, just not working on a case. Now it all seems so silly in comparison to the parents who have lost their kids.'

'Not silly,' Lily said. 'It's nice that you can do something with her on her special day.'

'The medical legwork on this case, is it almost done now, Lily?' Natalie asked. 'We know that it's tainted drugs. We simply need to know which ones. Or am I being too optimistic?'

Lily smiled. 'From here, it's going to need your police force more than ever. I don't have the authority to go back to the families of the deceased and ask them if they still have any of the drugs that were being taken so that we can analyse them. Would you be able to do that? You have the power to ask them for their leftover drugs, surely?'

'We could, yes,' Piet said. 'It would be a long process, but it is possible. We would have to do it carefully so as to avoid a panic. How do we organise the analysis of the drugs?'

'I want to send them to Australia, or Switzerland, where World Health have their headquarters,' Lily said.

'Why not a South African laboratory?' Natalie asked.

'To be honest, I don't know who I can trust here in South Africa. Having an independent source seems worth spending the WHO's money on. It's not going to be a cheap exercise.'

'You sure they will pay? If it is expensive, I do not think our police force will do anything about it. They might try to do the analysis themselves because we are so under-resourced,' Piet said.

'World Health will pay. But I'm still worried. We might have found what I think is causing the clusters, but about what happened to Ian and

Chelmsford? There's still so much unanswered. Too many loose ends dangling. I've been giving it some thought—why haven't any legal letters arrived at the house if Ian was looking to find a publisher for your book? What if he had a printout of your book in his possession when he was hijacked? It was important enough to be on that flash drive, so why no letters of rejection, or further contact requested?'

'What are you suggesting?' Piet asked, sitting up in his chair.

'I know the first thing I did when I saw your book was to begin checking patents on those remedies. Patents can be worth millions, and your book, it's not written by a tribe, but you, the medicine man of Platfontein. It's a representation of medicinal plants and the history of this area, and in the Kalahari. Surely Ian must have said something to you about the legal side of it if the money was to come to you or your whole tribe?'

'While I have a little knowledge about what has happened with the *Hoodia* plant, and the fight between the pharmaceutical company and the San, we never discussed anything like that. Just that he was going to find a publisher when it was done so that the knowledge never disappeared and the book would look good. It was never meant for a big sale, a wider distribution, just for our tribe, simply to keep the knowledge from being lost. Surely Ian did not try to sell it as more than that?'

'I don't know. I don't have proof of anything like that. I also don't have any proof of him approaching lawyers or publishers. Besides, something else about Ian is bugging me: there's the fact that he lived on such a huge property alone. Patients at my outreach clinic said they used to pay Ian, and yet that research clinic is supposed to be free. Where did his money go? It's not like he needed to amass a fortune, he always said he inherited money, lots of it.

'Despite all the evidence pointing to these tainted drugs, I can't find evidence that Ian knew about it. And I've read his notes about his HIV research. His research pointed to him looking into the under-reporting of HIV statistics. Not that he analysed everything in his files. There is no file with a comparison analysis like I did to suggest that he was aware of what he had stumbled onto,' Lily said.

'You don't think he knew about the drugs?' Piet asked.

'He might have. He definitely knew he was in trouble, otherwise why hide that flash drive? But I'm still not convinced that it was about pharmaceuticals only. When we first got here, Lincoln told me that Ian said to burn all the medicinal plants if they sold his home. Why would he say something like that to him, unless he knew something was going to happen?'

'You make a good case,' Piet said.

'You were attacked at the market after you gave Piet the flash drive, but also after seeing Mr Magaso and getting his list of names. Do you now think that it might be connected?' Quintin asked.

'I don't know. And I would hate to speculate and take us down the wrong path. The files are pointing to him gathering information on deaths and people who were ill, but who did he tell? That's my question,' Lily said. 'There's always been an element of danger coming here. I knew that when I took this job. Believe me, we have been in worse places in the world, with a lot more security around and still been shot at.

'The WHO are aware of a cluster of meningitis deaths in this area. Your files showed that there were prisoners all over South Africa dying too. These combined with Ian's folders show it is not a simple area cluster anymore, which means that this is potentially an epidemic spreading across the whole country. The WHO will want answers. And quickly.'

'World Health want answers? They can stand in line. I want answers,' Piet said, drumming his fingers on the table. 'It's all very well World Health sitting somewhere in an office in a foreign country, but it is our people in our country that are dying. And you are saying this could be an epidemic like it could spread the whole way across South Africa?'

'What I'm saying is that the spread of the contaminated drugs already appears to be countrywide. If the cluster was only in Kimberley, it would've pointed to something in the environment causing a sickness. When I added Dr Juliet's patients, we could already see that we have a much bigger problem. Once I tell them, WHO will bring in a specialist team that will handle this. It's getting too big for just one person.'

'Dr Winters, can I ask what made you suspect the drugs?' Natalie asked.

'Coti was not responding to the cheaper generic drugs, but when I switched her to original trade-name ones, she responded immediately, as she should have when she was on the generic ones. I went back and looked through all my other patients to see which medications were used, and I realised that while I couldn't tell between trade-branded and generic medications, there was a drug-identification problem in my research. We will need to take as many samples across many different companies, as well as do more in-depth research at the pharmacy in the hospital.'

'What are the possibilities of this being just one company?' Piet asked.

'I don't know what to think anymore. Look here,' Lily said, opening her computer and then at her spreadsheet. On the front tab were the pictures of some of the patients, and corresponding numbers for her files.

'You keep pictures of your patients?' Natalie asked.

'Every one of them. To me, they're more than a case study. They deserve more than just a number in a research sheet,' Lily said.

'That's so sad to see those kids' faces,' Natalie said as she looked at the thumbnail-sized pictures.

'Unfortunately, yes. My youngest in the study was little Milutin Nyatama; he was just eight months old.' She zoomed in on the photo, and a picture of a healthy baby filled the screen. 'This was taken about a day before he came into hospital.' Lily minimised the picture and enlarged another. 'I was perplexed with this one, Jenny Parkes, because from the notes she was already unconscious when she was rushed in from one of the farms. She should have been in our care long before she was admitted. She was a healthy thirteen-year-old, as you can see from this picture of her. No reason for her to contract bacterial meningitis. Jenny had an extremely isolated upbringing out there on her grandparents' farm; she didn't even go to the local school. She was home-schooled, but that didn't keep her safe in the end. So, something got out to their farm, the same thing that is in the townships, the old-age homes, the prisons and everywhere else.'

'Perhaps we should take a look around that farm,' Natalie said. 'Ask them for any of the medication she was taking before she became sick, and then what she had before she came into the hospital.'

'I called and they gave me all those details. Now I need to know if they have a sample still, without creating panic. A warning, the file says that medical personnel need to step carefully with her *ouma,* because she seemed extremely frail for a farmer's wife. I would like to meet them and come with you to collect the medication if they have it.'

'I'll treat them with the utmost respect when we get to meet her,' Natalie said. 'And I think it would be a good idea to have you along. The people in this country don't always see the police as the ones looking after them, rather the ones you run away from.'

Lily smiled. She knew that to be too true.

They heard the back door open as Bessie walked in and greeted them.

'Good morning, Bessie, can we have a cooked breakfast for everyone, please?' Lily asked.

'*Yebo*,' Bessie said as she went to the kitchen, and they could hear her crashing pans and banging pots.

'Lily, who else knows about the drugs and the potential for them to be contaminated?' Natalie asked.

'Quintin obviously. Nobody else has been told.'

'What are you going to be prescribing now that you have found out?' Piet asked.

'For now, I'll avoid generic drugs in the hope that the contamination is only in those. In reality, I cannot trust the drugs at all. I'll be avoiding them whenever I can. However, I can't take anyone off their HIV blockers. It's too dangerous for them. I'll be ordering in original brands for the clinic, that is a certainty. Hopefully, switching over the blockers now will not cause any panic.'

Piet was nodding. 'Right, let's see when narcotics want to get involved. I know a guy I worked with a few years ago in that department. He'll keep this under wraps, but he'll also be a big help to us,' Piet said. 'Before I do this, are you sure that you want to continue as a police adviser on this case?'

Lily frowned. 'Why wouldn't I?'

'From here, an investigation involved with the Narcotics Enforcement Bureau is going to take up a lot of your time. That will be time away from your clinic.'

Quintin squeezed her hand.

'I don't have a choice, do I? I either treat people, or I fight whatever is killing them. And I don't want to have it on my conscience that I prescribed a drug that killed one of my patients,' Lily said.

'Good, I had to check. Quintin, you okay with this?'

Quintin nodded. 'If it's what Lily feels is necessary, then I go where she goes.'

'Good,' Piet said.

Natalie ran her hand through her hair. 'Epidemic? You keep using that word.'

'Between our results, we've probably only scratched the surface across the whole of South Africa. It's across the whole population, and there's no hope of quarantining the drugs responsible, not until we identify exactly which drugs the contaminants are in.'

'I'll phone Colonel Vaughan Smith and ask him where he is and if he can get to Kimberley for a visit,' Piet said.

'Right, while he's doing that, we can clear the table for Bessie to set it for breakfast,' Quintin said. 'I'm starving.'

Bessie set the table quickly and brought through their breakfasts.

'Thank you, Bessie,' they all chorused.

'Tuck in,' Quintin said.

They had covered Piet's food with another plate to keep it warm and were halfway through their meal when he walked in from the lounge area.

'He doesn't look like a man with good news,' Lily said.

'Vaughan cannot come to Kimberley right now, so he has organised one of his team to speak with us. He also said that they had a weird tip come in, which he thinks might be related—it is from a drug company. Their informant said that somebody is messing with their manufacturing process,' Piet said.

'How did he put that together so fast?' Lily asked. 'If you've only just spoken to him?'

'Vaughan is in charge of the whole narcotics division of South Africa. We go way back to his time as a Recce in the Caprivi Strip. He always has his fingers on the pulse of his entire unit. He is in the middle of a sting operation on a big drug bust in Richards Bay. The sad news is he is pissed as hell that somebody tampered with HIV blockers—his son died of meningitis a few months or so ago, and now he is out for blood.'

'That's terrible,' Lily said.

'*Ja,* his son contracted HIV from a bad blood transfusion, and they thought that they would lose him, but he was still hanging in there. Vaughan is angry deluxe, with reason,' Piet said.

Lily nodded, and she put down her knife and fork.

Piet sat down at the dining-room table, but he didn't lift the cover off his food. '*Eish,* I am heart-sore. And after talking with Vaughan, I think that it is possible that Ian had come to the same conclusion as we have and was going somewhere with his evidence, and that is what got him killed. I do not have the authority to put a full-time police escort on you—we would have to tell our boss, Chetty, what is going on, and he has a mouth bigger than the Limpopo delta when it reaches the sea. Vaughan asked us to keep this tight, till he can be here, but that might take a little while longer than we want it to. Lily and Quintin, is there a possibility that you can hire private security contractors to help keep you safe while we investigate further? I can give you a number for a guy I know who operates out of Bloemfontein; his firm has extensive experience in the Middle East and across Africa. Bringing in a private security contractor for personal protection is now a priority. There is a definite escalation in the amount of danger you are in, and Natalie and I cannot protect you twenty-four-seven as well as try to investigate this case.'

CHAPTER 23

'HELLO, Ulwazi, lovely to see you again,' Anaya said.

Ulwazi smiled. 'It is good to be on my friendship bench, and it's good that you were here to talk with me again. How have you been since we last spoke? It has been a little while.'

'Very stressful, but the children are now at my new home—thank you for pointing me to Joanna for that—with the new maid you found for me. She is wonderful, thank you. I have the morning to myself before their swimming lessons, and I can think a little bit.'

'It is good to think, but sometimes it's good to share your problems, too. After all, that is what this bench is for.'

Anaya smiled. 'I have bought a new house in Sandton. It is so much bigger and better. Thank you again for sending me to Joanna. She had just the right house for us.'

Ulwazi clapped her hands together. 'This is good news. I'm so happy that I could help.'

Anaya chewed the inside of her lip. 'You have been so much help already. I really don't want to take up more of your time.'

'Blah, I love helping and knowing that I have helped. You still look troubled though. What else is on your mind? You will find I am a good listener. These old ears, they have heard many, many stories before.'

'Not problems like mine.'

'*Eish,* always you younger ladies think that you are the first to experience a troubled life. You look at us and see that the colour of the person's hair has changed, from dark to silver, from blonde to white, you look at our skin, once smooth like a baby's bottom, now wrinkled and sun-damaged, it's easy to forget that we oldies were young once, too. That is a fact of life. There are many things we know about that we can pass on to the younger generations. If they let us listen to what is happening to them, you never know, we might have an answer to help you. We have lived our lives already, perhaps experienced some of what you are living through now. Perhaps we can help you to avoid making the same mistakes we did, or perhaps we can look at your problems with wisdom and distance and show you a path when all you see is thick bush blocking your way. You do not know, unless you give us the opportunity and you talk with us.'

'Okay, then this is what's eating at me. I have moved away now from my sister-in-law. His twin. He didn't want to move, but in the end, I told him it was move or me, and the kids move without him. He didn't want that. But I'm still not sure how I'm going to get through to my husband. To make this life of ours happier and calmer. To cut her further out of our lives. I know that there's lots that needs to change.'

'Does he hurt you? Are you scared of him?' asked Ulwazi.

'Oh no. He would never, ever hurt me, or the children. I know that he loves me in his own way, and he will not raise one little finger against us.'

'So, you're happy together?'

'I would not say happy. We exist together. Walking on the same path next to each other with our children in between. And his sister, always his twin sister is there.'

Ulwazi was quiet for a moment. 'Do you love him?'

'We were an arranged marriage, but yes I do. I have always believed that he is stronger than he gives himself credit for.'

'Then you should show him that. You should show him that he is a strong man, so he knows it. You should make him your priority. He should be the one right next to you, because when your children leave it will just be you and him together.'

'You think he isn't my priority? I do everything I can to make him happy.'

'But he needs to know that. Remember when your children leave, and there is a big void, and you are alone at night, you will wish you had.'

'There's not much sex now,' said Anaya. 'There is no time.'

Ulwazi shook her head and clicked her tongue. 'That is a shame. We need to fix that. The way to a man's heart is through his penis.'

'I can't get to his penis if he is sleeping on it,' Anaya said, frustration in her voice.

Ulwazi shook her head. 'Last time you spoke to me, you said you wanted a better life with your husband, and you should have that. You deserve that. I am proud to tell you that in South Africa the woman—she might seem like the weaker sex, but in reality, the African woman is the stronger one in most relationships—it is the woman who controls her man, and who controls her family. It is the woman who keeps the mother-in-law in check, or in your case, look what you did moving away from under your sister-in-law's nose. Remember, there is no way that your husband will be getting sex from his sister; that's your privilege. Use it as a weapon. That is your biggest advantage over your man, and if you can keep your husband happy in the bedroom—even if you have to go through every page of the Kama Sutra—then that is what you do. And as you do it, you get him to talk and to trust you, and then you can help him with his problems from work. It's called pillow talk.'

'I never thought that people spoke about things like this,' said Anaya.

'Welcome to South Africa,' said Ulwazi, 'where women empower each other, instead of pulling each other down. Except for your sister-in-law, who seems hellbent on destroying your happiness and is not what the bench is about.'

'I like that,' Anaya said. 'So, you think that if I can control his penis, I can get him to talk about his work, and I can help him with his problems and make him less depressed? Less anxious?'

'Of course,' Ulwazi said. 'Once you own his penis, he will give you the world—not just diamonds for your fingers.'

CHAPTER 24

Reyansh walked into his bedroom after kissing each of his sleeping children on the cheek. 'The kids seemed so tired tonight; I didn't even get to see them awake before I got home.'

'They had swimming today; they are always tired after that. Now there's only you and me awake in this big, beautiful house,' Anaya said.

'Please, Anaya, not now. I'm so tired,' Reyansh said as he took off his tie and put it on his bed.

'Reyansh, you need to listen to me. I love you. I'm not leaving and going back to India, not unless you and our children are by my side. I just moved us into a bigger, better home.'

'I know that,' Reyansh said. 'I'm glad you like the new house.'

'Come and sit with me.' She led him by his hand and sat him down on the leather couch. 'I might be quiet and traditional, but I'm not a mouse. I listen to everything, what everyone speaks about. So, I know that there's something at work that you're not happy with, and I need to know what. I need to help you.'

'I can't tell you. To bring you into my darkness would take the light from your face,' Reyansh said.

'What brings me darkness is that on the day we married we promised to be together, for better or worse, and now you hide things from me. I know you've had some bad times, and your drug addiction goes up and down ...'

'You know I'm an addict?'

She stroked his cheek and he leaned into her hand then he kissed her palm. Her skin so soft against his.

'Everyone knows you're an addict. Even your father. He simply chooses to ignore it and only see you on days when the black dog isn't nipping at your heels, and you're not flying high in the clouds. I knew, before my father came and asked me if I could ever love you, that you were an addict. I just chose to accept it, until now. Now we have this new home, and I want a fresh start. A new beginning,' Anaya said, her hand holding his head close to hers.

'New beginning?'

Anaya shrugged and gestured with her hands to the room.

He looked around as if seeing their ornate bedroom in their new house for the first time.

She smiled. 'We're in a beautiful new house. A suburb away from your dominating family. Away from your manipulative sister and your mother, who you pander to all the time. We're away from your father, and even your grandmother, who seems to believe that you're a weak man and takes unusual pleasure in telling you she thinks that. But I know different. You're very strong. You can talk to me, and we can talk to a psychologist, and we can get your depression under control. When we do that, then the addiction will go away on its own. You'll not need the pills.'

'I wish it was so easy. What if I fail again?'

'What if you succeed? Then your three children will know the beautiful man you are inside, the one who is the hero, not the failure, in this family.'

'What are you suggesting?'

'Tell me what is going on at work. I know that something has changed in the last two years. You have been more stressed than ever before. What changed? You cry out in your sleep. It worries me.'

Reyansh tried to take his hand out of his wife's, but she held fast.

'I was young when I married you, only just eighteen, and you were already thirty. But now I'm thirty, and I've matured a lot. Now is the time to change. Trust me, Reyansh, show me you love me and show me that you trust me.'

She let go of his hands and put her palms upwards.

Reyansh knew that this was one of the biggest decisions he would ever make in his life. To trust his wife.

He looked at her hands. Although they were kept soft to the touch with creams and lotions, they weren't those of a young girl anymore. They wore the rings of a married woman, and many rings for each child that she'd gifted him. And if he looked at the other side, he would see that the diamond settings were kept pristine and clean, despite looking after three young children. Her wrists were adorned with gold.

He'd kept his wife well over the last twelve years, and she was right. She had grown as a person. He just had been so busy at work he hadn't noticed it. Until now.

He placed his hands in hers and her fingers closed over his. He wished that it was as if a dam inside burst its wall, but as much as he tried, nothing would come tumbling out. He opened his mouth to talk, then closed it again.

'I'm waiting,' Anaya encouraged.

'You live in a beautiful home, have a family. You have everything you want from me. Why can't you just leave it alone?'

'Because I don't have your trust. You think I'm still the giggling schoolgirl you married. You're blind. Blind. I live in a gilded cage of your making. Sure it's beautiful but it's still a prison. You shut me out of your work, and yet I have to have Mishti coming here and closing me out of my kitchen to speak with you. Secrets. Always secrets with your family.'

'You're moaning about Mishti again? We have rehashed this a million times.'

'No, you have shut the door a million times. Your sister's a Medusa. She turns men to stone. She's eaten her husband's soul so much that he can no longer be a man in his own house. She manipulates everyone in the family to do what she wants them to do. She plays your father and threatens to ruin his company that he set up from nothing. She forced him to retire early so she could run it. You're the perfect husband, and you deserve to be the CEO of your company. It's your birthright as the first male in your family to inherit it. I know that you do things at work. You sleep-talk at night. You say things like "more contamination". "More fillers". You said, "Mishti, this is a more creative way to make people sicker."'

'I say that? When I'm sleeping?'

'Yes. And much more.'

'Perhaps because I'm so worried that one day I'll take too many of the drugs and not wake from the deep sleep. I'm an addict, and I can't see a way out of this dark place.'

'You say in your sleep that it's because you are changing the drugs that people need to take, to make them a little bit sick. Is this true?'

Reyansh stared at his wife. She was using words, spoken while he slept, against him. He might as well come clean. Well, as clean as he could. With her hatred of Mishti, if he told her it was all Mishti's idea, he would just leave out his part in the story.

Lying by omission wasn't an outright lie.

'You're right. I contaminate the drugs and make people sick.'

'You? You would never do anything like this on your own. You're a kind man. This stinks of your sister's influence. Your sister's evil touch.'

'She's wicked—but she's powerful, too. She can take everything away from us with the snap of her fingers, Anaya. Don't think she won't just because I'm her twin. She's the CEO, not me. I might be the son, but it was Mishti that my father trusted with his precious company.'

'We need to make sure that she can't hurt us, that she's no longer a threat. It's time to milk the viper of her poison and leave her powerless.'

'How?'

'I've been giving it considerable thought lately, and I believe that now it's time that you begin collecting evidence of what she tells you to do. You need to go back in all your files, find every time you met, and write it all down. On paper. Never on a computer. Together we can find a way to catch her, and we'll bring her down. As the CEO, she's responsible for the company. We've got to be very careful; we don't want to destroy the company, only her. Not you, so that you can step up and take over as the CEO when she's out of the picture. I'm sure, with enough evidence, we can find a way to stop her and get her out of both our lives forever. Because you deserve this, my husband, you do.'

Reyansh lifted his wife's hands to his mouth and kissed them. 'I'm so lucky that you married me. You've always been so good to me.'

'You better believe it. Now let's talk about payment for helping you …'

'A price?' Reyansh frowned. 'What type of price?'

'I'm sure you'll be willing to pay it,' she said as she began to unbutton her top.

Reyansh sat in his laboratory. It felt right today. It was everything that he dreamed it would be, and more. He finally believed that perhaps all his years of university and work had been worth it.

Mishti was going down.

He was going to take over Ayurprabhu Pharmaceuticals.

Why had he never thought about overthrowing Mishti before? Why hadn't he come up with the idea? With her out of the way, he could inherit everything.

For the first time, he felt that there was light at the end of the tunnel. He and his beautiful wife had a plan to execute together, and they were going to defeat his sister and take over. The building would be his.

All the drugs would be his.

He was the son—the heir.

Ayurprabhu Pharmaceuticals should never have passed to Mishti in the first place.

It was his inheritance.

Despite Mishti telling everyone she'd chosen his wife for him, he'd loved Anaya from the moment he'd laid eyes on her. He'd thought she was beautiful when he'd first met her, although he'd been surprised to find that she still believed in most of the traditional customs of their culture—like it was her job to look after him and to make a happy family, and not to work. She was totally different in every way to his sister. And for that, he was eternally thankful.

But now, he'd discovered that not only was she patient, but she could also help him to own Ayurprabhu Pharmaceuticals. He suspected that he'd underestimated the power and wisdom of his beautiful wife.

His phone rang. Mishti.

He walked out of his laboratory, grabbing his coat on the way. There was no way she could check if he was ignoring her calls here. He would get back to her in his own time.

He walked past his new secretary.

'Good morning,' Vivaan said in an accent still strong enough to know that he was a child of an Indian immigrant, but there was enough South African mixed in there to know he was also a victim caught in Misthi's spiderweb.

'Morning. I'll be on the floor,' Reyansh said.

'There are messages from Mr Collins of the external quality-auditing company. I was told that you would handle them. He said that you have an audit coming up, and could you please call him back as soon as you can.'

'Call him and let him know that the date he suggested is acceptable. We'll be ready for him, and email Mishti so that she knows it's coming up and is expected to be here for the audit.'

He turned and walked away, down the steps of the factory to the floor beneath. He had plans to implement, and he needed no witnesses. The first step would be to get rid of the marionette in the suit outside his office, whom he knew was reporting his every move directly to Mishti.

It was time to begin unravelling the spider's web.

CHAPTER 25

Ulwazi sat in the Black Isle Shebeen on Florence Moposho Street on the very outer edge of Alexandra. The settlement was built for black people by the apartheid government, but they never anticipated that more than 70,000 people would live there, doubling the original estimated population. People were on top of each other, with little shacks surrounding the first homeowners' concrete houses. Although some of the original residences remained, their gardens had become rented-out shacks for family members and tenants alike as everyone attempted to live together in the small area. All for the convenience of being closer to the city than Soweto.

Ironically, it was right next to one of the most affluent suburbs of Johannesburg, Sandton, making it the ideal place for Ulwazi to run part of her business. Although she never saw clients at her home, much of her merchandise was stored under the floorboards of her room, where she'd made a shallow cellar for the weapons she sold.

Once she had feared the SADF—when she'd been younger, and before the new South Africa. Now she could either pay off the cop, and they would turn the other way, or get one of her staff to kill the law-enforcement officer who wouldn't leave her business alone.

Her business had been growing steadily along with all the other crimes in South Africa, especially in the Johannesburg region. The most significant part of her business, after weapons, were the contracts she took on to get rid of other people's problems. One of her previous customers was now sitting opposite her, and he didn't look happy. In fact, if he had a gun on his person, she suspected he might have pointed it at her.

'Mr Mbaya, your situation was dealt with. There was an exchange of money and the problem was removed,' said Ulwazi.

'My problem didn't go away. Now there's somebody else who is asking questions from Kimberley; it is like these doctors never give up.'

'The contract was completed. Unless you want to take out a new contract—which you will need to pay for—we have nothing to say to each other. You are aware that there is a big risk in removing two doctors who work the same job. Somebody will become suspicious, and you might get a cop on the force who cannot be bought next time. You might be creating a bigger problem for yourself. Perhaps, if you are a little bit patient, the problem will go away itself.'

'I do not think being patient will help. Not this time. There is too much at stake.'

'So, what are you proposing?' asked Ulwazi.

'I want a contract on the life of Dr Lily Winters.'

CHAPTER 26

KAMFERS DAM, KIMBERLEY

THE HOT OCTOBER sun beat down mercilessly on the flamingos nesting around Kamfers Dam. The heat shimmered off the water and bounced up onto their white feathers, which in turn reflected it off, keeping them cool.

Amahle could feel her unborn chick moving around inside the egg. Chirping, knocking, trying to break free of the hard shell that had protected it for a full moon cycle. Turning it once more with her curved beak, Amahle tapped it gently to let her baby know she wasn't alone.

Scanning the horizon, she looked for Msizi. She wanted him to be present when their chick entered the world. Its time was close.

The tapping increased, and she stood on one leg, watching the baby as it used its beak to crack the shell. The baby squeaked. Amahle reassured it that she was still there. Waiting. Encouraging.

Msizi arrived back with an exaggerated flap and walked to where their turret stuck out from the surrounding water. As long as they could keep their egg at a constant temperature, the baby would survive.

Together they turned the egg, using their webbed feet, gently helping their baby where they could to break free of its protective shell. Eventually, it was out. A bedraggled-looking bird with thick, stubby legs, a long neck, grey-and-white feathers slick and wet, and a small triangular beak.

Young-One's first sounds were unique, and her parents constantly talked so that their baby would learn to recognise their calls. So that she could always distinguish her parents.

The sun passed overhead, helping the baby's fluff to dry. She fed from both her folks, a rich red milk made from the algae in the water of the dam, but also the DNA of her parents, as it dripped from their beaks and into her waiting mouth.

Msizi fluffed himself up proudly, knowing now that he had the important job of protecting his chick from the hot sun in his shadow, and the hard rain that fell from the dark sky, and the lightning that zigzagged in the night.

Young-One rubbed her baby down against her mother's pink feathers. Amahle fluffed up and bent her head, stroked her baby with her beak, and fed her again. Already Young-One loved early mornings, when the sun touched the water and turned it pink, almost the same colour as her flock's feathers. She snuggled closer to Amahle and closed her eyes for a moment. Practising walking could wait. Soon, when she could stand and then walk without falling over, she would go and join the nursery, and play along the shoreline of the island with the other babies—trying to fly, testing their wings, attempting to stand on one leg. Making the small muscles stronger so that when she grew her flight feathers, they would be able to fly away, and onto the next stop on the migration route. Until then, she was safe with her mum, in the warmth of her feathers surrounding her.

Young-One heard the honk of Msizi as he returned to the nest after an early-morning foraging, and she looked out at the water. The shoreline was different; the island that her small family looked at was almost gone. Water lapped all around the turrets there, and just the tops of the nests were showing.

Those neighbours who had not managed to build their nests higher yesterday had been covered during the night. Young-One looked closer to her. A small ripple of water lapped against the edge of her nest, too, but it was only at the base and was not about to spill inside and saturate her young feathers.

Like all the other flamingos, she looked at the new addition of the water with fascination. The water was rising at night, and then during the day it was dropping fast, but it gave the flamingos a small reprieve to repair their nests where they could and abandon the dead chicks where they'd been unable to stop the flow of water into their homes.

She looked further up the water to where the humans on the shoreline stood with their fancy cameras and attempted to hide in the bushes, but Young-One could already recognise their scent. They smelled different from the freshness that was there before.

Something unusual was happening.

Something was definitely wrong.

She peeked her head out of her hiding place.

The island was now covered in water.

She watched as her mother reinforced her turret even more, determined to keep the water out. Still, more water rippled into the dam, and the level kept rising slowly against the side of Young-One's turret.

The whole day the flamingos watched as the water rose further and further, while desperately reinforcing their turrets in a losing battle.

Early the next morning, something ran along the land area that Young-One hadn't seen before. Its sleek body bobbed and ran quickly, its golden-red coat shimmering in the sunlight. As it got closer to the nests, parents were honking loudly, attempting to peck at it, challenging it, fluffing out their wings and their feathers, trying to intimidate the predator. It ran on, trying to scatter and scare away the adults. They had to be quick to get out of the way as it bared its sharp teeth and ran past the next nest.

Parents were sitting on their babies to hide them, but Young-One's father, Msizi, was still at the water's edge, not close enough as the creature ran towards her. Honking, Msizi swooped in and challenged the creature and received a bite on the leg for his troubles. For a moment, the creature and Msizi tussled as the flamingo shook his leg violently, trying to shake off the creature.

It rolled, bared its teeth at Msizi, and then continued its mad dash towards Young-One.

Her mother, Amahle, was at the nest, and she also challenged the creature, bending her neck and running at it, stomping her feet, but her gentle, curved beak was no match for the creature as it darted past her and grabbed Young-One from the nest.

Young-One felt pain.

'Piet, I have brought in a baby that was hurt today,' David said as he jogged into their campsite. 'It was damaged by a mongoose. I clobbered him good and don't think he will return to raid the nests again, but the baby was hurt.' He reached into the bag and handed Piet the fluffy white flamingo baby. It was silent.

'I do not think that one can be saved,' Piet said.

'But we're in charge of them; we're watching them. If I can't save it, why are we bothering to watch them?' David asked.

'No, I mean you should not have brought it here. We are not supposed to get involved; only watch.' Piet held the baby. 'See here? Its tail end is hurt. I can put some herbs on that, but it will need real help to make sure there are no bones broken by the mongoose. I treat humans, so does Dr Lily, but Quintin, he is friends with the vet, so perhaps if you take this baby bird to him, he will make sure that the vet checks it for us. But we cannot keep it when they have fixed it up, it needs to go back with the other birds and be wild again.'

'I'll take it to him,' David said. 'It will be a long walk to his house.'

'*Ja,* it will. Take Maddy with you and walk together, remember her parents have standing within the community, so it is good to have someone to keep you out of trouble. You kids are doing a good job, keeping the predators away from the babies that are left for this year. Such a small group of them, too. It is going to be a long three months until all the babies can fly and we have to keep the area safe. Let us hope that this flood is the last of the water. Cross fingers that the municipality stops more water coming into the dam and diverts it like they are supposed to. They should be diverting it—they are damaging all the work that the mine did to build the island in the first place. Do you remember the way to Quintin and Lily's house?'

'I remember,' David said.

Piet grinned and put his hand on David's shoulder. 'Tell Bessie that you want to see Mr Quintin right away, and that Piet sent you.'

David smiled. 'Come on, Maddy.'

Quintin was working in the garage, carving the wood to make the neck of a violin, when Bessie cleared her throat.

'Young David is at the gate with a friend. He said that Piet sent them from the dam, and they have something for you.'

'Please let them through the gate,' Quintin said, wiping his hands on a rag that was next to Tiger's box. Tiger meowed for his attention, and Quintin stroked the cat almost subconsciously.

Bessie nodded and walked out through the inter-leading door to the house, which was left open. He liked it that way so he could hear if Lily needed him.

Until Lily sorted out with the right authorities who was causing the medicine contaminations, they wouldn't leave. If they were not finished by June next year, they would have to though. Quintin was set to tour around at least eight countries with his new album, finishing up with his Christmas concerts in Vienna. But they would return here until her work was completed. While they had their own obligations, they always travelled together and didn't like being apart. Not even after all their years together.

Despite having full-time security guards at the moment, he was loving the big property and the quietness of the house. To his surprise, having Bessie in 'their' space hadn't proved a problem. Even Lincoln always pottering around in the garden hadn't disturbed him, as work on composing his yet unnamed album and his new project of making a violin himself was going well.

Sure, Lily had patched up his hands more than once, but he was thankful all the wood crafting he did, as therapy to get his fingers back in shape way back when, was coming in handy now. Even Piet had helped with the small carving challenges; he was a man of many talents.

He took off his safety glasses, wiped his hands, switched off the plug and walked towards the outside door. Opening it, he yelled at the top of his voice, '*Woza*, Lincoln, we've got a new plant!'

He walked back through his studio and to Lily's study to fetch the new digital camera. Lily was getting excited about the book as she'd sent out a proposal to a lawyer in Sandton to oversee the legalities, and she had also sent letters to a few of the South African publishing companies to see who was interested in printing it.

'Hello, David. Who's your friend?' Quintin said at the front door.

'This is Maddy.'

'Hello, Maddy, nice to meet you.'

Maddy didn't put her hand out; she ducked behind David as if she was a little shy.

'So, what type of plant did Piet send me? Come on, let's walk to the hothouse, and Lincoln can pot it up for us after we've taken a few pictures. You can tell me all about it.'

'Mr Quintin, it is not a plant,' David said as he brought his backpack to the front of his chest.

Quintin could see a small head sticking out from the soft webbing pocket in the front. The baby was wrapped in some cloth, and only its grey fluffy head was visible. Its beak not even curved yet. 'A baby bird?'

'It is hurt,' David said. 'The mongoose tried to steal her from the turret, but I saved her, and now she needs help.'

Lincoln walked up next to them, standing outside the door, and looked at David's backpack. 'I've never seen one like that before.'

'Whatever it is, let's get it inside, then,' Quintin said.

'It's a flamingo,' David said proudly.

Lincoln grinned. 'It looks too small to take away from its mother.'

'It is,' Quintin said. 'Come in, there's a box in my studio we can put it in.'

Entering the studio, Quintin lifted Tiger out and onto the bench. 'Come on, cat, I need that box.'

He put a towel that was on the bench into the box and then turned to David. 'Let's put it in here for now, so it can be safe.'

'Won't the cat eat it?' Maddy asked, seeing Tiger eye the bird.

'I hope not. I'll keep an eye on Tiger.'

'Piet said you know the vet,' David said.

'Let's call him. Maddy, your job is to make sure that Tiger doesn't eat the baby while I'm on the phone.'

She nodded.

He dialled Mason, the local vet who had helped him with the vaccinations of the horses. 'Hey, Mason, is there any chance you can come by my place, like now? I've got a baby flamingo. I'm not quite sure what I'm supposed to do with it, but it's here and I could use some help.'

'I haven't seen one up close for many years; I'm on my way—give me fifteen minutes. For now, keep it warm if you've got a desk lamp to shine onto the chick. It'll be in shock and needs to be snuggly. And put it in a box so it can't escape and hurt itself. See you soon.'

Quintin hung up and turned to the kids. 'He's on his way. Let's get Bessie to make us some lunch while we wait. I'm sure you're thirsty after your long walk?'

'I have plants that need to be tended to,' Lincoln said. 'Let me know if you need some hay brought in for the baby to sleep on.'

Quintin nodded. 'Bessie, please could you rustle up some lunch for these children, and bring us a drink,' he called out the door.

He could hear Bessie as she busied herself in the kitchen and he looked at the kids. He wasn't quite sure what to do with them. He wanted them here with him when Mason came, so that they could answer any questions he'd have about where the flamingo came from and how it got hurt.

'What shall we call it?' Quintin asked.

'In Afrikaans flamingos are *flaminke,*' said David. 'I wanted to call it Minke. That name can be a boy or a girl, but it's your flamingo, Mr Quintin, so you need to name it.'

'You found it, so you name it,' Quintin said.

'I think Minke is a nice name for it,' said Maddy as she stroked Tiger, who was now all over her, basking in the attention she was giving him.

'I think so, too. Minke it is. Let's see what we can do until Mason arrives. He'll know exactly how to help you, little one, and we'll do whatever we can to help make you better so that you can go back to your mother,' Quintin said.

'The baby flamingos only stay with their parents for a little bit, and then they go and make a creche,' said David. 'If we can get Minke to the edge of the creche, then it can go back in the wild again because flamingos are flock animals.'

'How do you know so much about flamingos?' asked Quintin.

'The man came to our school to talk about them, and I think they're beautiful birds, that's why I go with Piet on patrol to look after them, and to look after all the other animals that live around the dam. Before I came to live at Platfontein, I had never seen an oryx or even an eland, but now I'm learning all the skills that my ancestors knew because Piet is teaching us.'

'He's teaching me, too,' said Quintin. 'We're learning about all the plants from the Kalahari and also the Kimberley area that can help Dr Lily to get her patients better.'

'I call him *Oom* Piet because he's special to me, and he looks after everybody in Platfontein, and it doesn't matter which tribe we belong to. He sees us all as one tribe, one San. I like learning all the bush secrets from him because my mother is too busy to teach me,' Maddy said.

Minke squawked in the box, and Tiger immediately crouched down. His tail flat to the table, he crept towards the box as if he was hunting.

'Be nice, Tiger. The bird is not food—understand?' said Quintin.

Minke honked again. It was a forlorn noise, as if she was now calling for her parents and getting desperate.

Tiger stood up, and instead of hunting, he looked as if he was more interested to know what was in the box. He sniffed the air and walked slowly towards it. Putting his head over the edge, he peered in. Then he hopped into the box.

'You have to save the baby from the cat,' David said.

'Let's give Tiger a chance. He might not want to eat Minke; he isn't showing any signs of attacking it,' Quintin said.

Tiger meowed and wrapped himself around the baby flamingo and began cleaning it as if it was one of his own kittens.

'Well fancy that. Tiger seems to like Minke. Looks to me like he wants to adopt her,' Quintin said.

'Until we look the other way perhaps,' said David, 'then the cat will eat the bird. It is how nature is.'

'We'll have to watch them carefully, that's all,' Quintin said.

They heard the intercom buzzer and Bessie let Mason through the gates.

Maddy put her hand into the box and was stroking Tiger. He was purring as he continued to clean Minke. 'I think the cat likes the baby bird.'

'Hey, Mason, thanks for coming over,' Quintin said as he shook Mason's hand.

'Sure, let's see what we have here,' Mason said as he gently lifted Minke from the box, and Tiger growled at him. 'Be nice, Tiger, I'll give her back.'

'We've called her Minke,' David told him.

Mason examined Minke and then put her gently back with the cat, without putting any ointment on where she had been bitten. 'That's a great name, but we can't confirm its sex without a DNA extraction from its feather bulb. Which is an expensive test for us here in South Africa. I can't believe how this cat has taken to this bird so quickly, but I've seen instances like this before, where cats have taken in ducklings, or even chicks, and brought them up like their own. I never thought this fat cat had a paternal bone in his huge body. He's so big and such a demanding cat, it's so good to see that he's looking after little Minke. I'll get on the phone to the zoo in Pretoria to get the formula they use to feed their babies. They have a flock of Chilean flamingos there that they have been successful with. You're in for a lot of feeding for at least a few weeks. This little one right now needs fluid for sustenance and nutrition, and it needs flamingo milk or a close alternative to survive.'

'Let me know what we need and we'll buy it. We'll look after her until she's big enough to go back to her flock,' said Quintin.

'That's good because you cannot take it back now. Its parents would reject it—they are very fussy breeders. They abandon their chicks too easily when disturbed. That's one of the reasons that the island was built in the first place. It's interesting to know that some of the flamingos are being successful on the shoreline. The island was working so well before it drowned all the babies. The municipality has a lot of blood on their hands. But at least we can save this one little flamingo,' Mason said as he dialled the number for Pretoria Zoo.

He wrote what they needed on a piece of paper and then handed it to Quintin. 'Minke will need an egg-based and shellfish formula several times a day to substitute her mother and father's milk. I'll go collect this from my surgery; I have everything we need there. I'll help you feed it once I get back,' he said. 'Minke is going to need to be dropper-fed every two hours around the clock, which means you're not gonna get much sleep for a while.'

'We can help,' said David. 'The school closed early for another teachers' strike action, so we are on holidays again.'

Quintin smiled. 'I would need to speak to Piet about that, and David, to your sister, and Maddy, your parents. But I don't have a problem with you sleeping over and helping; we need to let Lily know. I'm sure she won't mind either.'

'Good, because you're going to need the help. Between you and Bessie, even having Lily helping, it's going to be a hard month,' Mason said.

'What's a few hours of lost sleep? It will be worth it,' said Quintin.

Lily crept into the studio for another peek at the newest member of the family as she'd done for almost a week now. That, and to tell Quintin it was ten-thirty and it was bedtime.

Tiger meowed as if to tell her he knew she was there, and he was still doing his job. She stroked both Tiger and Minke. Tiger purred. Minke made a noise that was a series of squeaks and honks as she fluffed herself up and pressed back into Tiger, tucking her head in against her little body.

'So adorable,' Lily said. 'Quintin, I'm still worried that the cat will eat this chick and we'll find it dead one morning. This is not normal behaviour for him. He always brings us all those dead-animal presents—lizards, geckos and even a rat—and now he adopts a baby bird?'

'Mason said this type of thing does happen sometimes. Tiger will be fine, he's adopted her.'

'And the kids—aren't they tired of babysitting a bird yet?'

'Probably, but they are taking this seriously.'

Lily elbowed him in the ribs. 'I know, but they seem so young.'

'Anyway, they're only on the four and six o'clock shifts at night.'

'Piet is amazing with what he is doing for these youngsters. Who else would do this type of thing?'

'Not many. He's a man in a million,' Quintin said.

'I'm really happy that Bessie has said that she could help by watching Diamond for David and Elise, and Elise can rest a few more hours each day. I'm worried about her; she's beginning to lose weight. I fear she's crossing into full-blown AIDS, despite taking the blockers. Her CD4 count was only slightly above two hundred last week. I changed her blockers to an imported make, and I'm hoping to see a difference with her resting. I feel like our house has gone from child-free to full-time parents.'

'I'll admit it's kind of nice having kids here, even if it's just for a while.'

'In another three weeks, we won't need to feed Minke so often, and then we can organise for the kids to go home at night. I'm sure we can manage the nights then between Tiger and us. We should have this little flamingo ready to fledge with the other babies in January or February. Piet said that there are a few hundred chicks which have survived, that were big enough to swim when the waters came in and covered the island, and others which bred on the shoreline.' Lily smiled and put her head against Quintin's arm. 'With everything going on, trying to find the cause for the clusters, and now everybody under our roof, I'm not sure how you're doing for your music time. It's become rather hectic lately.'

'Actually, amazingly well,' said Quintin. 'The flamingo is so sweet. I get hours of inspiration. Minke and Tiger play together so beautifully.'

'I love the pictures you've taken of her, the one of Minke curled up inside Tiger's legs, snuggled into his tummy. And the one where the kids are sitting back to back and Tiger is laying stretched out against them both, with Minke laying nose to nose with Tiger. They're such an unlikely pair,' Lily said.

'David asked to learn the violin while he was here. So, I've got him using one of my old practice violins. He's such a natural, he plays by ear. It gave me the idea to record all our sessions, and I've started a library of lessons for kids who can't spend time with their teacher. We've been working on it when Minke sleeps.'

'Have you finished any recordings for your album?'

'A lot of composing in pieces at the moment. Nothing to share with you yet. How's the data collection from the bereaved relatives going?' Quintin asked.

'Slowly.'

CHAPTER 27

Ulwazi put her hand over her mouth as Anaya gave her a large bunch of flowers. 'I wanted to thank you and give you something in appreciation. I've come to you for advice, and it's helped me. My husband and I are now talking all the time. I believe that I can help him because I'm much stronger.'

Ulwazi took the flowers and put her nose into them, taking a deep sniff. 'I do not remember anyone giving me flowers on this bench,' she said with a smile. 'I thank you because I am so happy that you have been able to sort out your problems.'

Anaya shook her head. 'I cannot believe that people do not thank you for helping them. You're better than any therapist. Your advice works.'

'It is like it is,' Ulwazi said, but she was still smiling.

'I hope I'm allowed to still come and sit here and talk to you as a friend sometimes even when I don't need help.'

'Of course you can.'

'Thank you,' said Anaya. 'I do have one thing to ask before I leave.'

'I am always listening,' Ulwazi said.

'My husband has a problem with his sister. She's causing us a lot of trouble because she wants to do things her way and her way is wrong.'

Ulwazi smiled; this is why she put in the time on the bench. This is why she spoke with women—they always knew what was happening in businesses, and she made it her business to know theirs. Since the first day that Anaya had sat on her bench, Ulwazi had learned that her husband was the head chemist for Ayurprabhu Pharmaceuticals.

Yebo, this was precisely why she sat on the bench, listening to stupid, whiny, spoilt women like Anaya.

'What type of trouble is your husband in with his sister?'

'Bad trouble. The type I want to go away, quickly. I like my new life with my husband. If I can make everything right for him at work, remove his sister, then perhaps there will be no reason for him to have to worry about her anymore.'

'There are people in Africa who can sort out problems like this for you. They can make your problems go away for only a little money.'

Anaya shook her head and with a wry smile said, 'Go away?'

'That depends on what you want,' Ulwazi said.

'I want her out of the picture. I want my husband to be the CEO as well as the head chemist. My husband is a good man, and she's a bitch. She's making him do things at work that he doesn't like, and it was all her idea. He said that soon he might take too many pills and not wake up because he is so stressed about what is happening.'

Ulwazi clicked her tongue. '*Eish,* she sounds horrible. Perhaps we need to take care of her for you and make your life with your husband even better. But that will cost you a little bit more than flowers.'

'I'll happily pay the price to be rid of her. I have money of my own. What do you suggest?'

CHAPTER 28

Lily watched the lights from Piet's *bakkie* as he stopped on the dusty driveway. The Acacia Ridge Farm homestead had a steep thatched roof and whitewashed walls. It had a huge veranda in the front, with large overstuffed sofas on it. There was a BMX bicycle laying on its side, and a doll sat on the low wall. There was a colourful line of flowers on either side of the path, and a lush green lawn between the driveway and the house. A garden swing was motionless under the big camel thorn tree on the right, which was alive with a buffalo weaver's nest colony that chirped constantly.

Lily got out and stretched her legs, happy to be able to move them after the long drive. In front of her, Natalie appeared to be doing the same. She saw Khanyi, her new personal security guard, on the other side of the Land Cruiser. He was tall, his arms bulging with muscles, and his broad shoulders strained against the constricting fabric of his shirt. She was glad he was on her side, having recently made a switch from the police force into personal security. She and Quintin had employed him to accompany her throughout the day, but once she was inside the security of the home fence at night, he was off duty. He was living in the little house next to the one that Piet used.

'Oh shit!' Khanyi said loudly.

Lily looked towards the house. An old man, probably in his late eighties, stood waiting on the verandah, two Rottweilers at his heels. They didn't growl or make a sound. But the look of him was menacing, as were the dogs and the shotgun that hung off his shoulder.

'You're on point, Natalie,' Piet said, 'you spoke with him on the phone. Go work your charms so that he doesn't shoot at us. Lily, stay behind your door until she has sorted this out.'

Natalie walked forward to the bonnet. 'Mr Parkes, I'm Detective Natalie Hatch, the driver is Sergeant Piet Kleinman and behind him is security personnel Khanyi Nzo with Dr Lily Winters. I spoke with you on the phone about visiting today.'

'You said nothing about bringing the whole police force with you.'

'Piet and Khanyi are Lily's security detail. Someone attacked the doctor a few months ago. They're not here for you, but to keep her safe on the road. I should've mentioned it to you; I apologise for that oversight. Would you consider putting your shotgun down and perhaps locking your dogs away?' Natalie asked.

'I'd consider it, except I'm not the hospitable type, so perhaps we can conduct our business with a little distance between us. That way we'll both be happy because I know that you won't be putting your firearms down. There's no reason that you should be armed when I'm not.'

Natalie nodded and took a deep breath. 'We mean you no harm. I'm happy to put my firearm down here on the bonnet,' she said, proceeding to do so.

'Natalie,' Piet cautioned.

'It's okay, Mr Parkes. I'm unarmed now. My colleagues will stay right here by the *bakkie* if you like and only Lily and I'll come talk to you.'

'I didn't say that I've got a problem with blacks. I have a problem with people being on my land.'

'If I come forward so that we can talk reasonably, instead of shouting, will I be safe from your guard dogs?' Natalie said.

'Here we go,' Piet muttered. 'Do better at your charm thing.'

Khanyi said, 'No, Natalie, just stay here, where we are all safe. You can hear him, he can hear you.'

Natalie shook her head and took two steps forward. 'Do I have your word, Mr Parkes, that your dogs will stay by your side and not harm me and Dr Winters?'

'Dr Winters's security needs to get back in the vehicle, and they can point those guns of theirs somewhere else.'

'Please, guys, if he wanted to kill me he would have done so already,' Lily said. 'Put your weapons away. Natalie and I need some answers, that's all.'

Both men pointed their weapons downwards and climbed back into the Cruiser, leaving the doors open.

'You have my word,' the old man said. Putting down his shotgun and stepping forward, he walked two steps in their direction. The dogs remained on the verandah. Watching her but not moving.

'You coming, Lily?' Natalie asked, and they walked together.

As Natalie got closer, she put out her hand. 'Thank you for agreeing to meet us. I'm so sorry to hear about Jenny.'

'The loss of my granddaughter was difficult to talk about. My wife, Philani, is broken about losing her. We have the other girls, but it's not the same without the four of them running around together.'

'Dr Winters wanted to ask you a few questions about Jenny. She's investigating several similar cases. While we understand this could be extremely difficult for you, your information might help save other children.'

'Jenny was a sweet girl, and she was my granddaughter; that's all I'm saying about her.'

'Mr Parkes, the medical notes on Jenny.' Lily gave her papers to him. 'The file is very clinical, and there are notes in it that I need to know more about. The information you give me might help save other children from the same meningitis death that you have all had to witness. Meningitis is an agonising sickness. Your help could save someone else's child from excruciating pain, even death.'

He nodded, then reached for the file and opened it, squinting, trying to read the writing.

'Try these; they may help. I'm also long-sighted,' Lily said as she handed him her reading glasses.

He put them on and looked at the file for a long time without moving a single page. A tear ran down his wrinkled cheek and dripped onto his shirt. 'Nothing will bring her back, but I'll help you do whatever I can so that another grandparent doesn't have to feel this emptiness. The pain that is left knowing there is no God, because he took your precious grandchild, even when you offered yourself in her place. No one should have to lose their faith and their grandchild before they die themselves.'

Mr Parkes returned Lily's glasses to her and wiped his eyes with a white hanky that he took from his pocket. It was embroidered in the corner with blue monogram initials. Lily wondered who had made it for him. His wife or Jenny?

'Mr Parkes, did Jenny ever go to the hospital other than when she broke her arm when she was five?' Lily asked.

He shook his head. 'Normally, Philani can fix anything. She can set broken bones, she can stitch the deepest cut, but the day that Jenny broke her arm we knew that she needed extra help, so we got her to the hospital. Philani removed Jenny's cast later, and she did all the physical therapy with her to make sure her arm was as strong as it had been before. That arm was perfect, or we would have taken her back to the hospital. Believe me, I would never let Jenny suffer any more in her life. After what she went through as a small child, she didn't need any more darkness in her world.'

'What profession was your wife in before you came to live on your farm?' Natalie asked.

'She was a nurse. She'd done a lot of work in the Baragwanath Hospital in Soweto. She gave up her career to live on my farm with me and to help bring up my sheep and cattle. She was a strong woman once.'

'Do you still have any of the medications left that you gave to Jenny when she was sick?' Lily asked.

'We might have. All 'my girls' are generally healthy and don't take many pills. I can ask Philani. She'll know if we have them. She tried everything to get Jenny's temperature down that day, even an ice bath. But she didn't respond to anything. We couldn't save her.'

'She was a very lucky girl to have you in her life,' Lily said. 'She knew that she was loved and that you and your wife were there for her.'

'I hope she knew,' Mr Parkes said. 'I hope she understood that we did everything we could for her. Come into the house, and we can talk with Philani. Bring your bodyguards with you into the shade. Phoebe. Themis.

Release,' he instructed, and the dogs got up and ran off down the stairs past her and into the garden, totally ignoring everyone.

Mr Parkes began to turn away from them. 'I need to put the shotgun away; I don't want it laying around where the girls can get to it.'

A frail old black woman walked onto the verandah. 'This is my wife, Philani. She'll see you to the lounge, while I put this in the gun safe.'

Mr Parkes's behaviour fell into place. They were an old mixed-race couple. They'd spent so many years hiding from the law, going to extreme lengths to conceal their relationship, that even now, after the apartheid laws had been demolished, they kept themselves isolated so that no one could rip their world apart.

Lily's eyes stung with tears, knowing that she was about to do just that when she told them about the contaminated medication they had given their granddaughter.

CHAPTER 29

As Lily drove towards home, Khanyi sitting next to her, her mind was on the bottles of drugs that they now had secured in the evidence bag in the police *bakkie* with Piet and Natalie. Her first case where she could be sure that she had the sample of contaminated drugs. Thankfully, none of it had been taken after Jenny had died.

Piet and Natalie drove behind her; she could see them clearly in her rear-view mirror. She called Quintin.

'Hello. It's the *umculo womuntu* speaking to his lovely *wifie*.'

She could hear his voice clearly with her phone on speaker, and it made her smile, despite everything going on. Quintin had always managed to do that. 'Hey, Music Man, your Zulu pronunciation is getting better. Just letting you know that Piet and Natalie are on their way to our house and are right behind me.'

'Are they staying for dinner?'

'I offered them a *braai* with us to de-stress, yes.'

'I'll get Bessie onto it. How was the meeting?'

'Heartbreaking. It was never going to be easy to tell someone that they bought the drugs that inevitably killed their loved one, without having some type of fallout. I feel strongly for them, losing Jenny was hard on them. But we left them with the knowledge that we were going to go hard after the killers.'

'Listen to your tough talk. Where is Khanyi, he's supposed to be the tough one?' Quintin asked.

'Sitting next to me, so don't embarrass me.'

'That's like a red flag to a bull. How far are you from home?'

'I'm coming back over the train tracks and up Midlands Road—Oh my God, Quintin, someone's lying on the road. It looks like a hit-and-run—I'm going to have to stop. I can't just drive past.'

'No. Drive!' Khanyi was shouting. 'Don't stop!'

She had already braked hard—Khanyi had his handgun out even as she slowed.

'I'm not leaving a person to die in the middle of the road,' she shouted at him. 'I'm a doctor!' She jerked to a stop and wrenched her handbrake upwards.

'It's a trap, Lily,' Khanyi said, trying to grab at her arm, but she twisted it out of his fingers and got out of the car, running a few steps.

Instantly, the body on the road rolled over, jumped up and ran towards her.

Screaming, she attempted to run back to the Cruiser. The man was faster. He reached forward, grabbed the edge of her blouse and yanked her. She fell hard on her back, her head slamming against the road.

Bitumen bit into her skull. She could feel the stones as they broke flesh.

Time slowed.

She tried to roll over, to get onto her knees and get up, and the move gave her enough time to see the police vehicle stopped behind her Land Cruiser, and that Piet and Natalie were running towards her. Khanyi was in front of Piet. She felt the man grab her firmly by the hair, but before she was even yanked to her feet, both officers had their weapons drawn and were shouting at him. They spoke in three or four languages, shouting, 'Drop your weapon! Let her go!'

Instead of complying, he brought her closer to his chest, pulling her hair so hard it made her neck strain at the angle that he forced it into.

She could smell the pungent aroma of an unwashed body. And his breath was hot as he shouted back at the police right next to her face, in a language she didn't understand. The smell of cheap tobacco surrounded him, but it was the coldness of the gun that he'd pressed hard into her temple that made her freeze.

Flashes of the pictures of Ian went through her head.

She was going to die.

'Put the gun down,' Piet instructed. 'Put it down and let her go. Now.'

'No,' her attacker said.

Khanyi came at them out of nowhere, a bull charging—knocking them both over. Lily could feel the pressure of the man's fingers in her hair loosen as he pulled her down with him. Taking advantage of his distracted moment, she broke free and rolled away. This time she managed to stand up and run towards the lights of the car. She could see the silhouettes of both Piet and Natalie, and knew that she would only be safe when she got to them.

She heard grunting and bone hitting bone behind her, but she didn't stop. She knew she had to get to the safety of the Land Cruiser.

Gunshots exploded in the night, and she threw herself down on the road, putting her hands over her ears. Trying to make herself as small as possible, she looked to see how far she had to get to the Land Cruiser to use it as a shield as she had been taught so many years ago before she went to Zam Zam.

She leopard-crawled towards the lights, which were not close enough.

'Lily,' Khanyi said, lifting her by her midriff and enveloping her in his arms as he ran to the back of the Land Cruiser.

Natalie and Piet were running past them, towards the man who had tried to kill her.

Opening the back door, Khanyi put Lily in the boot, pushed her flat and crouched over her to shield her. He was looking out, his 9mm ready. 'Stay down. And for God's sake listen to me this time.'

'You shot him. You shot him,' Lily said over and over.

'Not me. But that's the best outcome we could hope for. If they didn't, you would be dead by now,' Khanyi said. 'Stay low. Piet is checking the surrounding area to see if there are others out there. Natalie is on the other side of the road covering him.'

After a while, Natalie returned. 'Lily, you okay?'

'Not really, but I'm alive, and that's what matters.'

'Why did you let her stop, Khanyi? I thought you explained all this to her. I thought—'

'I did, she didn't listen to me,' Khanyi said.

'You should have shot him when you got out of the *bakkie* before he even got to Lily,' Natalie said. 'Not just smacked him a few times. The bastard got up again; he was coming for you. You didn't drop him good enough.'

'Will you two stop arguing!' Lily said. 'Let me up.'

'No,' Natalie and Khanyi said together.

'Oh great—they agree on one thing,' Lily said.

'Wait, continue to shield her,' Natalie instructed. 'Piet!' she called loudly. 'Anyone else in the bushes?'

'No. I found his vehicle but no other tracks. If there was someone with him they did not get out at the same point, and the likelihood is that they have run away.'

'Do we need to get the dogs?' Natalie shouted.

'Let me up,' Lily said.

'Khanyi, you best let her out of the boot because there is blood on the mat. I need to check her over.'

Khanyi moved from his position like an agile leopard.

Piet had just jogged up to them. 'I think it might be an idea. Can you radio this into the station? I am going to carry on looking for more signs of where the partner is. They normally work in pairs. Besides, we have discharged our weapons—we need to report in. Lily, you okay?'

'Yes, thank you, Piet.'

'I'm on it,' said Natalie.

Piet disappeared back into the bushes.

'Thank you for having my back,' Khanyi said.

'He's not getting up again, that I can assure you,' Natalie said.

'You killed him,' Lily said.

'Unfortunately. He was going to kill you, so I made a choice,' Natalie said. 'If we weren't so close behind you, you would have been dead. What were you thinking, stopping for somebody on the road? That's one of the oldest tricks in Africa. They make you think that they need help, and they rob you, kill you, or worse, rape you. You're from Africa—you should know better. Call it into the nearest police station and keep driving.'

'I know, but I'm a doctor—I couldn't just drive past. What if it was real and I could save them?' Lily said.

'*Ag*, man, I get you, but next time, please keep on driving. It's your life or theirs here. We might not be there to help again. Come on, let me look at you—where's this blood coming from?'

'My head—I could feel the stones when it smacked the ground,' Lily said as Natalie snapped on latex gloves and turned Lily around.

'*Eina, jislaaik*. There it is. Nice big cut, needs cleaning too. Will have that one seen to in the emergency room. That's going to hurt when the adrenaline leaves. Going to make sleeping on your back difficult for the next few days.'

'Oh my God, Quintin. He was on the phone; I didn't hang up. He would've heard all of this. I left him on speaker!'

'Quintin, you there?' Natalie said loudly, but there was no answer on the handsfree. 'Stay here, I'll go to the front and see if I can find your phone,' Natalie said.

'It was in my pocket,' Lily said. 'It's probably on the road somewhere.'

'Okay, will look on the road.' Natalie walked towards the dead body, and Lily watched her. She bent down and grabbed the phone, then jogged back, handing it to Lily.

Lily pushed the screen and it lit up. 'It's still working.'

'Right, you call Quintin. I need to go use my police radio. Khanyi, watch her closely. Shock's going to set in any moment. Perhaps get her a foil blanket out of the emergency kit; she's going to need it before the ambulance arrives.'

Lily's fingers were starting to shake so much she was struggling to put the code into her keypad to unlock it.

'Code?' Khanyi asked, calmly taking the phone from her.

She gave it to him, and he dialled Quintin's number, then put the phone to her ear. 'Hold the phone.'

She put her hand over it and held tightly. He dug in the back for the blanket.

'Lily? Lily? Are you okay?' She could hear Quintin's frantic voice.

'I'm here, Quintin. I'm safe now,' she said as she pressed her phone closer. She could feel the smear of blood on her phone from her ear, and she physically shuddered. 'On Midlands Road, about three kilometres from our turn-off. Someone tried to kill me.'

'I'm coming,' Quintin said.

Hours later, Lily still sat in the Roodepan police station. The building was painted what used to be white, but too many people had smoked indoors for it to have remained pristine, and now it looked like an eggshell light brown. There were big 'no smoking' signs up all over the place. Lily's eyes were drawn to the thick bars on the windows. She silently admitted to herself that she must live in a dangerous place when even the police station had bars on it to keep the criminals out.

After downing the last of the can of Coke that Piet had pushed at her and instructed her to drink, she lifted one of her hands. At last, the tremors had gone. Her stomach twanged with hunger. After being discharged from the emergency room with stitches in her head, she'd gone straight to the police station. And stayed there.

Although the hospital had cleaned her up, Natalie had taken her clothes and put them into an evidence bag, leaving her to wear the light-purple scrubs from the emergency room.

Quintin sat beside her, holding her hand in an interview room. Piet and Natalie were opposite her at the table, and Khanyi sat on a chair, next to them. In front of them was a binder with photographs and sketched pictures.

'Have you seen any of these faces before?' Piet was pointing to different people. 'Take your time, have a good look. Both of you.'

'Why am I looking at these?' she asked. She didn't recognise a single person.

'That was not a simple attempted hijacking. It was attempted murder. The man who tried to kill you is a known associate of a gang in Alexandra. If this man came after you, someone has put a contract on you. His name was Kagiso Dubazane, he is wanted for other contract killings. Usually he works out of Alexandra in Johannesburg, so he was a fair way from home.

Dubazane has gone to court once before, but he got off on a technicality—someone messed up in the paperwork, and not surprisingly he had an expensive and elite legal firm working for him.'

'He was a known criminal?' Lily asked.

'Yes,' Piet said. 'I am worried that they will send someone else to finish the job. A contract, or a hit as some would call it, is mostly paid upfront to the person who organises it. Not afterwards. Then whoever is organising the hit, only pays the money over to the hitman once they have proof that the execution has taken place. In a professional execution, there is always someone who pays, someone who organises and someone who does the deed. We now need to find out who the organiser is, and who actually wants you dead. And most importantly, why.'

Lily swallowed and ran her hands through her hair. Then flinched when she touched her wound. 'Do you think this is the same person who wanted Ian dead?'

'I do, and probably Chelmsford, as well. Too convenient, that style of hijacking. Now our jobs are to find out what you put your foot into. If this is about the tainted drugs or something else.'

'We can't discount any of our wild ideas now,' Natalie said.

'If drug dealers are angry with us for growing a few plants to make medicines, surely someone might have attempted to break into the property, try to steal them, burn down the hothouse. Not attempted to kill Lily first off?' Quintin said.

'I agree,' Piet said. 'But you have locked up your place pretty tight. It was as if this killer knew where you were going to be. He seemed surprised that you had company, but he knew your location, that you would come down that road. He knew your Land Cruiser.'

'People could probably set their clock by what you do,' Khanyi said. There were icebags across his fists, a reminder to Lily that he had gone into a physical fight with a killer to protect her. 'We spoke about shaking up the days, but it's really hard for a doctor—it's a lot to rearrange. And there is only one road into town from Lily's place. We found night-vision binoculars at the scene to look for you, ensure it was you before laying in the road. But then, he could have just got lucky.'

'Not that man,' Piet said. 'He did not have the brain capacity to get lucky. He was told precisely what to do, where, when and how.'

'We can't rule out that someone told him you were going to be on that long stretch of straight road,' Khanyi said.

'True. But we need to find who. Who knew? Our dogs did not find any other scents when they searched, and they would have detected another presence. Kagiso Dubazane was a cold-blooded killer. He would not simply take time out to randomly target someone. Can you think of who you told that we were going to Mr Parkes's farm?'

'I guess I might have said something to Jacob because he always likes to know where I am, and of course to June. I can't go anywhere without her knowledge for insurance. Actually, I asked Bessie if she had been near Hopetown and if there were any butchers on the way worth stopping at for biltong. But she wouldn't have times that I was travelling, and she never knew it was today.'

'One thing we got from him was his gun. If it is a match to other hijackings, then at least we have an idea of what his legacy with that was,' Piet said.

'Can I go home yet?' Lily asked.

Natalie nodded. 'Quintin can take you now; I'll grab my things. I'll take turns with one of the other policewomen from Roodepan and Kimberley police stations to keep an eye on you. As well as Khanyi. Just until he can organise to bring in more women personnel to protect you, be with you all the time for a while. Until we catch these guys.'

Piet said, 'We do not believe that this gang will stop coming for you. Even though we have killed one of the assassins, they will keep surfacing when least expected. We do not know how much time we have before they try again. We need to find some answers. Quickly.'

CHAPTER 30

QUINTIN COULDN'T RELAX, as hard as he tried. Neither could Lily. They were together in the lounge, Lily with her feet up on the couch, but they were both restless.

Tiger walked in and jumped onto the table. 'No, you get down, you are not allowed up there. Next, you'll be begging for food,' Lily said.

'Hang on, if Tiger is here, where's Minke?' Quintin got up and walked to the garage, Tiger and Lily following behind.

Quintin frowned. Minke was not in her little caged area. She had managed to hop out of it yet again.

'Where's Minke?' Lily asked.

They heard the kids laughing and went to the outside door. Opening it, they saw them in the little portable swimming pool they had bought for Minke, splashing around with the bird honking.

'Did that cat just dob them in for going outside?' Lily asked.

'I believe he did,' Quintin said, lifting Tiger up and stroking him. He was rewarded with a loud purr.

Bessie was watching them from across the way. Little Diamond was dressed in her bathing suit, and Lincoln was putting the hose away, having filled the small pool for them that he emptied daily.

'Well, at least they didn't go swimming alone this time. Looks like they got Bessie to jailbreak them,' Quintin said as Diamond took off towards the pool, where David helped her into the water with them.

Lily laughed. 'Those kids are going to miss that baby flamingo when it goes back to the wild.'

'Yeah and their excuse to stay here with us, too,' Quintin said.

Lily could hear a sadder tone in his voice.

'Unfortunately for David and Diamond, it might not be an option to go anywhere else when Elise dies. Piet says that their real family are gone. Those two will be all alone now. If they still lived in the desert, the tribe would bring them up together, but now welfare will take them, probably split them up and house them with foster parents if they are lucky.'

'Won't Piet take them on?'

'He didn't say he wouldn't, but he seemed to think that welfare might not think him a suitable candidate for adopting two kids. He has no wife, and he works all the time, and he already looks after his sister. Well, the financial burden is on him, he employs someone to watch over her when he's at work.'

Quintin hugged Lily close.

'I can't do this, Quintin, this knowing that they're about to have their lives implode on them. Knowing that we've all had a moment of happiness together as a family but it will end when Elise dies and they get split up. I need to get out, get away.'

'With me, I hope,' Quintin said.

'You're the only one I do want around right now. But I feel like every move we make at home today is being watched.'

'It is, but we can play hooky. What about a visit next door? Should we see if they can fit us into their private game reserve for a night or so?'

'Perfect. African animals in the wild and you, that will help me relax.'

Game reserves had always calmed Lily as a child, and as Quintin drove through the gates of their neighbour's game farm, she could feel the muscles in her neck relax. Just knowing that they were going to spend one night under the stars in tented luxury did that. But she knew it was also safety. Knowing that the farm's security to keep the animals in also kept the intruders out and was probably as tight as their own at home was, if not more with their anti-poaching units constantly patrolling.

They needed time alone to talk. To process. And to cry and laugh together in private. Once again, she had somehow escaped death, but she'd unintentionally put Quintin through anguish, too.

The thorn trees around the waterhole were green. If you looked closely, you could see some had almost silver branches and the mean thorns of the *Acacia* tree. There were a few large dead trees which stood in dark contrast to the blue sky behind as wispy clouds danced across the horizon in the distance.

In the trees sat two starlings, their blue-black feathers shimmering in the heat as they looked towards the waterhole, where the animals had trampled the grass and eaten it short like a suburban lawn. In the distance it was longer, and it was here that the tree line began in earnest, and distinct paths coming from the bushes down into the waterhole marked the terracotta earth where many feet had trodden before.

Lily could hear the wind as it blew through the treetops, making the leaves dance with a soft whistling sound. She looked into the shadows underneath the trees to the right, where she could see a small troop of baboons as they lay in the dappled shade. To the left, a tall giraffe plodded towards the water, its hooves making more paths of dust as it trod carefully, watching everywhere for predators while it nibbled at the morsels of green in the treetops. Its white and orange-brown colours were a stark contrast to the green behind them. Its strides were long, and soon it bent down in an almost elegant but ungainly way. Its legs splayed aside, it bowed its head into the water and then lifted it, showering everything around with droplets of silver. It swallowed, taking another look before going back to drinking. It was incredible that this animal had evolved to be so tall for the treetop foods, and yet still reliant on water which was at ground level, Lily thought.

Eventually it was full, and after licking its lips and nose area with a long tongue, the giraffe headed back into the tree line, and was soon camouflaged and almost impossible to see among the trees.

A couple of ducks were having an altercation and were running towards the water, heads down low to the mud, wings flapping. They made so much noise that other birds in the area turned to see what was causing the commotion.

She squeezed Quintin's hand.

A spotted hyena walked towards the waterhole and sat in the green shallows. His hindquarters were submerged, and then he flopped onto one side, his body half underwater, while he kept his head lifted out, the muddy ripples lapping at his bulging belly as he tried to gain some relief from the heat. Another hyena with giant jaws joined a small group as they slunk from the bushes towards their friend. They were a little smaller than him. They flopped into the water to cool down—obviously part of the same cackle.

After a while, they got up and walked together through the muddy shallows, keeping away from the deeper water before once again covering themselves in the sticky mud on the other side of their bodies. When the male had had enough, he strutted around displaying his dominance for all to see as he tried to attract the attention of the two females there. Eventually, he waded slightly deeper, seduced by the coolness. He looked around constantly, as alert as the giraffe had been earlier.

Along the shore, small birds picked at insects, and like the duck crew along the shoreline, they seemed too hot and bothered to be enticed by even the fat dragonflies that flew around. It was as if the heat had sapped everyone's energy.

The larger of the female hyenas coated herself in mud as she turned on her side, still panting. She was unconcerned about a threat from the murky depths of the water but continued to watch the shores for predators.

The male chose to move in further and was soon rolling over, with only his head showing as he immersed himself in the experience. His coat changed from striped and spotted to mud-black. His paws folded upon his chest when he was on his back, looking much like a dog's while he rolled around. Every now and again, Lily could see his tail mid-wag above the surface as he enjoyed the cool wetness. One of the females made her way over to him, submissive as she rubbed against him, but you could see that this was a family and there was affection between them.

Butterflies danced along at the edge of the mud, their wings opening and closing as they fluttered a synchronised dance as the male stood up.

He continued to scan the horizon as he walked towards the females and then over the grass and onto an animal trail and soon disappeared into the bushes.

The females lifted themselves up and surveyed the surrounds. As if realising they'd been left alone and were no longer safe, they bolted in their lopsided run towards the shade of one of the *Acacia* trees, then slunk further back into the brush.

Quintin passed Lily the water bottle, and she drank deeply before she gave it back.

From the bushes, a single impala took tentative steps beyond the tree line, and was suddenly followed up by a whole herd as they made their way towards the water. The waterhole was alive with a lighter shade of brown and flicking whitetails everywhere. Some of them frolicked around—testing their skills against each other.

A big ram with impressive horns walked up to a younger impala, and while they put their horns together, Lily could see that they weren't really sparring.

The impala drank deeply and continued to mill around. Many of them came away, their thirst quenched, but with long black stockings of mud coating their elegant legs.

Lily watched as an oxpecker landed on one of the impala necks and started to clean off the parasites. The bird moved among the herd and chose another host—it sat on its head and picked at its ear. Obviously finding something good to eat.

'It's an impala-cleaning station,' Quintin said. 'They came down to the water, and they get a drink and a clean at the same time.'

Lily smiled.

The impala stayed around for a while, grazing on the short green grass until slowly one by one they ventured up back into the bushes and disappeared again.

'I could watch these animals all day,' said Quintin.

Lily adjusted the way she was sitting and snuggled into him. 'Me too, there's something about them that's—relaxing. I'm glad you brought us here.'

'You always did relax when you watched the wildlife,' Quintin said.

'I'm sorry, Quintin. I really am. To make you worry.'

'Not really your fault.'

'I shouldn't have stopped. I should have listened to Khanyi.'

'No argument from me there; you should have listened to him.'

'Hindsight is a wonderful thing, isn't it?'

'Agreed, but you aged me a hundred years. I thought I had lost you.'

'How much did you hear before you were cut off?'

'It became all muffled, then I could clearly hear the gunshot, scratching sounds, then we were disconnected. I thought I had heard you die. I thought I had lost you this time for sure to Africa.'

'Oh, Quintin,' Lily said, hugging him tightly.

'When you rang, and I heard your voice, and I knew you were not dead, I couldn't stop shaking. I knew years ago that you were too free-spirited to be wrapped in a protective blanket. God knows our trips all over the world have proved that.'

'When I realised I'd left you on the phone, I panicked. I was so worried about you. I knew the anguish you would have gone through, and I'm sorry,' Lily said.

'Me too. Sorry you got hurt—again,' Quintin said, kissing her.

'Together,' Lily said against his lips. 'As long as we are together, we can survive anything.'

She felt him nod and they sat comfortably in silence for a while.

Nothing came to the waterhole for quite some time, and while Quintin and Lily watched the geese as they slept with one leg up, it wasn't riveting viewing. Until the lookout baboons barked. Lily sat upright.

'Something's here,' she said. 'That's a warning call.'

'Look,' he said.

Coming down to the water was a lioness, her beautiful tawny colour shining in the hot sun. She walked to the pool and went down on all fours as she began lapping at the murky water. She adjusted her weight distribution and moved her back legs further apart. She looked uncomfortable.

'Look at that fat belly, she's either just eaten her fill, or she's very pregnant,' Quintin said.

Flies buzzed around her head as her big paws sank deep into the mud as she drank.

'Can you see her body heave as she pants? It must be the heat,' Lily said.

The lioness half stood, her hind legs straightening, lifting her butt into the air, but she continued to drink for a while longer. Eventually, with one final push of her powerful feet, she stood up and soon vanished back into the trees.

'Do you think she's alone?' asked Lily.

'Looks like it.'

The sun was sinking lower. The tree line extended itself almost to the edge of the water as it cast long shadows across the ground. Quintin said, 'We need to go to the camp, have some dinner and then we can disappear into the tent for the night.'

Lily hugged him, and Quintin held her tightly.

'I don't want to go to the tents and be waited on like a tourist; I don't feel very touristy. I want to go home to Hacienda El Paradiso. You and me in our house with Tiger laying on our bed, the kids and Minke downstairs.'

'Your wish is my command, my *wifie*. Home it is.'

CHAPTER 31

Someone had decorated the police offices in the first week of December, complete with a tree in the corner with coloured lights, and a handful of vibrant plastic baubles hung on the fake fur branches. Piet tried his best to ignore the flickering of the lights and tapped his finger against the side of the computer printouts. Things were spidering away. Nothing was neat and tidy. It was typical of a South African case; nothing was ever simple in this country, not even the way to cook *samp* and beans.

It was as clear as day that Warrant Officer Sithole was signing off all his cases as unsolved hijackings. Not one of the vehicles in his cases had been recovered. Normally, a fifty-fifty split in vehicle recovery was considered normal, especially with the number of GPS trackers increasing in usage. The statistics were stacked against his cases. Sithole had his hand in the *koeksister* syrup right up to his elbow.

'Something wrong?' Natalie asked.

'I take it you saw that the report came back on the 9mm that Kagiso Dubazane used to try to kill Lily? It was the same one used to murder Hawthorne and was in a heap of those other cases that we have,' Piet said.

'I just saw that. It's about time we got a break in the case. Pity we can't tie it to Chelmsford, too.'

'Follow this chain of evidence with me.' Standing at the cork-board next to his desk, he put the picture of the 9mm in its evidence bag and pinned it near the bottom corner with his stapler. 'There is a 9mm that was used in multiple murders—one being Hawthorne, and now the attempted murder of Lily. Kagiso Dubazane had the gun when you shot him.' Piet put up a mug shot of Dubazane from a previous case.

'And?'

'Kagiso Dubazane is a family member of the Dubazane syndicate. If memory serves me, his mother, Ulwazi, is rumoured to be the head, but no one's been able to pin anything on her and make it stick. She's slipperier than a yellow fish.'

'She must be getting quite old,' Natalie said. 'Did she retire or does she continue to run them? Guide them along?'

He pinned up a picture of a police hat. 'This represents Sithole, in case someone in this office knows him.'

'*Ag*, man, I see where you're going now. So, you think that this is now two-pronged for us. We have to look at a crime syndicate, and we have a dirty cop who might be involved.'

'*Ja*,' Piet said. 'Technically, we should take this to Chetty, but I am happy to bypass him if you are? I think we need to reach out to both the Internal Affairs investigators and the Crime Intelligence Division. Give us some breathing space before Chetty finds out and opens that big mouth of his. I doubt that Warrant Officer Sithole is alone in his affairs in his office; no one can sign off on cases like this without someone else checking and knowing what he is doing. And there's clearly a link with the Dubazane syndicate because of the attack on Lily, and that's organised crime and falls outside of our jurisdiction.'

'This is getting too big for us to handle without help.'

'I agree. Who was his superior?' Piet asked.

'I've marked the part about Sithole's superior. For most of the years that Sithole has been in the force, he's been reporting to a Captain Arno Swanepoel.'

'You must be kidding me! That arsehole. When did they make him a captain?'

'You know him?' Natalie asked.

'Unfortunately. He was at Kokstad police station for a while when I was there. The laziest of all the police ever,' Piet said. 'A real user. Getting others to do his paperwork, never putting in extra hours like the rest of us. Bad attitude.'

'There has been no movement on either of their careers. Bit fishy, neither of them budging for over ten years. I know this is the new South Africa, but people still want to go up the ranks and get better pay. Do you think he's a person of interest?' Natalie asked.

'Probably. It is the type of reckless thing he would get caught up in, even if he claims innocence.'

'And not so innocent as the evidence is proving. Getting involved with murder is bad, but if you are going to do it, don't leave a paper trail,' Natalie said.

'Deep, Natalie. You should write that on a poster for the office.'

She grinned at him and he turned back to his computer.

'*Ja*, brilliant, my china,' Piet said a little loudly.

'What?' Natalie asked.

'They finally broke the encryption of Ian's drive. They sent us the files. I'm printing them out now.'

Piet passed Lily the papers. 'This is what Ian was doing when he was in Sudan with you a few years ago. He got himself involved in smuggling drugs and dealing in weapons.'

'He was smuggling in drugs for the refugees,' Natalie said. 'The documents on the drive were probably to help clear his name if anything happened to him. The weapons were used to fund the drugs and payments to the rebels in the region—to not attack the shipments that he was funnelling in from the north. He had used the profit to buy expired drugs for the refugees on the black market from India. This took brains and balls to organise. It's a side of Dr Ian Hawthorne that I, for one, never saw.'

'Expired drugs still save lives,' Lily said as she looked through the papers. This was the reasoning that had motivated him back then, that insistence that a plane with the drugs was coming which had almost cost them all their lives.

'All this was possible because Hawthorne skimmed off the top of the doctor's budget to finance the weapons.'

'World Health's money,' Lily said. She had the proof she needed to take it to WHO and get their apology, but it felt like a hollow victory. Ian was dead anyway, as dead as all those people they had left behind at Zam Zam.

'But why was he still hiding it? Why was he collecting money from the people at Platfontein at the free clinics? Why did he fill his house with artworks that cost thousands, antique furniture and imported rugs? Why was he amassing material possessions in Kimberley? What was he doing here?'

'See that bank account? It was still active,' Natalie said.

'Our accounting forensic team have now looked over all these files. It appears that he was definitely amassing money in this account again, but we don't know what for at this stage, and he did not have an explanation for the new sets of transactions, unlike his accounts for Sudan,' Piet said.

'Can I keep these?' Lily asked, bringing the paper back into a single neat pile. 'I'd like to share them with World Health.'

'Those are your copy, and we wouldn't expect anything less than for you to share that with them,' Natalie said. 'I'm really glad IT finally delivered.'

'Me too,' Lily said. 'It's a small win in the right direction.'

CHAPTER 32

ANAYA SAT down on the friendship bench and waited for Ulwazi. She'd never been late before, and she wondered where she was. Could something be wrong with the old woman? Another old lady walked towards the bench and sat down.

'Are you waiting for Ulwazi?' she asked.

'Yes, I meet her here every Tuesday morning for breakfast. I've bought her favourite, coffee with hazelnut and caramel syrup. Ulwazi has a very sweet tooth. It's going cold.'

'Ulwazi will not be on her bench today—she's had a death in her family.'

'That's so sad. She didn't have lots of family to lose. Is it possible to tell me who died?'

The old woman clicked her tongue much in the same manner that Ulwazi did. 'It is a sad day. Her son was killed by the police in Kimberley. Ulwazi went to claim his body so that she could bury him in a nice place in Fourways.'

'Fourways? Why would she bury somebody there?' Anaya asked. That was an expensive cemetery for anyone to be buried in, and Ulwazi had never acted like she had lots of money.

'That is where she owns a family plot. That is where everybody in her family who has died has been buried.'

Anaya passed the cup to the old lady. 'Would you like the coffee, otherwise it will go to waste. When is the funeral? I would like to go and pay my respects.'

The old lady took the takeaway beverage and sipped. 'Thank you. That is very thoughtful of you, but you cannot attend the funeral or the wake, which she will have for her child, because that will be in Alexandra and you should not go there. Perhaps next Tuesday you can give her an envelope with a little money in it to help towards the cost of the funeral and the wake afterwards. It can be very expensive when someone in the family dies.'

'I'll do that. And don't worry—I'll not be venturing into Alexandra. Ulwazi already told me never to go into that township even if I have somebody with me.'

The old lady took another sip from the cup. 'This is very nice coffee. Ulwazi is very lucky to have you come and sit on her bench every week.'

'I'm lucky to have her to talk to,' Anaya said. 'If you will excuse me—I've got shopping I need to do. Thank you for letting me know about Ulwazi. I do appreciate it.' She got up from the bench and left the old lady sitting there. As she walked away, she could feel that the woman stared at her departing back, watching her every move.

She wondered why, when Ulwazi was on the bench, she never felt as if she was being spied on but she did when she spoke to her stand-in.

CHAPTER 33

ULWAZI SAT at her table in the shebeen. Tears ran freely down her face. This was the wake for her last remaining son, Kagiso, her firstborn.

Her son was never going to walk through the door again, with a different woman on each of his arms. He was never going to be there to help her with her business either, to help her keep a low profile, despite being so busy. She still remembered the day that she gave birth to him and had known that she would never be alone in the world again because now she had her own baby, a son to be proud of and to love. And to have him love her in return, as a son should.

He'd been shot by the police in Kimberley.

In days gone by, she might have taken to the streets with a placard and demonstrated against the police, but those days were long gone, and there was no way now that she could draw attention to herself. She'd sent him to carry out the removal herself because she trusted him to get the job done.

Now he was dead—and the doctor still lived.

Sometimes his job was viewed as dangerous. But her son had been good at it. He lived for the risk and the thrill. It was the only job he'd ever excelled in. Killing.

Warrant Officer Sithole sat opposite her. He passed her two envelopes.

'I'm sorry for your loss, Ulwazi. I know how precious your son was to you.'

'Thank you. What is the second envelope?'

'The information you wanted on his shooting. I urge you not to take revenge when you see this police report.'

Ulwazi took the envelopes, folded them and put them safely inside her bra. 'I will not look now because it is my Kagiso's feast. But know that I will have my revenge. He was my son. I am Ulwazi, the head of the Dubazane family. If I do nothing, the people will not come to me for weapons or information anymore. People will not trust me to do things. It is my obligation to kill whoever shot my beautiful son.'

'This will not be easy. You are going against the police force; you know what happens when you become a cop killer? They hunt you, and they kill you.'

'I believe it was a very smart man that once said something to the effect of: "Unless you help find a solution, you perhaps are part of the problem." Sithole, either help me, or you get up from the table and walk away. Forever. You are only getting this pass because it is my son's burial feast.'

'Know for true that I am not turning on you, Ulwazi. I have always looked up to you. I have always helped you to cover your tracks when things have not gone right, and when things have gone right, I have helped you celebrate, and been the one to sign the files. I am in deep with you. I cannot walk away. We are business partners. We need each other to ensure that we can make money. Why was it so important that your son went all the way to Kimberley to try to kill the doctor?'

'She is stealing the secrets of the San community of Platfontein and publishing them in a book.'

'And? You are not a San, so why should you care?'

'A man from Ayurprabhu Pharmaceuticals cares about it. He says that he can make more money off those drugs than the San would ever get from the sale of a stupid book, and he will give me an ongoing share if I make this problem go away. No doctor. No book. Problem out of the way.'

'You accepted the contract.'

'I did.'

'But you know that covering up the last foreign doctor's death was difficult enough. Now you sent your son to a district where I have no power, no jurisdiction. I cannot meddle in Kimberley police cases and files. Even my captain would turn away from that.'

'It was foolish for him to try to kill her there, and not bring her nearer to Johannesburg first. I see that now.'

'Now is too late. The police can get to you through your son. They can get to me through you. Let me complete this contract for you, but in my own way. No more killing foreign doctors.'

'You think that you can finish what my son could not?' Ulwazi said.

'Why kill her if you only want the book?' Sithole asked.

'The contract was for her death so that she cannot make another book.'

Sithole sat in his chair. 'But she will leave anyway when she is finished her work here? In the police file it says that they have almost completed their work, and then she will go back to Australia. What if you had the book? You can auction it off to any of the pharmaceutical companies, and you could get more money than just from the Ayurprabhu man.'

'But then I will have broken a contract.'

'What exactly was the contract for?'

'The life of Dr Lily Winters.'

'See, that man from the pharmaceutical company is not clever. No. If you kill her, the book will still be there on her computer and in print. Another doctor will come and take her place, as she did already when you killed Dr Hawthorne. If you make sure she's finished writing the book, then you get the book yourself, instead of him, there is more power in that. You'll have the book. Knowledge. She'll go away to a different country. It's as good as disappearing under the earth. When she's flown back to Australia, you can then have the auction of the book and sell it to the highest bidder.'

Ulwazi was still for a moment. 'I see what you are thinking. *Yebo*, this is a good idea. I can have everything my way. Getting the book or her computer was not part of the contract. And when she leaves, she is as good as dead because she is so far away, no one from Africa can get to her. You are a clever policeman sometimes, Sithole. I hope that the people in your department never find out how clever you are.'

Sithole smiled.

'Once again, I know who my friends are, and who will stick behind me and keep me out in the shadows where nobody can find me. You can organise to get me the book. Now, this conversation is over. Today I drink beer, and I celebrate the life of my son. Although he never gave me grandchildren, at least I still have my two grandsons, and I have my great-grandchildren from them. I am not alone. I am Ulwazi Dubazane, and I've earned my place in Alexandra.' She took a swig of her beer and she put it back down. 'Where is my sister-but-one?'

'I have arrived, my sister,' Bessie said. 'I am sorry, but the train from Kimberley was late getting to Jo'burg, but I'm here, with you in your sorrow today.'

'Does not matter that you were late. You came to support your family.' She hugged her, then stepped back. 'Now we can eat. Where is that calf that they have been *braaing* the whole day? I am starving, and I am ready to feast with lots of salt in honour of my son's passing.'

CHAPTER 34

LILY HIT another pothole in the road and had to correct her steering as she swerved to the left.

'Slow down,' Khanyi said to her. 'You should not be speeding on this road. You could hit a buck or worse, a child.'

'Believe it or not, I'm going the speed limit. It's the limit that's too high for the state of the road.' She eased off a little on the accelerator. 'You have a point though, and I guess everyone will still wait for me. I just hate being late.'

'That they will. They love your clinic time here,' Michael said from the back seat.

She looked in the rear-view mirror and saw Michael smile.

A grey lourie flew low in the road, and she slowed to avoid it. 'Lots of morning traffic on the Platfontein road today,' she said. This road was never busy. She drove past the school towards the clinic. 'It's really dry again; we could do with some more rain. Look at how the crops are drooping.'

Neither of her guards responded; there was nothing to say. They would feel the heat the moment she opened the door and they were out of the air-conditioned car.

She watched as women and children came out from underneath the 'waiting room': the shade cloth that she had bought and insisted that Piet and the men put up outside the clinic, and the benches that they had made of heavy wooden sleepers and cemented into the ground, so they wouldn't be stolen in the night. They went to stand where they had left their shoes, keeping their place in the line. 'Look at that, a long line of women as always,' she said. 'I wonder how many of the men see Piet when he's here? I really should ask him.'

'Probably the same, only they sneak into his place and are not so open about seeing a doctor as the women. Some men are very private about things that need doctors,' Michael said.

Lily smiled as she climbed out of the car. Already her two helpers, Coti and her sister, had the door at the back open, and all the containers of supplies were being passed along a human chain to be put inside the little room at the clinic.

Lily could hear the excitement of the small crowd, that the doctor was there and they would soon be seen. The kids seemed to scream a little louder.

'Good morning, *Dokotela* Lily,' Coti said.

'How're you feeling?' Lily asked.

'Good. I am still taking the medications. I am feeling much better,' Coti said.

Lily nodded. A few months ago, Coti had pretended not to know English to avoid talking to Lily because she didn't know her. Now she spoke it to her all the time. It was as if Lily curing her meningitis had opened a door to the community. 'Just keep taking it. Thank you for organising all the supplies.'

She noticed that both Michael and Khanyi had sat away from the door, but close enough that they would be with her should she need them. The women of Platfontein sort of looked at the security detail as their protectors, too.

'Right, a quick wipe down with the sterilised wipes, then we can begin the clinic, Coti,' Lily said.

Soon they were ready. And the morning flew past until Elise walked in, helped by another woman that Lily had not met yet.

Lily felt like she was back in Zam Zam, only this time it wasn't hunger and violence that was sucking the life out of people as she watched. It was AIDS. Elise had lost a lot of weight, fast. Her shoulder bones stuck out cruelly and her T-shirt slipped from her scrawny shoulders. While she still had her hair done neatly, her head seemed too big for her body.

'Elise, why didn't you ask Piet to get me here sooner? You didn't have to wait,' Lily said.

'I was not here. I was in the big city. As soon as you took David and Diamond, I went to Johannesburg to see if I could make better money for them for when I die. I ran out of my drugs while I was there.'

'They have government clinics in Johannesburg,' Lily said.

'Yes, but I couldn't get a job; it was a lie. Johannesburg, the city of gold, is a terrible place. I had to watch my money and make sure I had enough to come home. It was a mistake to leave Platfontein. The new South Africa is worse in the big city.'

'When did you get back?'

'Yesterday. I need more pills, *Dokotela* Lily, and I need you to make sure that David and Diamond are safe. I thought the pills would stop this happening. I never understood that if I stopped them, even for a month, that it would eat my body like this.'

Emotion choked in Lily's chest, threatening to rise up. 'Elise, your HIV looks like it has become full-blown AIDS. You're very ill.'

'I do not want to go to hospital and die in a bed where lots of other people just like me died before. I want to die free. Where I know that people look after each other. Where I know that you and Piet will make sure that my brother and sister are looked after and are not put into an orphanage. That they will have a better life than I did.'

'I don't have the authority to promise you that, Elise, but I will do everything I can to help Piet do what is best for your brother and sister.'

Elise began coughing, and while she stood next to her, patting her back gently, Lily could see that it pained the girl's lungs to take the bigger breaths necessary for the cough.

'Elise, what if you come to live at my place? David and Diamond can then spend more time with you, and you don't have to look after them. Bessie is doing a good job on that front. We have a little house there that Piet uses, but I'm sure that he won't mind you living in it for a while. I can get someone to come in and help you, too, a friend if you have one you want close by. I take it David hasn't seen you, or he would have said something to me about the amount of weight you have lost.'

'I would like that,' Elise said. 'To see him and Diamond happy, playing. It will make my passing easier.'

'Enough about passing, you had a setback, that is all. We can get some food into you, and we need to get your CD4 numbers back up. Don't give up just yet. Your family don't want you to leave them. There are other remedies to take the pain away, too; promise me if you come to live there, that you'll concentrate on getting better, not only for David and Diamond, but also for yourself.'

Lily hated grocery shopping. But she wanted to make Quintin a special anniversary dinner, so to surprise him she needed to go to the shops. Khanyi walked beside her as always, but Natalie had decided to grab a few groceries herself and had put them in Lily's trolley so that she wasn't hampered by anything while they walked around the shop.

They paid for their purchases and walked out of Checkers.

'You ready for your big anniversary dinner cook-up?' Natalie asked. 'The evening is—'

The shots came out of nowhere.

Lily felt pain and heat as something too familiar tore through her leg. The agony ripped through her flesh for only a moment as she heard Khanyi shout, 'Down!' and he pushed both of them to the pavement.

Duck and cover. Get to safety. The training that Khanyi had been doing with her kicked in, and she rolled up into a ball as tightly as she could. She could feel his body over hers. The shots continued, coming from different directions. One hit the pavement near her head.

'We need to get under cover,' Natalie said.

Lily tried to get to her knees to crawl away, but only one of her legs would cooperate. More shots rang out.

'Shit, I'm hit,' Natalie cursed. She had her weapon out and was returning fire towards the two taxis shooting at each other.

'Where?' Khanyi asked.

'Shoulder. I'll be fine.' A bullet hit the steel pipe behind them, and shrapnel exploded around.

'They are definitely shooting at us,' Natalie said, getting her phone out and quickly dialling a number. 'Piet, we're under heavy fire in the parking lot at Checkers. Two taxis. Come quick.'

'Come on; we don't need to stay around and be shot at more. I'll cover you while you get under cover,' Khanyi said.

'No, you go first. Lily can't run, she took a shot in the leg. Carry her, get her out of here. Looks like a taxi war across the parking lot is picking up!' Natalie was shouting as she was returning fire.

People were screaming and running everywhere, the gunshots reverberating all around them.

'Ready, Lily. On my three. One. Two. Three,' Khanyi said as he half lifted Lily by her middle like a sack of potatoes to run while keeping low.

The war came to them.

Multiple shots could be heard, only this time instead of the *ting* as the bullet hit the concrete and ricocheted away, there were hollow *thwack*s as bullets sank deep into flesh.

Lily waited for the familiar burn of the bullet. But there was nothing.

He half threw her, half dropped her. She crashed on the concrete pavement, her head skipping like a stone across water on the hard surface, until she came to a stop, crumpled against the wall. 'Khanyi, you okay?' Lily asked.

Khanyi landed heavily on top of her.

From his weight, she knew that this time he was not trying to shield her.

He'd taken the shots.

'Khanyi!' she shouted. 'Natalie!'

Neither of them answered.

CHAPTER 35

ULWAZI WATCHED the television news in the shebeen.

'Detective Natalie Hatch died in hospital today, after being wounded in a drive-by shooting in Kimberley last week. It is with great sadness that she becomes yet another victim of taxi violence which has spilled out onto the streets of Kimberley, Upington and across the Cape Province this Christmas season. The Taxi Association is blaming the latest violence outbreak on ...'

'A fitting reward. She was no hero. Just because she has a badge did not mean that she was allowed to shoot my son in cold blood. Nobody stands up on TV and says that my son was shot by this hero. She gets away with murder because she wears police clothes,' Ulwazi said.

Sithole shook his head. 'Ulwazi, what have you done?'

'I am innocent. That was the taxi wars. They should have happened before. When she shot my son.'

'No, Ulwazi, this is one of your worst mistakes ever,' Sithole said. 'The man who is this woman's best friend is like a bloodhound. He will come looking for you. He will not stop. This man will get us even if he has to wait for his whole life. He is a patient but deadly policeman. I know this Detective Piet Kleinman, what he is capable of. He was part of a team who put a lot of powerful men away a few years ago in a gang-rape case that should never have gone to court. He has influential friends. Friends who know people. Ones who can operate on South African soil and have more teeth than the whole South African police force. He will come after you. Come after us. He will find out what you did, and he will not stop until you are behind bars.'

'Jail does not scare me,' Ulwazi said.

'Where he will put you should. If you even get there. You need to tell me who did this so that I can close the door, and they can never speak of what you did.'

'You do not need to "clean up" after me,' Ulwazi said.

'Actually, I do. You need me now more than you ever did before. Your son is gone. Your muscle. Your grandson Zenzele is already dying of the thinnings disease. Your other grandson listens to no one, and he is on a collision course for a bullet in his brain the way things are going. He runs around doing what he wants to like an American gangster living in Johannesburg. Neither of your grandchildren can help you with this. What will the taxi drivers do when they find that it was you who started it? That it was a hit on the policewoman and not a territory dispute, because that is probably the information you told them, wasn't it? When the retaliations began immediately after that, the wars started once more. Those are real men dying out there, in a dispute created from false information fed to them by you. You lied to the Taxi Association members; they will come after you.'

Ulwazi slowly nodded. 'They will not dare touch me. They all know better.'

'Once maybe, not anymore. Now they see you as old and weak. A grandmother who has no discipline for her grandchildren. This time you killed a cop, and you manipulated the taxi drivers to begin a war again without them having gained anything from it. The cops will hunt you down. There will be no business if the information queen herself is shot and killed. I do not want to walk away from you; this business brings me good money, and perhaps soon it can bring me even more because I will help you watch over your business until your great-grandchildren can take over. So, let me make sure that it continues to bring both of us good money. I need names. Ulwazi, who did you pay to shoot Detective Hatch?'

CHAPTER 36

PIET DRUMMED his fingers on his desk.

'One plus one does not equal five, no matter what the reality,' he said, looking at the pictures of the crime scene in front of him.

His best friend. Natalie.

It was hard to see the pictures, knowing that she was once so vibrant and active; now to anyone looking at the crime scene, she was a chalk cross and a dried blood pool on the cold concrete of the pavement. He touched the photograph where she had laid before the paramedics had resuscitated her the first time.

It hadn't been enough. She had died a week later anyway.

The twelfth of December was now burned into his memory as a day to remember the fallen.

If only he had been closer.

He wished there was a way to turn back the clock and change that day; he would give everything to have been there to prevent her death. Breanna had gone to live with her grandparents, and she had not sent Piet a single picture of a puppy since her mother's death. He missed the texts from his goddaughter. He needed to text her, check on her, but it hurt his heart.

There was more to the taxi incident, and he knew better than to look at it at face value.

'Detective Kleinman?' a young voice said next to him.

'Yes?'

'I'm Constable Makoni Namane. Acting Chief Chetty told me to come find you—I'm your new partner.'

Piet ground his teeth. No one in the police force was supposed to be irreplaceable, that was the nature of the work. But Chetty knew that he and Natalie had been friends, too, and he had hoped for more time alone. He had chosen not to take grievance leave on purpose; he would mourn his friend once he'd caught her killer. That was what he could do for her.

Get her justice.

He would not allow her to be yet another unsolved case in the growing pile of murders happening in South Africa.

'I have removed all of Nat—Detective Hatch's personal effects; the space is free.'

'I heard you had a special, long friendship, and that's exceptional. I wish I could have known her,' Constable Makoni Namane said.

Piet watched his new partner, who was putting his backpack on Natalie's desk. The skinny black man was perhaps in his early twenties, and his uniform hung on him from shoulders that had yet to fill out. His chest needed time to broaden. His hair was shaved close to his head, in the fashion of one who only recently got out of the police college. The poor *laaitie* had no idea what he was stepping into. Piet stood up and extended his hand. 'Good to have you on board. I guess it's a new year, new beginnings to us, then.'

They shook hands.

'Chetty said that you're working on a complicated case. He said that you would bring me up to speed. He also said that I had drawn the short straw being your partner. What does he mean?'

'Acting Chief Chetty is an idiot, and will be out the door within a month; then you will meet a real chief. Come,' Piet said. 'We can go into one of the meeting rooms, and I can get you up to speed on what's been happening. You are starting in the middle of a major investigation. Tell me, Makoni, are you good with computers?'

'Yes,' Makoni said.

'Good. I hate the things. We should get on well.' Piet picked up the files he had been looking at and walked towards the room with the big boardroom table in the middle. 'You coming?'

Makoni rushed to the room as if there was a fire behind him.

Piet closed the door, put the files on the table and started to bring Makoni up to speed.

About three hours later, Makoni said, 'In school, no one picked me for their sports team because I was too uncoordinated. But in varsity, people always wanted to be my partner, because they say I have keen analytical skills and can see things that others miss. In the police college it changed. People recognised that while I was skinny, I was also very fit. Those same people noticed that I could analyse things as a big picture, and still pick out the threads that held the ideas together.'

'Yes, so? As my partner, I expect you to have an opinion and to express it. It is not a partnership unless both of us work together. What do you see?'

'A big question on motivation.'

'What?' Piet asked.

'I understand the hijackings, the weapons, the link to organised crime. What I don't get is how did the information fall into the hands of Kagiso and his mother, Ulwazi Dubazane, for them to have a hit on the doctors? And if the medical-aid-fraud assessor is related—as the same MO suggests—how did Kagiso Dubazane know where to find Dr Winters that day?'

Piet nodded. 'Both good questions—I don't have an answer to either. We've been trying to figure it out.'

Makoni nodded.

'Here is another one for you. Look at the second part and the taxis' shootout photographs. Look at where Detective Hatch was shot, and where Khanyi took four bullets in his butt protecting Lily. What do you see?'

Makoni looked at the pictures. He then rearranged them on the table. 'Do you have any string?'

'Should be some in the drawer over there,' Piet said.

Makoni grabbed it and then began laying the blue string from the pictures back to where the taxis should have been. Then he put the pictures of where the shopping party were shot. And he laid the string from there, to the taxis.

'I am simply a constable and have only been out of the academy for a few months, but I have always loved forensic science. This wasn't a taxi war. This was an execution. No bystanders were injured, and both taxis got away with no casualties from either of them at the scene. They were likely not shooting at each other, but because there were no vehicles recovered, we can't be certain. The shells ejected out of open windows indicate multiple shots. You would expect some blood. Something. All the taxi attacks after this one, we have had bodies?'

'Every single one here in Kimberley was a bloodbath, drivers and passengers caught in the carnage. This incident is the anomaly. What else do you see?' Piet asked.

'One or two people have shot at a ninety-degree angle to where the other taxi should have been. Not at the taxis, but directly at the people shopping. They were either trying to get to the doctor, or Detective Hatch was the intended target all along.'

'Why do you think Detective Hatch was the target?'

'Organised crime. The file on your original attempted hijack on Dr Lily Winters. Detective Hatch was named as the policewoman who fatally shot Kagiso Dubazane. I would put my money on this being a revenge killing, made to look like a taxi war by the Dubazane organisation.'

Piet nodded his head. He had landed with a smart partner, young but intelligent, and not afraid to speak his mind either. 'I also arrived at that. It is good to get confirmation from a fresh set of eyes. Here is the picture I took, doing exactly the same as you with string earlier today.' He showed his mobile phone, and the strings were multicoloured. 'We have a cop-killing gang on our hands.'

CHAPTER 37

LILY SAT AT HER DESK. After her six weeks away on crutches to allow her leg to heal, she had been looking forward to getting back to work again. The shot had gone straight through her thigh and hadn't done much damage, but the shock of the incident had triggered nightmares again, as had happened after she left Zam Zam.

Now she knew she would have to face what was coming head on. There was no running from it.

Zam Zam had been life-threatening. She and Quintin had driven different vehicles out of there, carrying many of the nurses and doctors with them. They had fled as fast as they could from the rebels who had sacked the place behind them and killed many of the refugees, then tortured and raped many more. They had not got away unscathed, but they had been able to get away.

Those left behind had had nowhere to go to.

Ian's opinions on the situation had been valued over hers, because she was a female. Now she knew why he'd had such determination and been so adamant the drug drop would happen the next day. It burned her stomach to think that he had been so selfish on one hand, and yet, on the other, so giving, even if it was a risky move that he'd made for the refugees. She wished that he had trusted her enough to confide in her then, but the likelihood of her going along with his hairbrained scheme then was exactly nil.

She and Quintin were simply too law-abiding to get involved with anything like what Ian had been up to. And for that she was thankful.

She took a deep breath.

'Lily, you survived that. Quintin survived. Together you can do this,' she said quietly to herself. But the memories kept tumbling in like a movie that wouldn't end.

Back then, she didn't know Ian had been paying the rebels, who had turned on him anyway. Obviously, there was no honesty or integrity among thieves and rebels, of any sort.

WHO had supported his decision to delay the evacuation, even saying that Lily was overreacting when she had voiced her opinion about the delay. To give Ian credit where it was due, the drugs did arrive. A huge bomber airdropped the expected aid package. But the rebels followed the bombers and drove right into the heart of Zam Zam. And Lily and Quintin had had to flee and return to the safety of Australia, leaving the whole nightmare situation behind.

It was the first time as aid workers that they had abandoned a refugee camp. But that was not possible this time. There was no leaving. This had become personal. She would never outrun it.

She looked again at the comprehensive report from her MRI. But she didn't need to. The images were burned onto her brain already. She would never forget it. Well ironically, she supposed she would.

She gave a stilted laugh.

While her initial MRI had been done for a suspected concussion, the new comparison MRI was only a few weeks old. It was taken in the hospital after the attack at the shopping centre that had killed Natalie. Robert Mayer had called her into his office to deliver the results and discuss options with her, but even now, she could scarcely remember anything he'd said, even though it was only an hour ago.

These images showed much more than she'd ever expected. It wasn't good.

She walked over to the light box on the wall and clipped up her old plates, and one of the newer plates next to it. There it was—no brain swelling associated with a concussion in the second plate. Instead, clear as day in the comparison was the loss of brain mass associated with Alzheimer's disease, the shrinking hippocampus. A substantial decline in size, enough that she could see it, even without the helpful computerised ruler laid across it, giving her the accurate measurements.

She could not catch a break since coming to South Africa. She was a doctor, how had she not picked up the symptoms in herself?

Early-onset Alzheimer's.

Her fingers were shaking badly as she ran them through her hair, and she stumbled back to her chair. Taking a deep breath, she googled 'Ten signs of Alzheimer's'. Lily read it not because she needed to, but because she wanted to double-check. She printed the pages, waiting as they churned out one by one. Lifting the papers, she stacked them into a neat pile, then picked up a pen. She began to put dates and tried to remember when she'd first shown the symptoms. She knew she was going to have to see somebody else and explore further. Her usual doctor was back in Australia.

As a doctor, when a patient came to her, she'd normally recommend that the family get involved right away and she would check the situation between the patient and the family so she could assess exactly what it was and if the patient would need other support. She didn't want to upset Quintin, but she knew that she needed his hand to hold through the tests that were going to follow.

She didn't want to face this alone.

Robert Mayer had suggested she contact a specialist, Mr Neel Coetzee, in Johannesburg. Lily looked at Neel's number and swallowed hard. She'd studied for years to be a doctor to be able to diagnose diseases such as this in patients and help, yet she'd never dreamed that she'd be diagnosed herself, just shy of sixty, with early-onset Alzheimer's. Lily took a deep breath and let it out slowly before she reached for the phone and called the doctor's rooms.

After speaking with the specialist and making an appointment for Friday, she put down the phone. They'd discussed how he'd do a CT and PET scan—where they'd inject a low-level radioactive tracer into her blood in the hope it would reveal any peculiar features in the brain, like areas of low metabolism which would help him diagnose Alzheimer's or another type of dementia. And she'd agreed to courier the MRI and blood works she'd already had done to him.

Quintin, you at home? Got comprehensive results from MRI and we need to talk.

Sounds serious. I'm free NOW. Your clinic or home?

Home. I'm on my way.

I'm in my studio, as always. xoxo♥

This was one appointment she couldn't do alone—she didn't feel that she had the right to do it alone either. Having a patient diagnosed with early-onset Alzheimer's led to hard decisions for both the doctor and the patient. Many people didn't have enough time to process the knowledge that their loved one was about to be lost to them. She didn't want to do that to Quintin. He'd always been there—right next to her. He'd questioned some of her symptoms long before she'd even noticed them, and found ways to work around them, without ever making her feel inadequate.

As sick as she felt at the news, she had to share it with him. She knew that somehow, they'd handle it together.

The afternoon sun was warming the dining room, coming through the net curtains and making strange shadows across the glossy table. Sitting at the head of the dining-room table was Lily, and in the chair to her left, Quintin. Telling him the news, and seeing the love of her life having to process that ultimately she was terminal, was heartbreaking.

'You sure you want to do this here and not go home to Australia?' Quintin asked. 'We have the best specialists back home.'

'They have great specialists here, too. Besides, I can't leave. We're about to start closing in on the drug company, and I need to be here for it.'

'I know. I understand. But it was worth a try.'

She lifted her hand and cupped his chin. 'I love you.'

Quintin kissed her. 'Love you too. And you're not going to be doing this by yourself. We haven't done things that way in all the years we've been married, so we're not about to start now.'

Quintin held her hand as they walked into her appointment. Mr Neel Coetzee gestured for her to sit down and then he sat behind the desk. The office was light, modern—nothing like hers. It had plush deep-blue carpets, a set of leather chairs to one side and a huge glass desk that dominated the other side of the room. His Apple computer stood proudly on his desk, and as she looked around, the only personal item she could see was an old leather donkey sitting on its own shelf, away from all the books.

'Good to meet you,' he said.

Lily held her breath. Even facing the evidence of her MRI, she still held out hope that it could be something else. Something that she and the other doctors hadn't thought of.

'Lily, I've reviewed your results, along with your blood works, and they've ruled out a few other potential causes for your problems. Your thyroid is fine, and you have no vitamin deficiencies, although you could do with some iron tablets. We need to do one or two more tests, then I can give you my diagnosis.'

Lily nodded and squeezed Quintin's hand.

'Quintin,' he said, 'have you noticed if Lily forgets to do anything with her personal hygiene?'

Quintin shook his head. 'Lily wears a uniform to work, so it's a little hard to tell if it's the same one on consecutive days. But Bessie, our maid, would've commented on not having anything to wash. Lily's still looking after herself—she showers, washes her hair, brushes her teeth.'

Neel nodded. 'Lily, I need to do a physical exam to assess your overall neurological health.'

'Okay,' she said.

'Catch.' He threw her a soft stress ball from his side of the table.

Lily tried to catch it, but it slipped through her fingers.

'That's okay,' he said. 'We'll try a few other things for reflexes later. Why don't you go make yourself comfortable on one of the lounge chairs.'

As Lily walked across the room, he whispered loudly to Quintin, 'Do you think she can hear me still?'

'Of course I can hear you,' she said. 'I'm still in the same room.'

'Thanks, Lily,' he said. 'There're a few "obstacles" on the carpet behind the couch here; I want you to follow the numbers and do each one.'

She went to start the exercises. She'd never seen them done quite this way, but as she was doing them, she understood why—Neel was different from other specialists. He'd found innovative ways to test his patients.

Finally, she and Quintin were seated together again, and Neel was looking at her.

'Lily, there's no easy way to say this, but I'm confirming your suspicions. You definitely have signs of early-onset Alzheimer's. Thankfully, it can be managed. We can slow it down with drugs. But we can't stop it altogether. Don't go and resign or anything major. I recommend that you don't make any huge decisions alone anymore where your finances or your living arrangements are concerned.'

'I didn't want to hear that news,' Lily said.

'I understand why. It is never an easy diagnosis to deliver either,' Neel said.

Quintin said, 'I married Lily for better or for worse, so we'll face this together to the very end.'

'Quintin, you need to understand that these drugs won't make it go away. We've caught it early and can treat it, so we hope that we can push her to about a year, perhaps two, before Lily will need to stop work. By then she won't be capable of making her own decisions; it's all going to depend on how she reacts to the medications.'

'I'm still here,' Lily said. 'In the room.'

'I know. But sometimes I've found that for the person who has the ailment, it's easier to process the information when it's not directed at you, but through your spouse. You hear it all and process it, but if I were telling it directly to you, you would've thrown up a wall and stopped listening as soon as I confirmed your diagnosis.'

'Can I ask you something?' Lily said.

'Of course.'

'How long have I got? How long before I regress so much in my mind that I don't know Quintin and I've no idea what year it is anymore?'

'Realistically, knowing what is happening to you, the rate of shrinkage being substantial in your MRIs—within four years. We've diagnosed you early, and we'll have you on treatment. If you weren't on treatment, it might have been faster.'

'And how long do I have left to live?'

'Total shut down within six years. Unless you're extremely lucky. I'm putting you on cholinesterase inhibitors. Quintin, these drugs are to help preserve a chemical messenger that's depleted in Lily's brain by the disease. Also, Memantine, which will help slow the progression. I'm also going to prescribe an antidepressant.'

'I've never taken an antidepressant in my life,' Lily said.

'You're about to start,' Neel said. 'You'll thank me for them when they help lessen some of the side effects of the cholinesterase inhibitors.'

Lily opened her mouth to tell him that she was not about to take any pills that had been dispensed in South Africa, then shut it again. She couldn't tell him. 'Can you prescribe the genuine, not the generic drugs, please,' she said instead. She couldn't go public with her findings yet. There were still so many loose ends that she and Piet had to tie up. They were still waiting on the results from the drugs she had sent to Switzerland for testing.

And they were still on the hunt for Natalie's killer.

Quintin lay in bed next to his wife in the hotel in Johannesburg. She had turned her back to him, but he knew he needed to reach her.

'We need time to process what Neel said. We can't hide from it. We are going to have to face it,' he said, and kissed the back of her neck.

'I know it's not something we can run away from. But for now, I can try not to think about it.'

'You and I both know it doesn't work that way. You clammed up on me. You told me yesterday you didn't want to talk about it, and while you cried with me last night, we need to process your diagnosis.'

'I'm still too angry. Too sore.'

'I get that. But you need to tell me what's inside your head. It's not going away.'

'It's part of us until it fades from my memory and I don't know that I'm ill anymore. Until I don't even know where I am and who you are. But for you—it's going to be there until the day I die. You're going to lose me twice. Once when my mind goes, and I don't know you anymore, and again when my body dies. It's not fair, Quintin. It's not fair.' She sobbed as tears ran freely down her cheeks and she turned towards him.

He held her close. 'You're right—it's not fair.'

'I want to hit something. I want to scream at the world. Everything I've done in my life has been to preserve life, and then life throws this at us. I'm going to go from a doctor to a slobbering, uncoordinated body whose mind has checked out on her. An adult who needs her nappy changed.'

He kissed the top of her head as tears ran down his face. 'But you will still be my *wifie* and my best friend. You'll still be mine. And I'll still be there with you. Right beside you. I will make sure that those nappies are the best, and softest, that money can buy.'

Lily laughed despite herself, while the tears still streamed down her face.

'Just know I'll be there with you.'

'I keep having that song from *Evita*—"You Must Love Me"—play over and over in my head.'

'Lily, you know I would never abandon you. I promise you now that I won't. We're in this together to the end. And I'll love you always. I'm not going anywhere.'

'You say that now. But this disease destroys people. Confuses them. Erodes away everything decent that they were. Some people become violent, and they're so horrible to their spouses. What if I become so ghastly to live with that you need to put me in a nursing home in restraints? I've seen too many old people in those homes like that. I've seen how senior citizens get treated. Then what? You visit me on a Sunday between three and five for visiting hours, and forget I exist for the rest of the week? What if I treat you so badly when I love you so much, and I don't know that I'm being a bitch to you?'

'It won't be like that, Lily. We'll manage it together. And I couldn't put you in any aged-care facility. You'll stay with me.'

'Not if we go back to Australia. The authorities there have the right to remove a spouse from the care of their partner. I've seen it done before, where one is put into care and the other one only gets to visit.'

'If you're worried about that, then we'll stay here in South Africa, or we live somewhere else. We can afford to hire highly qualified staff and keep you in our own home. Believe me, they're not taking you away from me. Not now. Not ever. I'm sure that regulations like that don't apply to people like us, who can do better than what an institution can offer.'

'What if we run out of money?'

'We won't, Lily, we have more than enough. But I promise you, if it looks like we are going to, I'd rather sell everything, even La Angelique, and live with you in a shack than lose you. You're my world.'

'But I'm going to die on you! I'm going to leave you alone! Someone else is going to grow old with you and hold your hand, and it won't be me. We were going to be together when we were old. To walk naked on the beach at Cap d'Agde in France and shock the world with not caring about our wrinkled bodies.'

Quintin laughed. 'I can see us now, walking hand in hand, and the paparazzi turning away, not bothering to take a picture of the two oldies walking together with the saggy boobs and the shrivelled-up penis. We can still do that; we'll merely have to do it a bit earlier than we had planned.'

Lily smiled, and she brought his head closer to hers for a kiss. 'I cannot see how to go forward from here, Quintin. There are so many chemicals in these pills and so much uncertainty in the South African medication. I can't trust them.'

'Your tainted-drugs case aside, I understood what Neel was saying about the drugs not being a total cure. About the drugs just slowing down the disease. Remember, his dates are only guesstimates, too. But until the time that you're lost totally to me, we can't give up. I promise you that we're going to pack in as much living as we can. We're going to create more memories to stack into that brain and find ways to help you remember them when that mind of yours decides to forget, and we're not going to let anyone tear us apart. No matter if your body gives up or not. You'll always be with me.'

'You know I love you?' Lily said.

'From the moment I saw you on the dance floor, and I couldn't believe my luck when I opened my eyes in that hospital and saw you sleeping in that awful chair, even when you weren't in your doctor's uniform. I knew that I loved you, and I would love you till the very end. And if the end is coming faster than we planned, then at least we get to face it together.'

Lily hugged him tightly.

'I know that we're going to have to face the practicalities, too. I understand that. As Neel said, we're going to need to make plans to monitor you. I need you to promise that you'll tell me everything, and that you won't conceal anything. Don't shut me out. I'll need to know the whole shebang, from if you forget your meds, to if you experience anything strange. It'll mean changes for us—you've always been so independent—and now we'll need to pull together, and not let this destroy us.'

'I'll try, Quintin. I'll try.'

'Talking pills. After you went to sleep, I emailed that script to our doctor in Australia, and he's organising a courier to deliver your Australian-made drugs to the house within a few days. You will be safe from these thugs here who are tainting pills, no matter what. There are some advantages to being who we are.'

Lily kissed him again. 'Thank you.'

'So, *wifie*, are we okay?'

'Always. But I have lots of stomach-churning going on right now.'

'Understandable, given we just had our world blown apart,' Quintin said.

They turned into Hacienda El Paradiso. The stars had seemed so bright when they were driving. Lily sat outside in the driveway looking at the house. Bessie had once again put the lights on, so they weren't walking into a darkened building. Lily hoped Bessie hadn't stayed up and had gone to bed long ago.

The lights were also on in the security cottage, as expected, as they were in Elise's cottage. The main lights in the house also blazed out a welcome.

'Do you think the house knows that we've come back?'

'I don't know about the house, but I do know that there's a cat that ran out to greet us. Look. Here comes Tiger.'

Tiger came out of the bushes and was running towards the Land Cruiser. Lily opened the door, and the cat all but scrambled into the car as if it was a dog trying to get onto her lap and headbutt her.

'I would say that's a happy cat,' Quintin said. 'One that really missed you.'

The cat was yowling at her and then it jumped off her lap and into Quintin's to say hello to him. 'I've never known such an affectionate cat.'

'I've got to admit I'm as happy to see this cat as he is to see us. We're home, Tiger!' she said as he found his way back onto her lap. She wrapped her arm around him and, picking him up, she hugged him close as he continued to yowl like a set of bagpipes as she held him—all the time purring and meowing. After a while, she let him go and he jumped out of the car. She got out too, and as he headed towards the house, he stopped and turned around, as if to make sure that they were following him, all the while talking to them.

'That's the best kind of homecoming,' Lily said.

'I have to agree. It's lovely to know that an animal missed us, even if we were only gone for three days. Go inside; I'll bring the bags.'

Lily walked into Hacienda El Paradiso. It seemed so familiar—like she was walking into her own home.

Lily sat on their bed, her back against the pillow wedged between her and the antique cast-iron frame. She stared at the list of medications that Neel had suggested she begin, and all the side effects they could cause.

Tiger heard the crinkle of the paper and attempted to jump on it. Lily had to hold it up with one hand above her head to save it, as Tiger sank his claws deep into the other.

'Ouch. No, Tiger. I'm not on the menu.'

He let go of her hand and apologised by butting his head against her tummy. Then he jumped off the bed and headed out the door, towards the kitchen, looking for breakfast.

'The monster drew blood,' Quintin said as he wrapped a tissue around her fingers.

'It's okay, I'm fine. Just got a fright. I didn't want him to destroy the list. It looks like I'm in for some scary side effects.'

'We'll handle it. One day at a time,' Quintin said. 'That and our overzealous cat.'

'I love you, you know that?' Lily said.

Quintin held her hand against his lips and kissed it. 'I know.' And then kissed up her arm. 'I never get tired of hearing you say it. I love you too.'

Lily reached over and ran her fingers down his cheek, feeling the new growth of his beard. Sandpaper against the soft tips of her fingers. She shivered and whispered, 'You were asking about something before Tiger so rudely interrupted us.'

Quintin kissed her fingers before holding her hand captive in his and placing it on his chest. 'We're doing what we can. We'll take each new day as a gift. And when your mind forgets, we'll simply have to make more new memories.'

'Over and over again,' she said.

'Ah—but think of the fun we can have making them,' Quintin said.

Lily sighed mockingly. 'Okay, I guess we're just going to have to put some effort into making these memories decadent enough to make the brain neurons all light up together and work better.'

CHAPTER 38

SITHOLE SAT WAITING in the stolen 4x4, just up from the four-way intersection outside Ayurprabhu Pharmaceuticals. The street was so quiet it had the feeling of being abandoned. All the workers had scurried back to their shacks and houses across the city at this time of night. The buildings, lit by security lights, advertised false hope in their cheeriness, when in reality they were places that sucked the souls from every worker.

The standard six-foot fence topped with razor wire flew flags of plastic bags, blown there by the wind. Tattered until they decomposed, no one was going to clean them from the wire, and they would eventually be loose and catch on another obstacle, or land in the ocean one day. A legacy left by cheap disposable bags once used in this country.

The security guard on the boom gate opened the red-and-white barrier that was designed to keep out unwanted visitors, both in vehicles or on foot. Security cameras were mounted outside, pointing to where people would be expected: the driveway and the parking lot. The intersection was a dead spot for them. Sithole wasn't taking any chances though; his balaclava was pulled over his face. You could never be too careful.

He looked in the rear-view mirror, where he could see his captain in a stolen *bakkie*. Their getaway car.

Mishti Prabhu's silver Mercedes Benz coasted up to the security gate, and then through. He started his motor, ensuring that his lights were off. She drove out of the gate and towards the four-way intersection. He knew she'd go straight through, ignoring the road rules like most females at night. He'd watched her do it every night for the past week.

He looked about. There was no other traffic around. He pulled out into the road and gunned his engine, gaining momentum. If she saw him, she would break, and he would continue through the stop signage as if nothing was supposed to take place, but if she followed her habit, she wouldn't give him a fleeting glance.

He looked at his speedometer and pressed down on the accelerator. He could see her coming towards their intersection. He would hit the driver's side directly where she sat. An instant death was always preferable to the screaming of a woman. Or the impossible mission of attempting again in a private hospital to complete a contract.

He was confident that his vehicle was the bigger and stronger of the two. Her new Mercedes Benz was designed to crumple, to take the impact, but not this style of side-on collision with a weighted force.

He changed gears, his leather driving glove gripping on the knob of the lever, despite the amount of sweat from his palm that it held firmly inside. The engine responded, giving him more speed, even though it held a load of bricks on the back. The 4x4 was designed as a workhorse, its engine a coiled spring of energy, waiting to be unleashed.

If he couldn't drive away successfully, by the time the police came to the scene, many of those bricks would be missing, as news went out to those living close by that a truck with building materials had been in an accident. Looters were potentially his friend tonight. If it went south, his captain was there as a backup, as always, to pull him from the wreckage and remove him from the scene of the crime.

He allowed himself one more glance at the approaching lights and nodded. From years of experience, he knew that if it went well, they should collide. If not, there was always the next night.

Instinct was too strong not to swerve, but if you chose to avoid looking, you could trick your body and mind not to respond. He looked down at the speedometer, checking the temperature of the engine, and the small amount of fuel in the tank. Removing his eyes from the oncoming road, ensuring his mind was on other minor details. The pain from the collision would only last a few days.

The impact with Mishti's car threw him forward. His airbag deployed, cushioning him in an instant, before deflating again. The motion jerked him back in his seat as the seatbelt tightened up, holding him firmly in place.

He heard glass smashing. Then tinkling. Falling on metal as it made its journey down to the road. His hearing had become sensitised in the moment of impact.

Sithole let out a breath he hadn't realised he was holding. It sounded loud, ragged, even to him. He opened his eyes to look out.

The Mercedes in front of him had indeed crumpled. It looked like it had wrapped itself around the stainless-steel bull bar. He had hit it directly in the centre of the driver's door. His 4x4 was no longer running. The onboard car computer had done its job and immediately cut power to the engine.

He turned the key. It started again. He smiled as he put it in reverse and attempted to back up. The metal in the front groaned and complained; he gave more power to the engine. The metal gave way with a ripping sound.

He saw that the front door of the Mercedes was still attached to his bull bar, mangled into it. He could see the woman slumped over her steering wheel. She wasn't moving.

Eish, the things he would rather have done with this pretty rich Indian woman. But a contract was a contract. He did what he was paid to do.

Turning the steering wheel, his 4x4 responded. Everything appeared to be working. He drove around her smashed-up car and down the road. In his rear-view mirror, he could see that her security guard was running towards her car. '*Ag* shame, *gijima,* my china, but you are already too late to save her.'

CHAPTER 39

IT TURNED out that waiting for someone to come out of hiding and kill you, even when you'd employed the best security force available to protect you, wasn't actually so good for the mind. In fact, it was driving Lily crazy. She second-guessed everyone she met at the supermarket, the clinic, and even in her practice. She'd begun spooking at shadows.

According to Khanyi, that was normal and she was doing fine. She certainly didn't feel fine. But she was physically better than him. He was healing and had a little help from more staff while he was getting better, mostly coordinating the team now as he did his physical therapy and got himself moving again. He'd been lucky. Having fallen and hit his head, he'd been knocked out, so he now sported a new scar on his hairline for that, but the four shots he had taken in his backside and into the top of this thighs had miraculously missed every vital organ and surrounding bones.

Sunday was creeping past with the pace of a snail. Lily was walking back to the house after checking on Elise. She worried that the young woman would die anytime now. She was counting hours rather than days.

'Afternoon, Lily,' Piet said, waving as he got out of his *bakkie*.

She waved back and smiled. Only Piet could remain upbeat when the security company knew he was a policeman and yet still insisted on escorting him across the property.

'I am here for the camp-out I promised with David and Maddy. Mason said that he was going to join us for the fun of late-night fire and the marshmallows.'

Lily hit her forehead with her hand. 'Oh no, I totally forgot. That's okay; the kids will still love it as a surprise, I'm sure.'

Usually, she would organise nice food and snacks to spoil them when they were camping out, but this time they would have to raid the pantry and make do.

'Right, so, if we go tell them, I think they had Minke and were taking her for a swim at the dam by the willow tree. She's getting good at spreading her wings and trying hard to walk on water.'

'She is a flamingo; she should be able to do it naturally. But I am happy that they are exercising her, getting her ready for her release,' Piet said.

'I think they like the walk to the dam and taking bags of carrots to Perdy, Dee-Dee and Pedro, and of course, food for the ducks. I'm not sure what they are going to do when that bird goes back to the wild, they'll be so lost. Maddy's parents must think that we've taken her permanently.'

Piet smiled. 'In our culture, you can share children to help other people if they need a little space. To stop a husband and wife fighting, you can take their children to live with you for a few days so they can make nice and live in harmony again.'

'That's all very well, but we have had her … however long we have had her, but it seems a long time in my head. David and Diamond, that's a different story to Maddy. Have you given any more thought as to what will happen to them?'

'*Ja*, we spoke about this already.'

Lily looked at him. 'I'm blank.'

'I told you that I can't take them, not legally. I already have too many other responsibilities. At least when Natalie died, she had her parents still alive to take Breanna. If something happens to me in my line of work, they will be no better off once again. I think the best is to let them go to a foster home. Perhaps someone will be able to take them together. I hope so.'

'We did. You're right, now that you mention that, it's all coming back,' Lily said.

'You should increase your CBD oil intake. Let it help your brain more.'

'I will,' Lily said. 'I have to admit that I never thought I would be the one taking the oil, but there you go. I suppose stranger things in life have happened.'

'We need to make more soon. Lincoln and I will make it, and Quintin wanted to help this time.'

'I guess Quintin has never been what one might call a traditional husband,' Lily said.

'I will get the camping gear out of the big shed, and then find the children.'

'Piet, I have been editing your book, and it's looking good. Perhaps later we can sit and go through some of it—I'll print out another copy. For me, too, because the one I am using is starting to look quite tatty.'

'That would be good,' Piet said.

'Enjoy your camp-out. I know the kids love them,' Lily said.

Piet woke under the stars, next to the embers of the fire. The moon was at about three o'clock in the sky, so it was between two and three in the morning—the darkest hours. The noise he heard was not right. He lay quietly listening to see if it would come again.

There it was.

Opening one eye, he looked around. He couldn't see anyone close by. He opened the other and moved his head.

The person walked silently. He was good in the bush. The security guards had walked past a few times; they were not so soft on their feet; they didn't have anything to hide. But someone else did.

Piet sat up. The noise was coming from the direction of the gate. He looked into the open tent that Mason slept in. He was asleep on his mattress, and his soft snore was clearly audible. He checked on the second tent where David and Maddy slept. They were vulnerable if there was an intruder here.

The security company had not given him a button like they made Lily wear around her neck, to press for help if she felt threatened or needed assistance quickly. Silently, he crept into the children's tent. He had to get them to safety. Then he would raise the security company for help.

Piet put his hand over David's mouth and shook his shoulder. David opened his eyes, and Piet motioned for him. David nodded. Piet woke up Maddy the same way. When they were both awake, he signalled for them to follow him and keep silent.

He woke up Mason quietly, and he was up in seconds, ready to move. On his way past his bedroll on the ground, Piet picked up his bow and arrow quiver, and put it over his shoulder.

'Where're we going?' whispered David.

'To hide in the stables. There is someone here. If men come to you, then run fast to the dam and hide in the trees and the long grass like I have taught you. Make sure Mason stays with you so that you can protect him; he might not know how to hide well.'

'Seriously?' Mason said.

'I thought it would help keep *you* calmer knowing that *they* are looking after you, but ...' Piet said.

'Oh yes. What's happened?' Mason asked.

'Somebody has come through the front gate uninvited. We need to get you all to safety.'

'What about you?' asked David. 'What are you going to do?'

'I am a policeman, remember? Once I see you are safe, I will go and wake the security staff, and Quintin and Lily. We will give the intruder a big fright.'

'What about Diamond? She's sleeping with Lily and Quintin tonight,' David asked.

Still keeping everything at a whisper, Piet replied, 'I'll make sure she is safe, too. Do not worry, and we can check on Elise when it's all done, although even from here we can see her lights are off, so she is safe for now.'

'Okay,' David said.

Mason nodded his head. 'Come on, kids, quickly.'

They ran as quietly as they could for the stables. Piet leading them, Maddy then David and Mason at the back.

Soon they were in the outbuildings. Piet said, 'Go inside the horse stables and hide between the haybales.'

'Okay,' David said. 'Come on, Maddy, I'll make sure they can't see you at all.'

Maddy hugged Piet tightly before she was pulled away by David.

'Protect them with your life, Mason,' Piet said.

Mason nodded as he grabbed a pitchfork off the wall.

Piet crept towards the homestead. He knew that if he went into the studio, Minke would wake up and make a lot of noise, but he had no other way to get into the house. He stopped and listened but couldn't hear the man; he'd probably got into the house already.

He abandoned the plan to wake them, and instead headed to the security cottage, the second *ikhaya* that had been fitted out for the security company as a base station, and also had rooms for them to sleep. As soon as he got to the security office, he rapped on the door. It opened within a moment.

Whispering, Piet said, 'Someone came in near the gate. They are already in the house. I could use a weapon of some sort. I was camping with the kids; I only have my bow and arrows with me.'

The new security guard nodded. He tapped on his phone, and within a breath and a half, there were four of them standing with Piet.

'Nothing on the monitor, but if Piet says there is someone here, I'll believe him over our electronic equipment,' Khanyi said. 'Move out to the house. Someone give a spare to Piet.'

Piet held the cool 9mm in his hand as he ran in front of the team. He knew the property like it was his own home. He stopped at the back of the house—from here he could see both the downstairs kitchen and one of the big windows upstairs. A small light moved around in the office. He pointed. 'There.'

'Power is off in the house, and the battery backup is disconnected, or the security lights would have come on,' Khanyi said. 'Generator is disabled obviously.'

'On it,' one of the others said, disappearing back the way they had come.

The light moved from the window and Khanyi tried the back door. It was open. The team of three crept inside, checking each other as they went.

Piet stayed outside in the shadows. He moved his position slightly so that he could see both the back door and the studio exit just in case.

He heard Tiger meow as the door of the studio burst open and a man tumbled out. Minke was running after the man, honking and trying to peck at him, but with her curved beak, she wasn't actually doing any damage at all. The animals were clearly disturbed by someone they did not know being in their space.

The man ran right towards Piet, but behind him was one of the security guards. Piet couldn't take a shot with the 9mm in case he missed. He quickly took his bow off his back, notched an arrow and let that fly instead. He knew he would always be true with that.

This intruder was not getting away. Whoever had sent him had threatened Lily's life more than once already, and now trouble was there again. The perpetrator had forced her to get private security and live with them shadowing her all the time. Taken away her freedom.

That was something Piet knew a lot about.

'Fucking hell,' the man swore loudly as he turned and ran towards Lincoln's *ikhaya*.

Piet ran after him.

Suddenly, the light in Lincoln's home went on and he came out like a bull from a neck lock, shouting and beating on a tin pot, making a huge ruckus. '*Voetsak skabenga!* You keep away from this farm. Go away. *Voetsak!*'

The security floodlights lit up the driveway at that instant, and Piet could see there was a police car with Gauteng number plates parked at the front gates. He could hear the beeping of the security alarm resetting, and the lights in the house flashed on in his side vision.

The alarm started going off. The main gate had been forced open just enough for a man to climb through.

Lincoln rushed onto the driveway, a knobkerrie in one hand and the dustpan lid in the other, still screaming, '*Voetsak!*' at the top of his lungs. Bessie had come out of her *ikhaya* and was shouting too; she held a broom in her hand. There was total mayhem.

The security firm backup *bakkie* arrived behind the cop car, parking it in. One of the security guys was on his phone as he climbed out of the vehicle, and the other had got out fast and let his dog out of the back, and was waiting for instructions. The dog barked madly, pulling on his leash, knowing that this was no training exercise.

Two of the three security personnel burst from the front door of the house and ran towards the gate and the man on the phone. One had remained in the house with Lily and Quintin, and the other one, who had gone to fix the electricity, ran into the house. The security man who'd been talking on his phone nodded as another car skidded up behind the blocked driveway. A policeman was standing in the middle of the driveway, shouting orders, directing them towards the sheep pens.

The guard with the dog took off in that direction, his flashlight shining in front of him. His dog led the way on the leash as if he already had the scent of the men in his nose and was hunting. One other man followed, as did one of the security detail.

Piet shook his head. No way could the police have got there so fast before the private security backup. Something was amiss here. Under the bright lighting, he retraced his steps and followed the footprints as they ran first towards Lincoln's *ikhaya,* and then away again. They went through a flowerbed; here Piet picked up his discarded arrow. Then he walked onto the driveway where he found the blood trail. He bent down and smoothed the sand and blood spot through his fingers. 'He is bleeding from my arrow.'

'You shot him with an arrow?' Khanyi said. 'We lent you a 9mm for a reason. Why didn't you shoot the shit out of him?'

'*Ja,* you did,' Piet said, and carried on following the trail. 'But I did not want to shoot any of you guys by accident. I saw him only briefly in the shadows when he ran out of the house. Besides, you and I both know that I was hunting "only for the pot", and that's legal here; he just got in the way between that impala and me.'

Khanyi nodded and walked next to him. Piet went to the gate and then lay on his stomach and looked underneath the police car.

'He is not at the sheep pens, he is here,' Piet said, pointing to the policeman. 'And there is something under the police car.'

Khanyi motioned for one of his guards to go through the gates, but he pointed his weapon at the policeman. The other guards there followed his lead.

The policeman was shouting, 'How can you trust this little man? Why would he say something like that? I saw the *skabenga* run for the sheep pens when I got here. I was first on the scene.'

Piet looked at the man and stepped closer. 'So, Warrant Officer Sithole, we meet again. Been a few years, but obviously they have been better to this *little man* than to the cop who has been corrupted.'

'Who are you?' Sithole asked.

'*Doos*. You cannot lie your way out of this situation. You know me. Khanyi, the police car was here when the security floodlights came on. Then the headlights went on. I saw it,' Piet said. 'I was following Sithole.'

'I'm Warrant Officer Sithole. I was first on the scene after the alarm code sent a distress signal to the police station. This man's threatening me. You all heard him.'

'No he didn't, you *domkop*. Sergeant Piet Kleinman tells the truth, he's with us,' said Khanyi. 'Put your weapon down, now. Look at your own chest. See that laser marker. Know that if you let off even one round, the other laser tagged onto your forehead will blow your brains out before you can even attempt a reload.'

The guard who had climbed on his belly under the police car came out. 'I have what looks like a homemade book and a laptop.'

'This is my evidence. This is police property. That belongs to the police. I am Warrant Officer Sithole, and this is my case—'

Khanyi cocked his weapon. 'Shut up. Or I will shoot you.'

Sithole looked around. He seriously thought that he was going to run.

'I wouldn't run, look at that blood coming from your stomach, looks like you ran into something,' Khanyi said.

Sithole clutched at his stomach.

'You still die if you run,' Piet said calmly. 'You ran into a traditional arrow. It is dipped with poison for hunting. Do you not understand? You are already dying. I can follow you all night, and through the day, but before then, you will stop and you will die.'

Sithole dropped to his knees, his hands behind his head. 'Get me to a hospital. I don't want to die.'

Khanyi was on the phone again. He had it on speaker. 'The suspect has been shot with a poisoned San arrow,' he said.

The voice on the other side carried. 'Did you say an arrow?'

'Yes. You'll need to dispatch an ambulance quickly. The San hunting poison is deadly.'

Lily and Quintin, with Diamond carried close on Quintin's hip, were coming outside with the other two security detail as the real police arrived.

'Where are the children?' Lily asked.

'Hiding in the stables,' Piet told them.

'Lincoln, please go get the kids, get them back in the house. They must be terrified,' Lily instructed. Bessie stepped forward to take Diamond from Quintin, but the little girl cried to stay with him.

'Leave her, Bessie, she's fine here with me,' Quintin said, taking her back and hushing her. Diamond put her head down on his shoulder and wrapped her arms tightly around his neck. 'Go tell Elise that everything is alright and check on her for us instead.'

Bessie walked quickly towards Elise's house.

'What was he after? Why break into our house, but not come through our bedroom door? We were right there. Wasn't he here to kill Lily?' Quintin was firing off questions, adrenaline fuelling him.

'He had these. He threw them under the police car and then pretended to be here to help. Sergeant Piet Kleinman didn't get his master tracker's name for nothing. Lucky he was here, as that crooked cop disabled the security systems.' Khanyi proceeded to explain how Piet had tracked him down.

'The plant book? Why would he steal that?' Lily asked, taking her bound printout and flicking through the pages. 'The laptop I can understand, but the book?'

'That's one more thing that the police will have to ask him after they treat him for poisoning at the hospital. I'll go with them to make sure they don't go easy on him, just because he appears to be one of them. A crooked one obviously,' Khanyi said.

CHAPTER 40

THE POLICE STATION was fully ablaze with all the lights on.

'Where did you shoot him?' Makoni asked, standing next to the man handcuffed to the bed, but in the loading dock of the police station, not in the hospital.

'In his stomach,' Piet said. 'The poison has to go into muscle to work. And there is lots of muscle in the stomach area. It's also easier to hit than a leg.'

'*Eish,* glad I'm not the one to have to write that down in a report,' Makoni said.

'And I wish it wasn't our police station having to record it either,' Chetty complained as he walked to them. 'You two are nothing but trouble. It's four in the morning and I received a call from the Organised Crime unit to make sure that our police station was fortified sufficiently, in case the Dubazane gang came to claim one of their own—a dirty cop we are holding. Sithole. I take it this is him.'

Piet chuckled. 'The late Sergeant Natalie Hatch and I had already alerted Internal Affairs to Warrant Officer Sithole's dealings, and his superior—Captain Arno Swanepoel. They are both suspected of being with the Dubazane gang and are being investigated. Their call was probably to make sure your police station is ready in case it becomes an all-out war on our premises.'

'And?' Chetty asked.

Piet said, 'We need this good-for-nothing trash to flip on the gang, and fast. I suggested that we did not take him to the hospital, that we got the information from him first. I have now explained to him that I have never had to shoot a man before, so I do not really understand how long it will take for the beetle poison to kill him. In the bush, an eland can take a day and a half, and a rabbit, a few hours, so I guesstimated less than a day before he dies without help. We do not need to rush him to the emergency just yet. He can answer questions for us first. We have time.'

'Let's hope he doesn't die too quickly, then. Capturing this criminal, and you two taking down whatever is happening, is going to look good for my office when I retire in a few weeks. Do what you have to do to get him to talk fast, then take him to the hospital. We can't have a gunfight here. Repairing the police station is not in the budget.'

Piet smiled and shook his head. 'The odd thing is, it really does not look like he went there to kill Lily. He came out with her laptop and a homemade botany book. He had left the upstairs rooms when the security detail went in there. He did not try to hold anyone hostage, or harm anyone.'

'A homemade botany book?' Chetty said.

'*Ja,*' Piet said.

'How soon do you think you can get him to break?'

'He did not put up much of a fight when he was told he had poison in his stomach, so I think quickly,' Piet said.

Piet watched Makoni sit on the carton of goods in the loading bay close by and open his laptop. 'Ready.'

Sithole lay on the ambulance trolley bed. A drip in one arm, and handcuffs on the other which kept him firmly attached to the trolley, preventing him from running away.

'You awake?' Piet asked with a deep poke in Sithole's guts.

'*Eina.*'

'Do you have something you want to tell me? Or do I pull that drip out and let you die from the poisoning like you deserve, you waste of space,' Piet said.

'Wait till you have been on the force for twenty years and then pass judgement. Sometimes just helping someone out can get you into deep water,' Sithole said.

'I have been in the force longer than that. And I am still on the right side of the law. I am for the people, not for myself. I would never do what you have done. Are you going to talk to me? Tell me who sent you and why?'

'You knew me right away at Dr Winters's farm. How?'

'You do not remember? We worked together in Johannesburg. Surely you did not work with so many San that you forget them?'

'I don't remember you. You couldn't have been important, then.' He turned his head away as if to snub him even now.

The way he said the word 'then' had a venomous ring to it.

Piet recognised that after all this time as a policeman, the face that had turned away from him had been devoid of any expression, even when caught lying. Although he was confronting the possibility of dying, Sithole was incapable of any emotional response. He was a psychopath. '*Nee,* I guess I blended in with the environment and was just another cop then, but your life depends on me now. If I keep you here too long, that poison from my arrow kills you. I have heard that it is a painful death for the animals. Hope you are looking forward to it. Are you ready to talk more about why you were stealing a useless book and a computer from Dr Winters's house?'

'I'm a dead man anyway. There's nothing anyone can do about that. There is nowhere for me to hide.'

'Glad you see it my way,' Piet said. 'You do not mind if I phone a friend, a fellow cop so he can listen too? He is really interested because he said you have statistics stacked against you, and numbers caught up with you.'

'Do whatever you want,' Sithole said. 'I only have to answer your questions? Then you will take me to hospital?'

'*Ja*, and answer truthfully. If I have to check your alibi and I find information given by you here today was wrong, then I hope your death is far from unpredictable, because to many it would obviously still have taken too long. You are a dirty cop and do not deserve any sympathy from me,' Piet said as he dialled in Colonel Vaughan Smith and put his phone on speaker.

'Why did you steal a homemade book on plants and a laptop?'

'I was paid to steal it. And if I stole it, the contract on Dr Winters could be completed without her dying. She would finish her work and go home to Australia. Same end result: she would be gone from South Africa.'

'Why?'

'Because the book is valuable in the right hands, to the right people in the know.'

'And who would that be?'

'Ulwazi Dubazane and Ayurprabhu Pharmaceuticals. But there was going to be an auction for the book with the other pharmaceutical companies, too. It could go to the highest bidder.'

Vaughan said, 'Why?'

'Something to do with San patents and plants that printed money,' Sithole said.

'Patents. Oh God. This is all about money in the end,' Vaughan said.

'Always,' Piet said. 'Do you know the contact at Ayurprabhu Pharmaceuticals who wants the book?'

'Some big wig. I do not know which one.'

'Then who do we ask?' Piet said. 'Tick tock, time is running out.'

'Ulwazi Dubazane. It's her contact with someone in Ayurprabhu Pharmaceuticals. Apparently, there was a deal with her that if she got the company the book, she would get a cut of all the profits from new medicines. But things went wrong, and doctors kept finding the darn book and carrying on writing it. Wanting to take it to a different publisher and give the secrets free to the world.'

'Walk me through this. Ulwazi hears about a book on plants by a San. How did she find that out? It was not exactly public knowledge.'

'I don't know. I really don't know that part. She has her friendship bench, her whole plague of *igundane*, the women of the town who feed her all the information in her area. That is what she does, she trades in information.'

'How did Ayurprabhu Pharmaceuticals come to be working with Ulwazi, then?' Piet asked.

'Don't know that either. But now he works with her, he meets her in the bar, at Black Isle Shebeen on Florence Moposho Street, Alexandra. He's a black man.'

'Was it Ulwazi who sent someone to kill Dr Winters?'

'Yes, she sent her son. But your partner shot him. And revenge was sweet for a while for Ulwazi. But you know this already, it is in your file—I have seen it.'

Piet nodded. 'You are confirming that Ulwazi Dubazane sent someone to execute Sergeant Natalie Hatch? She started a taxi war to cover a contract killing?'

'You already know this to be true, so why are you asking me?' Sithole said.

'So Makoni here can type it up into your notes and we have it on file,' Piet said. 'Do you have the names of the people who undertook this job?'

'What does it matter, they are dead. I killed them.'

'I am not sorry they are dead, but I still need their names,' Piet said.

'Enzokuhle Ramathipela and Wekese Tsonga were the shooters. Dube Khoza and Jose Mabaso drove the taxis.'

'Now that was not hard, was it?' Piet asked, patting Sithole's stomach with a little force. 'Does your captain know that you are a dirty cop?'

Sithole closed his eyes, not answering.

'Worth further investigation, then. One more thing. Do you know anything about the contamination of drugs that is happening?'

'No.' He opened his eyes and looked at Piet. 'I know a lot of things, and I know where many, many bodies are buried, but nothing about that.'

'Best you start talking about those bodies fast, then, telling Constable Makoni here exactly where every single one is. Do not worry, he will ask you for a signature every few moments in case you die, so we have a legal statement. When you are totally finished, we will take you to the hospital. The nurses might have an antidote for you by then, or maybe not. If they do, you will be saved and made ready for when the Dubazane gang come for you for squealing. I wonder who will be faster, them or your captain to silence you. Me, I am in no hurry. Either of the three endings are fine by me, so keep talking, giving us this information. I know that soon you will get what is due.'

Piet did not bother telling him that as far as he knew, there was no cure for the beetle poisoning.

CHAPTER 41

Piet rubbed the back of his neck with his hand. He'd been sitting in the meeting at the Johannesburg office of the Narcotics Enforcement Bureau for hours. Lily sat beside him, chewing the side of her cheek. A very bored-looking Makoni sat next to Lily, not because he knew what was going on, but because Piet had told him to observe all the people in the room.

Noticeably absent from the gathering was their shiny-faced Acting Chief Chetty. When the Independent Police Investigative Directorate team had arrived, followed by a representative from the Narcotics Enforcement Bureau and Organised Crime unit in the Kimberley office, Chetty had guessed that Piet and Natalie had been onto something big. He had raked Piet over for going above his head, as Chetty had desperately wanted to be involved for his last hurrah.

Piet thought otherwise but knew not to say it out loud. Makoni was not as diplomatic, pointing out that the acting police chief was about to retire in a few weeks, and received his first official warning from Chetty.

Not one of the three units had accepted Chetty's offer to accompany the men. He was not wanted. Only his team. Piet believed it was karma because Natalie had always said the way he treated people would be done back to him one day. Piet thought that at last, today was that day. He was just sorry Natalie was not around to bear witness to it.

This was a critical moment in the narcotics investigation. The name of the drug company would go out into the police force during this meeting, and if there was a leak within the room, they might lose their element of surprise when they hit the company.

Piet looked out the glass walls of the office and could see an unarmed Khanyi waiting patiently for Lily, staring into the room, not even reading a magazine, often moving in his chair, walking around, taking the pressure off his recently healed backside. Watching over his client, even though she was in a highly secure police facility.

One day soon, Piet wanted out of the force, but he would hate to be private security. That wasn't an option he would ever take. He admired that these men and women could do it, but for him, he knew the waiting around would kill him. They were better than good at their job; they had kept Lily alive so far, and he silently asked them to keep her safe a little longer, so once the drugs were sorted, he could be part of the task force to take down the Dubazane syndicate.

Everything in its order.

He looked into the room and brought his mind back to the meeting. In front of them, laid out across the boardroom table, were the results from the tests that Lily had commissioned on behalf of the World Health Organization. The eight police personnel around the table each read the reports, drinking coffee and silently working through the information before them.

'Everyone finished?' Colonel Vaughan Smith asked.

There was a murmur of agreement, and then they all looked at their boss.

'Drug contamination. Not new to us, but this is on a big scale,' Vaughan said.

'Yeah, no surprises there. Contamination and also defective drugs,' Piet said. 'Dr Lily Winters has World Health standing by while we work to stop this. They are saying that with the information we have, we now need to act to sort it out and issue the recall on all the affected drugs. They were stressing again this morning how important it is to have the untainted replacements for them. We will need to get onto the other South African companies and check their stocks of the drugs and distribution. Remember that the people out there are still taking these contaminated drugs, and we need to get them out of circulation, but do it in an organised fashion. We cannot have chaos when this news breaks.'

'This is the proof we needed,' Vaughan said. 'If you look at the data Dr Lily Winters provided, on page forty-two, they have the name of the manufacturer and the pills that are involved from her sample. They're all from Ayurprabhu Pharmaceuticals.'

'Not only do we have proof of drugs which are nothing more than placebos, but there are drugs which contain bacteria and other pathogens to cause illnesses rather than heal the patients,' Piet said.

Vaughan was shaking his head, flicking the pages back and forth. 'Children's Panado has both a meningitis and a flu virus. HIV blockers have the meningitis strain of bacteria in them, flu viruses, *Helicobacter pylori*. Wow, even some of the drugs which they use for Alzheimer's. As for the placebos … *eish,* all these people with dementia who rely on the drugs to slow down the spread of the disease, are spending money, getting worse, and racing towards the end where their pain medication costs a whole lot more and complications always arise. They're speeding up people's deaths. This is one deranged fucker who cooked up this plan.'

'As per the report, Dr Winters believes that we're on the verge of a national epidemic—one of the biggest drug cases in South Africa's history,' Piet said.

'And she's right, looking at these trajectory graphs in this report,' Vaughan said. 'What do we know about Ayurprabhu Pharmaceuticals?'

'We made you a presentation on that,' Piet said, nodding to Makoni. He clicked his computer, and an image appeared on the screen of the meeting room.

'Thank you, Constable. This is their website picture of their manufacturing plant from the outside,' Piet said. 'Five years ago, Ayurprabhu Pharmaceuticals, a small but profitable family-run company, had a change in management. The daughter, Mishti Prabhu, took over from the father as CEO.' There was a picture of her on the screen.

'She floated the company on the stock exchange. Two years ago, they bought out another of our local larger drug manufacturers in Alberton, moved everything to that location, and they have rebranded all of the drugs as theirs. This company is now one of the biggest manufacturers and distributors of generic drugs in South Africa. Not only do they supply generic drugs, but they manufacture and supply the base components for the drugs, too, which other drug companies buy from them. However, less than a week ago this man, Reyansh Prabhu, her brother, took over as CEO when she was killed in a motor-vehicle accident.'

Vaughan sat upright. 'Convenient. Someone is cleaning shop.'

'Hopefully, we can get to them before they destroy all other witnesses and evidence,' Piet said.

'We need to get in there—fast,' Vaughan said.

'If this tampering is in the base chemicals, it could now be across all locally produced drugs?' one of the policemen on the left asked.

'I don't think so,' Lily said. 'The drug samples we tested were comprehensive—there's a full list on page seventy-five. It was not across base chemicals at the time I took the samples, or the other brands would have been affected and shown up in the testing. It might be an idea to look at them when you enter the factory though. It's possible that they are thinking bigger all the time.'

'The evidence only points to contaminations in their own branded generic drugs,' Piet said.

Vaughan nodded as he rubbed his hands over his face. 'Fucked up and in serious trouble is what we have here. Once we begin a full-scale quarantine, it will be extremely difficult to stop the spread of information to the public. There'll need to be a recall on the drugs. We'll need to ensure that we get the message out there on what drugs they need to return to their chemists for disposal.' Vaughan was rubbing his head. 'There have been drug recalls before; it's nothing new. Only not on this scale.'

'WHO warned that South Africa might get flooded with more expensive overseas drugs again,' Lily said.

'I hope not. And I do believe a bust like this will send a message to these overseas companies that think they can dump any rubbish drugs on to us, too,' Vaughan said. 'A clear message that South Africa is as sophisticated as the rest of the world. We haven't slumped into fourth world status yet.'

'Where do we go from here?' Piet asked.

'Firstly, we make sure that Dr Winters has everything double-crossed with WHO, and they will not move before we do. We need to do this right and arrest the people responsible for the contamination. No use us going in guns blazing at the new CEO when there must be others involved. We need to cast our net wide and catch everyone. Three days, people, we go into Ayurprabhu Pharmaceuticals. The whole company will be going into lockdown.'

'Okay, Dr Winters, you happy with that? You can make sure that WHO will wait for three days?' Piet said.

Lily nodded.

'We'll assemble the strike force to enter. I want legal ready, and TAKIES on site with us,' Vaughan said, tapping his papers together on the table to ensure they were neat and ordered.

'What's a TAKIES?' Lily whispered to Piet.

'Special Task Force unit. These are the guys you do not mess with in South Africa. The men that go into high-risk situations where normal police cannot and sort things out. The men you want watching your back.'

Lily nodded.

'Public relations will prepare the press releases that will go out once we have the factory in quarantine. We can tell the public that it is under further investigation. Let's stop those drugs we already know about. Save some lives. You're welcome to come with us, Piet and Makoni. Sorry, Dr Winters, police personnel only,' Vaughn said.

'I don't need to be anywhere near them, thank you very much. They've killed plenty of my patients and caused me sleepless nights. If I had to meet them face to face, I'm not sure what I would do. I'm so angry at them,' Lily said.

'Fair enough,' Vaughan said.

The people around the table all stood up and wandered off to perform their various tasks until only Piet, Makoni, Lily and Vaughan remained.

'Vaughan, I know for you this one will be personal. Are you okay going into this raid?' Piet asked.

'I really don't know,' Vaughan said. 'I tell you if that bitch CEO wasn't dead, I think I might have done it myself with my bare hands. But now, all I can do is ensure that everyone, and I mean every single person responsible for this contamination, pays. The audacity of this fucking drug company to come along and play God, targeting sick people.' He flexed his fists. 'I'm so proud of my son and the man he was able to grow into, despite that fucking virus, and they murdered him. I'll get justice for every single victim here, every single one.'

CHAPTER 42

Reyansh Prabhu sat at his desk. He wiped the tiny fleck of dust off it. Gone was all Mishti's furniture, and he had redecorated with glass and leather. Rather, Anaya had organised for the redecoration now that he was CEO. She seemed to be floating around happier than he had ever seen her since his sister's accident. And that happiness had spilled over into their bedroom, too.

'Excuse me, Reyansh?' the deep voice of his secretary said from the door.

'Yes?'

'There's a problem in the reception area, police—' He was cut off as two policemen appeared behind him.

'Can I help you?' Reyansh said. 'Please come in, sit.'

The policemen walked into the office. Two other officers were standing outside.

'What seems to be the problem?' Reyansh asked, putting his hands together to stop them from shaking. He had been off his drugs since the day he'd learned of Mishti's death, so it wasn't the drugs playing with his nerves. His dream of being CEO of Ayurprabhu Pharmaceuticals, at last, came true when she died. But right now, he wished that Mishti was alive to deal with the police.

The policemen were not sitting. Reyansh stood up.

'My name is Colonel Vaughan Smith, and this is Detective Piet Kleinman. As the CEO of Ayurprabhu Pharmaceuticals, you're personally responsible for all drugs manufactured and distributed from your factories. Do you acknowledge this?'

'Not personally. I run the company now, but I only recently took over from my late sister, may she rest in peace,' Reyansh said.

'According to the law, you're responsible. We want to ask you if you have anything to say on the counts that we are charging you with. Murder of at least fifteen South African prisoners and thirty-six civilians. Furthermore, it has been discovered that your company has been manufacturing contaminated and substandard drugs that did not perform their purpose, and your trading licence has been suspended. This includes all containers coming into South Africa as well as those already in transit. They will be seized on arrival, and the contents destroyed. It also includes all drugs on your premises and chemical compounds, and a raid is taking place there as we speak. The contents will all be tested, and anything found contaminated will be destroyed.

'You are also charged with the murder of Dr Ian Hawthorne, the attempted murder of Dr Lily Winters, and the attempted corporate espionage of botany piracy from the San community of Platfontein. Do you have anything to say?'

'I have nothing to do with any of that. I did none of these things that you accuse me of. Like I told you, I have only recently taken over from my sister. She would have probably been able to speak to you more about this; I do not know what you are talking about,' Reyansh said. 'You're welcome to search our premises. I can show you around personally, and you can take all the tests you want. I am the head chemist here, too, and if there were tainted drugs like you say there are, then they have to have been created away from our factory. Our factory adheres to strict standards; our quality is of the highest standard. As for botany piracy—I don't know anything about that either.'

'Do you want to call a lawyer?' Vaughan asked.

'Why? I have done nothing wrong. If there is this botany piracy you speak of, I would like to get to the bottom of it as much as you. If there are tainted drugs on our premises, then this is disturbing as it could damage our company. I've already told you, my company will give you full cooperation. There is no need to threaten me or any of my staff with your guns.'

Vaughan said, 'I would like you to assemble all the staff. Do you have an area where we can talk to them?'

'Yes, yes, of course, this way,' Reyansh said, and he walked out of his office towards the factory. 'Can I call them together on the PA system?'

'Yes.'

He walked to the main receptionist's desk. 'Holly, please call all the workers to assemble in the mezzanine eating area for a full staff meeting. This is all staff, administration and manufacturing.'

She nodded and pushed the button, and began calling all the employees.

'This way, gentlemen,' Reyansh said.

There were police and tactical soldiers everywhere. He took deep breaths to calm his nerves. He always knew that this might happen, but luckily with Mishti's passing, he could plead ignorance and she would take all the blame. Her name would be tarnished, and he might come out of this looking okay. Still able to run his company the way he wanted to, and hopefully without the need to taint drugs ever again, but for now, he needed to keep it all together and simply blame Mishti.

To his amusement, his sister who had had the perfect reputation in life was about to have it ruined in death.

The police surrounded them as he stood up and spoke to his workers for the second time since taking over leadership.

'This is Colonel Vaughan Smith and Detective Piet Kleinman. They have come here today to look for evidence that our drugs are tainted. Please cooperate with them as much as you can and answer any questions they have so that we can catch whoever is responsible. They will be located in my office and will call you all in to speak with them. Please do not be afraid. Help where you can. We can't afford to stay in quarantine for long, so the quicker we help the police, the better for all.'

Piet and Makoni sat at their desks.

'Something is not right. I am still missing a piece in this puzzle,' Piet said.

'What? Are you sure?' Makoni said.

'Do you remember the first day you came to work here, you asked me two questions. How did the information get into the hands of Kagiso and Ulwazi Dubazane for them to have a hit on the doctors, and then the medical-aid-fraud assessor? And how did Kagiso know exactly where to find Dr Lily Winters that day?'

'I remember that. We might not have answered those, but we have so much more. Organised Crime has invited you to be present when they interview Ulwazi Dubazane tomorrow after they picked her up yesterday. We have already been with the narcotics guys when they found nothing in the factory—no evidence of any tampering. The only person you could even consider arresting was the VP for his part in knowing about the book, but he said he was working on Mishti's orders, so that won't stick. Narcotics couldn't prove the contamination was happening there, but those affected drugs are off the shelves, and new ones are being supplied to those who need them. What more do you think is still unsolved?' Makoni said.

'I know, we have solved so much, but I still feel like there is this piece missing, like everything needs to link together somehow. I still haven't answered those two questions. But now I am adding a third to them: How did Ulwazi first come across the information that Ian and I were writing a book on plants?'

Piet's phone rang. 'Detective Kleinman.'

'You have a visitor. Please come through to the reception area.'

'Makoni, keep thinking on this. I need to see who that is.'

Piet settled Bessie and Lincoln into a private interview room. 'Right, this is a secure room, as you asked for. Why are you both here?'

'I know that Lily and Quintin said that we can always talk to them, but I don't know what to do. How to tell them,' Bessie said.

'Tell them what?' Piet asked.

'I think that I have harmed Dr Lily and Dr Ian without knowing about it. Lincoln thinks that perhaps we should tell you our story so that you know that we are not trying to keep secrets, but I was too trusting and blind with family.'

Lincoln held her hand in his, but her eyes were filled with tears.

'Would you like some water?' Piet asked.

'I think perhaps I just need to tell you before I can't,' Bessie said.

'I am listening,' Piet said.

'My sister—she is not a real sister, but my sister-but-one. We grew up together in the Transkei. It was hard. My father abandoned my mother, and then my mother died having another child. My aunty, Mary, she took me in and raised me like I was her daughter, too. My sister and I we were like this.' Bessie put her fingers together.

'I understand,' Piet said.

'My sister, she got involved with a bad man. I moved to Cape Town to be far away from him. I begged her to run away with me, to come and make a new life. But she would not leave him.

'For many years, I did not see my sister. Then I heard that her husband had died and she had taken over his business. I travelled to Johannesburg to caution her not to do this, that now he was gone, she could be free of him and his family. But she would not listen.

'Once again we parted ways. I met Lincoln and we got married. We were happy in our life in Kimberley. The family in the house before Dr Ian, they moved to Johannesburg and they invited me to visit when they moved, to help them before they could find a new maid. They would pay me to come back to Kimberley and carry on working for Dr Ian when they got a new maid.

'That is when I saw my sister again. She was waiting for me outside the new house in Sandton. When she saw me, she asked why I was working in Sandton, as no one worked in those houses unless she said so. When I explained my situation, she said she was so happy. Happy to see me, like I was her. We decided to keep in touch because everything else didn't matter; we were still sisters. We had to hold onto each other because we were all that was left of our Transkei family.

'Every week she calls me, and we talk about our lives. She tells me about her life in Alexandra and about what her sons and grandchildren get up to. My only daughter had moved away; I don't have family to talk about. I began telling her of the family who lives in Kimberley who I look after instead. About Dr Ian and what he was doing in his clinic in Platfontein. I was so proud that he was writing a book. A real book that one day I could go buy in the shop. I was proud of him, and of you, Piet. Of what you were making. I told her. But I did not think anything of it when Dr Ian was killed and the house was robbed. Then Dr Lily came to live in the house, and soon she had David, Maddy, Diamond, and Minke and all the guards, and I told my sister everything that was exciting and new in my life. How the sleepy house is so alive.

'Then my sister's child was killed—I did not know he had been killed in Kimberley. She told me her son had been shot by the police and I thought she meant in Johannesburg. I took leave from Dr Lily and I went to the funeral to support my sister.

'Then the man—he came to rob the house. The one you shot with your arrow. I remembered him from the funeral—he was very good friends with my sister. That was when the bells in my head began ringing, and I told Lincoln. We did not know what to do. But today, we decided to come tell you because she is dead now. I got a phone call this morning to say that she'd passed over. She had a heart attack. And now I must go to jail for telling her things about my family, even though I did not realise that she was hurting them. I thought she was my sister, all these years I treated her like a sister would, I cared for her and loved her, and in the end, she hurt my family. It must have been her who hurt Dr Lily and Khanyi and your friend Natalie. My sister, and her *igundane*, and her secrets and her lies. She used me. She took what I loved and she hurt my new family. She hurt them. And I am the one who talked to her on the telephone all the time, the one who was so excited that now I too had all this news to share with her.'

Bessie was sobbing. Lincoln had his arm around her.

The fine hair on Piet's arm stood on end. 'Bessie, are you telling me that your sister was Ulwazi Dubazane?'

Bessie nodded.

CHAPTER 43

It was another summer day, with clear blue skies overhead and the African sunshine warming those who chose to lift their faces up towards her. Only Lily was oblivious to the weather. Instead, she looked from Mason back to Quintin.

'Minke's feathers have enough waxing-waterproofing. A perfect day for her to be returned to the wild,' Mason said.

Piet stood inside the studio. The quiet man in the storm around him as everyone talked over each other.

'It can't be time already for this bird to go home; it only just got here,' Quintin protested. 'Who's going to be my muse when Minke is gone?'

'Tiger,' David said. 'He will still attack your bow, even when Minke isn't here.'

'Lily,' said Maddy. 'She's always your muse.'

Quintin laughed and reached for Lily's hand. 'Of course she is. But I'm going to miss this fluff ball.'

'I'm not going to miss cleaning up its poop,' Bessie said.

Mason laughed. 'We need Gentian Violet; if we spray a little on her head to mark her, then we can see her when she's in the creche at all times. For a few days perhaps. But she's ready to go wild again. She's very healthy and ready to rejoin her feathered family.'

'Do you have some handy?' Lily asked.

'In my *bakkie*. Hang on, I'll go grab it.'

'She'll have a purple head, so we can see if the other flamingo babies are picking on her?' asked Maddy.

'I guess,' Quintin said, nodding. 'Hopefully not though.'

'What about Tiger? He's going to miss Minke,' David asked.

'He'll get used to being alone again. Besides, he's a cat; he'll probably be happy to simply get back his box on my bench.'

'One without bird poop in it,' Bessie said.

Maddy laughed.

'True,' Quintin agreed.

Mason returned. 'Quintin, hold Minke while I spray her head.' He grabbed hold of Minke and passed her to Quintin.

Minke was not impressed. She honked at Mason and tried her hardest to get out of Quintin's arms.

'Come on, Minke, it's only hair dye,' Mason said, carefully spraying her head.

Quintin put Minke on the floor, and she ran to Tiger, who was lying in the doorway to the outside. She was honking still. Tiger stood up as if they understood each other, and he put his paw on Minke's foot. Minke lowered her head down to Tiger's level, and he began trying to lick off the purple antiseptic spray.

'Oh no, you don't,' Mason said, grabbing Minke. 'That stuff is bad for Tiger.'

'Are we ready to take her back to the dam?' Lily asked.

'Yes. *Ja. Yebo,*' all came collectively.

'Goodbye, Minke,' Bessie said as she reached out to pat the flamingo. 'You have been a good bird. Be safe in the wild.'

'Everybody in the Cruiser, or if you want to go in Mason's *bakkie,* climb in there.'

They walked out, Minke struggling against Mason.

'Put her on the ground. She'll come by herself. We got her used to the back of the Cruiser. Watch,' Quintin said.

Mason put the flamingo down.

'Come on, Minke,' Quintin said, and he clicked his fingers. 'Come-come-come.'

Minke ran to him and followed as he began walking towards the Cruiser. Her long legs were keeping up with him as she flapped her wings.

Lily sat in the passenger seat, and when everybody had piled in, Quintin opened the back door for Minke.

'Up, girl, up-up-up.' Again, he clicked his fingers. But instead, she walked right up to him. He bent down and hugged her. She rubbed her neck and her head against his neck and his cheek, and made a small guttural sound in her throat. 'I love you, too, you stupid bird. Now get in the car so you can go back to your family.'

Minke jumped up into the back and stood inside, looking out the window and then over the back seat, giving little nuzzles to David, Maddy and Piet's ears as they sat there.

'I'll see you at Kamfers Dam,' Mason said.

Quintin started the Cruiser and went to drive through the gate, but instead, he turned to Lily. 'Isn't it wonderful not to have to tell any security personnel where we are going or what we're doing? We can simply drive in and out of our own house without a thought in the world.'

'Pretty magical feeling. I don't think you appreciate freedom until you lose it,' Lily said.

They drove to the dam, and Piet got out of the Cruiser and opened the farmer's gates, as he had done so many months ago when Lily and Quintin had first seen the flamingos. They drove as close to the water as they could before stopping.

'Everybody out,' Quintin said.

Piet opened the back doors. 'Are you coming, Minke?'

Minke had settled down at last on her mat. Seated with her legs splayed either side, she honked at him.

Quintin went to the back and said, 'Come on, Minke, there are relatives of yours that want to meet you.' He clicked his fingers and immediately she got up, jumped out and ran to him.

'I think she knows she's saying goodbye,' Lily said, taking a photo. 'I've never seen her give you so many hugs in one day.'

'It's possible,' Quentin said.

David clicked his fingers, and Minke hugged him as well. Maddy had her turn, too, even Mason and Piet.

Finally, it was Lily's turn to crouch down. Without clicking her fingers,

Minke ran to her, honking and making little sounds in her throat as she snuggled close, all the time caressing Lily with her head, banging it against hers and talking to her.

'Time to walk to the others,' Quentin said. He reached for Lily's hand, and as she stood and began to walk, Minke walked between them and kept touching their hands with her head. They walked closer to the dam, and the noise of the other flamingos grew louder and louder.

They could see the flamingos wading in the shallows. Thousands of birds chatted and fed. Some flew around; others glided gracefully back to the water. There was movement everywhere. The older flamingos were further back along the shoreline, but the younger creche was right at the edge of the water.

Minke looked at her humans and then she looked at the birds which were like her. She seemed uncertain as to whether she should join the flamingos or stay with the humans.

'Go, Minke,' David said. 'This is where I saved you from when you were little, so this is where you need to be, with your own kind.'

Minke looked at him and then looked at Quintin. She went to Quintin for one last hug, then she walked with her strange gait, her wings flapping, towards the water and she joined the creche. She honked and talked to the other flamingos, and she swam around all the other fledglings, but because of her purple head, they could follow her clearly. She swam with the creche, and she mimicked them, quickly feeding in the water that was rich with nutrients as her instincts took over.

A few of the fledglings the same size as her were practising flying and not quite making it. They tried again and again. She joined in with them, running on the water in the shallows and flapping her wings, and then suddenly she was airborne; she was flying.

Maddy put her hand into Piet's. 'Do you think she's going to be okay without us?'

'A wise boy once told me that our imprint on her would be minimal when she went back with her kind, and I believe that he was correct. Look at her fly,' Lily said.

'She didn't even knock into any of the others when she landed, not like those wild ones,' Maddy said.

Quintin laughed. 'I think that it's a good thing that Mason had to come out here, too, and all our camping gear could be put in his *bakkie*. When Piet told me to pack the camping gear so we could continue to watch her for a day or so, or until that purple on her head wears off, I thought he was crazy, but now I can see his logic. Tonight, I'm going to hear Piet's story about the flamingos when we have a campfire, and guess what Lily brought? Marshmallows.'

'Yes!' David and Maddy said together.

Lily looked out at Minke, who had not made any signs of coming back to them. This was their first camping trip at the dam. Quintin had wanted to make another memory, and make sure that the kids could watch Minke for as long as they liked until the purple faded. She tried to enjoy it for his sake, but she knew that just like Minke, she too would forget the people around her.

And while Minke flew off into the sunset, Lily would take a different path.

Even at night, the roosting flamingos made a constant, distinctive noise. The fire's sparks flew up into the starlight above them. David lay with his head on Quintin's thigh, using him like a pillow, and Maddy was leaning heavily onto Lily's arm. Every now and again she would find she had slumped downwards, and quickly right herself again, fighting sleep, trying hard not to let the night end. Lily and Quintin sat side by side, holding hands. Piet and Mason sat on the opposite side of the fire.

Quintin smiled. 'So, Piet, have you made up your story for the flamingos?'

'I have been thinking about it for a very long time,' Piet said, throwing a stick into the flames and watching it catch alight. 'The San language does not have a word for the flamingo. Their wings remind me of fire at sunset, so for my story, they will be known as the firebird.'

'That's lovely,' Lily said.

Piet smiled. 'So it was that on the edge of the great Kalahari, where the sand does not move with the same incessantly as the central Kalahari. Here there were thorn trees that provided shade, and bush that provided cover, and grasslands where many of the animals ate food in the summer. Here it was that there was a *vlei* so blue that many would think that the monkey trickster god himself had made it because when you saw it from a different angle, it looked green. Many of the animals would get confused.

'This confusion was caused because inside the water was a special blue-green algae that blossomed, and it was the breeding ground for the many, many small shrimp who lived in the water. Humans would not bathe in this water because of the strange fishlike creatures. Together, these algae and the shrimp made the water bitter. The animals would not drink the water, even though it was so beautiful.

'Then, one day, a big, thirsty white bird that had been flying across the Kalahari for many, many hours landed in the *vlei,* and immediately drank the water. The big bird drank and drank, trying to quench its thirst. The impala beside the water said to the bird, "Do you not know that that water is bitter? No one drinks it."

'The big white bird said, "If our God Kaggen had made something so beautiful, why would he make it so we could not drink the water?"

'Then as the animals looked on, the bird started drinking the water again. As it did so, its beak began to change from straight to curved.

'"Look at your beak, get out of the water, it is melting!" the kudu cried.

'The bird shook its head. "Have you not tasted the sweet algae and the shrimp? My beak can filter them from the water; they are the best-tasting food that our God Kaggen has ever made."

'And as the bird drank more water and ate more food, its feathers began to glow red, and orange and pink, and a few feathers near its tail turned black as if they had been burned in a fire.

'"Look at your feathers," said the mongoose, "surely now you are burning, you are on fire."

'"Get out of the water!" the other animals cried. "If you stay in there, you will surely die."

'But the bird bathed in the water, and his legs and his neck grew longer as if they were both being stretched. "Look at this beautiful place that our God Kaggen made. I can drink this water, eat the food through my new beak, and even my boring white feathers have become beautiful. I think that this is the place I have been looking for all my life. I shall stay in this *vlei*, and I shall make my family here. You can all drink water somewhere else, but this water is good enough for me."

'"But look at yourself, now you look like a bird on fire," said the eland. "Run away; he is on fire!"

'The bird looked at his reflection in the water and indeed he did see a bird who looked to be on fire. But the look did not scare him. He had a long neck so that he could reach the water, he had long legs so that he could stand with only his feet in the blue water if he wanted to, and he had a curved beak that he could now filter the food in the *vlei* with. He was not scared of the bird in the reflection.

'"I am now a firebird, and after much travelling over long distances, I know this is where I belong. I have found a home all of my own. My long days of wandering across the Kalahari are over."

'The animals left the firebird in the *vlei*, and soon they migrated to new feeding grounds, away from where the water was green. The firebird looked at his reflection in the water often. He saw himself for what he truly was. He was different from what he had been, there were many changes about him, but he was content. He had almost everything that he needed in his life, right there in the *vlei*.

'A giant flock of birds, like he used to be, flew over. They did not recognise him.

'"We are so weary; we have flown far across the Kalahari. We are hungry and thirsty. Is that *vlei* any good for us to rest, firebird? May we share your roost?" they asked.

'"Come and join me, my friends, you are welcome. Come down here, rest on my beautiful water, shelter in the shallows here in this *vlei* where you are safe. You can eat the shrimp and quench your thirst. There is enough space to share this paradise with everyone."

'The whole flock settled into the water, and soon, they all looked exactly like the firebird. They had curved beaks, white, pink, red and black feathers and long legs so that they could stand in the blue water, and feed with their long necks.

'The firebird was happy. Now he had everything he wanted in life; all his needs had been met. He had a place to shelter from the predators, food to eat, water to drink, and he had a family to share it all with.

'The whole flock celebrated together by dancing and head-bobbing and head-wagging. They lifted their feathers erect as they danced, and made loud honking sounds in celebration that they too could share the beautiful place they now called home with the firebird.'

A tear splashed down from Lily's face, and she wiped at it with a tissue. 'That was beautiful.'

'You are quite a storyteller,' Quintin said.

'Is that us in the story?' David asked. 'Our people, we had to come far and change, but we found a new home?'

Piet nodded. 'The San always tell one story with another, and until Quintin challenged me to tell a story about the flamingos, I did not have a way to express my feelings. Then I started their story. Now their story will be like the footprints in the Kalahari, there for everyone to see.'

CHAPTER 44

WIENER MUSIKVEREIN, VIENNA, AUSTRIA, 2012

The fresh white snow on the ground made the old city of Vienna look clean. Lily climbed out of their luxury limousine for the last of the four charity concerts that they would be attending before flying home to Kimberley.

Quintin was standing there waiting for her, his hand outstretched. Taking her left hand in his, he made sure that she didn't slip on the small patch of ice before the red carpet started outside the Wiener Musikverein. Lights flashed as photographers took their pictures in the hopes of one of them getting a good enough shot to put in the papers around the world for the last of the charity concerts that Quintin held.

Lily should've been used to the lights and the microphones being pushed towards her face when she attended a charity event like those held here with the Vienna Philharmonic Orchestra. There was still a dinner to attend after the show, and that was where most of the money that they raised at the event came from.

'Smile, Lily,' Quintin said softly as he squeezed her fingers.

She plastered what she hoped was a radiant smile on her face. She wanted to scream at everyone in her immediate space to get away from her. Didn't they realise there were more important things going on in the world? She had wanted to back out of the last event, but Quintin had reminded her that despite everything, the money they would raise tonight was also important, and they needed to attend; for now, the show must go on.

She lifted her head and faced the crowd as best she could, even if she was crying inside. The old building was lit up with huge spotlights, and somebody had decorated it with what seemed to be a blanket of beautiful lights that danced across the front, making the grand entrance look even more impressive than usual. There was a huge Christmas tree to the left—decorated with thick ropes of tinsel, and thousands upon thousands of fairy lights twinkled on the new snow that sat on its outspread branches.

'I wish the children could see that tree,' Lily said.

Quintin looked at the tree and then took his mobile phone from his pocket. 'Come,' he said as they turned around and he took a quick selfie of them outside with the tree in the background and the Wiener Musikverein behind them.

'Quintin Cornelius Winters!' one of the reporters on the outside of the barrier called. 'Are you taking your family's Christmas photo?'

'Making a memory,' Quintin called back.

Lily looked at her husband. While he was wrapped in a beautiful soft wool coat, underneath was his clothing for the upcoming concert. He wore his signature leather pants that she never got tired of. Quintin still did things his way, and she loved him for that.

'Let's get in out of the cold,' he said after they'd spent another fifteen minutes or so milling around, smiling for the photographers.

'Fabulous idea,' Lily said. Her feet and calves were feeling the strain of wearing the stiletto heels. She thought of her sensible work flats sitting in the hallway at Hacienda El Paradiso. They walked through the front door and were immediately surrounded by people greeting them. Many of them she knew, but some of them she didn't—she should have. She stuck close to Quintin so that he could fill in names for her. Everybody seemed to be from the music world, and they were all there for a common cause—Quintin's charity concerts. A man walked towards them, and recognising him, she smiled.

'You always look stunning in your conductor's suit, Andries,' she said as she hugged her sister's husband fondly.

'Thank you, Lily,' he said. 'We've got a surprise for you tonight, too.'

'Surprise!' Piet said beside her.

The kids rushed her from behind and swamped her in hugs.

'Oh goodness, David, you look so debonair in that suit, and look at you, Diamond, that dress is so pretty.' She lifted Diamond in her arms and put her other arm around David, pulling him into a tight hug. 'I'm so happy to see you guys. Piet, oh my goodness, look at you; you're wearing a suit.'

'I am, for Quintin and you, and I got on a plane and used my passport.' Piet touched his heart then touched Lily's shoulder, and tears threatened in her eyes.

'Happy tears?' Piet asked.

Lily nodded.

Bessie and Lincoln were also there, and Bessie had never looked so radiant.

'Oh goodness, you came.'

'I could not let Piet look after Diamond, that is my job when you and Quintin are not around, so Quintin said we could all come and see him play. *Mywee,* I never imagined a place like this, ever.' Bessie was looking everywhere, her hand covering her mouth.

Lily embraced Bessie. 'You will get to see even more, too, I'm sure.'

'The whole family is here,' Andries said with an edge of excitement to his voice.

'How?' She turned and there was Rose, her sister, and her children, and her father, too. 'Rose.' She clasped her sister tightly. 'Thank you.' Her niece and nephew gave her hugs, and she could see them also embracing Quintin. Her dad enfolded her in his arms.

'We all flew in this morning as a surprise. Well, Quintin was in on it, but he swore me to secrecy,' Rose said.

'And we arranged for you all to sit together right in the front,' Quintin said as he reclaimed her hand.

Lily smiled. 'Thank you.'

Quintin bent his head and kissed her, and hugged the kids close between the two of them.

'I can't wait for the world to hear Quintin's new concerto,' Andries said. 'It beats every composition he's done to date. There's such passion, depth and sadness—and so much love in it. Have you heard it?'

'In bits and pieces,' she admitted. 'It's been a difficult time for us lately.'

Andries put his hand on her arm. 'I'm sorry. Hey, any news of your flamingo coming back again? What was her name? Micky?'

'Minke. And no. It's wild now. Besides, we don't want her pining for us. We wouldn't recognise her now anyway; she would have all her pink feathers and be an adult,' Lily said.

'But if she's been brought up with you, wouldn't she want to stay?' Andries asked.

'Flamingos, even when they're hand-reared, are flock birds, and no amount of imprinting can keep them with you. They go back to the wild—as they should,' David said.

'That explains the tone of the concerto,' Andries said.

A bell sounded, and Andries looked towards the entrance. 'That's our queue to go backstage and get ready. I'll see you all afterwards at the dinner.' He kissed Lily on the cheeks and did the same to Rose before he headed off.

Quintin hugged her. 'Are you sure you're going to get to your seat okay?'

'We'll be fine,' she said. 'You need to go and do your famous-music thing up on that stage and make everybody happy.'

'I love you, *wifie*,' he said as he kissed her before walking away.

Lily and her family made their way towards the door of the theatre that she knew so well. She chatted to people on the way, always smiling, always polite, even if she didn't remember who some of them were, only this time it was different. She had her children with her and Piet, who smiled at everyone and drew lots of stares. Lincoln and Bessie were looking stunning holding hands and dressed in their best clothes. For Lily, people's names and faces were beginning to fade.

She sat down in her seat, and Diamond climbed into her lap as the lights went down and Andries walked out. He looked handsome in his suit and did an exaggerated bow to the audience. He gave a little wave to Rose and their kids and smiled.

'He hasn't changed much since we were students all together in Durban, has he?' Rose said to Lily over David's head.

Quintin walked out onto the stage, and the audience reacted to him as they usually did. They screamed.

A rockstar in the classical world, Quintin defied all the rules and regulations of the traditions of the orchestra, and because of that, he'd won the hearts of millions of people around the world. They also respected his natural talent and ability with music and his violin.

When the noise had subsided, Quintin walked up to the microphone. 'Hello, ladies and gentlemen, and thank you for coming out tonight.'

The audience screamed again in response.

He played for almost an hour before he stepped forward once more. 'It's so good to see everyone here. I adore you all. I wanted to share with you a little about my years since I was last in front of you on this very stage. It is with great sadness that I tell you I'll not be doing another live performance for a while.'

There was silence in the Great Hall.

'I'll still be producing albums, and you'll still hear my music in movies and on the radio, but my darling wife, Lily, and I have decided to concentrate on spending our time together after she was diagnosed with early-onset Alzheimer's.'

People near Lily turned round. Staring. But Diamond had her arms around Lily's neck, and David held her hand, while Rose was patting her shoulder.

So, this is what he had planned.

Rose whispered, 'Focus on Quintin. Ignore them.'

'As many of you know,' Quintin said, 'my adorable wife, was instrumental in saving my hands after a vicious attack when I was touring in South Africa many years ago. It's where I met her. Together we have travelled the world—me playing my music and Lily healing people, as doctors do. We have been in many amazing places and some frightening ones when her work took us into war zones and refugee camps. We have always faced things together. So, we'll be doing the same now. The time has come for us to step out of the limelight. During the last two years, while we've had our lives turned upside down, we've had good times, too. Earlier this year, we became the official proud parents to David and Diamond, both of whom are here tonight. A little late in our lives to start a family, but now that we have them, we couldn't be without them. I'm sure many of you who are parents can relate.'

The audience went wild.

'We also became the recipients of a rescue flamingo baby, and while many people think of a bird flying in the sky that stands on one leg, there's so much more to these remarkable pink birds, which is almost what Minke looked like when we released her back into the wild. However, when she came to us, she was a dirty-grey colour and probably no bigger than a *boule*.' He showed the size with his hands.

'So tonight, I'll play for you, for the first time in public, a concerto dedicated to my beautiful wife, whose mind I hope to always reach with my music, no matter where it goes. To help me out, I'd like to bring the two other women in my life out on stage, La Angelique and Shirabe. Accompanying me today will be the amazing Li Shung, from the Japan Philharmonic Orchestra. Li is an amazing violinist, and she's one of the few other people in the world to also own a glass HARIO violin. We've played together before, and I hope that this won't be the last time. Please give a big round of applause for Miss Li Shung who will play on Shirabe.'

Li Shung walked on the stage, and people clapped for her as she bowed to Quintin and then to Andries.

'With thanks to my brother-in-law, Andries Johannes van Tonder, the conductor of the Vienna Philharmonic Orchestra, we bring you the first public performance of Concerto for the Flamingo.'

Quintin picked up La Angelique. Lily held her breath as he played the first bars, then Li Shung joined in. Tears streamed down her face as she recognised the pieces which she'd heard. Andries was right; it was the most exquisite music that Quintin had ever composed.

Two thousand guests in the Great Hall leaped to their feet, and thunderous applause cried for an encore as soon as Quintin had played the last notes of his concerto.

Quintin and Andries were motioning for Lily to come up onto the stage. Quintin walked forward to take her hand. Diamond saw him and immediately latched her arms around him, and David was still holding Lily's hand when Quintin took her other one and helped her up the steps, and then he kissed her in front of everybody.

'Thank you, everyone, for your support, your love and your loyalty. I appreciate all of you and all the kindness you show me. Please give a round of applause for my inspiration.' He opened his hands towards her. 'Lily. I love you. I always will.'

The walls of the Great Hall shook with the roar of the crowd.

CHAPTER 45

HACIENDA EL PARADISO, KIMBERLEY, SOUTH AFRICA, 2017

QUINTIN MANOEUVRED his Land Cruiser in the new garage on the opposite side of his house at Hacienda El Paradiso, and the garage door closed behind him. He grabbed the bunch of sunflowers he'd bought for Lily and the pink box from the back seat.

The sun was falling from the once bright-blue sky, the muted shades of sunset giving way to stars that would illuminate the inky darkness with their radiance. Lily loved this time of day. He increased his stride.

'Hey, Dad,' David said as he walked into the house. 'Did you remember?'

'Mum's flowers, of course,' he said, putting them in front of him and showing the teenager.

'No. To collect the corsage for my matric dance?'

'That depends, are you going to let me do your tie in a proper Windsor knot or wear it like a *skollie* like it is?'

'Dad,' David said, pulling it off and handing it to his father.

'Hold this,' Quintin said, giving the pink box to David.

'Thanks, Maddy is going to love this. Can't wait for her to see it.'

'As long as you are back by one in the morning, I won't come looking for you. You know I can track you on my phone.'

'Dad, you wouldn't?' David said.

'No, he might not, but I would as your closest uncle. I will come after you with the sirens on,' said Piet, walking from the kitchen. 'I have had many years of practice with nights just like tonight, and I do not want you out there after it wraps up. For some reason, boys think they are bulletproof after a night out.'

'Family! Who needs them when you're trying hard to date,' David said.

Quintin looked at Piet and smiled. Happy for the backup. 'You do. I trust you. You have earned it. We brought you up responsibly, so don't blow it now is all I'm saying. I know you and Maddy have been looking forward to this all year, but we all want you to go out there, have fun, but be safe. Okay?' Quintin said, putting David's tie over his head and tightening it up. 'There, it looks good. Like it should.'

'Sure. Thanks, Dad.'

'You ready? Your chauffeur awaits,' Piet said.

'Wait, we need a picture,' Diamond said as she ran into the entranceway, lifted her camera and took one of the three men together.

Piet took her camera from her. 'One of you guys,' he said as he took their picture.

'A selfie, all four of us,' Diamond said. 'Dad, you've got the longest arms. I'll set the camera and you hold it out, okay?'

They counted down the ten seconds, and the flash showed that they had taken the picture. 'Awesome, I'll show Mum in the morning,' Diamond said.

'Why only in the morning, young lady?' Quintin asked.

'Because I'm having a sleepover at Jessica's, remember? Piet is dropping me on the way to fetch Maddy.'

'Of course I remembered,' Quintin said. 'It's written on the whiteboard. Enjoy.' He kissed her cheek, and she took a moment to hug him.

'Love ya, Dad,' she said, then picked up her backpack and walked out the door.

'You take care, my son,' Quintin said, and he and David did a handshake that they had worked out years ago that ended with a fist bump.

'Look after Mum tonight,' David said.

'Always,' Quintin replied.

'See you,' Piet said. 'Tell Lily I say *howzit*.'

'Thank you, Piet,' Quintin said as he was left standing alone in the hallway.

He closed the door to the garage, picked up Lily's flowers and took the steps two by two.

'Good evening, Mr Winters,' Connie, the nurse, said as she sat reading near the door. 'I've wheeled Lily out onto the verandah so that she could watch the sunset. She's had a quiet afternoon, although she hasn't been able to eat anything. But she did have a little to drink.'

'Thank you, Connie,' he said as he walked past. 'I'm home now. You can take the rest of the night off. I'll see you at seven o'clock.'

Perhaps tonight would be better than this morning when her brain had taken her too many years away from him.

Perhaps she wasn't too lost tonight.

Perhaps tonight he could pretend that they were a regular couple on a regular date, and when he played their song, she might remember. She might recognise him.

His violin case sat on the antique dining-room table he'd chosen for her when they'd extended their house and bedroom. He couldn't bear the thought of her only having sterile medical equipment around. Lily had always been such a tactile person when she was there; he couldn't take that away from her now so close to the end. He gripped the handle and Fred, and walked out onto the verandah, where her hospital-style bed had been moved to, and handed her the flowers. 'Here you go, Lily, sunflowers, your favourite.' He kissed her forehead and smoothed small wisps of her hair away from her eyes.

Her hands didn't hold the gift he had placed across her chest, and her eyes didn't acknowledge he was there. He stroked Tiger, who sat with her on the bed and purred loudly, the hair around his mouth now grey with age.

Quintin exchanged the flowers for the wilted ones that were in the vase next to her bed, throwing the old blooms in the bin. He knew that she loved to spend the days outside, rather than cooped up indoors. Later, he would manoeuvre her bed back inside, next to his, so he could still sleep beside her.

He walked to where he had left his violin and took Le Angelique from her velvet case, before sitting in the high stool, one that used to be at the bench in the studio, and now remained upstairs instead. 'The kids have gone out; hard to believe they are growing so fast. It's back to you and me tonight, my *wifie*. While I was out driving today, I could see it was so dry, not just here, but everywhere. We need rain. Kamfers Dam is dropping quickly with the evaporation, but there is good news for the creche. There are still over five thousand flamingos there, and it looks like we have averted another disaster by diverting water in time to save those thousands of little chicks. I'm glad I could be here for the forward planning, and we were able to override those *numbskulls* at Sol Plaatje Municipality. Sometimes having money to throw at a project helps so much. The flamingos look like they are having another bumper breeding season.'

He lifted Le Angelique and Fred, and began a quick warm-up.

'She still sounds okay, even after all these years, don't you think?'

He looked at Lily and for a second he thought he saw a flutter in her eyes, then realised it was only the reflection of flamingos coming into roost in their landscaped man-made *vlei* that was fed with water from their borehole.

'Your flamingos are here, Lily; let's serenade them.'

GLOSSARY

ag shame – *ag* is a filler word like 'um'; *shame* is to express pity or sympathy; general slang term in southern Africa.

baas – boss; Afrikaans, but used as a general term in southern Africa.

bakkie – truck/ute; Afrikaans, but used as a general term in southern Africa.

boer – farmer; Afrikaans

braaing – cooking meat on an open fire; Afrikaans.

dokotela – doctor; Zulu.

domkop – meaning idiot; Afrikaans.

doos – a derogatory term for a woman's vagina—cunt; South African slang.

Dumelang – 'hello' when you greet more than one person; Northern Sotho.

aikona – no; generally accepted South African slang.

eina – ouch; Afrikaans.

eish (pronounced *eye-sh* or *eh-eesh)* – surprise/awe/shock/exasperation/excitement/resignation; generally accepted southern African slang (derived from Xhosa originally).

gijima – run; Zulu.

igundane – mice/mouse; Zulu.

ikhaya – hut/house; Zulu, Ndebele.

Jo'burg – shortened form of Johannesburg.

ja – yes; Afrikaans.

ja-nee – yes-no; a typical South African expression.

jislaaik – exclamation, usually for something unbelievable; Afrikaans, but generally accepted in South Africa.

Johies – slang for 'Johannesburg'.

laaitie – young person; Afrikaans.

ma-huang – a traditional Chinese medicinal herb.

Médecins Sans Frontières – Doctors Without Borders, a volunteer organisation.

Mywee – short for my *wena*—translates roughly to 'Oh goodness'; Zulu.

meva/Ameva – thorn; Zulu.

my china – slang for 'my friend / my mate'.

nee – no; Afrikaans.

Piet-my-vrou – red-chested cuckoo (*Cuculus solitarius*).

rinkhals – venomous snake also called the ringhals or ring-necked spitting cobra; Afrikaans.

SADF – South African Defence Force. The SADF was all the forces within South Africa: black, white, brown; everyone together under one defence label.

sangoma – traditional healer, practitioner of traditional African medicine. Often still holding onto the shaman aspect of mixing witchcraft with herbal medicines.

Shirabe – melody in Japanese.

skabenga – gangster; a Zulu word, but generally used in South Africa for anyone who is on the wrong side of the law / troublemaker / a bad guy.

slapgat – Slap-dash; Afrikaans

Spur – a restaurant steakhouse chain in South Africa.

SWAPO – South West Africa People's Organisation.

thinnings disease – in Africa, HIV is commonly referred to as the thinnings disease. People who lose lots of weight suddenly are more often than not suspected of having HIV. If you have the thinnings disease, it is assumed that you will be dead soon as there is not a lot of intervention by the government with drugs.

Ulwazi – Zulu name, meaning 'knowledge'.

woza – come; Zulu.

yebo – Yes; Zulu, now generally accepted South African term.

FACT VS FICTION

Fact

Kaggen—also referred to as Cagn or Kaang—is a trickster god of the San. The legend says that he created the moon, and this holds significance to the San.

Fiction

San have no ritual to want to die under the stars and the moon.

Fact

In April 2000, the !Xun and the Khwe San—who were part of the SANDF during the South African Border Wars—were relocated for the final time. For over twenty years they were moved around, from Omega base to Mangetti Dune, Namibia, and then to Schmidtsdrift in South Africa, and finally to Platfontein, where they now have a final settlement and home.

Fiction

This novel is not their story, and in no way reflects any of their views, or any of the people living within Platfontein.

Fact

The island at Kamfers Dam is real and was constructed by Kimberley Ekapa Mining JV (KEM-JV).

Fact

In 2019, Kimberley suffered with a drought and substantial mismanagement of the maintenance of its municipality equipment, eventuating in a flamingo chick rescue. That was driven by the private sector and individuals. People all over the world got on board quickly and it was reported that approximately 3000 chicks (this number couldn't be verified) were rescued and sent to different volunteer facilities across South Africa for hand-rearing. Many died, but many have now been returned to Kamfers Dam and released back into their wild flock. Thank you to everyone involved in saving these babies. This book was written before this event unfolded.

Fact

Tainted drugs are real, as are contaminated drugs.

Fiction

My South African pharmaceutical company using specifically generic drugs for their distribution and manufacture of tainted drugs.

Fact

In 2002, the number of HIV-positive people in South Africa was an estimated 4.94 million. By 2017, it had increased to 7.06 million. This is now an estimated 12.6 per cent of the total South African population (Statistics South Africa: www.statssa.gov.za/publications/P0302/P03022017).

Fiction

The South African Government attempting to cover up these statistics.

Fact

There is a list of known Stradivarius instruments made by members of the house of Antonio Stradivari between 1666 and 1737, some still survive today and are in both private and government collections, a few are still played.

Fiction

Le Angelique is not one of them.

Fact

HARIO's glass violins are real. They began their violin project in the spring of 2003, and production was at their Koga factory. The body of the violins are mouth blown by long term moulding experts from a heat-resistant glass material. However, while pretty strong they are still breakable. The necks are made of an acrylic material. The cost for a single glass violin: 5.5 million yen (US$55 thousand.) Their glass violins are mainly played for company events only.

Fiction

Shirabe is not one of their glass violins from their collection.

ACKNOWLEDGEMENTS

Once again, I want to thank everyone who journeys beside me as I take an idea and shape it into a book.

Brian Culver, man on the ground in Kimberley, South Africa, who talked to me about all things relating to the Kimberley and flamingos, at all hours.

Jenny Parkes, a reader who chose to go into a raffle to be my reader killed in this book. Congratulations!

Natalie Hatch, for friendship and because she's snarky and funny and gave me the perfect line to use: 'Murder is bad, but if you are going to do it, don't leave a paper trail.'

Antoinette Hermann, ex-South African Police Force, any policing errors are all mine—thank you for your guidance on procedure and all the different name changes etcetera.

Andries Johannes van Tonder and Vaughan Smith, two of my long-time readers. I decided to put your names in to make you both smile. As FIFO workers, thank you for your loyalty as you have continued to follow me from no matter where, Afghanistan to the Amazon, South Africa to Australia, wherever you are: enjoy reading this one.

Keyan G. Tomaselli, Distinguished Professor, University of Johannesburg, South Africa, for your help on HIV research and the San.

Ferdinand Veer Jr, for your on-the-ground information and research on the San.

John Jang, from HARIO Co. Ltd., for your information about the amazing glass violins you manufacture, and for allowing me to use them by name in this book. I hope you can hear that the music they make in my novel is as beautiful as it is in real life.

To the Quirk family who shared their story with me, and inspired the story of Quintin and Lily's love and their devotion to be together—always.

Debbie Kahl who named my glass violin, Shirabe, for me—and for her love of everything Japanese, culture, language and place.

The original publishing team:

The team at HarperCollins, Harlequin Mira, especially Rachael Donovan, for pushing me deeper and further in my stories, and, for the second time, naming my book. Thank you. My editors, Laurie Ormond, Chrysoula Aiello and Alex Nahlous, for not giving up on me and helping me make each story better than my last. George Saad, for my almost-pink cover! I love it!

My Independent Publishing Crew:

Line edits: Creative Ink.

Cover Design: Mecha.

Thank you!

My beta reader, Petro Grobbelaar, many thanks for your help in various edit stages.

Amy Andrews, long-time writing friend, for the idea to write a book with a 'flamingo in so I could maybe get a pinkish cover'. My male-dominated house now has a decidedly pink hue to it!

Robyn Grady, Gayle Ash and Alli Sinclair, who haven't fired me yet. To writing journeys—however windy the path seems to be.

To my readers who continue to buy my books, and who love wildlife, different cultures and stories as much as I do.

And my sons, Kyle and Barry, for putting up with me in my life between two worlds, and for being the most amazing young gentlemen a mum could ask for.

2019 - Lastly, to my husband, Shaun. For everything, always, but especially for the freedom to stretch my wings and fly beside you.

2024 – Shaun – Thank you for propping me up for this book that nearly broke me. From the disturbing research, then my mother's Alzheimer's diagnosis while drafting the story, right through to her passing during COVID from this horrendous disease. I love that you just accept whatever subject I need to write about – no matter what or how hard it is for me.

Milton Keynes UK
Ingram Content Group UK Ltd.
UKHW011126080124
435661UK00006B/588

9 798223 010760